Gender Wars

GENDER

Brian Fawcett

A Novel

and Some

Gender

Conversation

Wars

about Sex

28645311

and Gender

A Patrick Crean Book

Somerville House Publishing

Toronto

Canadian Cataloguing in Publication Data

Fawcett, Brian,
       Gender wars

"A Patrick Crean Book"
ISBN 0-921051-94-8 PB   ISBN 1-895897-09-2 HC

I. Title.

PS8561.A94G4 1994   C813'.54   C94-930179-5
PR9199.3.F39G4 1994

Design: Gordon Robertson
Printed in Canada

A Patrick Crean Book

Published by Somerville House Publishing,
a division of Somerville House Books Limited,
3080 Yonge Street, Suite 5000, Toronto, Ontario M4N 3N1

Somerville House Publishing acknowledges the financial assistance of the Ontario Publishing Centre, the Ontario Arts Council, the Ontario Development Corporation, and the Department of Communications.

Vancouver locations: 4 Wings Cafe, The Vineyard, Cafe Creme.
Toronto locations: Dooney's, J&R Steak & Ribs, Future Bakery.

People: Merrily Weisbord, Barbara Gowdy, Christopher Dewdney, and Judith Rudakoff, for their close edits and fact/reality checks, Michael Spragge for the anecdotes and slapstick, Gordon Robertson for pushing the design of this book beyond conventional limits, and to R. Murray Schafer, who taught me, years ago, that serious art comes from being prepared to dive into deep water.

The quotation from Albert Camus is from *Notebooks 1935-1942*, translated by Philip Thody (1963).

Earlier versions of several sections of this book have been printed in *The Vancouver Review*.

This book is for Leanna,
who changed (and changes) everything.

Contents

Gender Wars

Brian Fawcett

Gender **Wars**

The
*Mary
Smith
Memorial
Women's Collection*

Mexican Stan

A man named Ferris says to a woman named Annie:

"Now, get out."

He is moving toward her as he says this, his hands clenched at his sides, his eyes glowing with rage, his face a mask of violent intent. Annie senses what is to come, and picks up a heavy glass ashtray from the coffee table. As he lunges for her, she shatters it across the side of his face. He staggers momentarily, but as she tries to escape, he catches her wrist. He grimaces, paws at his face, and he straightens himself and jerks her smaller body against his own—and then thrusts her away, throwing her across the room as if she were a rag doll. As she slams awkwardly against the wall, she feels bones of her left wrist shattering. There is an instant and merciful numbness there and in her shoulder, and she crumples into a heap on the floor, nearly losing consciousness.

d-off

Ferris has his own numbness to contend with, and he does not pursue. Blood is pouring down his neck and inside the collar of his shirt, he can feel that, but nothing on the right side of his face. "Fucking bitch," he mumbles, touching a finger to his cheekbone. It comes back into his line of vision fouled with crimson.

Annie, meanwhile, is gazing at her purse. It is on the floor not more than eighteen inches away, fallen there from an overturned end table. She shifts her body slightly, groaning as she's forced to use her damaged wrist, and snakes her right hand toward the purse. She flips the snap open, gropes inside until her fingers close around the handle of the small black revolver she purchased last week. When Ferris, his rage not yet quenched, lumbers toward her again, she does not hesitate…

No. That won't do. It's a tempting opener, dramatic as hell, but I'm not going to resolve the conflict between these two human beings with stereotypes and/or clichés of violence. Their provisional here-and-now simply isn't like that, nor is it for anyone else who will figure directly in this narrative. That isn't to suggest that peace and love will reign in these pages. This is a book about gender, sexuality, and violence. But stupid violence, the kill-maim-jump-over-cars-brandishing-pistols kind, will figure as the ubiquitous threat it has become for each and all of us. For Ferris and Annie, it's a fairly distant threat, a lurking shadow—and I'm going to keep it, or try to, with me: under control.

Violence solves problems only on television and in the movies, where human reality must be declared, ciphered and closed within half-hour to two-hour segments. It pre-empts most environmental and emotional complexities and shrinks the history of ideas to manageable, acrobatic truisms. In the world, violence has none of those convenient properties. It is the cosmic sucker-punch that wounds every sweet human impulse, a direct pipe into the sewer of expedience that sucks down every notion we have of education, kindness, and decency. Between people it shreds every half-healed injury, tears open every annealed scar. And it makes people dead, and death is no story at all.

Which puts us back at the beginning again with Ferris's statement. What happens next? Well, nothing violent. A grey short-haired cat wanders in, senses the tension and scuttles through into the adjoining room, where it leaps onto an oak table to groom itself in a beam of sunlight. Ferris notes that a tree outside one of the windows appears to be marking time, its branches sinking and rising to an obscure rhythm of wind and cellular geometry—as if, he thinks, the world made sense, and things came to sensible endings. It's hard to say what Annie is thinking as she stares at Ferris. Her face and eyes are without expression.

This is a contemporary domestic tableau we're looking in on, and it is askew. Oh, the room in which it takes place is orderly enough. The walls are painted white, the north and east ones dominated by large wood-frame windows. The floors are covered with grey wall-to-wall carpet, broken up by imitation Persian throw rugs. A cheap off-white Bauhaus couch and chair are present, and a variety of hardy tropical plants in ceramic pots. On the walls are some framed Impressionist prints.

It is the two people here, the man named Ferris and the woman named Annie, that are askew.

Ferris stands by the couch, shifting his gaze from Annie to the tree branches, and back. She's across from him, sitting in the chair. She doesn't move, and she doesn't speak. All he can do is press his leg against the couch to steady his body, and will himself to remain as still and expressionless as she is. Long seconds pass this way.

Then, almost imperceptibly, Annie's eyes widen. He sees this and flinches. He knows what will happen next. She is about to become hysterical.

They're in the midst of a domestic battle, these two. That's obvious. I've already assured you that they won't trade acts of physical violence, and they've both been sufficiently liberated from the gender roles of the recent past that there's no chance they're going to start acting like characters from a television sitcom, either. Fists, ashtrays, and guns are out. So are witty children, neighbours, dogs, and irascible, irrational employers. That said, we can get on to everyday questions. Why are they fighting? And what are they fighting over?

Modern life, Annie will say. People, she'll explain, are frustrated these days, people—lovers—fight. Maybe lovers most of all. Relationships are difficult. Ferris's explanation will be more specific: She did this, he did that. And more personal: her fault, his fault.

They're young, civilized, decent middle-class North Americans, Annie and Ferris. Reasonably nice people. She's a health service administrator, negotiating the government's positions with—or against—medical professionals and their organizations. He's a city planner. Both are fully functional wage-earning citizens. They go to work in the morning, they come home at night, they don't take sick days unless they're physically ill, and they work overtime without expecting to be paid for it.

They're what sociologists are calling urban professionals, and each is accustomed to using her or his language skills as alternatives to—or as disarming devices for—violent confrontation. That's what they do for a living, in a way. But let's not let ourselves be fooled by sociology. An anthropologist would recognize them as warriors, front-liners, and yes, they do know how to fight. Their professional skills—and maybe the private psychologies that internalize those skills—are aggressive and self-protective at the same time, even though they're self-consciously unwilling to use—and perhaps even culturally incapable of using—the traditional resorts of their genders. He won't even *threaten* to use his physical strength, and she isn't going to employ the weapons women commonly use in domestic battles—passive-aggressive tactics like tears, or displays of real or feigned vulnerability.

Despite their credentials, they're in trouble here because neither has a plan of action or a common perspective. Ferris certainly doesn't appear to know what to do next, and Annie seems paralyzed that the argument has gone as far as it has. Usually, he backs away when he sees a confrontation coming—so he can attack later.

She's using the tactic that has worked best in the recent past, even though her instincts tell her that this situation has gone beyond the point where it will succeed. In her mind, of course, it isn't quite a tactic. The threatened hysteria is an emotional verity in which she is swept up and carried beyond control. To her it *feels* like a spontaneous reaction to his aggressive demand. He's *so* aggressive, really. What is she supposed to do?

From his point of view, her threatened hysteria is at least three things, maybe four or five. First, it is a tactical counter-move to his demand. But it's also a logical extension of her actions during the last few hours, and more: It is a manifestation of her total identity. And it is unfair, and cruel, god damn her.

Whatever Annie and Ferris believe separately, they're caught in a tableau that I, as their author, recognize as typical of their relationship. I could probably get them to agree on that much—and little else. They'd agree that this is an excruciating moment, and that it is important not to be the first to disengage, to break and run, or attack in some other way. They are prepared to fight about literally everything else in the world.

Without moving or speaking, Annie goes on staring at Ferris, and he keeps shuffling and glancing out the window. Never mind that in other parts of the world emaciated children totter through parched streets looking for food, or that in a half dozen locations across the world, artillery gunners are lining up their howitzers to fire on the homes of their enemies. Never mind that.

––––––––––

Granting this moment the importance it evidently has for both of them, what do you think is going on? Is Annie the maniac Ferris believes her to be, and is Ferris the aggressive male, the wolf dressed up in sheep's clothing Annie thinks he is? To a neutral party stepping onto the scene at the moment he tells her to get out, he might have appeared to be the aggressor. Yet if you look at him carefully, you'll see fear. Despite the tough words, his posture and his eyes betray fear of her and of the situation. Annie is less transparent. Her eyes and body are still but she's neither "transfixed" nor intimidated, and she and Ferris both know it.

Incidentally, you—the reader—have the best chance of neutrality. I'm thoroughly mixed up in this, too much to claim objectivity. That's why I've chosen to write about it. I may be the writer here, but I'm not, in the sense fiction writers so often affect—preposterously—the *omniscient creator*. I'm admitting—out front—that I have a destabilizing emotional stake in these proceedings. Having admitted that much, I'd better try to explain a couple of other odd procedures I'll be following.

I don't claim to be covering every aspect of this story. I'm aware that another person, given the same facts I have to work with, would undoubtedly see and interpret this differently. I won't pretend that the events happen exactly as I'm describing them. I might be missing an inflection here, misreading a gesture there, losing an important detail on focus, or underestimating the importance of, say, the walk-through by the cat. Because I'm a male, I will, some feminist readers will opine, inevitably weight things in favour of Ferris. They're at least partially right, so please calibrate. I'm sure that still other distortions pertain, ones that are less currently obvious. I can't identify them because they're internalized in my personal and cultural make-up—and in yours. Twenty years from now, these distortions will probably be blatantly apparent.

Such distortions are the rule in all human communications and their media, whether or not we recognize them through our idiosyncratic linguistic, emotional, and cultural glosses. But before anyone gets irritable or depressed

N ow that the Sexual Revolution is over and the counter-revolution is busily proselytizing the virtues of latex and reptiles, does anyone have a clear idea of what the Sexual Revolution set out to accomplish, what it did accomplish, and what it might have accomplished but didn't?

We can say with certainty that an attitude shift concerning sex occurred after 1960, that it permitted a generation of young and/or adventurous people to explore sexuality with a degree of safety and abandon previous generations couldn't risk. It also enabled—and tacitly encouraged—ordinary, sane people to fuck with relative strangers in more free and democratic configurations. Antibiotics and birth control pills created the safe zone, and a host of resistant bacteria and viruses eventually obliterated it—and ended the revolution.

Those are the facts nearly everyone will agree on. But they're not enough, somehow. They don't tell us anything about the goals, the accomplishments, or the

about being told this, remember that the gap between idiosyncratic perception and material event is also the *basis* of all human discourse, and that the difficulties of discourse are a large part of the unique joy of being human. We each have a choice to make. We can live our lives by swimming in the swirling currents of that discourse—which is also called narrative—or we can cover ourselves in ideology—where everything is reduced to bureaucratic procedures that align people, things, and events with the correct devotional ideas and their supporting hagiographies.

You probably know all this. But in a world that tries its best to ignore nonconforming imagination while relentlessly inciting us to believe in ideological consumerism and in the various police fantasies and military alignments that follow, we need to be reminded. So, as you wait for this story to crack open, I remind you of it. And I remind myself.

On cue, Annie shifts in her chair, and lets her body sink back. Almost odalisque now, she places her wrists carefully on the arms of the chair so that her fingers dangle from its edges. All this without taking her eyes off Ferris. It alters her appearance. Now, you can see her aggression, and perhaps you might also perceive an arrogant confidence. And you might, as the man standing across from her does, find her hands attractive.

Annie is a very small woman. She is barely five feet tall and she weighs less

failures. Those of us who were around for the Sexual Revolution seem to find it hard to get beyond the barest description of it. When the subject is brought up, most of us feel a strange mixture of nostalgia, terror, and embarrassment. Thinking about it is painful and humiliating, sort of like talking about the collapse of the left has become for many of us who were around in the 1960s.

I find it hard to separate the two subjects. Yes, social democracy, socialism, and every other permutation on out to the lunatic fringe seem to have been buried under the debris of the fallen Soviet empire—an empire that I was deeply gratified to see the end of. But I'm also frustrated by what has happened. People have forgotten that they adopted their leftist values not because they hated capitalism or believed in the Soviet bureaucratization of life, but because they believed that human beings ought to be treated decently. So also with the Sexual Revolution, which began not so much because everyone wanted to spend a weekend at a Plato's

than a hundred pounds. More important, her mane of red hair, her firmly muscled body, even her small green eyes, large, slightly protruding teeth, and full lips—all and each are to him, sensual incitements—and reflections of her power over him. Only her hands, small, with slender, tapered fingers, are delicate and vulnerable. And Ferris has the hots for them right here in the middle of a fight in which he's telling her to get out of his life.

"Stupid," he mutters, half aloud. It's a familiar feeling—too familiar—but admitting it to himself doesn't help. The attractiveness of her hands—their shape and position—has already undermined his resolve. He wonders whether he's really tried to order her to get out of his life or simply wished something that she can accept or reject as she pleases. Feeling weakened, but without yet resigning himself to retreat, he sinks down heavily on the couch to return her stare. He tries to force himself to relax, or at least give the appearance of being relaxed. This whole thing is (he thinks, as a means of distracting himself) a Mexican Stand-off.

Once upon a time, a Mexican Stand-off offered believable sets and a rule book: two swarthy sombrero-wearing Latinos face each other across a hot and dusty adobe square. Each brandishes two pistols, and across their shoulders are the familiar bandoleers of cartridges. They're drunk, and, of course, they're grinning at one another. It's Evil versus Evil, stupidity matched against stupidity, and there's something funny about it—damn the racist overtones. We sense these two will remain locked in these postures until after the death of Pancho Villa more than a decade into our own century, when the oppressions

Retreat group-grope or infect their peers with lethal bugs, but because they believed that sex did not need to be dirty and criminal and corrupting, that it could be rather beautiful and illuminating.

These days, nobody likes to admit that all the best things about the Sexual Revolution were utopian and well, "socialistic." But while it was happening, rational people actually believed that if we opened and improved our erotic practices, touched our loved ones—and strangers—without shame, and generally treated one another more generously, the world would become a better place. Now that capitalism has triumphed over every other political and economic idea on the planet, including common sense, we ought to be generous enough not to confuse those naïve erotic socialisms with those that informed the Soviet and other communist governments, none of which approved of any kind of pleasure unless you're willing to suggest that running your fingertips along slabs of concrete is a major erotic kick.

of civil life begin to become, for Mexicans, more like the ones Annie and Ferris face.

Ferris recalls that a woman once told him about an encounter her police officer-boyfriend had with a revolver-brandishing bank robber. Here in the midst of his own crisis, Ferris can't recall the exact details of the incident, just the geometrics and dramaturgy, along with the superfluous irony that the police officer didn't like guns, and it was his first day on patrol. As a matter of principle, the officer hadn't loaded his service revolver.

The stand-off that resulted, then, is quite different than the original Mexican one. It has an unarmed police officer facing a scratchy-faced one-hundred-and-thirty-pound armed bank robber. The bank robber is wearing a blue baseball cap, a Toronto Blue Jays fan hat, an Iron Maiden T-shirt, filthy blue-jeans and grease-stained Wallabies. It isn't Crazy Latino versus Crazy Latino, and it isn't quite upper-case Good versus upper-case Evil. More like lower-case nice versus lower-case nasty.

So what does Ferris have, here? At very least, a Mexican Stand-off involves two armed human beings pointing weapons at one another. So far, the parallels seem to hold all down the line—the Mexicans who invented it, the cop and the bank robber, and Ferris and Annie, maybe. But what are the rules? Presumably, in the real world, the standees in a Mexican Stand-off can't be expected to hold the pose forever. Sooner or later, one of them has to back off and lower his or her weapon, or fire it at the other person. Either action will end it. In a morally coherent universe, Good ought to triumph over Evil, and even in a Mexican

For about a decade now, the utopian socialist I still nurture at the core of my personality has wanted to deliver a eulogy for the Sexual Revolution. This seems like the only chance I'm likely to get, so here goes:

The privileged economic status most North Americans and Western Europeans enjoy has spared them the struggles against the kind and degree of sectarian and author-itarian political violence that have convulsed the rest of the world since World War II. We haven't gone through conventional revolutions and counterinsurgencies, where the ideas and the private choices are simplified by direct military and class violence, the ene-mies apparent and the dangers much more physical and immediate. Instead, we've been tricked into fighting amongst one another over issues of equality and social justice while the rich got richer and the International Monetary Fund supplanted the U.N. as the global arbitrator of values.

Whatever revolutionary ire and fire existed was consumed by personal and interper-

Stand-off, the more evil (or less good) participant ought to lower his or her weapon—or come second when the firing starts. But there isn't much evidence to suggest that this is a morally coherent universe, is there?

Another thought occurs to Ferris. If a weapon is fired, isn't it then just a gunfight? These days, as in old Mexico, life is depressingly full of those. In the cop versus robber stand-off, things ought to be black and white, but aren't. If the officer fires his gun, it becomes a "weapons incident," and a career-damaging inquiry by Internal Affairs will follow. If the bank robber is wounded or killed, particularly if he has ethnic or health-related properties, advocates of various abstract causes will make partisan statements to the media, there might be a lawsuit, demonstration, maybe even a riot. If the bank robber gets the first or best shot in, a whole different set of consequences will ensue. More years on his sentence, and if the officer is killed, calls for the death penalty, a solemn parade by fellow officers, and the Law and Order lobby gets a boost. Then there is the matter of bystanders. What if your daughter or your brother happens to catch a stray bullet?

Ferris doesn't remember how it ended except that the police officer survived. Actually, he did a little better than that. Soon afterward, he was transferred to the police department's community outreach branch, where he spent his days in the schools talking to kids about the dangers of crime and criminals instead of waving unloaded pistols at the criminals.

Well, this a fine distraction for Ferris. Cops and robbers may be an excellent arena for social drama or urban slapstick, but even in our flakiest moments,

sonal battles against opportunism and a shadowy venality that invaded every aspect of public life. Everyone else on the planet got political revolutions, military dictatorships, ideological warfare that most often turned out to be power-crazed fanatics in uniforms murdering innocent civilians, or power-crazed fanatics putting innocent civilians into uniforms and sending them off to be murdered by other power-crazed fanatics: Argentina, El Salvador, Angola, Afghanistan, Cambodia, Iran/Iraq. We got a revolution of sexual behaviours and habits, and we got consumer goods.

The utopian belief that fired the Sexual Revolution supposed that if the practices and protocols of private sexuality could be democratized, the exploitive political and economic structures of western society would automatically democratize and become egalitarian. During the mid-1960s, when the fires were more or less out of control, one could have got general agreement from anyone that the feedback from the private and inner democratization of sexuality was going to make the nepotism and exploitiveness of

male/female relationships have lost those properties. Ferris doesn't find this Mexican Stand-off amusing, and neither does Annie. And since nothing is happening, it isn't good drama.

———————————

Annie clears her throat, and her gesture brings Ferris back to wary attention. This is no set-piece, that much he's sure of. He doesn't have the slightest idea what she'll do next. He doesn't know what he's going to do either.

Business as usual, he decides, trying to shelter himself with the irony. Lord knows Annie has been unpredictable from the first moment. He's never been certain what will happen, and still less about what *should* happen. He can't say which terrifies him more—her unpredictability or his attraction to her. Once, not very long ago, he'd called both "love."

Annie has her theories about their confrontation—several theories. They're more general than Ferris's. One is that anger is unrecognized sadness, and that sadness is unrecognized anger. Another is that it is males, not females, who are obtuse and manipulative. Her examples are her first and second husbands.

The first husband had been an artist. Not a very talented one, she explained to Ferris, and he blamed it on her. Eventually, she'd had to walk out. What was she supposed to do? She'd got the art history degree so she could talk to him and his inarticulate artist friends. Was she supposed to paint his fucking paintings too?

our social and political systems distasteful and untenable, and that these nasty engines of business would soon collapse or wither away, to be replaced with more progressive and egalitarian behaviours.

What we got—men and women alike—was virtually the opposite. Even before the 1960s were over, most of the initial good will had been buried beneath an institutionalization of opportunity, and a market-crazed invasion of material and erotic entrepreneurs. We were spared the violence of factional and state terrorism, military coup d'états, death squads, and rightist and leftist ideological massacres, sure. But we got a rigidification and desensitization of our social, economic, and political infrastructure and a withering away, not of the state, but of the value and dignity of labour and of the concept of a responsible and responsive body politic. We got Ronald Reagan, Margaret Thatcher, and George Bush, and we got the total commoditization of life—the Global Village.

And her second husband, the lawyer. She'd acted the role of suburban housewife for him, waited for him each evening until he got home, cooked gourmet meals, put up with the horrible smelly dog he decided they should have. He enjoyed the garden she planted and weeded, the deep-freeze filled with shopping bargains and frozen home-grown vegetables. For two years she'd endured the isolation, the mouldy plastic suburban shopping mall, the afternoon Tupperware parties. Two years out of her life, given to him.

But after a year of this, she took the LSAT exam to prove to him that she could pass it. She passed, all right. Her score was higher than his. When she went back to school the next year to study public administration, what was his response? Resentment. Sneaky resentment, the fucker.

Ferris was predisposed to believe what she said about her ex-husbands. But eventually he discovered the true villain. It was her father.

"He never loved me because I was female and small and not an athlete, the bastard," she'd said. "He wanted a son, and when my brother was born, he did nothing but make jokes about me."

Ferris got to know the story well, if not the father, who kept his distance from Annie. She'd put up with his jokes until she reached her teens. Then she began to fight back, and when she did, one kind of cruelty stopped and another began. "You're like a midget version of your mother," he'd told her. "Equal amounts of venom and ice. You'll never be able to hold on to a man for long."

But Annie was anything but her mother, a tall and rather agreeable woman who, from what little Ferris saw of her, seemed to have spent most of the last

We also got AIDS to deal with, along with a terrifying array of other sexually transmitted diseases. We're still coming to terms with the painful truth that sexual contact is never casual, and that there are profound limits to the individual organism's tolerance for mucous membrane contact.

The Sexual Revolution was largely over before the 1960s ended, but the biological consequences didn't arrive in full force for another decade. (I suspect that a similar set of delayed consequences—political this time—will accrue to the collapse of the left.) Not all the consequences were biological, either. How about Michael Milkin and junk bonds as the perfect symbol of how absolutely the Sexual Revolution was co-opted and perverted by an economic system that captured its libertarian élan while tossing out the notion of rational brakes and discretion.

The Vietnam War convinced a few of us that we're now front and centre amongst the planet's bad guys, and that the price of our affluence and well-being is paid in

twenty years drunk or bombed on tranquillizers. Whenever Ferris encountered her, she was half-crocked and dozy, but never abusive or violent. And yes—Annie's father was right about one thing—she was a little cold.

Annie went out of her way to make sure she wasn't any of those things, least of all cold. "Men are attracted to me," she told Ferris one night when she was a little drunk herself. "They go crazy over me and always have. So fuck him. Women don't live to keep men, not now. And I can hold any man as long as I need to."

Let me tell you a few things about what Ferris believes about Annie. He has developed an elaborate *theory* to explain what she does, and how she does it. The basic premise of the theory is that she makes up her world and herself to meet each new circumstance. She composes each day, each hour, each minute, and each event or incident, and everything is up for grabs. She exists in a world of total opportunity. Every day, then, she wakes up to a different world and self, with open properties and prizes, adjustable goals and penalties. Around such persons, familiarity is not renewable. Only strangeness is. He believes that she makes him up the same way, and to her, he is always a potential or actual stranger.

In the beginning he mistook her inventions of reality for what they produced: accommodation and adjacency. It seemed as if everything Ferris was interested in or believed coincided with her interests and beliefs. At first he sentimentalized this as love's inexplicable mystery, an irresistibly compelling one. He was only slightly puzzled that he hadn't met her before he did. They'd lived

misery by the balance of the planet's peoples. This is depressing to live with, but it wasn't what did in the Sexual Revolution. There was a secret part to the Vietnam War—the assassination of the Kennedy brothers, along with most of the other imaginative public figures in American life—and it taught us that the only safe way to exercise imagination is to screw one's brains out. Sex became soma, and the media perverts took over, the pornographers set up shop, and the whole thing got creepy and prurient.

The globalization of information seems to have affected us least of all. Most of us, while we're fussing over fad diets, exercise programs, or whatever part of the consumer grid our private vanity is wired into at the moment, don't seem to connect our private body images with the children who are starving all over the Third World, or with the terrified refugees from whatever Eastern European or Asian country is trying to exterminate its ideological or ethnic enemies at the moment. We've become a nastier, meaner collective in recent years. The rich have got richer, and our own poor are

in the same city for years, after all, and travelled in the same circles. Must have missed her, somehow. Later on, he called it shape-shifting, an ability that she paid a high price for. So, eventually, did he.

When Annie told him she could hold onto any man she wanted, Ferris had flinched. He flinched again at the recollection. His mind drifted to the day they'd got married. There had been plenty of signals that it was a mistake. The conventional ones were obvious: her third marriage, and he'd had a string of short-term live-ins, none stable, none longstanding. Most of their friends, separately, had been vocally against it. It became a joke between them—to the point where they made a list of objectors and tacked it onto the kitchen bulletin board. But when it came down to planning the wedding reception, they kept the guest list short.

The ceremony took place in a suburban government office, with Annie's current psychiatrist and his wife (a friend of Annie's from school) as witnesses. To Ferris it seemed too casual and provisional—he'd had a stronger sense of occasion the last time he renewed his driver's licence. The reception wasn't much better. It was more like war-zone diplomacy than a celebration. Polite, grim-faced people deposited gifts as bribes to good behaviour, offered congratulations that sounded like condolences. Then they shook their heads darkly and left after one drink. To hell with them, they'd said.

They lived in an erotic cocoon, and within it the lucky adjacencies seemed secure. As the cocoon closed around them, Ferris saw his friends drift away, one by one. It didn't seem to matter—he breathed Annie in deeper. He was, she

poorer, and sex is being reduced to quasi-capitalist strategies for getting off without getting killed.

Well, that sounds so grand I almost want to click my heels and float off as one of Eros's admirals. Fine, except I never was anything but a rather cowardly foot soldier. There's something phony about a willing if not always conscious participant to events providing a lofty hindsight overview as if he/she were preparing the whole thing for a pic/edit coffee table book by the historians down at Time Life Inc. So let me bring this closer to home and describe what it was like for men like me—young, WASP, educated, and uneasy.

For young male heterosexuals with an instinctive distaste for the status quo, the 1960s were a confusing but exhilarating time. To the very simple-minded (which most young men are, and were then) the era offered an alluring, contradictory series of erotic promises. Theoretically, one could get non-coercive sexual gratification whenever,

said, a superb lover. He'd shown her pleasures she'd never dreamed existed, she said. Or maybe that's simply what he heard, up close—self-hypnosis, maybe.

Feminists won't find this much of a surprise, I suppose. Male vanity. But if he believed *her*, he didn't believe *it*, not quite. He knew what every man eventually learns, and he'd learned to control the panic of knowing—that someone is always a better lover, some other man is always bigger and better. Yet there was a little more to his disbelief than that. She'd had plenty of lovers before him, and she was telling him he somehow had something superior. Was it simply that he happened to be the man she was "holding"? What did that really mean? More important, who, among the shifting identities, was she?

———————————

He's slipping away again, she is thinking. His eyes are darting off here and there. What has he been thinking about? Other women, probably, other places to be. He's like the others that way, except more so. Too slick to be real. A shallow, incurable womanizer. But that's the game, isn't it? Well, she can play that game, too. She's played it from the beginning, to get him, and she'd played it since, to hold him.

This last thought makes her throat constrict. Involuntarily, she clears it again, beginning to tap her finger on the side of the chair. Get his attention, somehow, get control.

He *will* leave, she decides. Eventually. This bastard, like the others. Well,

however, and with whomever one chose. In effect, we were placed in an arena that was still patently testosterone-driven, invited to confront the stupidest, most banal, and superfluous elements of our personalities, and to construct a new reality from them— with our women partners as equals, har, har. There were no ground rules, no referees, no breaks in the action. In no time at all, we were the captives of our Oedipal neuroses—and we were infested with bizarre ideas and bugs.

Even the early results were, to put it mildly, mixed. Most of us learned something of female anatomy, something about female sexuality, and a few hints about our own sexual nature. Unfortunately, the percentage of dissidents was very small, the bugs were too strong, and women quickly made it clear that the revolution to equalize sexual opportunities and pleasures was going to be carried on with or without male participation.

No, that doesn't quite ring true. It isn't that it is inaccurate. I gave a fair descrip-

she has a few more tricks up her sleeve to prevent that. She's done it before. She can prove him wrong. She is *not* shallow. She can hold onto any man, for as long as she wants.

Ferris sees the anger welling up in her face and forces himself to drift again. He recalls their counselling sessions in the months after they got married. The psychiatrist was trying to teach them to "harmonize the relationship" through self-hypnosis.

Ferris forgets himself and smiles. Counseling hadn't worked quite the way it was supposed to. Annie appeared to go under at will, but Ferris found he couldn't. Partly it was the psychiatrist. He was strangely shifty-eyed, which made him, well, not much of a hypnotist. His chief technique consisted of telling Annie and Ferris to relax—and count backward from twenty. No dangled watches, no beady eyes, just good intentions, and good vibes that neither they nor the psychiatrist could manufacture.

Ferris faked a hypnotic trance once—successfully, he thought. But as he and Annie were leaving the office after one session, she accused him of not going under.

"No," he confessed, pushing the elevator button. "Maybe I didn't, quite. It's hard being hypnotized by someone who can't look me in the eye."

"It isn't his job to hypnotize you," she snapped. "This is *self*-hypnosis."

"Oh, yeah," Ferris answered. "Then why do we need him there? To cash our cheques and make it real?"

The elevator door opened, and when he saw six or seven people inside, he

tion of the conceptual elements, and I defy anyone to argue that the primary arenas of political struggle in North America didn't, for a pivotal period from the mid-1960s through the early 1970s, devolve to sexuality and to its specific practices and purposes. It doesn't ring true because I'm still refusing to be personal, to reveal the private data that confirm my own failure to come to terms with the biological limitation each of us has. So here goes:

As early as 1965 I had highly specific evidence to suggest that I couldn't safely sleep with everyone who caught my eye, stirred my lust, fired my utopian impulses. It was a beautiful thing, this piece of evidence, painful enough to give occasion for second thoughts, itchy enough to wake me in the night for thirds and fourths. It was N.S.U., nonspecific urethritis, a lower-case instance of Immune System Red Alert in which one's own plumbing system responds to habitual contact with foreign biofluids by aping most of the minor symptoms of the Clap. Each new lover I had caused an allergic reaction

regretted his smart remark. Once engaged, Annie would continue an argument even if the Queen of England were present. He gestured for her to enter the elevator, and she strode inside.

"It's easy to blame the whole thing on him," she said, her voice loud enough for everyone in the elevator to hear. "Why don't you work at it a little harder? You never let go, you know that, don't you? Don't you care about harmonizing our relationship?"

Someone behind them snickered, and Ferris turned to see who it was. A man smiled at him, and he accepted the conspiracy, rolling his eyes.

"I'd be happier," he said, leaning close to her and speaking as quietly as he could, "if we just treated each other decently and left the mumbo-jumbo to your shifty-eyed friend. Besides, it'll be a pretty fragile harmony if it has to be hypnotically induced. And anyway, what does Fuckface mean by 'harmony'? Do you understand his bullshit?"

"Of course I understand," she answered in the same loud voice. "It means we'd be in tune with ourselves. And his name isn't Fuckface."

The man behind them giggled again, and this time Annie turned on him. "This is none of your concern, mister," she bristled. "Piss off."

Ferris reddened and shrugged an apology to the man. Mercifully, the elevator reached the ground floor and the doors slid open. Annie stepped out into the lobby and stopped dead, hands on hips. She wants, he thought to himself, to go at it in front of even more people.

"Okay, okay," he said, still speaking softly. "But just exactly what does it

that would last anywhere from a few hours to several months. At the first few extended outbreaks of N.S.U., I collapsed into a state of panic, ingested massive doses of antibiotics, and turned in the names of my partners to my doctor. When the tests came out negative, and I realized that my doctor wasn't turning in my partners to the authorities, I demanded an explanation. He gave me, at least fifteen years before AIDS became a public crisis, a perfectly clear description of how the human body responds to too-frequent screwing with strangers. He told me that my autoimmune system can handle only a limited number of encounters without collapsing. Biological life is not, he said, private.

I heard him out, nodding at all the right places. It sounded altogether too much like what I'd heard from the church and state, and I went on doing exactly what I pleased. I suspect that hundreds of thousands of us received similar explanations.

Still, it's too easy for heterosexuals to say that the microbes won the war. For

mean to be 'in tune with ourselves'? I thought we were there to put ourselves in harmony with one another. I mean, look at us, for Christ's sake. We haven't even got out of the building and we're fighting."

"That's because you're an unco-operative, cynical asshole," Annie shouted at the top of her voice.

Ferris watched her storm off across the lobby, more embarrassed than penitent. He stopped to buy some cigarettes, then read a few pages of *People Magazine* at the newsstand to give her time to cool off—or brew up a real storm. He wasn't sure which.

He found her in the parking lot, sitting on the hood of the car. She was serenely fixing her make-up.

"You know," he said, "I think what that gerbil means by tuning into ourselves is tuning into his goofy brand of narcissism."

"That's just your ill-informed paranoid opinion," she answered without looking around. "And he isn't a gerbil."

She went on fixing her make-up, ignoring him. He got into the car and started it. "Are you going to get into the car, or do you want to pretend this is a parade float and you're a beauty queen? We could do that if you like."

"I'm not moving from here until you promise you'll start taking these sessions seriously."

"How can I take them seriously when they're not serious?" he said, nudging the car into gear and revving the engine.

She turned to face him, and when her eyes locked with his, Ferris lost his

us, there never was a war. It was declared, ignorant armies assembled and marched back and forth across the field, flashing their colours by day and discharging their weapons into the air at night, just as they've done throughout history whenever the stakes seemed to be high enough or lunatics were in control. The real battles have been fought, so far, in other people's bodies. There were serious skirmishes in what we erroneously thought were our private lives, some people wandered into minefields or into supply-line traffic, and some were killed or crippled. Some of us got frightened and most of us went home and became the chartered accountants, film makers, truck drivers, and supermarket managers we were expected to become.

The irony is that no one made it all the way home. There was no home to go back to. Knowledge possesses those who possess it, particularly carnal knowledge. One is changed, and so are the things one lives with and by. We know something

appetite for stormy weather. "I don't know," she answered. "But you'd better figure it out."

It took fifteen more minutes to get her into the car—and for him to "figure it out."

He tried to hypnotize himself for three more sessions. He tried to empty his mind, counting backward from twenty, nineteen, eighteen. He tried it from forty, then from sixty. Except for the time he fell asleep somewhere between thirty and twenty, he always arrived at zero wholly, consciously himself, unharmonized. After the third session he told her he simply wasn't suggestible, that it was a waste of time. He went a little further than that, actually, saying that he'd been right all along—the psychiatrist really was a fuckfaced rodent, and that all he was trying to do was to get them to run on his treadmill with him. But this time when Annie lost her temper and screamed at him in the lobby, it was Ferris who walked away.

She followed him to the parking lot, keeping up a stream of high-volume invective the whole way. He opened the car door, and watched as she perched herself on the hood of the car again.

"Did it ever occur to you that I've been going to these sessions just to keep you from screaming at me all the time?" he said to her turned back.

"I'm not yelling at you now, am I?" she snapped.

about the casualties of AIDS, herpes, the resistant strains of V.D. The moral casualties are different, and they are so numerous and complicated that no one will count them by any agreed-to method.

Yet it isn't all bleakness. Sexual life today is very different than it was in the 1950s. Those days—with psychic fire hydrants and gunshops at every street corner and at every rite of passage—were great fun and games for hetero males and no fun at all for everyone else. In fact, I'd say that sexual life today is better, despite its difficulties. Most of the improvements have occurred because women are much stronger than they were forty years ago. Even for men, this strength is a beautiful thing to witness—if you are not on the business end of the hostilities built into it. Of course, women understand the improvements better than men do. Many women are openly pissed off with men and with the deeper traps sexuality lays for them. And men are afraid of this anger. Some men cower, others

Ferris dropped the car keys on the hood beside her and turned back toward the lobby. When he arrived home three hours later, she was more furious than when he left her.

"I can't believe you walked away from me like that," she said before he was clear of the doorway, her voice at lobby pitch.

For a split second, he felt his self-control start to dissolve. He took a step toward her, and stopped. "I've had enough," he said, making his voice sound mild. "And you know I can't bear to argue in public. Do you really expect me to stand there and let you shovel shit on me?"

She wasn't backing away for a second. "So it's fine if you make a fool out of me?"

"You mean by walking away from you while you're out of your mind? You were making a fool of yourself without my help. I just refused to witness it, that's all."

"I'm talking about the counselling sessions, you stupid asshole," she yelled. "If you quit you're being disloyal to the relationship."

"Fuck the relationship," he said.

"Then fuck you," she countered. "If you won't go, I'll go by myself. If you won't help us, I'll do it alone."

He considered asking her how she intended to harmonize solo, but stifled it. "You'll do what you like," he answered. "As always."

---

glower, but no man has it right, and nobody—male or female—is very happy with our collective condition. And that is not a bad thing because what we thought was the Sexual Revolution was merely basic training for the real thing, the Gender War that may, depending on how intelligently we respond, make some sort of humane and pleasant reality of the socialist utopia people dreamed of as the 1960s began.

A sexual Counter-revolution, like it or not, is now in progress, and it is blurring the issues. For anyone who was on the front lines of the Sexual Revolution, this Counter-revolution is a nightmare. All the old enemies are in the ascendant— the chartered accountants who believe that life is a series of private-investment opportunities orbiting within a zero/sum universe; the authoritarians with their ordnance and their endless ordinances against disorder, abnormality, and noncon- formity; the fundamentalists—it doesn't matter where or what they worship—

Annie went off to the psychiatrist alone. After the fifth solitary session, she announced that the psychiatrist had hypnotized her into quitting smoking. She stayed off cigarettes for two days. Ferris kept right on smoking, even though he was having more and more difficulty ignoring the absence of harmony between them.

The private hypnosis sessions ended hilariously. Annie came home and announced that the psychiatrist had left his wife and run off with an ex-patient who was "into" astrology and witchcraft.

Ferris laughed. "What did you expect?"

"I expected you to take it more seriously. Did you know he's been making passes at me?"

"No," he answered, abruptly serious. "I didn't. Did he really?"

"Yes."

"Well, if he was making passes at you, why did you keep on going to him?"

"I thought he was just trying to make me feel attractive."

"You need a nutty psychiatrist to confirm that you're attractive? What does that make me?"

"Someone who only thinks about himself," she snapped.

At her urging, they moved into an upscale co-op in a more fashionable section of town.

who want everyone under the thumb of their peculiar ideology; even the bugs and viruses who just want to grow and know nothing of how beautiful human beings are in moonlight with a few buttons undone.

Whether we care to admit it or not, the ordnance for each and all of these enemies is the same: STDs as the conventional weapons, AIDS as the nukes. They speak of AIDS in precisely the same terms as the moralists of the pre-penicillin days spoke of syphilis, and, like their predecessors, they ignore the fact that the primary victims are the poor, the disabled, and the socially marginal. The God-fearing moral authoritarians of a century ago were politically resistant to finding a cure for syphilis at least partially because they recognized its uses. Like most visitations of the divine, it kept the poor frightened of one another, and it kept the marginal on the margins. I suspect that contemporary authoritarians—in a more subtle way—are playing the same game, hoping it will wipe out gays, drug users, and the

"We need a change of scene," she said.

The condominium was directly below that of a couple who were friends of hers, and to him it soon felt like they were living in someone's basement suite. He began to resent the place. Despite the increased floor space and the designer architecture, it felt crowded. There were more rooms than in their old place, but the spaces were smaller, the ceilings were lower, and there were no nooks and crannies he could second as his own. His complaints were symptoms of something else, and he knew it. The truth was that he was lonely.

It was a puzzling sensation. Except during working hours he was rarely apart from her. How could he be lonely?

In the colder light of this new condominium, Ferris began to notice that he and Annie had startlingly little in common. She protected her always-shifting identity—the one that only months before had seemed to fit in and around him like a glove—firmly and ferociously. Well, that was okay, he reasoned. She was an individual, wasn't she?

That was one of a number of rhetorical questions he comforted himself with: they couldn't agree on everything, could they? Wasn't this a democracy, equality of the sexes?

But some of the other questions, ones that hadn't mattered when they were first together, emerged in new and more urgent formulations. If she adored everything about him and the way he lived, how had they ended up in surroundings that were comfortable only to her? And again, why did he feel lonely?

sexually promiscuous. Back there somewhere, they're probably hoping it will also exterminate most of Africa and control population growth in the rest of the underdeveloped world.

Theories about the origins of AIDS—none of which are certain, and all of which are conceptually evasive—have the same revealing characteristics. Gay flight attendants, homosexuals en masse, monkeys, Congo pygmies, white South Africans, and the CIA have been blamed. The origin theories are typically hagiographic rather than empirical—they assign blame and hint at the appropriateness of the victims, and propose a coterie of authoritarian agencies to dictate and enforce improved behaviours. Together and separately, each of these origin theories misses the point. AIDS is the consequence of the cherished contemporary western practice of going too far too fast without checking either the scenery along the way or calculating the eventual trajectory. AIDS is a tragic consequence, but it

Eventually he admitted to himself that there were huge discrepancies between what Annie *said* she was and wanted, and what she *did*. For instance, at the same time as she said that her career wasn't important to her, she pursued it with single-minded intensity. Well, single-minded was her way of doing everything, wasn't it? But then why did she deny its importance, and why was she claiming that she really wanted to do and be something else—go back to school, write a book, take more time to relax and think?

The registration pins on this picture just weren't lining up properly, and however much Ferris fiddled with the accumulated overlays, the composite grew more fuzzy. First of all, ambitious, single-minded people don't stop to relax and think, and they don't stop in mid-career to write books or go back to school. In the swirl of her evolving and devolving identities, Annie didn't stop ten minutes in an average week to relax and think.

Second, her career—not his—was at the centre of their collective life even though she insisted that it bored and demeaned her, wasted her time and energy. This was the time and energy that she insisted should be devoted to some unspecified "creative" activity he could never get her to define. So which personality was the true one? The one that she said was entirely devoted to him, the relax-and-take-account personality she talked up, or the full-schedule executive on a career track that she lived?

Early on, Annie didn't seem to take herself very seriously. Now he noticed that she pursued a full-frame coterie of private habits the same way she did her career. Make-up and clothing rituals, swimming, recreational weight-lifting,

is part and parcel of the way our entire civilization operates.

In the midst of the hysteria, we've forgotten that the Sexual Revolution, despite its political naïvete and its brutal biological consequences, arose out of some fine and remarkably generous assumptions about what life ought to be like. One of those assumptions was mammalian, the other was humane and existential. The mammalian assumption was that there exists an unclammy order to human life that seeks to educate the senses and liberate (and gratify) new kinds of intelligence. The humane and existential assumption was that the point of bodily life is to achieve an environment free of violence, coercion, and manipulation. What I'm suggesting, as plague and new infestations of authority threaten to turn us into reptiles, is that the Sexual Revolution may have been the most admirable social experiment the human species has ever attempted, and its sweetest interlude from the cacophony of greed, coercion, and gleaming ordnance.

aerobics exercises, the too-many glasses of imported white wine with dinner. None were optional, all of them sucked up her leisure time. It wasn't that they were unusual, and they were hardly nasty. They could be found featured in the latest issue of *Self* magazine or *Cosmopolitan*. In fact, you could probably find them all there in any one issue.

So they made a banal kind of sociological sense, but he was reluctant to put them together with her. What was wrong with them—as she practised them? Nothing that he could argue successfully with her, or even with himself. Weren't they different people, she would say, from different social and economic backgrounds? Shouldn't independent people do what they like? Isn't everyone, after all, an individual? I'm okay, you're okay, right?

Of course. Everything she said was quite correct. But it was slippery, and her okay governed his okay. Even that wasn't hard to explain away whenever it became an issue: she was an active person, he wasn't. By his own admission, he wasn't big on socializing or career schmoozing. Activities had to have some reasonably entertaining or educative purpose before he'd get interested. Left to his own devices, he'd do little other than loaf and think. He was no athlete, for sure. The only sports he'd played were team sports—baseball, some hockey, a little soccer. To exercise, as she did, without some immediate goal in mind, struck him as, well, narcissistic. His body wasn't a temple, just a machine that he used, a space he moved around with his mind.

In the small northern town where Ferris grew up, people had to live together whether or not they had anything in common. It taught him the comforts of

In sharp contrast, the Counter-revolution plays to most of nature and civilization's nastiest impulses: paranoia, xenophobia, homophobia, anal-compulsive behaviours of all sorts, the lust to control and bully others. It feeds the rancour of the thwarted, the cheated, the terrified, the sick, and the hypochondriacal, and it comforts those who suffer sensory disability, deprivation, or perversity. The Counter-revolution supposes that order is never generous, that only the strong and aggressive have the right to survive, that sensory experience through layers of latex is a sensible alternative to life as a thinking, sensitized mammal. Worse, it believes that the point of bodily life is to avoid cohabitation and symbiosis, to achieve and maintain body integrity even if the price is total isolation. These values contradict the utopian ones of the Sexual Revolution utterly and implacably, and they ought to be rejected because they constitute a profound devolution of the species—precisely at a point in history where we desperately need to make a vast evolutionary leap ahead.

being alone, or in a community based on co-operative activities, usually physical and short-term. Social and technical education wasn't left to professionals. From early childhood, you worked alongside your family and friends, you helped them, and they helped you. That was how you learned. And you didn't only learn about things. You learned who you were that way. While your shoulder was against the wheel, your elders bent your ear on how and why things were done.

"Nail this frame wall to the next one with four-inch spikes."

"Why four-inch spikes and not three?"

"Because three-inch spikes won't hold the wood. And if the wood doesn't hold, the house will fall down, and if that happens, we'll go out of business, and if that happens, the Commies will take over."

The short-form social code was simple: Die for your friends, kill your enemies, and be polite to strangers. Most of the time it worked that way, but when it didn't, there was another, more ominous code: *Cheat, Lie, Steal, Fight with Pipe Wrench.* Either way, Ferris still lived by those codes despite the reactionary political and economic values that went along with them. He preferred practical problems, and he wasn't much interested in collective activities unless they involved some sort of physical work, such as helping a friend rebuild a fallen porch, rewire a house, or repair a defective automobile carburetor.

To be fair, there was a dark side to this idyll. You can't always work, after all. And when the work was done, Ferris had seen his small, physically dependent

Much as the authoritarians would like us to believe that we're confronting an either/or choice, we're not. There is a third alternative to self-dooming revolution or an insurgent devolution to the repressive social instruments of the past. Maybe there is an infinity of choices open, but I can see at least one alternative that is more sensible and humane than the choice between suicidal promiscuity and sensory deprivation currently being offered up. That third alternative, long overdue, is to grow up.

To do that, we'll first have to stop whining about the sanctity of the preconscious and sociopathic wellsprings of individual sexual identity. Our erotic impulses aren't sacrosanct. They only seem to be because our access to them is so thoroughly polluted by self-inflicted ignorance and egomania. For more than a half century, the therapy industry has encouraged people to let their childhood traumas and Oedipal slag fester to the point that permanent emotional adoles-

community pressure its members in some very ugly ways. He'd seen those pressures make couples who hated each other stay together, and he'd scrambled across the rubble all too often—drunken, violent men, crazy, manipulative women, their loony offspring. It was one reason he left, and even still, the slightest hint of domestic squalor sent him running for cover.

Annie's background couldn't have been more different. She'd been raised in an upper-middle-class urban suburb, in the kind of family where money, multiple television sets, and community facilities both enable and enforce the sense that life is best lived by professional procedures and standards. Her parents drove big American cars, dressed expensively if not particularly well, and thought of themselves as having a "lifestyle." As far as Ferris could see, this had meant that her father played a lot of tennis, her mother drank a lot of gin, and both flew to Hawaii several times a year so they could pursue their avocations under a fashionably hot sun.

Ferris gathered, from Annie's disparaging descriptions of childhood, that her upbringing consisted mainly of watching her parents sitting around a barbecue with their professional colleagues and enemies—they were one and the same—bitching about the selfishness of their employees, the bad taste of their social inferiors, and the unscrupulousness of competitors—and trying to figure out ways to get one up on them, the banks, and the rest of the human species.

There was more to it than that, of course. Her parents had provided her with a social education and an outlook, mostly by sending her off to be trained

cence has become a basic human right. In a sense, the main achievement of modern psychology is the discovery that there is a part of us all that hasn't quite climbed down from the trees or crawled out of the cave and/or womb—a discovery that has been turned over to the motivation researchers and the marketeers rather than to us.

Instead of using our immense material wealth and technological sophistication to free ourselves from this paranoic simian origin, psychology and the therapy industry have merely reshaped civilization into a more comfortable approximation of the environments we inhabited at the threshold of consciousness—network television high in the trees, showers and toilets for the womb, nuclear weapons guarding the mouth of the cave. What a waste. Human consciousness is a unique gift, a miracle, and our disposal of it involves an inherent and progressive contract: The field must be extended and refined. If it isn't, it will devour us.

at a hundred summer camps and after-school classes. Over the years, these saddled her with a series of recreationally defined identities. She'd been a figure-skater, a swimmer, a skier, and she'd participated in a succession of business-oriented organizations from Junior Achievement to Christian Girls in Training. Her parents, obsessed with their own idle pursuits, seem to have gone out of their way to make sure she'd never had a moment to herself.

It explained several things about her. In the midst of her need to be constantly active, she had no way to distinguish between work and play. It was no wonder she was in perpetual pursuit of some exterior goal or another.

Meanwhile, she wasn't interested in the co-operative physical projects that Ferris found so comforting. In her sense of how things were done, one joined a committee that then hired other people to do physical labour. The Categorical Imperative, which filled Ferris with a kind of democratic awe, induced a yawn of indifference from her. "Unsophisticated," she once described it.

And what was Annie thinking while Ferris was running her through this microscope? Until she realized he was examining her, she thought about other things. The job. The new car she wanted. The senior associate at work she thought was about to start hitting on her. And she thought about the relationship. Was it working? Was it growing?

To extend this contract, we'll have to get our erotic hearts and minds around the two parameters that the Sexual Revolution ignored: violence and will. In an otherwise-sensible recent London *Sunday Times* article on the sexual revolution in Britain, for instance, comes this Manichean line: "The pleasures of sex are inextricable from its darker side; that goes without saying." We hear that message reinforced at every turn, without much sense of what, specifically, awaits us in the darkness or who is responsible for keeping the lights from being turned on. It's easy to dismiss this attitude as nothing more than the 1990s' version of "sex is dirty," but it has become more complicated than that. Few people today believe sex is dirty, but what we do believe is perhaps worse. We've been bamboozled into believing that sex and violence run together—with roughly the same certitude as people in the fourteenth century believed that the world was flat.

The link between desire and violence may spring from the same chemical

The fights didn't bother her. On that count, the psychiatrist was affirming what she already believed. Fights were signals of passion, of commitment. What was it D.H. Lawrence said? Love and hate aren't opposites. They're aspects of the same passion. Indifference is love's opposite. Or something similar. If the fights were to stop, that would be real trouble. For her, real life was a series of crises.

Then she woke up one morning and discovered Ferris sitting on the edge of the bed, staring at her. When she demanded to know what he was thinking about, he wouldn't—or couldn't—explain. He got up and left the room, made his breakfast and left without a word. He'd never done that before.

She began to see things differently. What had she glimpsed in his eyes, across the bed? Love? Hate? Something else? Not indifference. Not that.

The questions snowballed in her mind. Why wouldn't he talk or fight? Was he still committed to the relationship? Was she was losing him?

When he declined to engage with her, she began to worry publicly, going out for the evening with her friends and filling their heads with stories about her husband's strangeness, his lack of commitment, his insensitivity.

"Why don't you leave him?" they asked. "If he's such a bastard, why do you stay?"

She couldn't answer. "He'll have to leave first," she said. "Don't ask me why."

When she returned home, usually late, they'd fight. "If I'm so awful," she'd say, "why don't you leave?"

source—testosterone—but desire and violence are different phenomena and have infinitely different relationships with our biological infrastructure. Desire is a basic component, while violence is a symptom of system failure. Intertwining them is like assuming that because we run our sewer pipes close to our water pipes, shit is going to come out of tap as often as clear water. That doesn't happen in our cities because some sensible people have recognized that even though sewage and water mix easily and are handled by similar engineering procedures, it is unhealthy to get them confused. Much earlier, we decided that it was wrong to permit people to murder one another because the civil costs were too high. We're now at a similar point with sexual violence. It costs too much—in destroyed or dysfunctional people, in the harm done by victims taking revenge or repeating the cycle of cruelty in successive generations—for us to continue treating sexual violence as an unavoidable fact of life.

"I don't know if you're awful," he'd answer, keeping the microscope trained on her. "I'm not sure who you are."

———————————

Now, since this story is about a Mexican Stand-off, trying to decide which of them is the villain isn't as important as deciphering their attitudes toward language and violence, since eventually, some permutation of the two will be used to break the stand-off. Here's what I think:

Annie uses language as a manipulative tool, and in the absence of long-term strategies, she employs verbal violence as a strategic device to gain immediate tactical ends. She'll say whatever gets the effect she needs or wants, and she'll scoff if you suggest that there's any profound connection between this and people hitting one another. Like many middle-class people who've never been subjected to violence, she'd admit that verbal abuse can be damaging, but it's different. Violence is terrible and ugly, and it's strictly physical. It's something that happens to, or between, other people. And she steers clear of those sorts of people.

Ferris believes that language is a political tool, one that most resembles a double-edged blade, and he manipulates it with more circumspection. He thinks its primary function is to serve as an alternative to physical violence. He's seen plenty of violence, he's hit other men in anger, and he's been hit. In his experience, the borders between language and physical violence tend to

Exerting unwanted physical or emotional force against others was evil two hundred thousand years ago, and it is today. We're so busy censuring it in others, hiring more police officers and protecting our private asses from proximity to it that we've forgotten that political and social violence are symptoms of failure—indictments that we lack, as a collective and as individuals, the imagination and skill to find alternatives—and to educate one another about them. In the erotic arena, the borderlines are elusive, but they are nowhere near as fuzzy as we make them out to be. We lack the will to define them accurately and forcefully, that's all. When we blame our sorrows and erotic dysfunctions on childhood wounds inflicted by incompetent or malevolent adults—usually our parents—it frees us from having to confront our own specific incompetences and malevolences. If the opprobrium attached to sexual violence were more firmly assigned—both in civil terms as crime and psycho-socially as *inexcusable stupidity*—much of the non-psychotic violence

disappear pretty easily under stress, and he believes that he has a personal responsibility to make sure they don't. If he can't do that, he's nothing more than another wild beast. He's troubled by the psychological violence he and Annie use on one another—troubled quite a lot. He tells himself that he mind-fucks her only to defend himself, but he doesn't quite believe it. The reality is a little more complicated and unpleasant, and he knows it. He thinks she's trying to provoke him into being physically violent with her. And the truth is, he's come close.

Too abstract? Okay, let me give you an illustration. On a weekend trip to the United States, Annie nearly sideswipes an oncoming car by pulling out of a parking lot without looking. The driver of the car, a husky, bearded man with a potbelly, pulls up beside her, honks his horn until he gets her attention and then curses her out. Annie sticks her hand out the window, middle finger up, and curses back at him. Fat fucking turkey.

The man stays behind her, and at the next stop sign, he gets out of his car and gives her a terse, obscenity-filled lecture on driving etiquette and the stupidity of foreigners. Annie rolls up the window while the lecture is being delivered, and at the end of it, gives him the finger once more, even though there's only a thin sheet of safety glass between them.

Ferris is pretty sure how she will respond, so while the irate motorist is speech-making, he carefully opens the car door, gets out, and walks to the rear of the car. His plan is to distract the man and—one way or the other—draw him away from Annie. Or, if things get truly nasty, Ferris intends to be in a

that makes women despise men would probably evaporate. Aggressive pathologies could be treated and the victims could be healed and/or compensated. Our current collective failure to retool our institutions and to redefine ourselves is without excuse.

Sexual violence should be defined by unequivocal prohibitions against inflicting physical injury or emotional trauma. We know that, but we can't quite seem to get at it. Why? Because for all our liberality, we're too damned prudish when it gets down to the fine, physical details.

We know that some people, for instance, like to stick their fist up their lover's asses or vaginas. Within my definition that seems quite okay—provided the recipients consent to it not only in the passion of the moment but also four to six hours later, and provided that no long-term injuries result from the practice. People can tie up their lovers with ribbons or ropes or chains if that's what they go

position to jump him before he can harm her. At the precise moment that she lifts the finger and mouths the expected "Screw off," Ferris says, "Can we deal with this back here?"

It works. The man slams the top of the car with his hand and lumbers back to confront Ferris. Ferris, meanwhile, calculates whether to hit the man without warning as he approaches—get the first punch in. He decides not to, and leans on the hood of the other man's car, keeping his right hand in a position where he can unload a quick punch if it comes to that. He bows his head and speaks so quietly that the man has to lean forward to hear what he's saying. "You'll have to excuse her," he says. "She's pregnant."

It isn't a rational excuse, of course, but it works. The other man's moment of psychosis has passed, he's respectful of pregnant women, and all Ferris has to do is listen to a much calmer lecture about good driving. All three escape unscathed.

As Ferris and Annie drive on, she asks him what he said to the man. "Nothing much," he answers. "Guy talk. You know."

She explodes. "Oh, that's just wonderful. This fat goon threatens to hit me, and you act like he's your best buddy?"

"Did you want me to get into a fight with him?" he counters. "What if I'd lost? Where would that have put you?"

"I'm sure you wouldn't have lost," she answers, clearly believing what she's saying.

"You shouldn't confuse what you'd like to believe," he says, "with what's safe

for—as long as there are no bruises or burns afterward, and the aggressor doesn't end up losing control and stabbing his or her lover with an icepick. Short of harm, such practices are private consensualities, and accurate utilizations of metaphor.

Where we foul up on this is in the utilization-of-metaphor part of it. We need to understand the nature of metaphor much better than we do, and respect its immense powers. Metaphors are intellectual devices that permit us to operate in complex environments without resorting to literalness and confrontation. They are the honeyed human packing we have placed between ourselves and the violence and arbitrariness of nature, they are the nurturing fog that keeps the inherent loneliness of being at bay, the disguise we drape across otherness so we don't exterminate it out of fear.

Given this absolute prohibition against violence I'm proposing, I'd say we

to believe. It isn't safe to believe that I can protect you no matter what you do. This isn't," he adds after a long pause, "that kind of world. And I'm not that kind of a man."

Still too theoretical? Well, I'm trying to record some of Ferris's confusion as he tries to figure Annie out, and to decide what he should do with this Mexican Stand-off. For him it has come to this: He doesn't approve of her, and there is no friendship and little common interest between them to bond them to one another. But there is her warm and sweet-scented body in the bed next to him each night, and there is a terrible vulnerability to her heedlessness, to her head-long inventions of herself and the world. For her, I'm not so sure what there is. Panic and too much certainty, as before, as always, jumbled together. I do know it scares the hell out of Ferris.

_____

Without the psychiatrist and the bogus but neutral forum the sessions with him provide, Ferris and Annie begin to argue and fight even more. At first, the fights are confused and confusing. Annie accuses Ferris of trying to destroy her sense of herself. Ferris tries to argue around that, but eventually he admits that unless he can shake out her self-inventions, he'll never know who she is.

At this she becomes hysterical, weeping and raging at him at the same time. "You're driving me crazy," she says. "If you don't stop it I'm going to have a breakdown. I'll collapse. Then what'll you do?"

ought to proceed by leaving the erotic field both wide open, fairly well lit, and frequently swept by our considerable tools of intelligence. Yet because we haven't the courage or will to investigate our sexual pathologies or practices, we seem prepared to plunge ourselves back into a darkness that is more egregious and aggressive than the one we've recently escaped from. Where sexuality connects with metaphor, we indulge our societal vice of separating art from life, and where it is rooted in infantile attractions, we mystify it for ourselves, check our personal investment portfolios and turn away when others start behaving strangely. We remain hung up in the kaka universe bowdlerized from Jung and Freud—even while we're making fun of it—because it permits us to climb back into the trees or the cave, where we can nurture our clandestine, inexcusable adolescence.

Men are worse offenders in this than women are, partly because testosterone is

"Go ahead and collapse," he says. "Maybe we'll find out who you are."

She accuses him of withdrawing from her. "You're a passive-aggressive," she says. He replies—angrily—that he can't see any alternative.

She recoils from his anger. "You're an essentially violent person," she claims. "I never understood that until now."

He's contemptuous. "Get to the real point," he says.

Her tone changes from confrontational to seductive. "I'm dying inside," she whispers. "Our relationship is dying, and it's your fault."

He ignores the shift in tone deliberately. A small light has appeared, a light from outside the cocoon they've built around them.

"I love *you*," he says, fixing on what he believes is a crucial error in her thinking. "I do not love our relationship. I'm tired of hearing about it, tired of talking about it. It gets more attention than either of us. I get into bed and there it is, between us, around us, telling us what to do and what not to do. If we don't get rid of it, it is going to suffocate us."

The look on her face tells him she doesn't understand what he's saying, so he elaborates. Or tries to. It's an elusive notion he's trying to pursue, and she isn't going to help him.

"It's like there's this gooey substance between us, and I can't get through it." He reaches over her shoulder as if to tear at it, pull it down to show her. She doesn't see it, but she does see the frustration in his expression.

"I can't take any more of this," she answers. "You hate me, don't you? You think I'm crazy. Don't think I can't see it. I can. And you'd better remember what crazy people are capable of."

Ferris is stopped dead by this. What is she saying? Is she threatening to kill him, kill herself, what?

It doesn't take long to find out. The next morning at breakfast, Annie swallows a handful of pills in front of him. He forces her to stick her finger down

more poisonous to rationality than estrogen is, but mostly because when sexuality is brought up into the unfriendly light of responsible causality and common sense, darkness serves the anticonscious habits and traditions of males better than those of women. Various therapies might help us to understand those habits and traditions better, but only if the therapists stop coddling neuroses, which are about the least interesting of our spiritual and intellectual possessions. Ultimately it is our personal and collective will that is going to decide whether we enjoy this miserable, misery-making mess too much to change it.

her throat, and discovers that the pills are only aspirin. He threatens to take her to the hospital to have her stomach pumped, and she promises not to do it again. The incident ends where you'd expect—in bed. It's the only place they're comfortable.

A second suicide attempt several days later is serious—or at least, it is a little more protracted. They fight over some small thing—their arguments are now a daily ritual and might concern anything from his failure to notice a new perfume to her lateness to dinner. This argument is little different, except that it escalates to name-calling: "Authoritarian prick," she calls him; he replies with "Bourgeois bitch," etc.

Annie leaves the apartment weeping, without a coat or purse. She gets into her car and disappears into the night—he thinks, to drive around the block for a few minutes, then to return as she has done before, unapologetic but seductive.

This time she doesn't return. A few minutes become an hour, and then two. Somewhere in the third hour Ferris receives a phone call from one of her friends, a woman he barely knows, one of her co-workers.

"Annie's psychotic," the woman says, after establishing that she's phoned the correct number. "Can you come down here and get her? She says she's going to jump out the window if you don't."

Ferris can hear Annie screaming obscenities in the background and feels his earlier anger rekindle. "Take her to the emergency ward," he says, naming a hospital close to the woman's apartment. "I'll meet you there."

"I've already tried to get her to go to the hospital," the woman answers. "She won't go. She says this is your fault, that you have to come and get her. Just a minute…"

He hears the two women arguing, and then the sounds of furniture crashing around in the room, then their voices again, quieter now. The woman returns to the phone.

"She just tried to jump from the balcony. You'd better get here right away."

Before he can answer, she hangs up. He doesn't have anything to say, anyway.

Ferris tries to force himself not to hurry, but in the end he does. He double-parks in front of the apartment block and runs up the steps three at a time. Luckily, someone is leaving the building as he approaches the front door, and he is able to slip in without having to buzz. Inside, he checks the tenant register to get the apartment number: 302. The indicator light on the elevator reads "3." Too slow. He takes the stairs four at a time.

It comes to him as he knocks on the apartment door: Since the ground slopes sharply upward from the front to the back of the building, and 302 is on the back side of the building, the distance from the balcony to the ground can be no more than about ten feet. He begins to giggle as the woman opens the door. She looks harassed and tired, and her expression tells him she doesn't think his merriment is appropriate. His wife—he reminds himself of her identity—is lying on the living-room rug, her clothing rumpled, hair in a tangle.

September 12, 1981

BELFAST, NORTHERN IRELAND: Twenty-year-old Alan Clark, a locally recruited part-time member of the Ulter Defense Regiment, was shot to death from a passing car as he walked along a suburban street.

ATLANTA, GEORGIA: The National Center For Disease Control reported that a penicillin-resistant strain of gonorrhea "imported from the Philippines" is spreading through Dade County, Florida. The Center's spokesman also noted a 33 percent rise in syphilis cases in the U.S. during 1980.

Her back is toward him. "Once she knew you were coming she quietened down," Annie's friend says by way of explanation. "She's been like that for about ten minutes now. If you don't mind, I'm going to leave while you sort things out."

"That's probably a good idea," he says to her. "Thanks for helping." He brushes past her, stifles his giggles, and bends over Annie as he hears the door close. "Annie," he says.

He sees her body tense. Her body is in a very awkward pose, he notes, probably designed to create the maximum visual impact on him when he entered.

"What do *you* want?" she snaps.

"You're the one who had me come down here," he answers, touching her shoulder with his hand. "Why don't you tell me what it is *you* want?"

Annie recoils from his touch and struggles to her feet. "Don't you try to fondle me, you bastard! You made me do this! You put me into this with your goddamned Mister Cool shit. I never want to see you again!"

Her ferocity strikes him as silly, and as he tries to grab at her arms to restrain

36

her, he begins to laugh. That sends her into a frenzy, and he lets her go. She makes a dash for the sliding glass doors that lead to the balcony, jerks them partly open, tries to dive over the railing. He grabs her around the waist as she falls and pulls her back behind the railing.

"I'm not laughing at you," he lies, holding on to her. "It's just that I didn't think you were serious."

"I *am* serious, you fucker!" she screeches, and struggles harder to escape from his grip. "Let go of me!"

He turns her away from the railing and leans out over the balcony to avoid her flailing fingernails. As he turns his head and looks down, he sees that it is less than six feet to the ground. If she fell, she'd land in some shrubs. Just for a second he considers calling her bluff—letting her make her suicide leap—but he decides against it. She probably won't hurt herself, but later on he'll have to deal with her humiliation. He doesn't want to face that.

She keeps on struggling, and he begins to understand that despite the ridiculousness of the suicide site, this isn't slapstick or melodrama. But it isn't quite drama, either. He isn't sure quite what it is, except that he's caught in it. And the woman struggling against him is not quite Annie, the woman he lives with, his wife. This is someone—something—else, something out of control. His laughter dies.

He carries her back into the apartment and sits down on the couch, forcing her to sit on his lap, his arms still around her. She continues to struggle, screaming at him now for treating her like a child, demanding that he let her go. He holds on, and gradually, she grows quiet, and the tension in her body eases. When he releases her from his grip, she slumps onto the cushions beside him, exhausted.

"I hate you," she says.

"Fine," he answers. "Are you ready to go to the hospital?"

"I'm not going to the hospital," she replies, her tone suddenly cool. "All I did was take a couple of tranquillizers. I must have had an allergic reaction."

He tries to sound as reasonable as he can. "Let's let the people at the hospital sort that out. Where's your coat?"

"I don't have a coat," she says, this time sounding indignant. "I was too upset when I left your place."

"Don't blame that on me. And it's our place, not mine. Remember? We're married."

He waves his left hand in the air, wiggling the finger that carries the ring

The Author's Official Plan, and the Disclaimers

Starving people don't think about sex. A few days ago, a man named Mohammed Osman slumped down behind the hulk of a burned-out truck only a mile from the gates of the U.N. relief camp outside Mogadishu, Somalia, curled himself into the foetal position and gave up his struggle to continue breathing. As he lost consciousness for the final time, he was definitely not thinking about, say, the colour of Madonna's pubic hair curling out from the edges of her high-cut panties as she fondled the breasts of two skin-headed lesbians in front of a photographer there to take pictures for a book of erotic photographs. He certainly did not imagine her labial

she'd insisted on having made for him. She stares at the ring for a moment as if she's seeing it for the first time.

"Okay," she says. "Let's go to your fucking hospital, if that'll make you happy."

———————

At the hospital reception desk, Annie sticks to her story about the tranquillizers and refuses to let either of them sign admitting papers. A doctor arrives, a young intern.

"So." He asks pleasantly, "What's all this about?"

Annie explains that she's taken two of the pills, just two. "It didn't seem like a lot," she adds, turning to glare at Ferris. "I was very upset over an argument I had with my husband."

Ferris can see that the intern believes her. Still, the intern is cautious about it. "A reaction as extreme as this should be taken seriously," he says, mostly to Ferris. "I'd recommend that she remain in hospital overnight for observation."

Annie is utterly composed now, and insists that she has to go home. Ferris catches himself hoping she'll let herself be admitted, and argues the intern's position.

"For what it's worth," he says, "*I* think you'd better stay overnight."

Annie gazes at him as if he's betrayed her all over again. "I don't want to

curvatures, nor the aromas wafting through the room, and he did not wonder idly what happened after the photography session ended: Did a kinky triad take place, or did Madonna snap into some other persona, say, "Thanks, girls," and get on with the business of being famous?

I did, though, just now. Now I'm thinking about a newspaper photo of a Croatian militiaman, hair close-cropped and decked out in military camouflage probably designed in New York and manufactured in some ManuZone in Mexico or Singapore, ammo bandoleers draped around his shoulders. The man was not genuflecting, and you didn't exactly get the impression that he was wishing he could return to his old job as, say, an accountant or an auto mechanic. Quite possibly he was thinking about killing someone. There's an even stronger possibility that he was thinking about sex, and, if he wasn't,

stay," she answers, her voice just above a whisper. "I've got to go to work in the morning."

Ferris loses it. "For Christ's sake!" he shouts. "You were a wacko for five hours, and even if that's because you poisoned yourself, you're still poisoned. You can't go to work."

"Yes, I can," she says. "I will, too."

He gives up when she agrees to see her own doctor the next afternoon. He would have argued more vigorously, but he recognizes that she's completely outwitted both him and the intern. Ferris's motives aren't quite pure anyway, and he knows it. He wants her to stay at the hospital because *he's* exhausted. He wants to sleep alone so he can think through what has happened without being distracted by her—or by the attractions that he knows, even after this incident, will still be there. What troubles him here is that an unpleasant new dimension has been added to their life together. Whatever they've fought about up to now has stayed within the boundaries of rational behaviour—sort of. He's been fighting with her as if she's a reasonable being. Now only one certainty exists— that she's irrational. Cold comfort.

They drive back to the condominium in silence. Out of the corner of his eye he sees her gazing at him. Oh Christ, no, he thinks. She's trying to seduce me.

"Don't," he says.

"Don't what?"

"You know what I mean. Don't try to pretend none of this has happened. It did happen."

it's damned sure the photographer who shot the photo thought he was pretty sexy.

Mohammed Osman, now deceased, Madonna with her erotic video and coffee-table book, and the Croatian militiaman getting his Warhol Fifteen—all appeared in the same newspaper on the same day. The photo of the militiaman made the front page, big and lascivious, Madonna led off the paper's entertainment page, and Mohammed Osman was a brief anecdote for a wire-service story about the difficulties of providing basic necessities in a country where everyone who isn't malnourished is a gun-toting hood-lum. And we all know which of those three persons, over the next few days, will occupy the public's imagination.

I think it's time we came to terms with where our attentions and our priorities lie these days. Mine as well as yours, of course. I'm admitting mine as a prelude to setting

"So I get the silent treatment, is that it? Can't you think up something new?"

"You've got nothing to be righteous about. Give me a break."

"Neither have you. Why don't you give me a break?"

God damn her, Ferris thinks. She's ready to start all over again. Where does she get the energy?

———————

It's a rhetorical question. He knows where the energy comes from. Even in the midst of a psychotic blowout, she's at home. This is a universe that has no one else in it, no one and nothing that can't be re-manufactured by mid-morning tomorrow. She *will* go to work, just as she says.

Annie isn't a basket case, so don't get the idea from these domestic flame-outs that she can't cope with everyday life. She always has, she can here, and she'll continue to. Better than most people, actually. If you saw her on the street or at work, she'd strike you as thoroughly, perhaps excessively, compe-tent.

Ah, but wait a minute. This is what *I'm* seeing—as the writer—not what Ferris saw. The question he asks himself about her isn't rhetorical at all. He's wondering, as he sorts through the rubble of the incident, whether she is like one of those black dwarf stars that contain only negative energy—is it anti-matter?—that draw in whatever drifts into their path. Such stars simply

down the basic ambiguities of authoring a book about sex. I think you deserve to know the basis on which I have proceeded thus far, and how I intend to proceed.

My book is a novel. All resemblances to real people, living or dead, are purely coincidental, blah, blah. Sort of, anyway. Not that I propose to make this a "quick cheap holiday" from reality as Stephen King and most novelists now have it. Given the difficulties of my subject matter, there is no other way to proceed. Throughout my lifetime, it has been the wonderful and terrifying mandate of novelists to imagine the essential details and structures of our collective condition. A novel ought to be *relevant news without the ridiculous pretense of institutionalized objectivity.*

Okay, I hesitated before using the expression "institutionalized objectivity." I tried out some other terms, but they were even more ridiculous and pretentious. "Self-

devour, and they aren't altered by anything. They remain imploded and black in their unshakable density. To him, it's an appealing metaphor. He parks the car, feeling victimized and embattled—so absorbed by it that he's almost enjoying the sensations. Black dwarf. Hmmm…

Before he can take the key out of the ignition, Annie jumps out and slams the door, striding up the walkway without him, trying to recapture her dignity. As he watches her, he sees how ridiculous his thought is. She's no dwarf black star. She's the woman he's married to, a human being, twisted around, maybe a little crazy in certain situations. And he's going to follow her, into the house, into bed, straight into hell. He reaches for the door handle, and stops.

Oh, no. There's more to it than that. Her display of bravado in getting out of the car is like everything she does. It is deliberate, staged. She's not irrational at all. In fact, she's perfectly rational, given that rationality is a projection of force driven by narrow assumptions. It's just that with her, he never knows what the current assumptions are because they change to serve the situation.

He remembers having read somewhere that the more neurotic a person is, the less spontaneous his or her actions. Psychopaths literally never do anything spontaneously. Everything is for effect. Is that the problem? Is Annie a psychopath?

He relaxes into the seat and begins to fiddle with the car radio. A sentimental love song blares, and he takes it in, feeling his resolve soften. Then he slams it dead. No, Annie isn't a psychopath. That's too easy. Still, it's true that she never does anything spontaneously. She's even planned this fiasco. All the

proclaiming objectivity" got the most serious consideration because it is the chief, and ridiculous, technical pretence of conventional novelists—the idea that if a framework of authentic characters in a coherent landscape is set up, the puppeteer pulling their strings will become invisible and thus achieve a sort of gestalt objectivity. Fuzzy, doily-festooned metaphysics, to my mind.

By now everyone knows, or ought to, that an objectivity of any sort has the same chance of surviving motion and time as a snowball in hell. Yet we all want to create or experience the cooling harmonies of objectivity anyway, don't we? We want this because without objectivity, there's nothing out there but the hot sun and the throbbing heat of blood—our own, temporarily safe inside our skins, or someone else's trickling into the gutter after an artillery barrage.

wacky behaviour he's seen tonight can be related back to an initial intention: Win the fight, prove the logic.

Absurd. She isn't a monster, and she isn't a logic machine. She's a woman, flesh and blood and bone. Maybe nothing but. Maybe that's the problem. Maybe she's merely a wild animal, incapable of ingesting complex feedback. A sobering thought occurs to him. Maybe they're the same that way. Maybe everything he's thinking is a cover-up for his own twisted assumptions.

Annie is standing at the door with her hands on her hips, waiting. Ferris's defences go up again: *not this time she doesn't*. Her bravado isn't attractive. It's criminal, stupid. Yet despite everything, she's attractive, damn her.

He gets out of the car, feeling hopeless, and follows her path across the parking lot.

"I want to get my car," she announces.

"We'll get your car in the morning," he answers, wearily. "You're still too drugged to drive."

"I want to get it now," she insists. "You won't want to drive me there in the morning."

He pushes past her and unlocks the door. "I'm not going to drive you any-where right now," he says, flatly. "And I'm not going to let you drag me into an argument over it, either."

He stands back to let her enter. Instead, she reaches out and touches his arm. It makes him want to grab her and throw her inside, but he doesn't. Instead, he brushes her hand away and enters the darkened apartment himself,

It's a frightening thing to live in Heisenberg's indeterminate universe rather than in an orderly one governed by a superior, omnipotent being. We still want to love, to be loved, and to be forgiven for our endless screwing around. But in Heisenberg's universe, no one can forgive us, and there's no guarantee that loving and being loved has a purpose. Those of us who want some measure of things have to run alongside the locomotive of erotic desire, wondering where it's going. For some of us, it's more frightening still to realize that the only things that will stop the locomotive—aside from a seat on the stock exchange—are starvation and death.

Admittedly, sex isn't a new topic for a novel. But gender relations in the last thirty years have taken on a dimension that hasn't been seen since the end of the Neolithic Era, and perhaps not even then. A massive shift in structure is taking place, and much

suddenly unsure if her gesture meant she wants him or merely wants to get her car.

———————

In the weeks that follow, things get worse. The metaphor of the black dwarf star stays in Ferris's mind, try as he might to rid himself of it. It's a scary image and, half-consciously, he finds ways to make himself invulnerable to its attraction.

Annie interprets his remoteness as an act of war and begins to treat everything he does or says as an actual or potential hostility. Sometimes she pleads with him to love her as he used to, other times she berates him for not loving her the way she wants.

For Ferris it is war too, but he fights guerrilla fashion, avoiding confrontations, making chippy remarks when she isn't expecting them. Constantly and with occasional cruelty, he is testing her composure. He succeeds in bringing her insecurities closer to the surface. He doesn't recognize it, but one result is some fairly decent farce, as with the following routine:

"Do you love me?" she asks.

"Yes. For what it's worth."

"Do you find me attractive?"

"Sometimes. When you aren't yelling at me. You know I find you attractive."

of the news is uplifting. Brute force, size, and capacity for violence are no longer the social and political assets they once were. In fact, given the overcrowding on the planet and its recently revealed fragility, it is becoming evident to many of us that trying out other methods of governing ourselves and one another isn't really optional. But the old habits are dying hard, and for the minority of us humans who are not condemned to scramble for food or superior military weapons, gender relations and sexuality are in a state of destructive and violent confusion. This isn't merely the self-inflicted crisis to which I abandoned Ferris and Annie. Our whole culture is locked in a massive Mexican Stand-off.

Which gets me back to where we are, and what has happened so far. My imaginary narrator is sitting in an apartment living room in Vancouver, B.C., wondering how to get

"You don't like me. You never liked me. Not as a person."

"What in the hell is a 'person'? How am I supposed to like you? I love you. Isn't that enough?"

"You love me but you don't like me."

"Have it your way. You don't listen to anything I say, anyhow."

"But I want you to like me as a person."

"I have trouble seeing you as a person or anything else when you bullyrag me like this."

"You never tell me you like me."

He has to answer this one carefully. "I don't," he says, "because you aren't a very nice person. And anyway, you always ask me before I can say it. Do you want me to come and tell you how much I like you every five minutes?"

"No, really. Be serious. Do you like me?"

"Not when you have to ask me questions like that. You know the answers. Leave me alone."

Soon she's back at him: "Do you love me?..."

It isn't always one-sided, and most of the time, it isn't remotely funny. For instance, Annie cuts her wrists. They're cuts, not slits or slashes, not deep enough to sever an artery. But they're deep enough to require bandages, and more than deep enough to make the threat real to him.

A few days later, fifteen minutes before she knows Ferris will arrive home, Annie opens the oven door, blows out the pilot light and turns on the gas, then sits on the floor while the kitchen fills with fumes. Ferris arrives on cue, shuts

through the next five minutes. He doesn't have a clue that I'm here, and that I'm about to send him on a journey through his sexuality, past and future. Back there, it's about 1980, and he's got a long journey ahead of him, one that will take him backward in time, and then forward to where we are.

Me? I'm sitting in a cafe on Bloor Street, Toronto, Canada, September 7, 1992, watching an elderly woman at the fruit market across the street trying to find a ripe cantaloupe among the many in front of her. Aha, yes, she has one. I can see her smile of pleasure from here.

Even though we occasionally look and think alike, my narrator and I are not the same person, and this is not a sexual autobiography. To attempt one of those would be to engage in an absurdity almost equal to the pretence of general objectivity—that of

off the gas and airs out the apartment, and tries to think of something to say to her. He's convinced neither act is a genuine suicide attempt, but he's still frightened. And the terror grows.

At the height of an argument, she rushes into the bathroom, slams and locks the door, opens the medicine cabinet, and stuffs pills into her mouth: vitamins, antibiotics, ASA, the tranquillizers she's obtained a stock of. He recognizes what she's up to, kicks open the door, and forces her to spit out the pills. She doesn't swallow the pills. She's content to fill her mouth and passively let him remove them by pounding her on the back and then thrusting his fingers into her mouth while he holds her in a stranglehold. This allows her to accuse him of being a violent man, a brute, and provides fuel for further recriminations. He begins to hide the more toxic pills and locks away the old straight razor he's kept as a keepsake of his father in the drawer of his desk. He puts the disposable razor blades he uses in with it, even though he's pretty sure she couldn't take them apart to use them.

She learns the trick of leaving an argument in mid-sentence to go to the bathroom. She closes the door, stands beyond the impact zone in case he kicks it in (which he does several times) and waits there until he comes to the door demanding to know what she is doing.

"I'm going to the bathroom."

"You don't sound like you are."

"Am I supposed to grunt and make rude noises? Would that make you happy?"

supposing that sexual experience is generic. And anyway, the specifics of my private life are not under the scope here. Still, I want—even need—to write a novel about the corner of sexuality and gender I inhabit, one that gets written with my libido stored in the hold and my gender ego tossed overboard at the beginning of the voyage.

Why those conditions? Because men don't talk about sexuality that way, and they haven't thought or written about sex and gender as a civil, non-mysterious activity. Instead, they've made it into a circus. The reactionaries are still around with their hard-hats, their hard-ons, and their dark blue business suits, and they're still telling dirty jokes to one another like they've always done. But there are now poker-faced male feminists in Birkenstocks who don't laugh at anything, exuberant gays, nostalgic refugees from Planet of the Guys wearing loincloths, talking dirty and trying to rescue their

"Yes. Never mind. Just come out of there."

She opens and closes the medicine cabinet several times before she comes out. He is standing outside, his face strained with tension.

Ferris isn't always the passive victim. The constant tension, which in some ideal world should have made him patient, just as often makes him cruel. For instance, he starts the argument with which this story began by asking her, without provocation, why, if she is serious about killing herself, she doesn't buy some serious poison.

"Do you have some sort of practical suggestion," she asks, archly, "or are you just being your usual nasty self?"

"I'm being practical," he says, smirking. "Isn't rat poison the standard? You could get that in a nice little brown bottle with the Jolly Roger on it so you won't mistake it for cough medicine. You'd be able to get into the medicine cabinet and drink off one of those before I could stop you."

"You'd like that, wouldn't you?"

"No," he admits, "I wouldn't like that." The smirk disappears completely. "But I'll tell you this: I've had it with you jerking me around like this. I can't have my life being run by your crazy threats. If you want to kill yourself, I'm not going to stop you."

"Well, don't worry. I wouldn't give you the satisfaction."

wounded-poodles-within from the horrifying truths that their parents were very busy people and not entirely competent at child rearing. The vast and loveless industry geared to choke the appetites of the lonely with pecker-massaging aids has been liberated from most of the restraints that all those tight-collared pecker-choking Presbyterians have held over it, etc. But somehow, men are still assholes, right?

It's true, I admit it openly. We're up Shit Creek, and we still don't get it. The progressives drift toward the falls singing "Row, Row, Row Your Boat," the Good Old Boys furiously paddle upstream, and the rest of us are flopping around in the current, getting nowhere.

I'm aware that I'm not the first male to write a novel about sex and gender, and I'm pretty clear that I won't be the last. The inspirational books lie because their authors

"Good," he says. "Now what?"

"I don't know," she answers, a new challenge in her voice. "But I do know you can't influence what I do."

He thinks about this for a brief second. "You're right," he says. "But I can do something for myself, and I can do it right now." And as you already know, in this askew contemporary domestic tableau, the man answers his own question.

He says, "Now, get out."

But this only bumps a momentary confrontation to a new plane. It certainly doesn't complete this story. The Mexican Stand-off is still on, and important questions remain unanswered. Does Annie leave without a fight? Of course not. Does Ferris leave? He acts like he wants to, and probably he ought to, but will he be back tomorrow or the next day, wondering which goddesses he's offended, ready for more?

Do these kinds of stories ever end simply, and if they do, are the players aware that their story has ended? I'm back to an earlier question, an abstract one: How does a Mexican Stand-off, once engaged, end? More important, can it end without total violence?

There are no set answers, clearly. People die, sometimes very quickly, as with the bandoleroed Mexicans of yore, but in a contemporary domestic stand-off like this one, most people stay with their hellish co-dependency and wound

have too many cheap answers and too few hard questions. The novels fail because their authors get so dizzy circling the cosmic fire hydrant at the heart of male sexuality that they lose control of their materials—along with their libidos. Acceptable practice a few decades ago, but, like I said, times have changed.

Here's what I know for sure: We (the millions of the leisured few, men, women, and all the gender inflections between) have created a civil crisis with our obsession with sexuality and gender. It is making everyone thoroughly miserable and violent, and worst of all, it is making civility difficult. The only other thing that occupies as much of our attention these days is money, and that doesn't interest me at all. I've had money figured out for twenty years: piles of rectangular pieces of paper that fly all over the place if you remove your brick from atop the pile to hit whoever it is you suspect wants to steal

each other until one or the other crawls—or is carried—off the field: defeat by a million tiny cuts. And what a monumental scale of misery that is, and how stupid. And it is the embrace the majority of both human genders are now locked in.

But I must remember that I have Annie and Ferris waiting for their drama to be resolved so that their, er, personhood can grow or diminish. I accept that they can't point their weapons at one another *ad infinitum*. Their arms will tire, their hearts will give out. Having said their piece, common sense dictates that they are unlikely to sit in this room and stare at each other for longer than, say, another twenty minutes. But I also believe they are trapped here. They've got nowhere to go even though they think they do. What worries me about them is this: Given the choice of inventing a wholly new and more just universe or staying where they are, I think they'll try to remain in their Mexican Stand-off until eternity.

It's hard to see what Annie wants from Ferris. At the beginning, I think she might have recognized in him an alien, divisible individuality large enough— or thick-headed enough—to mistake or ignore or withstand her inventions of herself and her environment. Maybe his imagination of her is infectious and has destroyed her ability to imagine herself independently of him. It's been known to happen, and it explains, to some extent, her attempts to harm herself: semi-suicide, destroying the parts of herself that originate with him or are nourished by his needs and behaviours. It has a bizarre logic, doesn't it? Despite everything, she loves him as best she can.

it from you. Not a very interesting way to live, and finally, just another by-product of centuries of male dominance.

Do I have any private motives? Sure. I want out of this silly creek I'm up. The speedboat I was given in lieu of a birthright is full of holes, and it wasn't a very nice boat to begin with. Too noisy, not very manoeuvrable, and now it is out of gas. That's what this book is about. I don't want to paddle it "home" because I don't know where that is. I'm afraid that home is filled with men like my Croatian militiaman and his pals, fantasizing about hitting their enemies in the face with their rifle butts, or about Madonna. So let me just scull close to the bank here, toss out the tools and weapons of my gender into the murky water, and see if there's some sort of human handhold.

Aha, yes! Here's one... No, several...

Ah, that's far too romantic. What power can her specific attraction—call it love, even—to Ferris have when she is condemned by her upbringing and personal experience to despise and distrust any and all men? It's a little too Freudian somehow. But if she's trying to find a daddy—and destroy him—I'd say it's justifiable for Ferris to refuse to play.

I have a better idea of what it was about her that attracted Ferris. Stated in its most lunatic way, it was the darkness of her individuality. If it's now me sounding like D.H. Lawrence, that's an appearance only. Lawrence imagined that he saw the bright pulsing blood at the heart of sexuality. All I can see, as the squalid underbelly of this turns up to the light, is opaqueness, the thick, distended veins returning to the heart with their depleted charge.

If you're a Romantic, you'll say that Annie and Ferris want to be near one another, sort of like savages around a campfire, moths around a flame. That implies that successful human love is impossible, which is the fatal flaw in romantic thinking. Still, it has an up side: We love anyway, most of us. Often badly, destructively, and without wisdom, no matter. Like most people, I'm moved by this, by the bottomless optimism of it.

But when I get to the specifics of Ferris and Annie, my romanticism disappears. I see no dignity anywhere in their confrontation and depressingly little intelligence or purpose to it. It offends me, because they should do better. Annie and Ferris are in this Mexican Stand-off because each demands the same thing. They want to be loved uncritically, but expect to live unaltered by love, or by the people they love.

The most likely scenario will see them leave the room, I suppose, retreat to fight another day. If they were more courageous, they would disengage and leave this marriage. What they can't do is resolve the Mexican Stand-off because we're all in it: Annie and Ferris, me, you, our friends and our enemies.

I have to emend that last statement. Not everyone is caught. Just those of us—a small and shrinking minority of the planet's human population—who get enough to eat, have roofs over our heads, and don't have to worry about incoming artillery shells, drought, or that twenty-year-old militiaman heading over to hit us in the face with his rifle butt. I suppose if we were more cognizant of the problems faced by those who don't have the luxurious safety to be able to struggle with the things we do, the Stand-off would dissolve in a puff of smoke. I'm not holding my breath for such a shift in consciousness. Are you?

There's another way of looking at it. It's possible that this Mexican Stand-off might be incipient in gender, fated. I'm suggesting that it has existed from the beginning—not just of Ferris and Annie's relationship, but from the beginning of human civilization, an inevitable evolution of the collision between bodily life and consciousness. Never mind that too many of us wallow in it as stupidly and unproductively as Annie and Ferris do. While we keep a nervous eye on the rifle butts, I think this is our true battleground, and what we do with it will be, in the long term, more important to the evolution of the species than the effects of a hundred thousand rifle butts or artillery barrages.

So, because I am the author of this story, I am going to force Ferris to make a decisive, characteristic move: I will cause him to break the Stand-off. Beyond that, I'm going to make him investigate what's behind it.

"Look," he says to Annie. "I won't live this way. I don't know who the hell you are. Most of the time I don't think you're anyone at all. You've tried to fix it so I won't be able to think about it, but I've learned how. Don't ask me why, but I can't seem to think about anything else."

She sneers. "Oh, really? And just what are your precious thoughts?"

Unlike you and me, he is not pondering the generalities of human life, love and gender, and for once, he is not thinking about how attractive she is.

"Like I said, I'm wondering who you are," he answers slowly. "And I'm thinking about what you and I are going to do in the next five minutes."

"Well, let me tell you who I am and what I'm going to do," she answers, rising from the chair and looking around for her purse. "I'm me, and I'm gone."

It seems important for him to have the last word: "Leave your key," he says, too quietly for her to hear.

He hears the door slam behind her. But in the silence she leaves behind, he hears the shattering of glass, the click of a plastic bottle being opened, the snick of a breechbolt being raised behind a gleaming brass cartridge. And in that instant, Ferris and I both look up, and recognize that specific things too often seem to have no resolution, that there are times when life leaves us hoping against all the things we want, demand, and hope for, that we really are alone, at last.

PORTRAIT OF

Fred

Ferris

Moral

His name is Ferris, Fred Ferris, although no one ever calls him by his first name. For a joke, he tells strangers his parents named him after Ferris Fain, the baseball player who won the American League batting titles in 1951 and 1952. Knowledgeable baseball fans eventually realize that our man was five years old before Fain won his first batting title, but they rarely notice the first-last name crossover. When they do, Ferris reminds them that "true" means bullshit with a straight face.

In case you think Ferris and I are one and the same, let me fill you in on some key biographical differences. He's from a small town in northern British Columbia. So am I, but his home town is about seventy miles south of mine, smaller, and more stunk up by its pulp mills. Both his parents were dead before he was twenty, while mine are still hale and hearty in their eighties. He grew up with a lone sister who lived with a distant aunt during the years when they might have bonded usefully. He hasn't seen her in more than twenty years. I have three siblings I see all the time.

Still, we have some uncomfortable similarities. In his twenties, Ferris called himself a poet, having come of age when a male with a functioning brain had two basic choices about what he called himself. You could be a communist sympathizer, or a poet. To Ferris (and to me) the latter seemed slightly saner. Having grown up amidst the then-vast forests of the north, he was interested in trees but not lumber, uniqueness rather than productive inevitabilities. Poetry was easier, too—you didn't have to go to as many meetings, and you didn't have to calculate anyone's distractions but your own—and occasionally the distractions of beauty. On such things he and I still agree.

Like me, he was an urban professional for a while, a student before that, a child for many years—some say, still—and once upon a time he was an infant nestled in his mother's arms. Eventually he became a travel writer who wonders if his mission in life is to provide his readers with a coherent description of nowhere. On most days, that's where he believes he's headed. Here we differ. As you know, I'm writing a book about him.

He has his peculiar set of erotic preferences and quirks, and an assortment of intellectual preoccupations he fiddles with because he can't hold up to being a

O n October 10, 1937, twenty-four-year-old Albert Camus made the following entry in his notebook:

To be worth something or nothing. To create or not to create. In the first case everything is justified. Everything, without exception. In the second case, everything is completely absurd. The only choice then to be made is of the most aesthetically satisfying form of suicide: marriage, and a forty-hour week, or a revolver.

From the spring day in 1961 when I first read these electrifying words in an eleventh-grade Social Studies class, to the darker day in August 1980 when I reread the passage while I was lying in the intensive care ward at Vancouver's St. Paul's hospital recovering from a massive stomach ulcer hemorrhage, I thought that absurdity was the multi-tempoed dance with death and despair that goes with philosophical curiosity and a lack of religious convictions.

I had, as Camus demanded, tried to be worth something. I'd read and thought myself out of nearly every comfort my culture offered, and much of the time I simply felt lost—it is hard to assign value when one's reference points have been obliterated. Value, it seemed to me, was situationally defined. I had also tried to create, but all I'd succeeded in creating were a few poems and stories that even in my own mind seemed of little consequence. They were little more than a public diary

sober-minded accountant or a leering salesman. Again, similar, but hardly unusual.

I should also point out that, like me, he's a WASP male hetero, and therefore the perpetrator, demographically if not personally, of nearly every social, political, and interpersonal imbalance, injustice, exploitation, and misappropriation of human and natural resources going. Demographically at least, he's the villain of North America's gender war. He has the grey-green eyes for it, the fair skin and hair you'd expect, and he's over six feet tall. He'd be taller still if his legs weren't disproportionately short.

From there some of the more conventional traits of villainy reassert themselves. His build is slight, and his face is hardly handsome. The nose is long and narrow and there are signs that someone, somewhere, broke it for him. Between you and me, it's been done more than once. His brow is furrowed, his eyes quick and, some say, elusive. A four-inch scar railroads across his left cheek, a gift from a teenage car accident. I won't inflict the details of that on you. There are things that happen in a life that are nothing more than accidents, and this was one of them.

There is one more similarity I ought to of my philosophical self-adjustments and self-serving emotional epiphanies. They'd been worth thinking, and worth writing down, but they were only barely worth publishing. And I knew it.

I'd faced the revolver a couple of times, and won easily, saved by the sanguine temperament I inherited. I'd faced marriage and a forty-hour week several times, too, and, I thought, I'd at least fought them to a draw. I'd planted myself on a half-coherent trajectory that systematically resisted the orders-of-the-day that occupy most people's lives, and I'd trained myself to ignore most of the bells and whistles that seemed to direct the up and down and back and forth of those around me. But along the way, I had come to recognize something that wasn't in Camus's idealistic program: creation and absurdity simply aren't contraries. No matter what we do, we are walking up and down, back and forth. No matter what I did, I was *of the devil's party*. And so was everyone else.

So it was that I arrived, strapped into an elaborate system of medical tubes and conduits, at the understanding that ended my youth: *Everything*, whether I create or not, is completely absurd—and *nothing* is objectively or even empirically justified by external principles. Nothing consistently justifies or explains consciousness, and only force, will, and cunning justify what we create with our minds and bodies—and then only

point out. Neither of us has been subjected to military training or violence. Neither of us has experienced war at close quarters, or, for that matter, any other form of violence more regimented than, say, a hockey game or a free-for-all in a bar. We've seen wars on television and in movies, but like nearly everyone else born in Canada, we know nothing about its discipline or its (alleged) ecstasies. That makes us part of a very tiny and privileged minority of the people currently living on this planet.

So let's ask the question: What will Ferris have on his mind or in his life that's worth anyone's serious attention but mine?

Try this, for one: When a system ceases to work, revolution-minded folks tend to dismantle its machinery and send those who own and operate it off to be retrained or shot. But before that is done, sensible people try to find out why the machines didn't work, and they question the operators to see if they have any ideas about how to rebuild. No matter that this has never been done. It ought to be.

temporarily and amorally. Albert Camus had been wrong, and his system for dealing with the absurdity of existence was in error. And since I believed what he wrote, so was the system I'd modelled on his.

I shouldn't have been shocked by this recognition. Camus was only twenty-four when he wrote those words, at an age when a man's testosterone-loaded will provides a virtually impenetrable shield against intelligence. At twenty-four, I'd been little more than a series of (extremely inefficient) inputs for experience, so busy opening new ones or securing incoming data for future examination that I was more or less incapable of interpreting what I was getting. Now, in my mid-thirties, I would have to change. "At age thirty-five a man throws away his crutches," Dante said. Reluctantly, I tossed away the crutch Camus provided and began to make an inventory of what I'd learned about the world and about myself in it.

I had to admit that things weren't too bad. Despite the permanent existential anxiety Camus had taught me to carry, I had been an essentially happy person, and I had a feeling that given a little

When it comes to gender relationships, questioning the old bosses may seem distasteful. Some will say, humiliate the oppressors, let them feel what the wheel is like when luck and some sunshine, I'd continue to be. Yet it seemed to me that I *shouldn't* be happy. The world was a mess, I had a meaningless but lucrative job, my second son had just been born, and I wasn't getting along with my then-wife. I was, in short, a fairly ordinary contributor to the collec-

it's on their necks. Others will go further: exterminate them, and get on with the revolution. But after the abject failure of a hundred virtue-crazed revolutions, maybe we'd all better look around. A revolution is too often nothing but a turn of the wheel. Given that life in the 1990s is an eighteen-wheeler, what wheel are we turning? Is it the steering wheel, or is it merely an inside dual on the left rear quad?

On the subject of revolutions, let me wax technical for a moment longer. Most systems are predicated on cumulative generations of technology and the habitual practices they, er, engender. Left to themselves and their ambitions, the managers of such systems usually emulate their predecessors until the sys-

tem collapses or is torn apart by its own internal stresses. Worse, most revolutions in the twentieth century are nothing more than a new set of managers taking over and rebuilding a slightly more efficient (or ruthless) version of the old system. If that is done with the reconstruction of gender relations, life will be no more just and peaceful than it was before the recon- struction— except for a tiny, stupid and Stali- noid vanguard whose only improvement on the WASP males who created the current mess will be that they're tive suicide we're all en- gaged in. I was thinking of quitting my job, and I was pretty certain the marriage I was in was going to fail, even though I cared for my wife. She'd asked me, indirectly and without quite under- standing what she was saying, to choose be- tween my new child and

my son from a previous marriage. I understood her maternal will, but she was asking me to make a choice no father is per- mitted to make for any reason. I couldn't find a way to make her under- stand that. It was one of the several crises that had put me in the hospital.

I really didn't mind being in the hospital, be- cause it gave me time to think over what I'd been doing since I made my strange pact with Camus in that high school Social Studies class as a seven- teen-year-old. As my

body healed, I went over every piece of ground I'd passed by, over, through in the years since the pact with Camus had been set, and discovered that what didn't make sense was sex. It bridged absurdity and creation, yes, but then it made the connections ridiculous. I'd used sex to sever my connection with the geography and cul- ture that brought me to it, and it'd come to nothing.

Over the years, I'd loved several women as best I knew how (which was not very wisely or well) and I'd been loved in return, often generous- ly, and in retrospect sometimes with more wisdom than I could muster. My experiences had taught me that sexual love has no cosmic pur-

different individuals. Some or most of them are likely to be women but it won't matter. They'll still be, front and centre, and in the last analysis, authoritarian assholes. As avowed enemies of our own gender and demography, Ferris and I don't believe this will be good enough.

One last difference between Ferris and me. He has a long-standing interest in washroom graffiti I don't share with him. We argue over it fairly often, actually. He says that whatever men find worth writing about while they're fondling their own genitals ought to be a reliable source of information about male erotic consciousness.

I've told him that graffiti are irrelevant, the by-product of semi-literate vandals defacing property. He's willing to argue about it with anyone, particularly the authors of the graffiti themselves. He tries to answer graffiti where and when it gives offence, sometimes writing long answering notes on the same walls.

Last week, for instance, he found this cryptic note pencilled between the tiles in the washroom of his favourite breakfast hangout: *The new waitress* it read, *wants her tight pussy fucked hard.* He noticed the new waitress himself when

---

pose and contains no inherent justice or superior reason. It didn't aid me or my partners, and it had made no significant contribution to the education or the happiness of the species. I'd discovered these things, but I hadn't accounted for them, because I was still riding on Camus's too-simple philosophical package. But what redefinitions were necessary?

More than a decade has passed since that crisis. I still haven't succeeded in making the redefinitions, and I don't have a consistent philosophical system to replace what Camus gave me. I've settled for a situational empiricism, of which the following observations about sexuality, at this time, seem to be supported by compelling evidence:

1. Mutual sexual gratification with another human being is the most profound pleasure life offers, even if the pleasure does not stay with us very long, and is not applicable to anything but itself, except very indirectly. It provides interesting metaphors, but contains no general or specific wisdoms, except that love-making is sweeter than war. It is our deepest means of entertaining our senses, but that's all it is.

2. Sexual pleasure doesn't help us to be kinder or wiser human beings, and the love that sometimes arises out of it can carry no social or political load. Those who force erotic love to do so permanently cripple the relationships they are in and may cripple themselves. Sexual pleasures

he came in. She's an attractive woman in her early twenties with auburn hair, a swimmer's broad-shouldered build and a cheerful disposition. She works the graveyard shift, and judging from the thick textbooks she pores over when things are slow, she's probably a university student trying to make ends meet while she gets her degree. As far as Ferris can tell, she's making the best of a lousy job, and doesn't need the fantasies of a vermin-headed shithouse philosopher-with-a-hard-on.

Herein rests the dangerous part of Ferris's self-appointed mission: He must imagine what the philosopher has imagined. Here, Ferris imagines the philosopher mounting the waitress, probably from behind, without preliminaries, pushing his cock into her vagina and then ramming her, repeatedly, brutally. Ugly, ugly stuff. Her grimace of pain tells him the waitress doesn't enjoy this in any way, and the grin on the philosopher's face says he doesn't care. Ferris grabs the collar of his shirt and throws him backward across the room. Then he removes his own coat and gives it to the waitress so she can cover herself. End of counter-fantasy.

Over the past few years Ferris has killed men for things like this—in his imagination. Only rarely is he likewise offer no rewards outside their situational arenas. They just *are*, and we've all got to make our political and social lives out of firmer materials.

3. Sexual desire is not only recurrent but inevitable, and so is pleasure—sometimes by unfortunate and degrading pathways. What I mean by that is that our sexual pleasures are amoral and addictive. Some few men derive intense sexual pleasure from, for example, nailing the foreheads of young girls to the floor and then having intercourse with their dying or dead bodies. But while many—even most—of us are twisted erotically, we are also moral creatures, and reason (which in the sensorium is experienced as generous love) demands the safety, dignity, and well-being of the other as a precondition to interpersonal or public acts of sexual desire. Privately we can ream out one another's sexual organs with masonry drills if we want to, and consent to it. But we remain politically responsible for the safety of the other.

4. Safety of the other involves quite a lot more than using condoms and practising safe sex. The current generation of safety-crazed urban professionals, in its efforts to protect the public (and one another) from AIDS and from other life- and health-threatening viruses and bacteria, has forgotten that without intimate physical contact there can be no true intimacy, and without intimacy, no one feels, or is, safe.

tempted to take their place. Being tempted is the difficult part, the greatest danger. Whenever he feels it, he admits it to himself, but as he's become more skilful with the fantasies, it happens less and less frequently.

Once he's figured out what's behind the fantasies, there are things to be done. Erasing the graffito isn't enough. That leaves the space open for the original philosopher or new ones to improve on his fantasy. The trick is to eliminate the fantasy within it, block it, break it down.

Ferris considers three addenda: One is *I think she's really interested in track & field.* Not quite right, because it makes the waitress seem invulnerable. It might also be mistaken to suggest that she's a lesbian, something that will spur the philosopher on. Ferris doesn't think the waitress is lesbian, judging from the affectionate kiss he saw her plant on a young man who wandered in a few moments ago. And she certainly isn't invulnerable. In any event, female indifference isn't something that will register on shithouse philosophers like this, since for all intents and purposes, they don't recognize that women have extra-genital identities.

He tries another: *Women don't like to be fucked hard.* Close, but not right, either. It has a mistake in it. Some women do like it, sometimes. Not the way this guy has in mind, but sometimes, usually with men they don't like much or approve of, a woman will seek a hint of brutality to confirm the alienation she's feeling—and has experienced most of her life. Don't give the philosopher anything he—or others—can argue with, as in "maybe not me, but someone else." Ferris's third effort is the best, and he pencils it along the tile seam behind the original: Forget it. She has a nice boyfriend who understands that women aren't dogs.

He's tempted to add a line suggesting that the boyfriend is sitting in one of the booths, but he doesn't. The trick is to keep the rejoinders short, not get too moral, and not give a sick fantasy anything to grow on. This reply does the trick, if not brilliantly. It allows the philosopher to imagine the waitress and her boyfriend. But it also implies that the philosopher himself will be most at home screwing his dog, and that's good, except where it might endanger the canine population.

Satisfied, Ferris leaves the washroom. On his way out, he drops an extra large tip, even though the new waitress's shift is over and she won't get it. Someone will.

People do what they can. Sometimes, quietly.

An Archaeology →

of
Head
and
THREE

Ferris's male elders imparted two pieces of official wisdom to him about sex while he was struggling through his official adolescence. One was that women were inferior and dangerous. The second was that sex is a messy business. The first wisdom was entirely obscured by half-truths, niggling paranoias, and rationalizations. The second wisdom carried two implicit corollaries: (a) Female anatomy is gross and malodorous, and (b) Get lots, give little.

The first wisdom was everywhere Ferris looked, but it got delivered officially when he was sixteen years old. One afternoon, an older man undertook to explain a secret of marriage to Ferris and one of his friends.

"Show me a man who doesn't go down on his wife," the older man proclaimed, "and I'll show you a wife anyone can fuck."

This was mystery piled upon mystery to Ferris. He hadn't thought much about what wives were or did, still less about how—or if—wives fucked or got fucked. Didn't marriage permanently assign those rights and duties? "Going down" presented a still greater mystery, this one with rather pleasant implications. He saw himself sinking down against the body of his future wife, nestling his head against her stomach and falling fast asleep.

"I guess," he said, hoping that the older man would reveal the exact dimensions of going down without him having to expose his naïvete, "this must mean you go down on your wife all the time."

"Christ, no," their adviser yelped. "She wouldn't stand for that." Ferris's equally mystified friend tried a different tack, asking if his wife went down on him.

"Don't I wish," the man said wistfully.

In a world governed by logic, the following conversation would have ensued: "So, I suppose you're going to tell us who-all is screwing your wife?"

"No one. Nobody else goes down on their wife. And we're all married, see? Or anyway, I'm not about to let anyone who isn't near my wife."

That conversation didn't happen because Ferris and his friend already understood that when it came to sex, their elders were bull-shitters, and their wisdoms applied strictly to others, not themselves. In the Zen of enculturation,

Head

As one of my women friends has been saying publicly for some time, *No head, no orgasms.* She isn't quite saying that head is an absolute prerequisite to her pleasures, and, sorry about this, guys, she isn't talking about blowjobs. But she isn't offering it up tongue-in-cheek, either. For her, the aphorism is an antidote to the endless mystifications men make of female sexual behaviour, and it addresses the attentional misfocus we've all suffered from for, oh, let's see, the last seven thousand years or so…

I'm completely convinced that she's right about the importance of cunnilingus. But since I'm not a sociologist or a social worker, I'm also completely disinterested in current theories about which cultural, racial or income groups do and don't characteristically perform it. The only insulting generalization I'm willing to go along with is this one: *Stupid men don't give their women head.*

a declared wisdom is a delicate matter. It often leads to a story, and the two need not be precisely related. And sure enough, their wisdom-giving elder deflected further questions by relating a tale about the prostitutes he and another man hired during a recent business trip. The hookers went down on both men in the tale, and although the older man didn't mention whether he and his friend had gone down on the hookers, he implied that a good time was had by all.

It was a fine, incomprehensible tale, and Ferris and his friend didn't disbelieve or believe it. They listened carefully (in the part about the prostitute the elder revealed at least part of what "going down" involved) and they stored away the information, undaunted but unenlightened by the details, and bemused by the whole. Ferris's instinct was that the older man hadn't really been with a hooker, but someone had, sometime. The other instinct he had was that this must be something that men dreamed of doing.

This doesn't quite follow the textbook procedure for enculturation, but it was how male sexual culture was passed on, and—notwithstanding television and our plague of caring professionals—still is. Whether Ferris and his friend actually believed the story or accepted the wisdom made little difference. They were getting a full blast of an already familiar subtext: Male sexuality involves lying about what you do and don't do. There were several smaller items they also ingested, this time with more scepticism: (a) When men took trips "out of town," the sexual behaviour of women somehow became far more exotic; (b) "Real" sex was the contrary of that which was familiar,

Turn that around, and you've got one of the three absolute truths about sex that aren't subject to cultural relativism. I'd list my woman friend's as the second. The third is that clitoridectomy is evil, bad, and wrong.

I'll add a fourth: *Human females are capable of multiple orgasms and should be given every opportunity to have as many as they would like.* After all, a severe deficit has built up over the centuries due to various male practices and malpractices, and redress is in order. It isn't certain that women who have multiple orgasms are nicer or easier to get along with than those who don't. At this point in gender history, men shouldn't be demanding a direct behavioural payoff. It's enough simply to suggest that women who have multiple orgasms—or, for that matter, single orgasms after extended stimulation—experience greater pleasure than those who don't.

I can think of several purely selfish reasons why men should give more and

domestic, and intimate.

Ferris wasn't entirely uncritical. His upbringing taught him to treat women with a respect that precluded using them as pieces of potentially recalcitrant sports equipment. His father died before he reached adolescence, so he was raised almost entirely by his mother. When she died several years later, his grandmother and older sister took over. All had strong personalities. He went to women when he wanted information on important matters, and he'd been given no occasion to believe that they were the chronic liars men were. They could be tricked or bullied, but it was harder to delude them than one's fellow males, and Ferris saw few reasons to.

Still, there were limits to what he could learn from women. In Ferris's world, they stayed at home, and their zone of control (and often their wisdom) ended at the doorstep. It was enough to satisfy a child, but as an adolescent, Ferris could see that their strengths and virtues didn't count for much out in the world. There, men were in control—even if they controlled by strutting, by bull-shitting themselves and one another, and by using physical violence to solve most of the problems that confronted them.

Did Ferris want to be a woman? No. He preferred their company and their more generous style of wisdom, but he didn't want their vulnerability and powerlessness. Did he want to be a man among men? No, but he couldn't see any alternative.

The incident that delivered the second wisdom led him to begin actively seeking alternatives to both kinds of wisdom. He was eighteen or nineteen

better head than they do. First, human beings are still close enough to their mammalian roots to be powerfully moved by olfactory stimuli. Since, compared to most animals, we have very poor olfactory equipment, it makes sense to get our noses as close as we can to the main source. Second, vaginal ciprine is tasty, and when it originates with the right woman, it can improve male intelligence and productivity. It enhances sensation, and in rare cases, it can produce hallucinations. Even if you're an insensitive, erotically challenged jerk, giving head will make the later entry of the penis easier and more pleasant for both partners.

I'm told that it's very difficult for women to predetermine whether a man will give head, still harder to prejudge whether he'll be any good at it. Contrary to rumour, race and class have little to do with it. On the other hand, men with bristly or waxed moustaches are unlikely to be very successful with the practice—

years old, sitting in a bar with two married couples who were then probably in their late thirties. He was there by invitation, and considerably more interested in being able to sit in a bar and drink for free than in any wisdoms the couples might care to impart. He looked younger than his age, and getting into bars wasn't easy. The couples knew this, and the husbands were teasing him about his youthfulness.

One of them asked him the inevitable vulgar question: Was he getting any? Mortified, Ferris countered the question with one of his own: "Am I getting any *what?*"

"Pussy," the second husband answered, to the conspiratorial titters of the two wives.

Before Ferris could reply—he wasn't going to answer truthfully, having already learned to lie about such things—the first husband began to editorialize on the original question.

"Pussy," he said, his lip curling in distaste. "I wonder why anyone would call a dirty filthy thing like that a pussy."

Ferris glanced at the women, too mortified to engage their eyes, and half expecting one or both to clout the offender or walk out. To his surprise, they seemed oblivious to the insult, apparently accepting the judgement of their anatomy and personal hygiene as if it were a matter of casual fact. The other husband joined in, and what they had to say in the next few minutes was very ugly. Words like "dirty" and "disgusting" and "holes" were used. The women remained silent, apparently unoffended. Ferris excused himself after a few min-

or interested in it. And because the skin on women's thighs is extremely sensitive, men with heavy beards are unlikely to deliver well—particularly those ninnies who think it is fashionable to wander around with two or three days' growth.

On the metaphysical side, there is real delight to be gained in surrendering one's head to one's beloved—physically and emotionally. I don't want to get too mystical about any of this, because the human brain is most effective when fully engaged with every sense organ and muscle in the body. Suffice it to say that male erotic intelligence is far higher when the male brain is located below the female, not the male, navel.

Effective techniques for producing cunnilingual orgasms vary from one woman to the next, and some women, when prompted in a subtle enough way, will give explicit instructions. These are worth listening to since there are as many

utes of this, not quite sure if he was offended or merely embarrassed. The free drinks were fine, but this conversation was costing everyone a little too much. He needed fresh air more than anything this foursome had to offer.

———————

From those two anecdotes, and from other incidents in his childhood and adolescence that carried the same basic information, it is possible to draw a composite picture of the older males around whom Ferris grew up. They were liars who maintained their sexual and social dominance by insult, intimidation, and violence.

By paring their behaviour and talk down to essentials, Ferris deduced that these men recognized just two types of women. First there was the type of woman they married and presumably loved: socially passive and manipulating, sexually repressed, and unclean. They had only generalized images of the second kind of woman, probably because they'd never encountered such a woman except in their own and other men's fantasies—or as part of mutually demeaning economic/athletic exchanges with prostitutes. Their fantasy woman was the contrary of the women they lived with and loved: She was erotically aggressive and apparently unjudgemental. The only similarity between the two types of women was that they were both unclean.

There may be darker truths here: One is that in these men's imaginations resided a single woman with a split personality, and each man lived in terror

optimum routes to an orgasm as there are women. It's also worth noting that effective technique has no relation to what can be learned from pornographic movies. There, all the techniques are subservient to camera access, and, anyway, the last things of interest to the film makers are the female orgasms. They appear to think that female orgasms can be identified by a few exaggerated moans and the occasional shout of "more" or "harder." And outside of lesbian pornography, has anyone seen or heard of a blue movie where the cunnilingus went on long enough?

Since technical information on the subject remains curiously sparse, let me be as clinical as possible for just a moment. Female clitorises are usually small and fugitive, and if a man can see one, he's not in a position to give it much pleasure because it is going to be touching his nose. A woman can be aroused by licking and nibbling her labia and clitoris, or by penetrating the vaginal cavity with the

that they might marry her, and with the secret hope that every other man had. Another is that no older man Ferris knew ever once spoke of going down on any woman they were willing to name. They may have done it gladly, but they didn't admit it.

Since these men seemed to be fools in most other ways, Ferris didn't pay much heed to what he'd been told about women when he began to have sexual experiences of his own. Half by instinct and half as an act of defiance, he performed cunnilingus on the second woman he made love to, the first he managed to get into a bed. He discovered, in that instant, that the generation of men that preceded him was very, very wrong. Ferris's women weren't unclean or dirty and they most certainly were not malodorous. They were fragrant and delicious, and he decided, then and there, that he wanted to experience as many of their different aromas and flavours as he could.

This made him feel as if he were a traitor to his gender, a woman's man, and he eventually discovered that he was living a strange and painful exile from men and male values. It wasn't that he was alone in what he knew, or ashamed or fearful of knowing it. He was neither. But he was alone *with* it, because heterosexual men simply didn't speak truthfully about sex and women. Not ever. Maybe they didn't know what the truth was. For certain, they didn't appear to care.

He was alone for another, more personal reason. Both his mother, while she was alive, and his grandmother were richly, articulately contemptuous of men. They thought and spoke of men—quite openly, where he was concerned—as emotionally and erotically incompetent beasts.

tongue. But to bring a woman to orgasm, light, direct pressure on the clitoris is usually necessary. This is best achieved by placing your lips over the clitoris, and alternately sucking on it and flicking the tongue rapidly back and forth across it, or by pushing the tongue gently up, into, and over it until you gain entry into the rhythm of her pleasure. If you can cadence your own rhythm of stimulation just slightly below hers, you can prolong the ascent, and give her more pleasure. But when a woman wants to come, help her—and then pull back slightly as she does, because the tissue often becomes sensitized after an orgasm. If multiple orgasms are the goal, move downward to lick and stroke the labia, very gently, while the spasms ebb. Since women's orgasmic capacities bear more resemblance to a Bach fugue than to the *1812 Overture* men tend to expect, this music can be played again, to infinitely changeable tonalities and volumes and altered pitches.

Their judgement coincided with Ferris's own data. Men *were* beasts. But since he was a male himself, he too was therefore at least potentially a beast in any and all erotic and social circumstances. To live with that knowledge, he tried to learn what a human male beast was and precisely what constituted its beastliness. He set out to separate himself from those qualities by thinking through every erotic event and encounter he engaged in. It was, of course, an absurd undertaking, doomed to failure on a practical level, and dooming him to a schizophrenic experience of gender and sexual relationships.

———————

At this point, reader, you're probably aware that the boundary between Fred

Ferris, character, and me, the author, is occasionally as thin as the paper this is printed on. The question on your lips is a perfectly sensible one: Is this getting excessively personal?

No, it isn't. I'm not revealing these details about Ferris in order to make a public spectacle of either of us, and I don't want him (or me) to be a special, forgivable case. Rather, I want to lay the groundwork for some questions about sexuality that, in the middle of a war between men and women, need to be raised and that can't be registered accurately if these are simply the words of a private individual at a public confessional.

Ferris is my invention, sure. At every one of his acts and insights, I am his witness. Metaphysically, we are trying to break the gender isolation that impris-

(Specific and local instructions *always* supersede the foregoing.)

Some heterosexual women prefer digital stimulation, likely because that's how they learned to have orgasms—alone. Their men should be selfish and try to convince them that the human tongue is a superior and more sensitive instrument, and that the orgasms it can produce are deeper and richer. Combinations of digital and oral stimulation are a good way to bridge this gap.

On the other side of this, women often aren't any more skilful than men at giving head. As with cunnilingus, fellatio requires technique, and it is often hard for men to explain the relatively simple truths of male erogenous location. Most women are too tentative when they give head. They often use only their lips, or expect the male to irrumate (to fuck them in the mouth)—a practice that defeats the best purpose of fellatio: to effect an erotic surrender in a male.

ons us—and to dispel the ignorance that shields us from reality. The next question is mine, and it is crucial to everything that follows: When did I invent Ferris? I *named* him several years ago, when this book became a psychic necessity. But perhaps I *invented* him years before, at the moment that I uncovered the gender and sexual contrarium I have just described him discovering. And since then, he has been inventing and informing me, as the embodiment of T.S. Eliot's insight that there is an absolute distinction between the artist who creates and the person who lives and acts in the world. Leaving aside, for the time being, the unanswerable question of which one of us is talking to you, these are the questions about sexuality we are here to address:

What comes from the head? What comes from the heart? Where and how do we learn, separate, store, and employ those knowledges? Why do men remain stupid in this supposedly information-rich era? How can the toxic civil war men have invoked be ended without inflicting still more humiliation and violence on both genders?

Except for a tiny percentage of men—largely professionals and artists living in our major cities—sexual experience hasn't really changed over the last forty years. For young males (or for stupid males of any age) complicated questions about the nature of male and female sexuality don't get answered because they are never asked. It's the same old shit dressed up in disco/BMW costumes: Men still think getting laid is their basic human right, and they still live in a world of sexual tactics that forfends both intimacy and understanding. If there is any improvement in the way most men perceive sex, it can be accounted for by the

The best fellatio combines a certain amount of firm suction, and a lot of tongue work on the glans, which is located on the lower side of the penis just behind the head. Other techniques involve gentle hand pressures on the shaft coupled with oral stimulation of the glans, or angling the head so that the basic pressures are on the underside of the penis. A really good fellatist can bring a man to a mind-bending orgasm with only the slightest movement of her head. It isn't, incidentally, necessary to deep-throat the penis, a practice that is just a filmic circus trick. Unless the woman knows how to do it, it just results in a lot of gagging, which will upset a man unless he's a jerk.

Increasing numbers of men say they don't enjoy receiving head unless they're sure the woman enjoys it and is aroused by it. If this is true, it's a singular signal of progress. Sexual pleasure shouldn't have anything to do with duty, and it seems to

fact that more women no longer pretend to be the passive and pliable subcreatures they once were forced to be.

Even there, the news isn't all good. The potentials for violent sexual outbursts by males are probably greater today than they have been for a very long time. It isn't that the database has improved, or that a higher percentage of incidents get reported. Men are feeling cornered, under censure. Their sacred élan—the right to remain ill-informed and oblivious—has been defiled. Most animals, when cornered…

And so it goes. Personally, I'm not quite convinced that the various "men's movements" are much more than sneaky insurgencies. Some elements appear to think it's enough to crawl around on their knees making a nuisance of themselves with self-aggrandizing public guilt. Underneath the façade, they strike me as the same old guys—excellent candidates for the sort of psychotic episodes we're all trying to avoid. Others, the ones running around with rhetorical spears and loincloths trying to liberate the "warrior (or wounded poodle) within" are more a signal that men are feeling the pinch than that they've seriously recognized they've got to change. It's probably better that they're acting their aggressions out symbolically rather than brandishing real spears—and other stiff, pointed objects—at women, but it still makes my skin crawl and, I suspect, it does the same to most women.

A very large part of the problem lies in the fact that men still do not speak with any clarity or directness about sex, and thus are half-witted and empty-headed as well as half- or empty-hearted. But must men remain half-witted in

me that the damage created by anyone engaging in any sexual practice out of duty will become still greater as sexual values become more egalitarian.

Still, why is head technique important in a gender war? With an increasingly sensitized male population to match an already sensitized and often angry female population, the penalties for incompetent sexual behaviours are going to become severe in the next decade—for both genders. Incompetent sexual technique is already inexcusable, not just because there's no reason for it, but because it's a signal of a general inattentiveness. Women and men who are not turned on by the sexual pleasure of their sexual *other* just aren't going to make themselves available. They won't stay in bed, they won't stay in relationships. And the pleasure of the *other*, along with the sweetness and communal duration of the melodies we learn to play is what sex is about, and for.

what they know about women, and of sexuality? What of the other kind of knowledge—the wheres and hows of how we might learn, separate, store, and employ accurate and respectful knowledges of ourselves, women, and sexuality?

Ferris and I don't think anyone can afford to stay closed and silent, men least of all. We've come to trust just three things—openness, specific knowledge, and laughter. Where sexuality is concerned, openness and laughter require an existential act of faith, and the knowledge that translates best is bodily knowledge.

What men know (or half-know) about this (and most other sexual subjects) is still too often thought of in the same terms of disgust Ferris heard in that bar conversation so long ago. It remains unspeakable, shrouded in subterranean rhetoric. Since openness has to start somewhere, Ferris and I are going to put our notes together and to speak of what we've learned, about ourselves, about women, and about what passes between them. What we have to say might strike some heterosexuals (gays and lesbians don't have this problem) as gross or excessively clinical. My answer to them is this: Only shared, even clinical—even embarrassing—knowledge will enable heterosexual men to break open their empty-heartedness. Above that in the main text, in the more transformative medium of fiction, is Ferris's progress through a world that is occasionally familiar to us both.

The

Ferris got it a few weeks after his eighteenth birthday, and it changed everything. It wasn't the girl, Diane, although she was part of it. It wasn't quite sex, either. That was as it had been—something else. No, this was *it*, something in the air, something vast and complicated, in his mind. Or was it in the world?

Ferris's world wasn't complicated. He walked up and down, he walked back and forth. Through the winter it had seemed enough to want Diane, or, more bluntly, to want her to take off her clothes. He didn't see the details—that her hair was thick and midnight dark, that her body was warm and sweet-scented, that they were surrounded by parents, siblings, common friends, blah, blah. Too fine for Ferris, such things. He wanted a female body, below the neck and without clothing. That would be fine, just fine, and there wasn't anything else to life, nothing better in the world. No past or future, not himself, not the girl named Diane, just the here and now and its demand.

You and I can say, far off as we are in future time and geography, that Ferris should have sensed the presence of a woman in Diane, but he'd never seen a woman. There were girls, mothers, sisters, some ladies—most of them old. A few, mostly girls, had body parts and zones that interested him. With our advantage, we can say he should have sensed something beyond gender differences and his own desire long before he did, something of himself and her, and of the world—something unborn, and mysterious. Maybe he should have, but he didn't. Life was simple: He mauled, she resisted. He was sure it was fun, sure. What else was there?

Well, a northern summer, for one. They have their own primal intensities, their own intentions and meanings. They mean that winter has been survived, that for a few months everyone can forget grimy survival. A northern summer intends to celebrate itself with abundant light—dusk that lingers well past the local curfew at ten o'clock, dawn before the last drunks have stumbled from the streets four hours later.

That year summer came late and reluctantly. But as the deep snow melted into the usual muddy spring, as the spring rains built the makings of a leafy paradise, Ferris began to sense a change. Wild lupines, buttercups, and Indian paintbrushes filled the meadows, yellow twinberry and thimbleberry blossoms in the thickets. Everywhere he looked, blue-backed swallows were building nests and swooping through the streets with open mouths to feed on insects, oblivious to the complaining crows. Things of his childhood, these, and for years he'd lived as if they'd vanished from the world. But here in this ascending summer of change, they returned unbidden.

One night toward the end of June, Ferris and Diane were parked in a borrowed Volkswagen out in the pine groves at the edge of town. The still-grey twilight was sweet and crisp and filled with humming insects, and he'd been wrestling with her panty-girdle for almost an hour. He felt a weariness sweep through him. He wanted to get her clothes off, yes. But the weariness made him want to gaze into her eyes. It hinted that something, something precious, was there, obscured the same way her body was hidden, locked up in her clothes.

His weariness wasn't so abstract as, say, the accumulated weight of failure. In the limited universe of boy-girl tactics, his failure to get what he wanted from Diane wasn't really failure. Panty-girdle wrestling was a sport, a game in which neither player was expected to win. Ferris had played the game willingly, because everyone did. His friends did, he assumed that his parents had once played it, maybe his ancestors had played it in the caves. He knew the game rules and so did Diane. For him the object was to come to a draw, to kill time, and to grow older and, mayhaps, more skilled and experienced. He wasn't sure what the object was for Diane, but he suspected that she wanted to keep her clothes on until she decided what to do with her life. And since Ferris wasn't offering her a life, she'd remain fully clothed for the foreseeable future.

Ferris didn't have many skills, and almost no useful experience at all. Sure, he could dismantle a brassiere with one hand. Who couldn't? But a panty-girdle was different. The rules dictated that it *couldn't* be removed inside a car, at least not in a Volkswagen. So far, Ferris had been satisfied by getting his fingers inside the waistband of Diane's panty-girdle, sometimes front, sometimes back. She governed how far in he got, and she had strict limits.

But suddenly, the game seemed awkward and demeaning. In the buzzing dusk of the pine grove, something changed, and the rules with it. He found that he had no idea what would or should happen. Maybe this game would end, and another would begin. Another game? Something better than a game, he was sure.

Strange new ideas and words were bubbling up in his brain. Oh, they were words he'd heard before. Parents and elders used them, sometimes older friends. Now they sparkled and glimmered just beyond his grasp, promising a strange new species of sensation more dumbfounding than Diane's fortress of Lycra and elastic. He leaned back, just a little, against the car seat.

"Diane," he said, "I love you."

Her grip on his wrist loosened and became a caress. Magic words, evidently.

"Hey," she answered. "I love you too."

Ferris didn't take advantage of her relaxed grip to push his hand deeper inside the panty-girdle, but his gaze did drop from her face to the front of her green sweater. Beneath its fine, soft sheen, he could see her nipples, and just above them, the bunched fabric of the brassiere he'd demolished half an hour ago. An odd thought came to him: I must have a soul. (Years later, when he came to read Dante, he would recognize the poet's description of the soul in crisis—the shadowy trees, the blood-dark lake of the heart, the sense of constraint and confusion—and recall this moment. But here, he was simply inside the moment with this word, the way a diver is when poised in the air before the downward descent into the water.)

Until this moment encountered and devoured his intentions, he'd had little interest in matters of the soul and saw no purpose in having one. Now, both its existence and its purpose were brilliantly clear. *It* had created and then spoken the magical words. And here he was in their deep, subtle waters, far from any shore he recognized.

He extricated his hand from inside the waistband of Diane's panty-girdle, and stared at his fingers. He flexed the muscles, partly to restore circulation and partly in wonder. They were still the same fingers he'd always had, but they were about to do something new. He took Diane's smaller hands, enclosed them within his, and raised them to his lips. Awkwardly, tenderly, he laid kisses—first on his own knuckles and then, learning the trick of unclenching his fists—across her slender fingers.

He still wanted something from her, oh, yeah. But now that he had a soul he didn't have the faintest idea what it was he wanted. Abstractly and experimentally, he began to search for an appropriate focus. Her sweater with the protruding nipples and bunched brassiere? No, that was the old world. A soul brought responsibilities with it. But what *were* they?

Ferris was a logical young man, and in his puzzlement, he sought out the single source of light. The moon was lifting itself above the horizon, making a brilliant paradise in which every common object, from the pitchy pine trunks and gravel roadways to Diane and his own sprawling body, were illuminated. He repeated his fabulous declaration, more slowly this time, testing its inflections and tones, articulating its swirling nuances.

Diane was watching him carefully. "Try to speak up," she said. "You're mumbling."

---

78   Okay. Maybe it didn't happen like this. While *Ferris* remembers it this way, hours or years later, the odds are it happened quite differently. Some of the specifics are a little suspicious. For instance, he may be assuming that the declaration took place in a car because he came from a culture where everything important was done in a car. His soul could easily have emerged in a restaurant or at a high school dance—except that those locations would hardly trigger his recollection of a lack of circulation in the fingers of his right hand immediately after making his declaration of love.

His clearest memory datum is the one that is most likely to be fabricated: the bright golden imprint of the moon through the black pine trees. Meteorological probability doesn't give Ferris and his full moon much of a chance. More likely it was cloudy that evening, and even if it was clear, the moon could have been new, waxing, or waning. It might have been the wrong time of night or the wrong directional orientation. And, lest we forget, there's no moon in a restaurant or at a high school dance.

It doesn't matter, really. Human memory and statistical probability operate in separate universes. In Ferris's version of events, the moon damned well *was* present and full. *Something* cosmologized a common girl-mauling episode on a small-town back road, and *something* woke up his soul and made him a lover. He believes that it was the moon. Up yours.

I'm prepared to trust him on this because his other data are precise and thoroughly idiosyncratic. He remembers the soft look in Diane's eyes, although not their colour, and he remembers the soft rumpled texture and green of her sweater—a forest green Dalkeith cardigan, buttoned up the back—but he can't tell you what colour her eyes were. Green, he thinks, maybe hazel.

It's only a small kindness to grant him this unlikely collection of verities. Certainly in his mind, he deserves them. Until this moment every rite of adult passage has failed miserably to meet his expectations: first date (he was eleven, the girl was four inches taller than he was, talked like Donald Duck, and forced him into the date by threatening to break his nose); first serious kiss (he can't remember that at all, probably because it was on that first date, and he was afraid he'd be swallowed whole); first time he touched a girl's breasts (this was years later, and the girl had thick, un-airbrushed hairs around her nipples); first "time" (in the front seat of his father's car in a drive-in theatre where it was so quick he wasn't sure if it really happened and neither, he's pretty certain, was the girl). He'd seen and fondled more female undergarments than female skin, and the undergarments, especially the panty-girdles nearly all women then wore, young or old, had become a metaphor for the mysteries locked up inside them.

But now he'd gotten it, and it was delicious. Did Diane have something to do with the way it happened, he wondered? There was a strange connection between her and the moon that night. The moon was smooth and shining, and so was Diane's face. No, Ferris decided, that wasn't correct. Her face was round and more or less thoughtless, and the moon was round and, as far as he knew, thoughtless. And here was a remarkable thing: He'd never really examined the moon carefully before, not so he would notice, as he did now, that it wasn't silver. It was golden. Why hadn't he noticed this until now?

Another new thing happened. The boundary between thought and speech collapsed, and Ferris began to speak as he had never spoken in his life. The words were spilling from him, cascading over and around Diane, a jumbled torrent of speculation and description. He had new words to speak to her, strange ideas to communicate. He'd seen the moon, really seen it for the first time, it was golden, not silver, and she resembled the moon. He told her everything he was thinking, except,

A Science Note:

Ferris's "golden" moon may be a side effect of atmospheric smoke from forest fires. Such occurrences in June are unusual, since fire season rarely begins before July. Perhaps it is a dry year, or a small early fire is burning close to town. And, perhaps, the colour is in his imagination.

discreetly, the part about her being thoughtless.

"Don't be silly," she said, looking in the rearview mirror. "My face isn't that round. Is it? And who ever heard of the moon being golden?"

"Look at it," he said, pointing out the car window.

She looked into the rearview mirror more critically. "Do you really think so?" she asked, sweetly. "Do you think it's attractive?"

His heart ached with newly discovered romantic formalities. "You are a beautiful woman," he said. "You're the most beautiful woman I've ever seen. You're the most beautiful woman I've ever even thought about."

"Don't be silly," she said, not taking her eyes from the mirror. "Do you really think so?"

He did think so. And to prove it, he started the car, navigated the Volkswagen through the pine grove, and drove her home in the full, rich, golden moonlight.

It was still before midnight when he dropped her off, so he drove over to the café where he hoped his friends Donnie and Artie would be waiting. All three had recently completed high school—or, more accurately, Donnie and Artie had completed it successfully, while Ferris had been released and asked to take his carefree insolence elsewhere. The compulsory part of their education was over, and for the first time in their lives, they were free to come and go, work or not work, sleep or not sleep—which is to say, they were under every covert and maleficent pressure adult society could exert on them.

Ferris breezed into the restaurant, found his friends sitting in one of the booths and launched into a description of the remarkable things that had just happened to him. His revelations weren't greeted with much enthusiasm.

"Oh, shit," Artie moaned. "I suppose you want to get married."

Ferris considered it, but only for a moment. Adults got married. He'd seen no evidence from their behaviour to suggest that marriage had anything to do with having a soul or being in love, and even less to do with sex.

"No," he said. "I'm not crazy."

"Have you screwed her yet?" Donnie asked, assuming that being in love must have some practical purpose.

Ferris couldn't think about Diane in practical terms. Not now. Love was serious and spiritual and mysterious, whereas sex—in this instance, *having sex*, had been suspended somewhere in the frivolity of tactics and chance.

"I copped some tit, but that's all," he answered, trying to sound nonchalant but feeling uneasy at the remembrance of Diane's tangled undergarments. "There's a million years for that sort of crap."

His two friends stared at him suspiciously. Only a few hours before, the three of them had been in agreement on how the world worked and what was important, particularly when it came to the subjects of love and sex. They didn't know what love was, and they didn't care. On the other hand, reliable information about sex was scarce, but they had plenty of theories on the subject. Their main theory was that sex was an illegal and dangerous substance possessed by females. They were quite willing to steal little bits and pieces of it whenever they could, but they stayed away from full-scale engagement with it or with those who possessed it. Sex also meant getting girls pregnant and getting them pregnant meant getting married, which meant all kinds of responsibilities they were trying to avoid. They wanted experiences, not responsibilities. And despite endless attempts by their parents and teachers to get them to believe that experience and responsibility were the same thing, they damned well knew better. Ferris had been drummed out of school for practising what he knew.

"What's the point of being in love with Diane if you don't get to screw her?" Donnie persisted.

"It isn't like that," Ferris answered, uncomfortably. "This is bigger. You can screw anyone, but you can't be in love with just anyone. It's different."

"Different how?" Donnie scoffed. "And since when can you screw *anyone*? You haven't screwed anyone that I know of, unless you just got into Diane or something."

He was headed in a direction Ferris didn't like.

"If I ever do," Ferris sneered, "I sure as hell won't tell you guys about it. Don't you ever think about anything except getting laid?"

Before either of his friends could make the obvious answer, Ferris got up from the table, stomped out of the restaurant and went for a long walk in the (alleged) moonlight. Later that same night, he wrote his first poem.

Sorry. He doesn't want that to appear in print.

He strolled down to the park, thinking hard. Before him was a difficult question: Now that he'd declared, publicly, that he was in love, shouldn't he alter—generally—his behaviour? The answer was obvious, but the specifics of how weren't. The park gave him no clues. Despite the moonlight, it was just a bunch of grass and trees, too neatly arranged to suit his disorderly soul and his new hungers. He walked up and down through the streets of his town and tried to imagine the other lives that were being lived around him, until the night sounds settled into the pale hush of dawn, suspending the moon's traverse in mid-heaven.

Having a soul turned out to be easier than he thought. His first move was to become more, ah, *spiritual* toward Diane—and to her cumbersome undergarments. Instead of the scheduled twice-weekly maulings, he began to phone her several times a day and visit her daily. He was curious about her, and it was beginning to stir in his mind that she might have thoughts about the world. He also tried to *talk* to her. He was seeking conversation, but mostly what resulted were rambling monologues, and lectures.

First things came first, of course. "Why do you wear a girdle?"

Diane laughed, nervously. Ferris kept silent. "I don't know," she answered, after a pause.

"My sister says you'll lose your figure if you wear a girdle."

His older sister had said no such thing, but he was pretty sure Diane wasn't going to ask her about it.

Although Diane didn't realize it, the girdle had become almost an academic issue to Ferris. Gradually, he stopped mauling and groping her. When he did she was vaguely relieved, if not quite grateful. And Ferris, like a dog being cured of a lust for the chicken coop, wistfully wondered why she didn't offer him her body the way she'd offered her love. But when it didn't happen, he discovered that he too was relieved.

They began to take long walks in the park beneath the golden moon. Because there is a rule in small towns that makes it a major deviation from normality for anyone with a driver's licence to walk any distance farther than two blocks, this was an unusual thing to be doing. Parks did not get a lot of business, least of all for evening strolls. What got the business were secluded parking lots and the pine groves at the edge of town. But Ferris had lost his taste for business, and even for cars. When he and Diane weren't walking, they stayed home at Diane's parents, talked with her older brother, or played with her two younger sisters.

After a few weeks of this, Diane and he were able to have reasonably successful conversations, almost as if they were friends. Her parents liked this.

Until then, they weren't entirely sure that Ferris spoke English. Meanwhile, Ferris did some scientific research. He learned the phases of the moon, and about the effects the weather had on it, and he explained these to Diane. Meanwhile, he thought about love and moonlight and he talked about them incessantly.

He wasn't spending much time with Donnie and Artie, and when he did see them, he used them to practise his treatises on love and moonlight. For a little while, they were amused by his nonsense. When the novelty wore off, they went to ground on him, refusing to talk about anything but sex and cars and other elements of their previously unquestioned agreement about what constituted the real world.

Ferris shrugged them off. Barbarians. What did they know about the real meaning of life? What he didn't see at all was Diane's growing impatience. She had an imagination of her own, and a strong sense of what mattered and what didn't. Both were lodged in succinct practicalities. She wanted an education before she married and had her children. In fact, her body was sending her urgent messages that it was time to get on with the part of that education that Ferris had apparently lost interest in. For her, his silly talk about love and moonlight was gibberish, a return to childish stuff. And so, with some collusion from Donnie and Artie, she turned Ferris's new world on its ear.

———————————

By now July was ending, and the rich heat of late summer was making Ferris anxious. He could feel the summer moving past him, and he wanted its traverse arrested so he could stay at the beginning, where he'd found his soul. When he wasn't with Diane, he slept late and went to sleep early. What else was there?

Then, one morning, Donnie rousted him from his bed.

"Come on," Donnie said. "We're going to the lake."

Ferris was grumpy. "I don't want to go."

"It'll be fine," Donnie coaxed. "My parents are out of town, and we can swim and fish and all that shit."

"I'm tired of shit," Ferris replied. "What'll there be to do?"

"Artie's coming. I'm sure you'll find something. You can stare at your goofy moon all night if you want. But you're coming with us."

Ferris couldn't think of a good reason why he shouldn't go, and at least one reason to go. Diane's parents owned a cottage not far from the one Donnie's parents owned. She wouldn't be there, but it would give him a new target for his meditations.

"Okay," he said. "How soon do we have to do it?"

"Soon" was immediately—Artie was waiting in Donnie's car with five cases of beer and some fishing rods. Fifteen minutes later—ten of it taken up by Ferris's apologetic phone call to Diane—they were on the road.

Ferris sat in the passenger seat and gazed out at the passing countryside. He'd been out to this lake dozens of times, maybe hundreds. When they were kids, Donnie and Ferris had sat in the back seat and made jokes about their parents, plans about what they could do to elude them once they arrived at the lake. Now they were free as birds, and doing what they liked.

They had five cases of beer to drink, and they had to drink it all. They'd let themselves be guided by whatever accidental insights (and physical accidents) the beer produced. They understood that it would probably only guide them to and from the nearest latrine, but since they didn't have any other firm plans for the evening—or for their lives—this was fine, okay, a normal route to whatever tomorrows they would have. For a while, Diane didn't exist.

At the lake they sat on the cabin's porch, drank one beer after another, and talked. Donnie and Artie talked about how drunk they were getting, with occasional passes through the subjects of trout fishing and sex. Ferris couldn't concentrate on any of it. He talked about Diane and love and moonlight.

"I'm about full up on bullshit," Donnie said after a couple of hours of this. He picked up a fishing rod and half-full case of beer and wobbled off to fish from the dock. Ferris yakked on into the smoky dusk until Artie couldn't take any more, either, and got to his feet, tottered inside and fell asleep on a couch. Ferris was left to chat with three empty beer cases.

"To hell with you," he muttered, and staggered off the porch in the direction of the dock.

Donnie wasn't there, but a three-quarter moon was rising above the lake. For Ferris, it was companionship enough. He stumbled to the end of the dock and lay down on his back to gaze at the moon's mysterious golden face, thinking how much like Diane's it was, and how beautiful both were.

This moon had another property. Gently at first, it began to spin. Ferris sat up. There were reflections trembling on the still water. As he tried to focus on them, the reflections—and everything else—picked up the same spin. He closed his eyes and, seconds later, fell asleep.

Or sort of. He dreamed that he was running in a pack of dogs, a hound among hounds in the frenzy of the chase. He didn't know what he was chasing, but it didn't matter. It was enough to be swift and alive as he ran across grassy hills, through wooded groves of trees, into and across streams.

Next he was alone, tiptoeing silently among the trees on slender hooves. In the distance, he could hear the baying of hounds, the sound of their feet on the earth, a soft thundering. He began to run, heedlessly, as the hounds drew in behind him, tearing at his flanks, catching at his hooves. He fell—not down, but into a spiral that seemed to lead in all directions at once.

It took him downward into complete darkness, and for a time, into nothing at all. When it began to carry him upward, toward the light, he heard Diane's voice shooing Donnie and Artie out of the cabin. He didn't open his eyes, and a moment later he felt her body next to his. It wasn't wearing clothes. Neither was his.

He didn't open his eyes as she nudged him, not too gently, to respond. He did, sort of, and they made love, sort of. It was blurry and swift, and he couldn't shake fully loose from the dreams he'd been having until it was over.

When he did, he found that the walls of the cabin were spinning, and all he could think of was getting himself out of the bed and outside. He crashed off the porch and made it almost to the lake before he lost it. He vomited in the reeds beside the dock until his throat was raw. The retching finally subsided, and he stripped off his clothes, leaped off the end of the dock and swam in the jet black water, real water this time, trying to clear his head.

He had to swim a long time. When he crawled back onto the dock and stood up, Donnie's car was gone, and Donnie and Artie with it. Not far away was the pickup truck Diane's older brother must have lent her.

She was sitting on the bed when he returned, fully dressed. Ferris was a little relieved that she was.

"Hi," he said, awkwardly. "Are you okay?"

She didn't answer for a moment and didn't meet his eyes. "I'm fine," she said, quietly. "I love you, you know."

"I know," he acknowledged. "I love you too. God, was I drunk."

"You don't have to explain anything," she said. "It was my idea."

"I know," he mumbled. "I mean, Jesus, you can't believe how drunk I was."

She didn't confirm or deny this, and he, prudent for once, let it go. He drove the truck back to town, also prudently. The severe light of dawn was drawing shapes from the dark by the time they reached the outskirts of town. They hadn't had much to say to one another as the miles peeled by, but she held his hand all the way. Ferris felt an odd calm settle over him. Love had found its way, even if the way had been pretty awkward. He was grateful that it hadn't found its way in the front seat of a car.

A few weeks later Diane left town to go to university, and Ferris woke up to the fact that he didn't have that option. At first it didn't appear to present any serious problems. She assured him of her undying love and for the first several weeks wrote him long gushy letters every single day to prove it.

Ferris, meanwhile, was footloose again and hanging out with Donnie and Artie. Vaguely aware that the nights were getting longer and that the cold weather would soon put an end to their fun—maybe forever—they took to staying up all night, going at it with gusto, and with a touch of desperation. But for Ferris, nothing was quite the same. The town seemed smaller, the streets dingier. Something was starting to move past him, and he didn't know what it was. Even the moon was changing. It was less golden now, more the silver moon of other people's stories.

As the golden light faded, Diane's letters came less frequently. Every two days, then every third. When a week passed without a letter, the moonlight took on a distinctly metallic glint.

"She's down in the Big Time now," Donnie said. "Two more months and she'll probably be married to some Joe College type with a Corvette and rich parents."

"Screw you," Ferris answered, still secure in the power of love. And anyway, he told himself, absence makes the heart grow fonder, right?

"You'd better stop believing in your own bullshit and start figuring out how fast you can get to the Coast," advised his always-practical friend.

Ferris didn't receive a letter for two weeks. When one finally did arrive, it was just a single page.

"I'm having a wonderful time here," Diane wrote. "I'm meeting all kinds of interesting people." One of these interesting people, she went on to say, reminded her of Ferris. He took the advice he'd been given, packed a bag and bought a bus ticket south.

As the bus rolled south and Ferris gazed out across the forested hills and valleys, it came to him that whatever he was headed for, he was also leaving home. All his life he'd been secured by familiar people and things: family, friends, the rooms he'd slept in, the tables he'd eaten at, even streets he'd walked through. He'd taken home for granted because that's what everyone did—that's what you *can* do when everything is known.

Ferris's estrangement had been growing for what seemed a long time—before the summer, maybe before Diane. Now, he felt as if he didn't know any of it, and didn't want to. There was a world out there, the real world that Diane was in. And when he—or was it his soul?—picked her, he and it picked the world. Never mind that Ferris also felt put upon, victimized, a goof headed for the glue. Home was receding in his mind more quickly than the bus was eating the miles south. It was gone by the time the bus reached its destination.

Ferris parked his bag with a distant cousin, who provided him with a room to sleep in and a not-too-subtle warning that the less he saw of Ferris, the better. That was fine with Ferris. He set his new routine the next morning, hitchhiking to the university, where he busied himself with protecting Diane from anyone and everyone who got near her.

November 8, 1964

SAIGON: South Vietnamese President Ngo Dinh Diem reportedly commits suicide in the back of a troop carrier while soldiers transport him to prison in the aftermath of a CIA-backed coup. Subsequent reports suggest that he was shot or stabbed to death by soldiers.

NEAR BON ARFA, MOROCCO: Several thousand Algerian infantry attack a Moroccan encampment from the surrounding hillsides. After nine hours of fighting and heavy casualties on both sides, the Algerians withdraw to their original positions.

BEIJING: The Chinese government announces the roundup and execution of 300 Taiwanese "agents."

What else could he do? The interesting people she'd been meeting were smarter and older than he was, and they had more money. As a matter of fact, there was just one unusual thing Ferris had that they didn't. Overnight, he developed a startling ability to get into—and win—fist fights. He didn't start the fights. He just threw the first and last punches.

"You've got to stop following me around," Diane told him, unimpressed after he'd spent an entire weekend with his hackles raised. He'd gotten into three different fights. In one, he'd knocked a member of the university's football team cold for asking Diane to dance.

"And you've got to stop picking fights with every guy who talks to me," she added.

Ferris didn't try to argue. He was flat broke, and he'd already realized he was going to have to get some sort of job. As for picking fights with all the people who were trying to steal her from him, he agreed that he'd stop them—if they would. He didn't like the fights much more than she did, although he was secretly impressed with his winning record.

"Okay," he said glumly. "You won't be seeing me for a while."

He didn't tell her he'd be looking for a job. Too mundane. He left it vague so she would worry that he was going to abandon her. He wanted her to beg him to stay.

"Oh, fine," she said, cheerfully. Then she caught his hurt expression and explained that she had several tests coming up and needed the time to study. "You'll be back soon, won't you?"

"Sure," he answered, still not revealing the reason for his mysterious disappearance. He noted her momentary frown when he said that he wouldn't be gone very long, but before he could digest what the frown might mean, she was hugging him, patting him on the back and pushing him out the door.

"I'll be lonely," she said from the doorway, her eyes darting past him to something in the street.

By the next afternoon Ferris had a job. It wasn't much of one—he'd be driving a delivery truck. The job didn't pay very well, and he had to work long hours, but it renewed his confidence. He had money, or soon would have. He'd be able to rent an apartment of his own, and then, who could say?

On the Friday after his first week at work he borrowed some money from his cousin, bought six small cream-coloured roses—his sister told him that no girl could resist roses—and, without phoning, hopped a bus.

He knocked on her door, and as he waited for her to open it, his confidence evaporated. He'd imagined her studying quietly, as if she'd gone into a nunnery during his absence. The loud rock and roll he could hear inside wasn't exactly church music. The door opened, and a tall, dark, smooth-looking guy stood in front of him, hands on hips and question marks all over his face.

"What can I do for you?" he asked, as if he owned the place.

"Is Diane around?" Ferris countered, not sure whether to punch him now or to give in to his rising panic and run for it. He saw Diane enter the room and the look on her face told him the right response was panic. Another guy and a girl followed her into the room, looking as if they'd been wrestling.

"Oh," Diane said, putting her hand in front of her mouth. "Ferris. It's you."

Ferris couldn't decide if she was suppressing a yawn, or if she was surprised—amazed—to see him. Something was amiss, and his brain went on a sudden vacation. "Yeah, it's me." Pause. "Nice night." Pause. "I got a job." Pause. "I brought you some flowers." The words felt like bricks in his throat.

Diane composed herself. "This is David," she said, pointing at the now-smiling Oilslick, who was holding the door open. Ferris instantly forgot the name. She motioned behind her at the other two. "This is Robert and Elsa." Ferris forgot those names just as fast and didn't notice that Diane didn't introduce him by name.

Oilslick stuck out his hand for a handshake and invited Ferris inside. He tried to crunch Ferris's fingers, and Ferris did it back. Oilslick winced, and Ferris brushed past him into the middle of the room, trying to catch Diane's eye to reassure her that he wouldn't start a fight—unless Oilslick provoked him.

Diane didn't seem to want eye contact. Ferris didn't have anything to say to Oilslick and the others, so he began to inspect the walls and floors.

"We were just, uh … they were just going to a movie," Diane said. He saw her glance at Oilslick. "Please. Take off your coat."

Ferris handed Diane the roses he'd been holding behind his back. "Oh … you shouldn't have," she said. "They're so cute, so tiny…"

He thought he saw her melt a little. For once, his sister had been right about something. "I have to talk to you," she said. "Will you stay for a while?"

"Sure," he replied, grinning. "You're what I came for." He was winning. The others were leaving, and he would have Diane to himself.

"Nice meeting you," Oilslick said as he put on his coat and began to ooze toward the door with the other two.

"Sure thing," Ferris answered, smiling confidently in Oilslick's direction without bothering to meet his eyes. "Another time maybe we'll talk."

———————————

Diane and Ferris had their talk, or rather, Diane talked to Ferris. She mentioned the things she was doing at school, and how much she liked her new life and her new friends, and then she talked about how much she liked Ferris and how much she respected him. She went on for an hour before Ferris realized that it was she and not he who was talking. He tried to think of something to say, but his brain was still on vacation. Then she got up, sighed, and began turning the lights off. It wasn't the right time—nothing here was right—but he didn't stop her.

She lit a candle, and as he watched, astonished and mute, she undressed in front of him. It was only the second time he'd seen her without clothes on, and the first time when the world wasn't spinning. He knew he should have been aroused by it, but she did it without modesty or fanfare. It was strangely unerotic.

As he pulled off his own clothes he saw with shock how beautiful her body was, how independent her beauty was of his gaze. He also saw—a deeper, more fearful shock—that her eyes were wet with tears. He tried to think of something to say, something *right* to do, but she pulled him down on the couch and locked her arms and legs around him and held on to him as if she were drowning. He felt himself enter her, but it was a too-easy admission without welcome, and he told himself no, not now, but his hips were pumping him into her independent of his will, and it was still wrong, his awkward bumping and pushing was pulling her under, dragging her down when it should have been helping her, pleasing her, lifting her clear, making her safe. And when he tried to slow himself, to pull away and stop, to comfort her, kiss her breasts, her neck, her face, she clamped her legs around his hips more tightly still, dug her nails into his back and urged him on, averting her face, and there was no stopping it, no time to think of love, no time at all until…

She held him captive for a long time after he finished, alternately stroking and gently pummelling his back. Then, for what felt like an eternity, she was absolutely still and silent.

Ferris wanted the eternity to continue, at least until he had some idea what was beyond it. But he could make no headway on the future, here, and there was no past scarred enough to cling to. There was only the present, and it was tilting, tilting against him. Eventually Diane took a deep breath, untangled her limbs from his, and reached across him to turn on the lamp that overhung the couch. Life was going to go on.

He wanted to talk, to tell her how beautiful she was, that her body was the only human body he would ever love, but an instinct told him to keep silent. She dressed quickly, striding around the room as if the physical activity of doing so was preparing her for a more arduous task. She left the room and returned with two glasses of lemonade, and sat down next to him, not quite touching.

"I have to break up with you," she said, handing him one of the glasses without looking him in the eye.

"What?"

"I want to stop seeing you."

"Why?" he asked, numbly. "Jesus. We just…"

She cut him off. "You're a nice person, and I care about you as a friend, but it…"

She trailed off into silence and stared at the floor in front of him. Words may have deserted her, but there was a determination in her face that told him that the decision had been made. There was nothing for him to argue against, no terms to negotiate.

It didn't make the slightest sense, but he believed her. What else could he do? She had said it. But even as he believed her, he tried to tell himself that it couldn't possibly be true, that it must mean something else.

"Is this it?" he asked, shaking his head incredulously. Then he repeated the phrase, exploring its unfolding flavours, expanding them. "Is this all? Is this all there is to it?"

"I think so, yes," she said, getting up and standing in front of him with her hands on her hips. "I'm afraid so. I'm really sorry. Please go. Please."

Ferris pulled together his clothes and put them on. She handed him his coat, helped him on with it, and stood aside, as if he were a leper. He steadied himself, squared his shoulders, and walked out into the night. Against all the evidence, he hoped she'd be watching, and that she'd relent, tell him it was a stupid mistake. He made it to the end of the sidewalk before he turned around. The door was closed, and she'd already clicked off the porch light.

A hundred yards down the street he was in an ecstasy of self-pity. I've been defeated, he told himself. Outclassed, rejected, and humiliated. But who is the villain, and who is to blame?

Not Diane. But if not her, then who? He tried to convince himself that Oilslick was the villain, but it didn't ease the humiliation. Sure, Oilslick probably had a car, money, was in university, and was at least three years older than Ferris. He could do everything Ferris could, and do it better. Ferris made a fist, and then opened it, stretching his fingers to the limit. No, this one wasn't the kind he could get through by fighting. He'd lost, and he was lost.

Aimlessly, he drifted over to the park Diane had taken him to the day he arrived in the city. It had been raining that day, and the trees had been in full fall finery. Now he found that the branches were almost bare, but a full moon shone down on the last few survivors. He looked up into the branches, his mind suddenly sorting at breakneck speed.

It was a chilly night, and the wind was scattering leaves across the grass. Ferris began to circle the park, telling himself he didn't care what became of him, that his fate was set. He would never love again, that was sure. He was a broken man—and, hard to explain, he was very close to laughter.

Laughter? Why now? It didn't seem right, but it felt good. He was supposed to be tasting the crushing defeat, savouring his humiliation. The last thing he expected to find in them was laughter. To keep it back he banged his head against the trunk of each barren tree along the margin of the park. By the time he finished, his head ached and a small stream of blood was running from his scalp across his cheek. He leaned against the last tree and recited his litany, this time aloud, raising the volume each time until he was howling. *Is this it?* Yes! Thump. *Is this all?* Yes! Bang. *Is this all there is to it?* Yessssss!

But as he listened to himself, he felt the laughter bubbling up anyway. Sure, it was cruel and unjust. Yes, he would always love Diane—cruel bitch that she was. But there was more to it than he had previously imagined, and now he was at liberty to pursue it without distraction. It wouldn't heal his wounds or set the world right, but there was a deliciousness to it he could taste, an elusive satisfaction he'd never felt before.

He chased it out across the wet grass of the park as the images of the last hours did their reruns on him: the look on Oilslick's face, the tears he'd seen in Diane's eyes while they made love, and here and now, the cold wet earth, the trees, the moon, the moon…

It was beautiful, poignant. He wept a little, not from grief or loss but from the sheer abundance of the sensations passing through him. Stretching before him were decades and decades of broken, shimmering liberty, a field without rules or boundaries, where the hounds would run in every direction, where the does would grow horns and chase the hounds, and where there would be no end to bloodlust and bloodletting.

He lay down on the grass and let the wind blow some leaves over him while he secured it permanently in the new sensorium. Somewhere in the distance he could hear a dog barking—a hound, baying at the moon, the real moon. More tears filled his eyes, and when he looked up, the silver sphere shattered into a hundred—maybe it would be a thousand, a million, a billion—fragments of pleasure.

Preda

June is staring at Ferris with her brilliant blue eyes, chin in hands, across the chipped grey Arborite of a café tabletop. Well, one eye is staring at him, at least. The other one he's not sure about. It's off wandering, pondering God knows what. Maybe the nature of the universe, but more likely the whereabouts of Ferris's competition, Ethan—that rat-faced son of a bitch. Or maybe the eye is considering John, her born-again Christian doctor ex-husband.

Probably not the latter. The eye, along with everything else of June except a small sentimental part of her brain, would enjoy watching John being flattened under the wheels of a bus. But she's looking too pleased with life to be thinking thoughts that evil right here.

"What about it, Ferris?" she's asking. "What do *you* want to do?"

Mostly he wants to keep his balance—and her off-balance—but he can't tell her that. He can't even admit to her that he's spooked. She'll be annoyed, and rightly so. He has, after all, been pursuing her like a hound since they met. He's supposed to be an educated adult WASP male, closing in on thirty, virtually the perfect cultural product of the Church of England, and theoretically at least, a man born with a ticket to capitalism's board and ballroom. He's *supposed* to be decisive and self-assured, high-fiving the world on his way to purchase a new BMW.

Trouble is, he doesn't feel it. He's never quite been in tune with his demographic persona, and right now, he's not properly tuned to anything, least of all himself. It's not quite that he's spooked by June or by *what* she's asking. No, it's how direct she's being about it. Because he still doesn't have a clue what he wants out of life, he gets nervous around women who do know and are out front about it. He'd have preferred to go on tiptoeing around the big issues a while longer, keep it light and breezy, you know? Call this extended adolescence if you need to. He calls it common sense, even though he can't see the sense of it right now.

It's true that June knows what she wants, but it hasn't always been that way. While she was a young girl with white-blonde hair and blue eyes, growing up in a small town, she knew. Gazing out across the flat white vistas of a prairie winter and thinking that something so cold should have polar bears and ice floes, she decided that someday, somehow, she'd live among polar bears and poets. That's a quote, her own words.

No one can be a child forever, and June was no exception. The white-blonde hair begins to darken to the colour of honey, and adolescence arrives, with hormones, breasts, and awkwardness. A few more years pass, the honey of her hair deepens to the colour of amber, some beauty settles onto her bones, offset only a little by the wandering eye. She graduates early from high school, then university, works at several jobs that don't use a tenth of her education or intelligence. Eventually, she meets John and marries him at twenty-four. From there it is into the dark suburbs of a city a long way from home.

For seven years, June's story is John's, even in her telling of it. *He* finishes university, *he* goes to medical school, *he* interns successfully, *he* joins a thriving private clinic in their suburb, *he* wears the suits and buys a silver car made in Germany. For him it's a portrait of a conventional marriage, and June occupies a predictable niche in the lower right-hand corner, a niche that seems to diminish in importance and focus as each year passes: *she* goes to work to support them while he's at school, *she* cooks the meals, *she* washes the clothes, *she* takes his suits to the dry cleaners the one day a week he allows her to drive him to work. For too many women, that's all she wrote. Not for June.

Lodged in an obscure part of the top left corner of her and John's portrait, in the spot reserved for collective dreams and aspirations, rests a time bomb of white bears and poets. You see, John wrote poems when June first knew him, and he told her he would always write poems. He also promised that once medical school and interning were through, he'd take her to the far north and set up a practice where a doctor was really needed. In the fog of being twenty-four, his promises and the occasional verse left on the night table are enough to nurture her.

But John turns into a busy young doctor, becomes a slick young doctor, and one day, June wakes up and discovers that she's thirty years old, living in the suburbs, somebody's—a doctor's—wife, and the bomb detonates: She *still* wants to live among polar bears and poets, and nothing less will do. When she reminds John about his promises, he laughs. He's forgotten these and a lot of other ones he made to himself—and anyway, that was schoolboy stuff. Time to grow up, and he's ready, even if she isn't. He doesn't say this, but he isn't about to give up a week of his thriving practice to go off and holiday with a bunch of ice cubes, let alone give it up completely so June can live near some dangerous and unpredictable predators. June hears it anyway, and she decides that her dreams are more important than the bullshit he's gotten her stuck in.

To help her with the decision, John acquires some funny ideas of his own. He gets religion and starts hanging out at a fundamentalist church called the Temple of Jeremiah, Prophet.

In June's telling of it, the word "prophet" ought to have been spelled "profit." "Their idea of heaven," she tells Ferris on their first date, "is a cross between one of those hypo-allergenic bubbles and the Stock Exchange. They think that God's Will is to see that a few white middle-class people make a lot of money, don't touch one another very often and wave bibles at everything that offends them."

June isn't hesitant about explaining herself and what she wants from life.

Her dream sits proudly on the prow of who she is, a finely carved figure that she's teaching to steer the ship. She's not quite so clear about how her marriage ended, except that she leaped from lower right corner straight out of it, and she put her foot—deliberately—through the canvas along the way. She left John, God, Church, and medical practice—along with the house, German car, and most of the other assets—and moved into the city. Within a few days, she had a job working in a bookstore—best place to meet poets. And that's where Ferris came in. Literally. One thing led to another, and here he is, staring at her across a café table, sipping coffee, and feeling vaguely frightened.

What does he think her question means? He believes there are several questions. *Does he really care about her?* That's easy. Yes, sure. *Is he really a poet?* Ferris writes poetry, for what it's worth. He makes his living at a less sensitizing occupation, but what poet doesn't?

Well, Ethan, for one, according to June. But Ferris knows Ethan only *appears* to make a living at it. Ferris didn't tell her that the little fuckface cheats. He got a job as a go-fer in a truck assembly plant a few years back, hung in just exactly long enough to get a union ticket, and is now traipsing around as a union organizer, representing the Revolutionary Working Class at cocktail parties, making speeches about the Dignity of Labour and writing extremely sensitive poems about truck motors for the union newsletter. The little fraud doesn't know enough about trucks to change a tire on a tricycle. That isn't the kind of thing June would notice. Alas.

> November 12, 1976
>
> BUENOS AIRES, ARGENTINA: Twelve "leftist guerrilla suspects" were reported killed today in clashes with army troops and police. The 1976 death toll from political violence reported through official Argentine channels is 1,243.

June knows that Ferris likes her, but they both know that the road to hell is paved with the good intentions of poets. So maybe the question that has Ferris crawling for cover is this one: *Will you take me to live among the polar bears?* He doesn't have a clue how literal she's being about these polar bears. Worse, he suspects that Ethan understands this question quite well, and that he's feeding her the right answers. Never mind that the scrawny little bastard wouldn't make a decent afternoon snack for a polar bear, even if Ethan's mother were to let him out without his mittens.

Well, Ferris can't worry about Ethan, anyway. He has a few questions of his own that need answering before he can give June any answers. They're big ones, too. *What is it that women really want from men? And when do they mean what they say?* These aren't new questions. He's been puzzling over them since he got out of Pony League baseball. So far, he's made a career out of coming up with the wrong answers. But something tells him that with June, it's time to get them right.

June's eyes bore in on him. It's an unsettling experience, like being examined by two different people. One of them will shoot him if he makes a wrong answer, the other is already distracted, looking for alternatives down the street. If he wants her, he has to come up with the answer—*right now*. It's deep water.

He takes the plunge. "I want you," he says, gazing back into her left eye, the one on the conventional track. "I want to sleep with you, I want to know everything about you." For a second, the water feels warm and soapy, like a bubble bath. Then it closes over his head.

"Okay," she says. "Let's go to my place."

He's trapped himself. He can't quite hear the bars clicking into place, but he imagines he does. He has no idea if it locks him in with her, or the rest of the world out, reality with it. He suspects it is both, and the sensation is exhilarating and frightening at the same time.

He manages to get the check, pay it, and pull on his coat without his teeth chattering audibly. Yippee shit, he's thinking. I'm going to get it on with June. And also, holy shit.

She takes his arm and leans against him, shyly possessive, as they walk across the parking lot to his car in the chilly November air. It catches at his heart, but so does the wind blowing from somewhere, probably the northeast, where the polar bears come from. This is typical. Ferris never quite knows what he's doing, but for some reason women think he does. *Sensitive and in control* seems to have got itself stencilled across his spiritual behind. He opens the door for her, making that learned Anglican gesture as always, and as she climbs in he glimpses her shapely legs and ankles, realizes he's probably going to have them around his ears in a few hours, and hopes, in a thoroughly un-Anglican way, that he'll be able to make them quiver with delight. A gust of wind slaps his face, and he runs to his side of the car, shivering, and climbs in. Does everybody's life run so close to panic? he wonders. Can I do this? Can I please June? For once, this last question is more important than the other ones.

Apparently he can. An hour later he's removing her clothes, slowly, almost delicately, more calm than he's been in weeks. This, at least, he understands. There is a right and wrong way to proceed, and he knows what the right one is: touch her without urgency, don't be in a hurry, let no skin remain uncaressed, make the intimacy created be a gentle one. She is standing beside the bed, and he sits on it so that his mouth is even with her nipples. He pulls the shoulder straps of her brassiere across her shoulder and reaches behind her to unsnap the rest. As it falls, he leans forward and runs his tongue from her breastbone across to her right nipple. It stiffens between his lips, and she sighs.

"I don't need a mechanic, Ferris," she says. "Be real with me."

He freezes. No, even this isn't going to be simple. Be real. Be a polar bear. He hasn't a clue how to do either.

June pushes him backward onto the bed and climbs onto his chest, tickling him. He pushes her off, onto her side, and she kisses him, pushing her tongue into his mouth, laughing at the same time.

"Be real with me," she says for the second time, this time more playfully. "I've already said yes, so quit trying to blow me away with your silly *technique*."

Evidently he *doesn't* know how to make love to her, so he lets her teach him how. It's nothing he doesn't already know, it turns out, but it is sweeter her way, and strangely easy, once he gets the hang of it. He can't explain what the difference is, except that after they're finished, they aren't finished. It goes on and on, it becomes conversation, listening, seeing, smelling, as if everything around them is intelligent and clamouring to have its part of their attention.

It's the best he's had, but it isn't

Orgasms

Female orgasms are more important, interesting, and more variable than male orgasms. Everyone knows this by now, but yet an amazing number of heterosexual women are in their late twenties before they take possession of this fact, and most men ignore it until late in their thirties. What a waste.

1. Common sense tells us that the best sex is the kind that engages the maximum number of our senses, and oral sex confirms this. Cunnilingus is easily the best and most reliable method of bringing a woman to orgasm, and for determining if, when, and how well she's having one. Contrary to legend, the male sex organ is a poor instrument of empirical or aesthetic judgement. It simply doesn't have enough nerve endings. A head-giver has a superior tactile, visual, and olfactory vantage point, and a human tongue has more interesting textures than a penis, finger, or vibrator.

2. The intensity and variety of

female orgasms appear to be relatively limitless, subject to a number of general factors:

a. Direct and isolated stimulation of the clitoris produces intense, localized, and "high-frequency" orgasms that some women find painful. This variety is equally (and sometimes more) easily produced through digital stimulation or with vibrators. In most cases the clitoris emerges from subcutaneous tissue and becomes erect only with or shortly prior to orgasm, and both orgasm and clitoris rapidly subside. This variety of female orgasm is similar to male orgasm.

b. A more indirect orgasm can occur if the labia and surrounding tissue are stimulated orally, or if oral play is coupled with interrupted penetration and copulation. The result (occasionally) is a labial and vaginal engorgement, along with greater, more gradual, and more long-lasting clitoral erection. Orgasms are longer lasting, more "low-frequency," and almost never painful, and subsequent intercourse is a wholly different and usually more pleasurable experience for both female and male.

3. Orgasms that coincide with labial and vaginal engorgement are probably the source of what some researchers have called the "vaginal orgasm." They can be explained physiologically. With engorgement, nerve synapses in the engorged tissue recirculate sensation, diffusing (and sometimes extending) it,

quite like dying and going off to heaven, like they say in the books. The earth doesn't move—for either of them, he suspects. Ferris is still who and what he was before June introduced him to paradise. He remains alert inside his own mind, and a part of him stands aside from this, making comparisons, tallying experience, trying to figure out just what these sensations are and what to do with and about them. Still, his earlier fear that something awful is going to happen has evaporated completely. He's himself, June is herself. And a very sweet conduit exists between them that makes the unshaking world friendlier, richer, more evenly verdant, and emptied of predators.

Paradise, his inner note-taker observes, isn't perfection, and neither is June. Her lovely body has flaws. She doesn't seem to have any hipbones, and her breasts are larger than he imagined they'd be, and firmer. Through their transparent skin run thick blue veins that don't seem to go anywhere in particular, like meandering blue streams. He discovers this because she teaches him to trace their path with his lips. He makes the exploration willingly, but he also continues with his private inventory.

June sweats a lot, and it is different in each body zone. A heavy musk exudes from beneath her arms, at the small of her back, at the nape of her neck. Below her waist the scent changes. There is honey to it, and milkiness comes up through the musk. It's unlike anything he's encountered, and for someone who uses his nose in the erotic zone the way most people use their eyes, it's something.

There are other irregularities. Her skin is rough here and nubbled with body hair there, satiny and transparent elsewhere. Her pussy is the best, like a bell, the labia rich and darkly flared, her clitoris jutting from their apex.

He's intoxicated by all these particularities, but they don't blind him to what is truly unusual about June and her basement den. Because a den is what it is. At the top of the unusuals is a huge, thick fur robe that is draped across her king-size bed. The robe is white, big surprise, and too big to be a polar bear skin, although he can detect no seams that would expose it as a hundred dead rabbits. The bed dwarfs everything in the bedroom, which is the largest room in the small apartment. Not that there's much to see around the margins of the bed. Everything has been painted white—everything: lamp shades, chairs, tables.

The effect of the room is perfectly intentional, although she doesn't say so. This is her private memory theatre. It is the prairies in winter, with their chilly iridescent panoramas, her personal refuge from the unrelieved

and thus the orgasm is more indirect than when surrounding tissues are not engorged. This is probably what latter-day sexologists mean when they talk about "G-spots." What seems to have eluded them is this: What produces a woman's orgasm is not so much a location but a carefully manufactured event that exists temporarily in a woman's mind and body—and in a man's head.

4. Labial engorgement is the physiological equivalent of male erection. (Vaginal engorgement has no male equivalent.)

5. A small percentage (ten percent?) of women experience spontaneous labial engorgement, while another ten to fifteen percent experience it during "normal" penetrative intercourse (depending on a number of tactile and non-tactile factors. The size of a man's penis is fairly far down the list.). Most women require five to fifteen minutes of skilled stimulation to achieve labial engorgement, even when the level of interpersonal intimacy and trust is very high. The most effective and pleasurable technique, again, is cunnilingus. Vaginal engorgement is rarer and seems to be a nexus of physical and psychological effects. If "female" mysteries exist (and they clearly do), this is one of them.

6. Some women, as a side effect of labial engorgement, exude aromas that can addict their partners for anywhere from twenty minutes to thirty years.

greenery their present mossy climate offers to the senses. It is also, Ferris suspects, the trap he's been looking for. When June sleeps, she's at home, and her dreams—she strokes his back as she dozes—are a wonder. That's where the trap waits. This is also the Arctic sea, an invitation for polar bears to romp, hunt, sleep at her feet. Or between her thighs.

Ferris discovers himself relaxing. Fuck the trap. It is cozy here, animal-warm, like being inside the skin of an animal that is more than the sum of the fur robe and their two bodies, male and female, more than the perfumes of sex, even. He turns toward her, hunkers down beneath the robe, and feels his stupid male ego with its erectile electric fences give way. In the perfumed darkness he begins to touch her on her terms, with his hands, his lips, his tongue. When she stirs from her nap and arches her back, he can feel the firm muscles of her stomach flex, sense her Achilles tendons stretch, her toes clench and unclench. She pushes him onto his back again, but he squirms out from under her, and begins to lick her skin as an animal might, grooming her, across her shoulders, flanks, the small of her back, down the crack of her ass and into her pussy, which is dripping with the protein of his come. He can feel her shuddering orgasm as he mounts her, she is the bear now, and he doesn't know what he is, and doesn't much care.

Male orgasms are fun, too. They're also a lot more variable than is generally recognized, particularly when they aren't confused with ejaculation. For some men, this variability comes with aging, because they learn that withholding an orgasm can be at least as much fun as getting it off and done with. Unfortunately, fear too often becomes a factor at this point, and the result is impotence.

Still, male orgasms are almost always less intense than the orgasms women have. A wise uncle once told me that St. Augustine took the following comparative measure:

If the measure of pleasure were divided into ten, nine would go to women, and one would go to men.

My wise uncle went on to suggest that men, mistaking an empirical calculation for a hostile political slogan, have historically responded to St. Augustine's formula by insisting on a nine-to-one orgasm numerical balance in their favour to even things out.

———————

Later on, they talk. Gazing out across the snowy fields, she tells him all about her childhood, and he tries to make a sensible narrative of his. She makes complete sense to him now, but his life is barely coherent and thoroughly un-sensible: a happy, uneventful childhood followed by an interminable string of refusals to co-operate.

He's tried to tell the story before. It's about a normal, happy person who is lost, restless, in exile. He talks about his green forests and blue rivers, and he talks of their destruction. He talks about the pale midnight skies of the high north, and how he can never forget that they have been filled with nuclear attack bombers all his life, how he grew up expecting the brilliant flash of light that would end his life—and everyone's at any moment.

It occurs to him that this half-darkened room contains no such threat. It is making his self-drama sound silly. So do June's questions. "Really?" she asks. "If you love it so much, why don't you go back?"

Out loud, he pushes that question back and forth through his mind, one moment talking about his fear of exotic places and things, the next, about his craving for them. "I don't know why," he admits, finally. "It's as if it's gone, destroyed. Or it's somewhere else, some *thing* else."

I reasoned that since Augustine was a saint, the versified measure he took (and who knows what was lost or added in the translation into English) was a theological truth and I didn't question it for many years. Now I think that the true ratio is about seven to three in favour of women, and I steer away from comparing the two kinds of orgasms. Between the two genders there is an infinity of individual pleasure gradients with so many contributory intangibles that only a fool would make a serious attempt to quantify them.

Women are capable of multiple orgasms within a single erotic encounter, while for most men orgasm terminates the encounter—often with extreme abruptness. In a sense, then, all male ejaculations are premature, and sensible men learn to pursue other erotic goals. Alas, sensible men are almost as rare as wise men, who treat the quality and intensity of their orgasms less as material for self-epiphany and more as an indicator to the quality of their treatment of their sexual partners.

She's listening more carefully than others have, and more carefully than Ferris does himself. "That's so abstract," she says. "Tell me what you enjoy. What do you hold on to?"

"I like holding on to you," he answers. "That's easy."

She thinks he's joking again. "We'll see about that," she says.

He does like holding her, more than he can say, and maybe more than he wants to admit to himself. He likes it so much that he doesn't sleep. And as the hours pass, a familiar irritation creeps in: How important can this be? How long can this magic last? Isn't there supposed to be more to life than this?

June is convincing evidence that this *is* all there is. When she's awake, she's either talking, listening, or zipping up to or down from lovemaking or from sleep. Not a wasted moment or motion. Even when she's asleep, deep sleep or REM, she appears to be engaged. There are no groans or mutters from this woman, no pushing him away, no claws. She's simply unafraid, in there, at home. If she senses him at all, it's as a fellow creature to grasp or stroke. He could just as easily be a polar bear—or Ethan.

When dawn breaks, Ferris is wide awake, telling himself he has other responsibilities, other species and specimens to investigate. He gets up quietly, dresses still more quietly, and is about to sneak out when he recognizes that no, he can't sneak out on this woman. Not that she's stopping him. She's absolutely unconscious, lying on her side with the robe down to her waist, and he can almost see a superior life form, the future coursing along inside those blue veins he's just spent hours tracing across her skin. He removes his coat and returns to the bedside, leans over and nuzzles her neck.

"I've got to go," he whispers. "Work."

June opens just one of her eyes. It's the one that wanders, but this time it bores into him like a drill. "You're a lying son of a bitch, Ferris," she says. "It's Saturday."

Outside, the city looks luridly green and overgrown, as if the world, overnight, has been encrusted in a bryophyte invasion. He's nostalgic for June's snow fields before he gets to the end of the sidewalk. Then he remembers the polar bears, and isn't so sure.

Well, he tells himself, things have just got much more complicated. He

Some other items concerning orgasm to ponder: 1. What *is* the point of a quick orgasm? 2. If the total number of female orgasms on the planet could be doubled or tripled, it would solve most, if not all, of the world's problems. Wars would cease, the general level of violence would diminish, sensible economic and political activities would flourish, and women and men would be infinitely happier. No, I'm not suggesting that

corrects himself instantly: His life may be a thing confounded by other things, but this woman, June, isn't *a thing*. Thinking of her on those terms is an affront, as if she's nothing more than a connected system of body parts. Ferris reminds himself that she's a serious woman, a person wanting to get on with a new kind of life, and not as a satellite spinning around the polluted planet of male behaviours. Fair enough.

But of course, whatever Ferris thinks last night was, he's aware that it was also a job interview. Along the snowy trails, June lets him know that Ethan is an equally serious contender, and she hinted that he's hungrier. As she talked about Ethan, Ferris made a half-serious plan to break the little bastard into small pieces, but he kept his trap shut. Which one of them she'll choose depends, partly, on what he does, and he won't be very successful if he does it to Ethan.

And never mind Ethan, what to do about June? It would be immoral to exploit her need, immoral to exploit her in any way. The choice is hers. Helplessly, he returns to the idea of polar bears. Sleek, bullet-headed, beautiful, deadly. As he starts the car, one leaps from an ice floe, he sees the huge soles of its feet as it disappears gracefully beneath the icy water. If that were me, he thinks, I'd be hypothermic before I could crawl onto the next floe. As a test, just for a moment, he imagines that he's become her polar bear mate. When he resurfaces, there's a small seal in his jaws, its broken neck lolling to one side. Ferris notes, as he pulls the car away from the curb, that the seal looks like Ethan.

If it's a bear she wants for a mate, Ferris is the only real candidate she's got, that's at least clear. It's just that he's not enthusiastic about *polar bears*, that's all. In his wildest dreams he might imagine that he's a grizzly, and in his nightmares he occasionally suspects he might be nothing but a stuffed panda. But a polar bear? Never.

———————

women are the cause of our collective troubles. Men are. But if everyone made doubling and tripling female orgasm rates a priority, men would be spending too much time in bed to get into trouble. They wouldn't have time for war and other sublimations, and while they were in bed, they'd learn the sensible arts of compromise and conversation.

Okay, I know, I know—be practical. But if something so eminently sensible isn't practical, why isn't it?

During the next month he spends about half his nights under the white robe, soaking her up, drinking her in. The rest of the time he does his best to forget that she exists. He has to, because Ethan is hanging around, getting his—whatever that means. Ferris doesn't ask, and June doesn't provide any details.

He learns that June really does want to live in the Arctic with him, not as polar bears, but as *something*. She wants her life to be a triumph of human warmth over all the ice and snow in the world, a grand adventure, and she's got it in her head that she's owed it. In her mind, adventures are what men are for. That's a problem for Ferris, in several ways. He feels like he's being asked to pay for something her ex-husband promised and didn't deliver. And besides, Ferris isn't exactly David Livingstone. Just getting to work in the morning is adventure enough. And so on.

He takes a couple of weeks off to think things through, and he doesn't do it right. He disappears, doesn't call her, lets things slide. He goes to the bar every night, actually, drinks his face off and comes home too pissed to worry about responsibilities or bears or leaving the field to Ethan. He knows what he's doing, he even knows what it's called—Fear of Commitment, Failure to Communicate, Boorism, Indifference. A little of each, maybe a lot: stupid behaviour. He tells himself he's hibernating.

Before he knows it, the two weeks are two months, and when he finally wakes up, June has moved from the basement apartment to a downtown highrise. Eventually he calls her at the bookstore. She doesn't seem angry, but she's characteristically direct.

"Where have you been, Ferris?" she asks, sounding more curious than hurt. "I missed you."

He mumbles some excuses that don't make sense to him let alone her, but she lets them by. She's happy to hear his voice. They make a date to meet the next day at a café not far from his office. Subtly, she lets him know that he's a jerk, but that she forgives him.

The moment he hangs up, he turns into a bear. There are no snow fields or ice floes this time, no white fur, no mangled Ethan disguised as a seal. This is maverick grizzly bear stuff—overturned logs, clawed tree trunks, hump-shouldered charges across the meadow at anything that crosses his suddenly myopic field of vision. Everyone at his office thinks he's lost his mind, because he's snarling at co-workers and visitors for no apparent reason, kicking furniture, banging his shoulders against every doorjamb he passes through. He ends the afternoon sitting at his desk alone, growling audibly. No one dares come near him. He's the Original Bullgoose Loony, the Fire-eyed Silvertip King of the Mountain, the Badassed Brute No One Dares Tangle With. Why he's behaving this way he has no idea, but it feels so terrific he doesn't care.

After work it gets even better. He comes within a hair of ramming his car into the tail end of a Volvo driven by some poor accountant foolish enough to have made an impolite lane change in front of him. After that he skips dinner, goes to the bar, drinks too many glasses of Scotch and gets into his first fist fight in six years.

The next morning he calls in sick, and he's advised to take a couple of days off. He agrees, probably to everyone's great relief.

He doesn't show up for lunch with June, naturally, and he doesn't call to cancel. He knows damned well he's trashing himself, but all that does is fuel his anger. He spends the afternoon watching soap operas. So he's an asshole. So what?

June isn't about to let it go at that. At six o'clock she calls him.

"Where were you this afternoon, Ferris?" she asks, without a trace of complaint in her voice. "I waited for you for ninety minutes."

His anger evaporates. He feels contrite and guilty, but those aren't helpful emotions. He can't explain himself. There's no possible explanation other than that he's nuts, but that isn't the reason why he can't. He can't bring himself to apologize. It's all slipping away from him—his self-respect, his shot at June, maybe his sanity. He can squeak out just one coherent thought. To him it's a perfectly clear one.

"June, I'm just not a polar bear. I'm a grizzly—a woodland grizzly, and there's nothing I can do about it."

There's no possible way to translate this into sense, and he doesn't try. A series of images is buzzing around in his head—a solitary bear threading his way along a leafy, trout-filled stream in dappled sunlight. He knows the bear is headed downstream, away from something, but what it is eludes him.

"What?" June doesn't get it. "Say that again?"

"Never mind. Are you going to be there later on?"

"Yes, but…" She's catching on that he's cracked and tries to get out of it. There's this, there's that. No mention of Ethan, but other things. Her hair. She'd like to take a long bath and do some reading. She's tired. She's human.

"Just for a little while," Ferris pleads. It is suddenly of extreme importance that he see her.

She gives in, agrees to nine o'clock, not a long visit, just a cup of tea and talk. He has to ask for her new address. It feels like *her* fault he doesn't already have it.

———————————

If this were only Ferris's story, I'd make him chicken out a final time and leave him genuflecting on his moronic behaviour. That would be a predictable outcome, replete with the banal transformations of a Danielle Steel novel but minus the syrupy ending in which to drown the characters: Man meets Woman, Man avoids Woman, Man imagines Grizzly Bears but more resembles a Deranged Chicken. It's more tempting to toss the entire mess into the wastepaper basket and remind myself that no one needs more evidence that men can be jerks.

But there's more to it. Wherever we are in this world, cowardice has an absolute price. In our part of the world, the price is usually paid by women. What I'm saying is that this isn't just Ferris's story, and I don't intend to let him off the hook for what he does in the next several hours. Hence, I'll describe it, but I won't dramatize it. To do that would be to sanction it, excuse it, perhaps even encourage it. Better to make it a confession that far too many men might make, and elucidate the specific consequences it has for Ferris.

On this night there is no robe of white fur, no imagined snow fields, no warmth kindled and kept, and no thought of bears. June and Ferris start in her living room, formally, a cup of tea, averted eyes—three of them, anyway. He makes small talk: how hard life is, how awful it is to be human. June is guarded, Ferris morose and unresponsive. Eventually, her hopeful nature breaks through her reserve.

"Are we going to talk," she wants to know, "or are you just going to come around like this now, with your needs?"

It's his last chance to be human, but the only part of him he can reach is his own misery, his needs.

"No, no," she says and makes excuses. Her period, just over. Not now. She wants more, as always. He wants her body, insistently. And eventually, she lets him use it.

His "usage" is brief and brutal without being violent. June lets it happen, but she doesn't participate. When it is over, and Ferris's need used up with it, her expression as she ushers him into the hallway tells him what the price will be: She will close herself to him, permanently. She is determined beyond any other ambition to let herself be used by no one. Since he already knows that, he's not surprised at the cost.

We could look at this from another perspective. Ferris has raped June. He himself almost recognizes this despite the depths to which he's sunk. Almost, but not quite. There are enough supervening social baffles to protect him from that recognition, not the least of which are in June's mind. To her he still exists as a lover, one who has proved to be unworthy. Her revenge, a small one but adequate to the times, is that Ferris will now exist in his own mind by those definitions. As he leaves he excuses himself, dimly, by telling himself he has exercised the comforts of a predator. Such comforts will never offer him much pleasure again, but it will be ten years before he, and the world he lives in, see through them.

June and Ferris, needless to say, never sleep together again, and he doesn't ever ask her what it was *she* thought happened that night. He doesn't get the opportunity. Soon after, she moves in with Ethan. She keeps on working at the bookstore, because Ethan doesn't take her to live with her beloved polar bears either. He isn't up to it, not even for a visit. And maybe she's lost her taste for bears.

SIX

A decade passes. Ferris meets and loses Annie, quits his planning job, gives up poetry, becomes a writer of things he never imagined he'd write about: first, travel articles for magazines, then tourist brochures and books about cities and countries he barely knows and interest him not at all. It's a living, and it permits him to wander.

So, How *Did* You Like

I can summarize these years with a question: Why do human beings turn themselves like corks in the neck of a bottle—trying to see what's inside—while ocean waves pound the shores, glaciers calve and drop into the sea, single oxygen molecules combine with their carbon and hydrogen counterparts in ones and twos?

For Ferris, the question is neither poetic nor rhetorical. Over the decade it sends its tendrils into every corner of the obvious and the commonplace. It is a question he can't answer, but for which he eventually arrives at an *understanding*—a contrarium built of the question's dimensions and complexities. The contrarium is this: Everything twists—it's the way we are, and a way we can't afford to be any longer.

Some of the routes he travels can be explained by way of his question. It suggests that we are twisted by things more compelling than sex and gender, that sex and gender don't explain everything, that there are interiors and glacier slides moving among us we do not see, or that seem to be something—anything—other than what they are.

For instance, contiguous with the historical period this book encompasses, roughly 1960 to the present, we—as a species and as a political collective, if not as selfish individuals—appear to have ceased making plans for the future. The end of Ferris's career in urban planning coincided with the death rattle of the North American century's attempt to make cities something better than places to make money and commit crimes. When Ferris recognized that our collective political will to protect and/or improve our condition had disintegrated, he quit the profession. He didn't want to be part of what has become a combination of near-term profit trajectory-tracing, crisis management, and lying to the general public about what the future holds—flexibility, governments call it. Better, he decided, to hit the road and stay there as long as the new rules of flexibility permit.

Ah, you wish to know more about "flexibility"? It is the process by which intelligent people sit in their machines, gazing at the dials, and never looking up to see where the machine is taking them. And the corollary rules of urban life it has engendered? Well, the first rule is that everything is permitted, up to, and until, the results cause inflexibility (or looking ahead)—or the banks foreclose. The second rule is that we do not, in the end, have our dreams fulfilled. The third rule is that things twist in such a way that we forget what our dreams were, and we become either victims or opportunists. Pardon my sermon.

Testosterone

Germaine Greer has described testosterone as a "race poison," by which I take her to mean that it is poisoning the human species from within. She's right, and my only criticism is that she doesn't pursue her insight far enough. Human males carry around massively excessive loads of it. It makes them violent, stupid, hairy, and bald, and it no longer has any offsettingly positive purpose. It is a dangerous drug that, left unchecked, will eventually exterminate us and destroy the planet along the way.

While we were still in the caves or in trees, testosterone provided human males with the aggression necessary to fight more powerful, larger or more numerous animals, and it helped stronger individuals breed successfully while natural selection was still a biological necessity. Short of the kind of protein-poor environment inhabited by the Yanomami in the Amazon, no human environment that I know of requires this degree of aggression and violence we subject them to.

Civilization makes the human qualities engen-

For instance, June didn't get what she wanted. She didn't get her poet, and she didn't live among polar bears. She ended up, as before, driving a German car. Not long after she and Ethan moved in together, Ethan gave up poetry, dumped the Revolutionary Working Classes and the attempt by the Vanguard to surround them with state-owned concrete apartments and boloney sandwiches. He went back to school. What did he study? Three guesses: Heavy Mechanics, Poetic Theory, or Dentistry.

Wrong if you guessed Heavy Mechanics or Poetic Theory. Ethan had arrived at the truck factory all those years ago with pre-med qualifications, and when he and June got married there appeared, as if by magic, the predictable pressures for him to "get serious." If most of a whole generation hadn't committed this kind of about-face, it would be hard to explain Ethan's. Ferris didn't try very hard. He told himself that Ethan was an ordinary guy responding to ordinary pressures. In his cynical moments, he had another explanation: Maybe, screw the Revolutionary Working Classes, Ethan was secretly just another guy who wanted a wife to pick up his dry cleaning every Friday in a BMW.

Ferris hadn't decoded anything from June's demands that would have encouraged—or permitted—Ethan to become a dentist, but Ethan's ego must have heard something. After all, Ferris was phobic about polar bears when there weren't any within several thousand miles, so maybe Ethan hallucinated dental chairs, root canals, porcelain bridges shining in the morning light. "Ethan, I want you to build root canals to link a nation of candy-heads" isn't any sillier than Ferris hearing "Ferris, I want you to be a polar bear."

Whatever. June quit the bookstore when they got married, and Ferris heard they moved to the 'burbs. That was that, life went on, and if not exactly up, then back and forth and up and down.

Ferris didn't think much about June, to tell the truth. At first his ego wouldn't let him. Later on, when it sank in that what he'd thought was merely crappy, boorish male behaviour actually bordered on indictable crime, it was hard to think of her, and morally dangerous. The years passed, he was travelling a lot, and eventually he didn't think about her, or it, at all.

It was a matter of luck that he happened to be in town when the woman who owned the bookstore where June used to work sold it to a multinational chain and, strange behaviour, married the lawyer who negotiated the sale for her. Ferris knew her well enough to get himself invited to the wedding. June and Ethan were also invited.

Ferris wasn't fond of weddings, not when WASPs were involved. He'd grown keenly aware of how his fellow WASPs had lost all grasp on formal behaviours. They were simply unsure of what to do at a wedding—or at any other ritual

dered by testosterone vestigial and counter-productive. In the crowded quarters in which we live, the presence of excessive amounts of testosterone has created environments like the Bronx, Somalia, along with virtuals like the World Wrestling Federation and Pro Football. It precipitated the arms race, kept the Cold War spending us into bankruptcy, and it will be the true source of whatever geopolitical lunacies rain down on us in the near future. It's no accident that seventy percent of the acts of violence committed in North America are perpetrated by men between the ages of seventeen and twenty-four, when male testosterone levels are at their peak. It is the non-behavioural fuel behind male violence against women and children, the banana skin on the floor at every male interaction in the world. It is rape-gasoline, plunder-Wheaties. If anything on this planet is going to survive, we're going to have to make a radical reduction in the amount of human testosterone circulating in it.

Am I being silly here? No. I'm completely serious about this. It takes

occasion—fine for the toaster and Lazy Susan industries, but it was a drag when no one knew who was supposed to toast the bride, or when, or if the groom got toasted and whether it was best delivered burnt or half-baked. To Ferris, WASP weddings had become one long solecism, with everybody either uneasy or insulted, and with the poor victims of this cultural disarray wandering off to live with nothing sanctifying their alliance but a bank of appliances they would probably sell off at their first anniversary garage sale—or give back to the donors if they were foolish enough to undergo the same indignities.

Wisely, he sat out the ceremony for this one with a Scotch and soda in a bar a few blocks from the Unitarian church where it was held. Someone had warned him that it was going to be one of those write-your-own affairs where the bride and groom tearfully read off their favourite platitudes in front of a Unitarian whose priestly qualifications were a degree in sociology, having found Anglican liturgy too authoritarian. Religious beliefs? They consisted of wanting everyone to "have a nice day."

Better to sip Scotch and amuse himself by imagining the ceremony:

Do you take this, er, person to be your spouse, to love, uh, honour—no, that's a little heavy—cherish and treat as well as you feel up to, until—sorry, can't mention death, too negative—until it doesn't feel right or your career paths diverge, or until you've got better things to do?

Oh, sure.

And do you promise to try to be civilized at the divorce hearing, and not make unreasonable demands on one another's assets?

---

very small amounts of testosterone to provide human beings with enough aggressive energy to get out of bed in the morning, and only a very little more for us to have a normal sex drive and act like decent people. About the amount that women have will do just fine. Both men and women produce small amounts of testosterone in the adrenal gland. The superfluous stuff males have is manufactured in the Leydig cells of the testicles, right next door to the also biologically superfluous sperm-producing cells.

Please relax. I'm not about to suggest general castration of our male population. But it's now common practice to regulate (allegedly for reasons of women's health and well-being—the kind that benefit males) the amount of progesterone and estrogen women have in their bodies. Why not regulate the levels of testosterone males carry? It would be extremely easy to justify the public and individual benefits. Crime rates would drop dramatically, sexual violence would become a rarity, warfare would become rarer still. Sure, razor

Why not?

That being the case, I pronounce you—what are your names, anyway?—husband and wife, or wife and husband, in the name of—what day is this?—yeah, Saturday.

Ferris did go to the reception, mainly because he knew June was going to be there. He was curious about what had become of her and Ethan, and when he RSVPed he asked to be seated with them.

He got a little more than he expected. The guests weren't arranged around the expected eight-to-ten-person tables, but at nice, intimate tables of four. When he arrived, the other three at his assigned table were already there, June and Ethan, and a woman named Phyllis—someone had thoughtfully made her his date for the evening.

Ferris knew her, but not well. She was the recently separated wife of a university professor, a pleasant enough woman, and for the circumstances, safe, easy company.

June stood up as he crossed the floor toward the trio and met him with the appropriate formal embrace and peck-on-the-cheek.

"Nice to see you, Ferris," she said.

Ferris caught her scent and, without thinking, breathed deep. "My pleasure," he answered. Ethan was standing behind her, staring at him. Ferris extended his hand to him. They shook hands without embracing, and he moved on to Phyllis.

"You're looking well," he said to her, turning up the charm a little. "Can I take it that being single again agrees with you?"

blade and male hair-replacement sales would drop, the NHL, NFL, and a number of other blood sports would fall into a steep decline, and a few already insecure guys might feel more insecure because their balls are smaller and a little less bouncy to the touch. Small price to pay for survival of the species.

The problem, of course, is that no government could be trusted to regulate testosterone. They would turn testosterone into a political commodity, and we'd soon have a worse nightmare on our hands than the one we're currently trapped in—everyone in the Third World wandering around in a testosterone-free daze, testosterone-loaded armies and militias fighting in specialized war zones, bozos mainlining synthetic testosterone for the business and recreational advantages. Still, Greer is right when she says it's a poison and it is therefore only logical to at least make a public identification of testosterone, and perhaps even to invoke our education system to encourage sensible people to download their individual excesses.

"It was a shock," Phyllis replied, a little more earnestly than he thought was warranted. "But I'm starting to like the idea."

Ferris sat down and began to chat her up while he took in June and Ethan. June looked good—terrific, actually. She'd grown handsome, as some women do in their forties. Her face had thinned to reveal the strength and character in it, and her hands, through the rougher skin, shorter nails, had become the precision instruments of the will within. Her eyes were still blue and (at least the one that tracked) piercing, but somehow they lacked the old sense of expectancy. Maybe, he mused, that was because the expectations were gone.

Ethan was a mess. He'd ballooned, his hairline was receding, and of course he wasn't any taller. The bulk made him seem smaller, slighter, probably because his intensity was gone. Yon Cassius had gone yonder, and now he simply looked vacant. He was a middle-aged dentist now, denizen of the prime suicide demographic, and his eyes reminded Ferris of a pig in a slaughterhouse. There was a paranoic deceitfulness in his expression, as if he were trying to think of ways to trick the hammer and the knife. Ferris, in other words, didn't like him any better than he ever had.

Ethan, unfortunately, seemed to like Ferris just fine. In fact, from the moment they sat down together, Ethan treated him as if he were the only interesting person in the room, June notwithstanding. He wanted to know what Ferris had done yesterday, last month, last year. And while he was asking, he was guzzling the party-swill like a thirsty kid gulping Kool-Aid at a summer birthday party.

After several hours of this, Ethan's eyes were looking distinctly like June's wonky one, and June was rolling the one she had full control over. When Ethan went to the washroom, she pulled her chair closer to Ferris's.

"Don't encourage him, Ferris," she whispered. "He's a little stressed out these days."

Phyllis, who had been watching Ethan's antics with a great deal of interest, discreetly excused herself and headed for the bar.

"Why would I encourage him?" he answered, when Phyllis was out of hearing range. "You know Ethan isn't my favourite person. What's stressing him? Excessive tire wear on his BMW?"

"Dentistry isn't fun," she said, without irony. "And he thinks I'm having an affair."

"Are you?"

"That's none of your business. Let's just say Ethan hasn't got anything to complain about." Her last sentence implied that if he didn't, she did. Ferris could imagine.

Ethan returned, looking suddenly relaxed and a little spaced out. When he sat down next to Ferris, the spicy aroma of marijuana told him why.

"You ought to know better at your age, Ethan," Ferris said. "Booze and dope don't mix the way they once did."

"Very smooth stuff," he said, slurring the "s" in "smooth." "Very fine. 'Sno problem."

June got up, made a barely decipherable signal to Phyllis, and they marched off, presumably to the washroom. While Ferris wondered idly what they were going to talk about, Ethan moved in.

"So," he said, his voice a confidential whisper, "how did you like fucking her?"

Ferris was too startled to answer. He pushed his chair back a little and stared at Ethan.

"Phyllis?" he queried, feigning surprise at the question. "She's just a friend. I don't really know her well enough to say."

He waved his arms impatiently. "Not her, for Christ's sake. She's just a cunt. I mean June. How was she?"

Ferris took a deep breath.

> **August 15, 1987**
>
> JOHANNESBURG, SOUTH AFRICA: In separate mining incidents, 21 blacks have been killed and 79 injured in the past two days. In one, a bus carrying 100 black mineworkers crashed into a rock face, killing 20 and seriously injuring 49 more. At another location, police fired on a group of striking mineworkers said to be "under the influence of narcotics and a witch doctor," killing one and injuring 30 others.

"What's this about, Ethan?" he said, trying to think of a good way to handle him. "That was a long time ago. Twelve years, almost."

Ethan's eyes were glazed. Apparently there was no good way. "Piss on all that. I wanna know if you thought June was a good fuck. I mean, fuck, man, you been all around the world. You probably pumped every kind of broad there is. I wanna know how my old lady rates with all that exotic shit."

"Look, man," Ferris said. "I don't think this is, uh, appropriate."

Ethan waved his arms impatiently. Appealing to his discretion was pointless. He was into it, obliviously squirming around in some private muckpile of jealousy. "Aw, don't give me that guff. Guy to guy: Was she hot?"

Ferris felt himself reddening. He scooped a wineglass off the table and got to his feet. "I need another drink," he said. He leaned over and pulled Ethan's empty glass from his fingers. "I'll get you one, too."

He stayed at the bar until he saw June and Phyllis return. He watched them sit down, chatting amiably. They were ignoring Ethan, who looked like someone had pressed his "pause" button. Ferris returned, pushed the refilled glass toward Ethan and made himself very attentive toward Phyllis. Just as Ethan seemed ready to launch again, the bride and groom joined them for a few minutes. Ethan's agitation seemed to subside. He appeared to be interested in something across the room—or in some other dimension.

Until Ethan's performance, Ferris really hadn't been very interested in Phyllis, but all of a sudden, she was fascinating. In the next half-hour, he listened to her tell him in detail what a jerk her ex-husband was, and how horrible it was to be alone after fifteen years of companionship. Ferris nodded agreement at the right junctures, stroked her arm, held her hand, did everything possible to convince Ethan he wasn't interested in June. Did the stupid ass think, after all this time, that Ferris was having an affair with her?

June evidently hadn't told Ethan what really happened between her and Ferris, or why she'd chosen Ethan instead of him. Or maybe she'd told Ethan just enough to let him stew on it, and with their present troubles, he was serving it to Ferris because he didn't know how to serve it up to June without losing her. Ferris couldn't tell which it was, and he didn't much care. What he did care about, very much, was finding a way to keep Ethan from spilling it all over the reception.

Ethan stumbled to his feet and started rummaging in his pockets. "Lez go outside for a joint," he said. "I've got some fine weed here."

June looked disinterested, and Ferris ignored him. Phyllis *was* interested.

Hygiene

For reasons of efficiency, most animals use the same body zone for sexual reproduction and for waste removal. Since human beings are among the few species that fiddle with one another's genitals for the sheer fun of it, efficient animal design can present aesthetic problems and may even be a design flaw. What I'm saying here, in a roundabout way, is that the practice of personal hygiene is an important part of human sexual pleasure.

Okay, I know the counter-arguments. If there had been a few showers in ancient Judaea, the Song of Solomon never would have been written, and the perfume industry never would have got off the ground. But there's another way to see this. A rutting bull moose is drawn to a cow moose by the scent of very specific hormones, not to the fecal detritus attached to the mating thereabouts. And it is difficult to deny that if personal hygiene had been a common practice in the ancient world, there would have been a lot more fucking, more oral sex, more female orgasms, and

"What a *great* idea," she said. "Just what we need."

Ferris thought it was a lousy idea, but he couldn't think of any way to say no without precipitating the scene he was trying to prevent. The four of them trooped outside to a sheltered balcony, Ethan leading the way, June guiding him. Ferris brought up the rear, careful to keep Phyllis between June and himself.

It was a warm night, moonless but clear, and the few stars Ferris could see dotting the smoggy heavens grew brighter when Ethan lit the joint and the four

a whole lot less fighting and killing. Let's face it. Except for a tiny, strange minority, there's nothing erotic about lousy hygiene.

It has always astonished me that so many women—and, I'm reliably informed by my women friends, even more men—are so careless about hygiene. Since erotic pleasure operates by its own dynamic rules and not those of factory production lines, political debates, or abattoirs, it seems like common sense to start erotic encounters at olfactory neutral, and to let it power up by the specific olfactory secretions of arousal. From that point, artifice can blossom as each of us chooses, and the blossoms will be larger, finer, and better perfumed.

Personally, I like a moderate degree of artifice. There is no olfactory nexus more pleasant and eroticizing than the illumination of vaginal aromas and secretions through expensive French perfume. Other people may prefer baby powder, tomato paste, pine needles, axle grease, or even cleaning fluids. I've heard of couples who like to roll around in horse manure while they're screwing, and we've all heard about occupational aids affecting olfactory incitements—it explains the popularity of high colonics among members of the medical profession, and high incidence of golden showers and glass coffee-table defecation routines in the upper echelons of the legal community.

I can't say if this is true of males, but each human female body generates a signature aroma under the genial stress of sexual activity, and a man who doesn't pay close attention to these is an inadequate lover, a sensory moron, and a fool. I have a theory that it is possible to tell what is happening to a woman—even to discover her specific and essential sexual character—by her scent alone. Likewise, sexual dysfunctions and ambivalences are also recognizable from hygiene and olfactory conditions and attitudes. In my experience, erotic ambivalence in women invokes a scent and taste that distinctly resemble that of copper sulfate. Similarly, the range of musks women produce is extraordinarily variable. In some women it can smell like woodsmoke, while in others it is cut with the scent of milk. Others give off a faintly vinegary scent. Bacterial presences, mild or endemic, also influence sexual aromas,

of them took turns sucking on it. It was strong dope, smooth and immediate, not at all like the throat-scalding reefers of yore. This was lab-grade cannabis, the kind a BMW-driving dentist would buy from his friend and patient the plant geneticist. Ethan tossed the roach into the shrubs below and pulled another joint from his shirt pocket. Ferris went along, calculating that more dope might turn Ethan's itchy Eros into a sleepy Cupid.

Big mistake. The second joint made June dreamy-eyed—an interesting phenomenon by itself. Phyllis became amorous, and Ferris got hungry. The mistake was with Ethan. He went into hyperspace, talking a mile a minute, and accelerating. Feeling doomed, Ferris excused himself and wandered off in search of some wedding cake. No luck. Ethan followed.

As Ferris leaned over the cake table to lift a chunk of sugary white cake onto a paper plate, Ethan launched into it.

"So, Ferris," he said, this time loudly enough for a dozen bystanders to hear. "Did you go down on her? Did you ream her out good?"

Ferris ignored him, but Ethan was undeterred.

"C'mon man. I know you know. How was she to fuck, Ferris? I mean, did she get hot? Did you make her howl and moan?"

Aw, Christ, Ferris thought, what now? Thirty or forty wedding guests were staring at them, and more were drifting curiously in their general direction. Silence wasn't working, and Ethan's mouth was just starting to roll.

"I mean, I *know*, Ferris." He was now enunciating each word with startling clarity. "I *know* you had my wife down on her back with your tongue in her up to the navel. You fucked her, reamed her, did it all. I think I have a right to know how good she was, God damn it."

"Shut the fuck up, Ethan," Ferris whispered, trying to sound firm and

as do deodorants, which I happen to dislike intensely because they are aimed simply at paralyzing the sensorium.

One more note. Clinical hygiene is more important in casual sexual relationships (and in stable but marginal relationships) than for people in the early stages of a love affair (or in any stage of a Grand Passion). This is because the beloved (male or female) exudes an addictive substance that grows more characteristic and powerful after it has rested in or on the body. This is why people who are deeply in love often like to make love in the late afternoon or in the early morning, while most long-term and casual affairs are most satisfactorily consummated late in the evening, after bathing.

threatening without raising his voice. "Or I'll drill you right here."

"Oh, sure, Ferris," Ethan said, turning the volume up high enough so everyone in the hall could hear. The music stopped. "You fuck your brains out with my wife and I'm supposed to keep quiet. Well, screw you. I wanna know if you enjoyed her. So did you? Did you en*joy* her enough? Would you like her again? Why don't you fuck her now, lay her down on the table and plug her right here so we can all enjoy it?"

June appeared behind Ethan and put her hand on his shoulder. "That's quite enough," she snapped at him. Ethan froze.

She turned to the onlookers. "My drunk husband is upset about something he thinks happened a long time ago. It's none of anyone's business, so everyone please go back to what you were doing and try to ignore him."

Amazingly, the onlookers did what she requested. Ethan shut up, eyes were averted, and the assembled crowd—everybody in the hall by now—backed away and went on with celebrating a wedding. Ferris heard the music restart, a loud, fast dance number. Across the hall, June was coaxing a now-docile Ethan out the door. She turned as she reached the doorway, grinned at Ferris, utterly unembarrassed, and rolled her eyes. It was the only time he ever saw both of her eyes move in unison, and for a split second, it made him wonder if she'd set this all up to get revenge on both of them.

It didn't quite make sense. On the night's evidence, Ethan was his own punishment. Fair enough. But when Ferris turned to Phyllis and saw the way she was gazing at him, he understood that the jury on him wasn't in, and the evening wasn't over.

In the next few minutes, he learned some things about Phyllis he hadn't expected to and would have preferred not to. She told him that her main complaint about her ex-husband was that he was, well, an overly fastidious man. She didn't have to tell him that she'd heard nothing nasty in Ethan's wacky accusations. Quite the opposite. She heard that Ferris was just the thing to help her get over being alone, and she knew exactly how he could do it.

"I think," she said, "we should get out of here. Would you like to come over to my place for a nightcap?"

I hope I haven't been misleading you about Ferris. Although he's not the same man he was the last time you saw him, he remains essentially similar to most males of his generation. If you get him drunk enough and place a willing female in his vicinity, he'll boogie all night long, even if the partner has the intelligence and charm of a bedpost.

But when Phyllis suggested a nightcap, Ferris hesitated. He scanned the ceiling for a moment, then gazed around the room. Something was telling him to say no to this offer, but he was having a hard time listening. He wasn't all that far from the condition Ethan had been in, and here was Phyllis, a perfectly attractive woman he didn't know at all, asking to boogie.

"Nightcap?" he answered. "Sure. Why not? Let's have another glass of wine and see how it sits."

Pheromones

About a decade ago I found a tiny item in *Scientific American* about an exotic genus of moths that use a complex array of hormones to defeat sexual competitors and attract sexual partners for mating and reproduction. It was the first time I came across the idea that sexual chemistry was more than convenient folklore—that it had a wide empirical basis in nature in the form of chemicals called pheromones—or were they *pheronomes*? When it came to writing about them for this book, I decided to go back to the evidence that brought them to my attention. I spent at least twelve hours in the public library rereading back issues of the magazine trying to relocate the reference, but in the end I didn't find it. Still, the search wasn't a complete failure. I did determine that they are "pheromones" rather than "pheronomes," something that had confused me from the moment I discovered the existence of these powerful inducements to obsessive behaviour.

Actually, I gave up the search because I recalled that the moths I'd been looking for used a combination of visual display *and* pheromones to accomplish their goals. Inducements are powerful, in other words, but they're never quite pure. About the same time, I rediscovered something I'd known all along—that the empirical causalities that govern sexual attraction in human relationships are so oblique and multisensory that to account them to pheromone secretion would be an obfuscation and a diminution.

Still, even if I'm not quite prepared to follow fashion and load all human behaviours onto a biochemical bandwagon, I am willing to make the modest assertion that pheromones do play a larger role in human sexual relations than is generally credited, both at the onset and as a glue to keep people attached to one another. Beyond that, I become sceptical. Pheromones are a cute concept that seems to explain the intangibles of mutual attraction, but in the real world they're usually (and mercifully) superseded by a variety of other factors such as common interest,

Phyllis reached two fingers between her breasts and came out with another incentive. Before Ethan went off the deep end, June had taken away the remainder of his dope. She'd given it to Phyllis.

"Never mind the wine," Ferris said. "Do you have a car?"

Phyllis didn't drive, so they took a cab across the city to deep in the East side, where she'd recently rented a spacious apartment on the main floor of an old house. She had two joints. They smoked one while they waited for the cab, the

Oedipal circuitry, mammal/reptile balances, interpersonal skill levels, and good old-fashioned will. Chemical theories of behaviour have severe limits, and it remains to be seen if the current interest in pheromones is much more than a peripheral aspect of the larger reductionist fad of human beings as agglomerate chemical compounds, with pharmaceutical balances that require the attention of an expert to keep in line—thereby turning the vast problem of human cruelty and stupidity into an industrial opportunity for the drug industry. In the end, such an approach isn't much more informative than insisting that God or the devil is behind everything we do.

On the other hand, a couple of years ago I walked into a crowded party, made casual eye contact across the room with a woman I'd never seen before, and received (and evidently sent) a palpable stream of something so powerful that I became and have since remained for all intents and purposes "under the influence." In other words, I fell in love at first sight—or first sniff. I'd had similar, if less intense, experiences earlier in my life, and in each of the previous cases the consequences hadn't been pleasant. The pheromones disabled my abilities to think and act rationally, usually when I desperately needed them. Most of the time, I felt—and acted—like a moth drawn to a flame—empty-headed and blinded as the heat and light increased.

Yet notwithstanding past experience—mine and that compiled by science, which indicate that one is as likely to be pheromone-compatible with Charles Manson or Lizzy Borden as with Mr. Rogers or Mother Teresa—this time things worked out just fine. What began as an extremely intense exchange of pheromones turned into a humane, permanent relationship between two reasonable beings. The woman involved is not a maniac, and neither, apparently, am I. The pheromones helped, but there are also vast zones of coincidence between our backgrounds, personalities, and values, and we appear to be mature enough to protect the wholly

other over the promised nightcap, which Ferris had trouble remembering even while he was drinking it.

For the record, Phyllis was quite a lot more intelligent and charming than a bedpost. She was also extremely explicit about what she wanted from him and quite clear about how it ought to go. She didn't seem to mind at all when Ferris kept calling her June and asking her what was in the refrigerator. She fed him an apple, several different kinds of cheese and several more nightcaps. And then she took his head in her hands. "I want head," she said. "Now."

He got down to it, and he thought it was fine. Not a great moment in his life, but pleasant enough—until the room began to spin. When he began to salivate uncontrollably—a dead giveaway that he was about to drop his cookies—the

human state of goodwill that exists between us—and cunning enough. We've succeeded in bonding in ways that go far beyond the hormonal Bacchanalia that originally got our two heads spinning in unison.

I'm hollering "*Whoopee!*" here, sure, but don't miss the serious caveat I'm also lodging. A human being who has just gotten a heavy dose of pheromones from another ought to pay attention to them (actually, there isn't much choice if the dose is substantial). Just don't quit your day job when it happens: We still have to live in the "real" world, despite the pheromones.

So, given all this, what are my conclusions concerning pheromones? Mainly, they have to do with the differences between moths and human beings:

1. All moths are adult, an achievement that manages to elude most human beings.

2. Moths can and do send and receive pheromones across distances of up to several miles. Human pheromone transfers have a much more limited range, probably no more than about ten metres. Alas, with our added neural complexity, some human beings (nearly all of them male) are much more powerfully attracted to non-chemical instruments when it comes to giving expression to their sexual impulses. These are extremely important on hunting trips, military invasions, and around automotive race tracks and rocket-launching facilities.

3. Moths are instinctual, stupid creatures engaged in a simple cycle of nature. Early in their cycle, they eat their faces off. As adults, they sip a little nectar, fly into light bulbs, screw, reproduce, and then die. It remains to be seen if human beings, as a species, are capable of much more than that.

What makes us so interesting is that we have a shot at expanding the cycle. Our best shot will involve learning to give greater value to the twin miracles of con-

not-great-but-pleasant erotic moment suddenly began to turn into a genuinely bad, awful, humiliating one, much worse than the public one Ethan had delivered.

Bad, awful, and humiliating Ferris could live with. He had before. Call it gender guilt or simple consideration, but in the midst of his physiological crisis, he had a moment of genuine, displaced empathy. He did not want Phyllis to find out what it would feel like to have a man vomit on her while he was giving her head.

I can't do this, he told himself, willing back the whirling sensation. That changed its direction, clockwise to counterclockwise. What will she think, and what will it do to her self-esteem? As a newly divorced person, she is fragile. What edge will this send her over?

sciousness and wilful relationship to others. And if we're not to become a colossal mistake of nature, we had better get more skilful at demonstrating that consciousness is not a superfluous mutation, and that human sexual relationships are not merely a misery-creating eat-fuck-smell-the-roses-and-die evolutionary dead end. For our species, it isn't enough to poke our noses into the occasional flower and then act like wild animals until the bloom is trampled. We have to protect nature, improve it, cultivate it. To do that we'll have to understand the ground and conditions in which things and people blossom far better than we do at the moment.

4. Moths live for a very short time and are not neurologically equipped to be aware of what they're doing. They are therefore unable to administer feedback to the one-dimensional genetic mission nature has programmed them for. Human beings live quite a long time, and we can and occasionally do experience an environment-improving strain of self-consciousness. We are therefore fully capable of installing feedback loops that can alter or even transform destructive or cruel mission enactment. We don't do it often enough, that's all.

5. Except for their attraction to light, moths are almost wholly governed by their genetic mission. There are reductive explanations for this usually self-destructive attraction, but none of them quite accounts for the phenomenon. I would like to propose the idea of phero*nomes* as the human equivalent to the heliotropism of moths. These are empirically undetectable hormones that instruct human beings in how to behave in the presence of light, and for the existence of which there is no empirical evidence whatsoever. Notwithstanding, phero*nomes* may yet prove to be the true determinants of conscious human sexuality (not quite an oxymoron), and the intelligence and imagination of our response to them may turn out to be what separates us from moths.

The spin on the whirlies tightened. Somehow, he got his salivating mouth out of her crotch, his body out of her bed, and stumbled out of the bedroom in the general direction of the bathroom.

"Excuse me," he mumbled. "I'll be back."

Luckily, the bathroom was just down the hall from the bedroom, the first door he blundered into. With more luck he got the door closed and a tap running to cover the sound of barfing. Then his luck abruptly failed. He missed the toilet and projectiled the first two heaves directly into a floor-mounted hot-air register that happened to be next to the toilet. He got his head positioned over the toilet and lost count of the heaves when they ceased to bring anything up.

When the dry heaves let up, he passed out. When he came to, the room was spinning, it stunk, and the toilet was filled with vomit. He heard Phyllis outside the bathroom door, rattling the handle.

"Are you okay in there?"

Twenty-eight years ago, or four complete body-cell changes ago, this was the only sexual subject that interested me. There was a compelling knot of delight on the underside of my penis, and I wanted to unravel it, to play out the strings and revel in its apparently endless capacity to retie itself. Back then, everything created or caused (I wasn't sure which) an erection, and many of the creators/causes were mysterious. It wasn't limited to women or erotic stimulations. Certain types of sunlight gave me erections, sure, but so did cloudy weather, the sight of books, the spelling and pronunciation of exotic or new words. Car profiles gave me erections, sports statistics gave me erections, the topology of hillsides gave me erections, and so did dogs, cats, bears, deer, several species of birds, and one or two tree species. That's what it's like to be a young male.

I was attracted by power, symmetry, and movement and overly impressed by my instinct to plant my perpetual erection into the midst of any and every physical site of those three things, without regard for relevant species or technology and mucous membrane interface compatibilities.

Male barnacles have that same instinct, I've since learned. Among barnacle species, the penis sometimes constitutes four-fifths of the body mass, and if barnacles were of a size comparable to that a human male, their penises would be between nine and twelve feet long. How impressed are you by that animal?

Do I digress? Yes, but deliberately. What I want to say is this: Male erections aren't an absolute prerequisite to male sexual pleasure. They're an often-inferior instrument for giving women pleasure, and quite frankly, men (and occasionally

"Yeah, I'm fine," he answered, repressing another heave. "Sure, I'll be out in a second." He modulated the tap to make it sound like he was washing his face.

He knew, rationally, that Phyllis must have realized that he'd dropped his cookies. Rationality be damned, he was going to clean up the evidence. It wasn't going to be easy, or pleasant. A healthy portion of the evidence, remember, was down the hot-air register beside the toilet.

He looked around his still-spinning environment and found a nail file from the medicine cabinet with which he could remove the grate screws on the hot-air register. That didn't work very well, so he poked through a dish of trinkets he found in the towel closet and found a dime. With the tap still running to cover what he was doing, he removed the grate, pulled it off, and carefully, painstakingly, cleaned up the mess. He used a washcloth for the operation, and when he'd finished, he carefully washed the washcloth with a bar of soap. Then

women) should stop worrying about them all the time. Having said that, I should stick to the empirical spirit of this inquiry.

What do I know about erections? Well, they seem to be of three relatively distinct varieties: infantile (or barnacular), engorged, and reluctant.

The first variety is the one that, with inexperienced men, is the only kind: the polymorphous, infantile kind of erection small boys amuse themselves and their parents with on the diaper-changing table. These recur more or less unaltered in their character into late adolescence (however long this goes on) as a means of attacking the world. This "barnacular" erection is an instrument of singular, simple, and fundamentally onanistic pleasure. Women should beware of men who only have this variety of erection. They're likely to have other personality traits of barnacles. In the end, the woman will be better off with a dildo or a vibrator, because at least then the person on the operating end of it will be capable of caring for them.

There is another kind of male erection. This one has a mind connected to it, and it has some anatomical characteristics that several informants tell me are distinctly superior to those of a "barnacular" erection. It is slightly softer and, occasionally, larger, and it is the direct product of a successful male recognition that he has a partner. When a male really desires a woman and is experiencing her pleasure and not merely brandishing himself and his erection, the erection will reflect that in subtle ways. It will come and go, alter its degree of engorgement in response to the always altering textures and engorgements of the tissue it is in contact with, and it is rarely on a binary track toward orgasm. In fact, it may not end with an orgasm at all,

he cleaned himself up, shut off the water, left the bathroom and padded back to the bedroom.

The room still wasn't entirely stable, but his stomach was empty, and the effects of the dope had overwhelmed the alcohol—at some point in the clean-up, without his recognizing it, the RPMs dropped to within governable levels.

Two hours had passed, and Phyllis was sleeping peacefully. The booze and dope, happily, had simply laid her out cold. She was lying on her side with one hand tucked between her head and shoulder, her fingers entangled in a lock of hair. Snoring a little.

She looked happy, childlike, although Ferris knew better. He considered that for a moment. No, he knew nothing at all, really, except that her bathroom hadn't been so clean since the house was built. He took a sip of wine from a half-empty glass beside the bed. She rolled onto her back, smiled, and gestured sleepily for him to join her.

Ferris finished what he'd started.

which is, after all, only a biologically vestigial inducement in the male to the perpetuation of a vastly overproduced species.

As men grow older, a minor integration of mind and body occasionally occurs. This, together with a mind that has become as active as the body, can create reluctant, or partial, erections. No, this is not an oxymoron. Nor, when such erections occur, are they occasions for panic. They do not necessarily signal that one is getting old, or "going over the hill." They may have something to do with age, but there is still no cause for alarm—unless maturity is an evil. Like any other kind of refusal to co-operate, reluctant erections are occasions to think things—and people—through. They might be messages that one is overeager, or that one's partner is unprepared or even inappropriate. They're signals of ambivalence, in other words. And ambivalence, wherever it appears, demands circumspection and patience, both of which this world badly needs—more than it needs brainlessly erect penises, or the still more brainless reproductive drive of barnacles, that's for sure.

a

starling's

SEVEN

journey

Ferris staggered out into the faint light of dawn, his head aching like he'd spent the night in Phyllis's microwave. As he crossed the boulevard, a flight of starlings settled around him and began to poke their skinny beaks into the turf, looking for crane-fly larvae. Mornings-after weren't what they once were. They were bigger, longer, and more painful, and the robins had been replaced by starlings. He knew this morning-after would stretch into the late afternoon, perhaps even to tomorrow. He also knew he'd screwed things up again—none of this should have happened at all.

The starlings lifted off as he stepped onto the tarmac, to re-alight on the boulevard across the street, directly in his path. Flying wharf rats, someone had called them, just a few days ago. Or was it pigeons they'd been referring to?

Starlings—they were almost pretty when you got up close—were imports from Europe, brought here at the turn of the century when a misguided culture enthusiast released, in New York's Central Park, three breeding pairs of every bird mentioned in Shakespeare. Most of the other importees died within the year, but the starlings did just fine, thanks. Now there were billions of them, an avian plague that migrated slowly across the continent, arriving on this part of the continent's west coast in the late 1960s. With their arrival, the robins disappeared into the deep forests, unable to compete. Now seven hundred and fifty thousand starlings nested beneath the city bridges—and the last virgin forests were about to be clearcut.

Ferris picked up a small shard of broken pavement from the road, aimed it half-heartedly at the starlings, but didn't throw it. We're all immigrants here, he thought, why pick on them? And anyway, they reminded him of something he couldn't quite get his mind around, something connected to last night. He dropped the shard on the next boulevard.

He was tired, sure. That had been the price of admission, and he'd paid it often enough. But this tiredness seemed to go deeper. He felt ruminative, chastened, as if this, and maybe the accumulated adventures and misadventures with it, were about to deliver some new message.

Why *now*, he wasn't sure. Maybe it was just Time's Winged Dumpster hurrying near. If that were all, it wouldn't be unwelcome. He'd been a young man far too long. He walked a couple of blocks the way he imagined an old man would, slowly, stopping once to pull a sprig of lilac from a bush that overhung the sidewalk. He pushed the sprig beneath his nostrils and breathed deeply. A cab swung around the corner, and he lifted the sprig above his head to hail it.

As he crawled into the back seat, the driver peered over the seat at him with mock contempt. "You want to go to the floral show," the cabby said. "Am I right? The only one I know of is at the cemetery. And you look about ready."

"Very funny," Ferris answered, tossing the sprig of lilac into the front seat as he gave the cabby his home address. The cabby nodded without looking back and left him alone.

Ferris didn't want to talk. As the cab slipped through the silence, he began to go over his internal map. For him, this had become a city without a centre, without politics or progress or community. It was zoned by faces and bodies and sometimes voices. Some of the zones radiated from houses or apartments he'd lived in with different women. Others—usually smaller—were defined by bedrooms he'd spent a night or a dozen nights in.

It wasn't the city he'd lived in a few years ago. That city had a public character, along with a history and a future in which he'd actively participated. Somewhere along the line, he'd given up that city for a private base-of-operations

All through my extended adolescence—i.e., possibly until last week—I heard the following statement trotted out as if it were gospel truth: Men learn love and desire from their mothers, just as women learn desire and love from their fathers. Depending on the degree to which we grew up in a typical nuclear family, this is *sort of* true. It would be truer still if Freud's sexual universe were an accurate model and we also lived in a just and gender-equitable society—or in a laboratory. Erotic life would be pretty simple.

Since erotic life obviously isn't simple, just as the world we live in isn't just, gender-equitable, or circumscribed by our Oedipal impulses, we have to sort out our parents and our erotic wiring in more specific or situational terms, even those of us who did grow up in a fairly typical nuclear family.

Most of modern physics is premised on the notion that reality is smooth and continuous. Because space flows through and across and around objects, and because one event seems to be connected to another, with an erotic history and a not-very-bright present—together with a tourist atlas of the world.

He knew that neither his psychic base-of-operations nor his world atlas bore much resemblance to the physical world. But where his global mappings were defined by places he'd generalized and abstracted clean of specificity, his local map was all specifics. Whole sectors of it were darkened by the stupid things he'd done—or things, not stupid, he'd failed to do. Still others were rhinestoned by pointless and temporary erotic events. The rhinestones had been created by things like last night—moments of impulsiveness in which both he and the women he'd been with got used. Each had created its own cheap, gleaming darkness, some large, some no more than the room or house in which the stupidities had been committed. Put together they'd blacked out much of the city.

Ferris couldn't say for sure when he'd ceased to pay attention to the city he walked and drove through in his daily life, and until this moment, he hadn't understood why. He'd taken to avoiding the dark zones, and not just in his mind. He literally avoided whole parts of the city, subconsciously driving around them on the way from one place to another of them, avoiding restaurants and passing on social gatherings that happened to fall within them. This, he realized with a slight shock, was why the physical city he lived in from day to day seemed to be shrinking.

So last night he'd created another of those rhinestone-dark zones. It didn't matter that for all its absurdity, last night was without malice. Darkness had

we assume that space is at least omnipresent and that time is linear. Most of us operate on the expectation that experiential reality has those same properties. Renegade physicist **fallen because last night was like too many other nights. It had begun with a combination of lust and curiosity without anywhere to go, nothing to find, nothing of himself to secure. A** misadventure, merely. It ended with what it began with.

Edward Fredkin has a different theory. He thinks that the space/time continuum is composed of bits of discrete digital information, and that their essential nature is agglomerative and granular rather than linear and smooth.

I've discovered that applying Fredkin's physics to parenting and to the Freudian system of *maleficent causalities by*

which we deduce that our parents are responsible for our bizarre erotic needs and behaviours and for our extra-rational erotic dysfunctions can be quite liberating. When I apply it to my own mother, it instantly frees me from having to tell another horror story about incompetent nurturing or to indulge in the whinings of a wounded child.

Maybe it is just luck, but at the worst of times I have no axe to grind against my mother. Not a single hostile thought crosses my mind when I think of her. Mine was one of the good mothers,

Once he would have thought it an adventure, part of an accumulation that had seemed necessary. For years, he'd covered himself with the slightly mystical (i.e., unexamined) idea that there was an erotic databank out there somewhere—and that he couldn't process the data until the bank was full. Another rationalization, he now decided, bleakly. The bank existed, all right, but it wasn't quite a databank, and what he'd been depositing was erotic capital, believing it would grow and multiply, as wisdom. An illusion, apparently. After each deposit this bank got robbed, or the capital withered or leaked away. Whatever it was, it was a bank that always proved bankrupt when he tried to make a withdrawal.

Out the cab's back window Ferris glimpsed the first rays of sunlight break over the horizon, and with them, his black mood began to lift. It wasn't quite that he hadn't thought about the women he'd been with, or the things he'd seen and done to and with them. He'd thought plenty, more than most men he knew. But it was only as a pastime, a prelim to more, a way of eluding the silences created by the comings and goings. Somewhere, women and sex had become entertainment. Without ever quite recognizing it, he'd come to believe that fun excused nearly anything.

a decent, sanguine woman with a quick temper and a bottomless fund of cheerfulness and physical affection that made her instantly conciliatory of every wrongdoing—both her own or that of the people she loved. But a few years ago, a therapist-aided regression exercise enabled me to unearth a parenting event that explains quite a lot of my erotic behaviours.

When I was three, I ran away. I didn't go far for my adventure, merely across the street to sit in a neighbour's darkened garage. But when my mother called me, I didn't answer. Who can say why I decided to ignore her call? Probably it was some childish recalcitrance, or perhaps the dark spaciousness of the garage reminded me of something that would make a Freudian say "Aha!" Whatever the why, the dark garage was an ecstasy that I couldn't bear to break just to answer her call. I sat in the splendid darkness for an eternity before she located me.

I remember the garage door swinging open, the light pouring in, and her grim expression as she entered. She saw me, called me to her, but still I didn't answer or move. It

Some fun. Here he was, hungover and sick, surrounded by a lifetime of erotic anecdotes and mishaps that clouded everything they'd touched, blotted out most of a city. Was there a pattern to the anecdotes? Sure. He tried to sort the anecdotes to see if there was a decipherable pattern.

Some were moral tales, but the morals were largely undetected. Others were mysteries, but the mysteries were unresolved. In all of them, he sensed there were other human beings, richly vulnerable and complicated, that he hadn't got to. They'd been personal stories, his alone. Or were they personal? Too often he'd merely allowed himself to be the agent of action, the grid upon which the other lives, for shorter and longer durations, touched down to make their casual or profound connections.

Well, it had caught him, hadn't it. Willy nilly, the matrix was now lighting up inside his brain. And as the city, backlit by the morning sunlight, slipped by the windows of the cab, he caught a glimpse of just how gorgeous the matrix was. It wasn't the world, and it wasn't quite reality, but maybe now it could be a source of light, maybe even enlightenment. It was time to stop wandering, to settle down. But to what? And how?

He had the taxi drop him off at a restaurant called The Vineyard. It wasn't his favourite breakfast spot—in fact its only three virtues were its name, that it was open twenty-four hours a day, and that it was within walking distance of his apartment.

Rays of sunlight were flickering in the treetops by the time Ferris got out of

wasn't that I couldn't. I didn't want to. I had been in the darkness, outside her zone of omniscience and yet somehow pleasantly inside it at the same time. I forced her to enter the taxi. The restaurant's sidewalk tables had been left out overnight, and on a whim, he poked his head inside the door and asked if they'd serve him breakfast outside.

The waitress gave him a look that said she'd rather be at home sleeping. "Sure," she said. "Grab a table and I'll be out to take your order in a moment."

He snuck a glance at himself in the mirror behind her, and stopped cold. He looked like he'd been dead for two days. His eyes were hollow, his hair matted. Wow. But for all that, he felt curiously alert, ready to get on with it, whatever it was going to be.

the garage, pick me up, and carry me all the way home. Through it all, I didn't feel any fear, and no shame. I was, on the contrary, blissfully unapologetic, or unapologetically blissful. And she knew it.

She lived in a very rational universe, and my strange behaviour troubled her. To cure me of this irrationality, she employed a little magic of

her own. To keep me from running away from her, and to make me fearful of dark, strange places, she told me that if I ever ran away again, she would not be there when I returned.

My mother didn't ever carry out her threat, of course. No doubt she forgot about the whole thing in a couple of days and was reminded of it only because throughout my early childhood I checked constantly and compulsively to see *if she was still there.* It became one of those stories she told her friends over tea—isn't my child amusing? She still recounts the

He sat down at the table. A soft breeze was blowing along the boulevard, and he could hear, through the intermittent traffic, starlings in morning song. A few doors down the street, a middle-aged woman was gazing intently into the window of a kitchen shop. She was carrying a paper bag in one hand, and she was surrounded by starlings. The day, on its own, promised to be a fine one. For now, it was enough to watch it develop.

So what, Ferris asked himself as he poked through the sickening mess of scrambled eggs the waitress set in front of him, was last night's moral? He could see there was more than one, and more than one kind. There was the very simple variety, such as *Stay away from old lovers,* or *It isn't a good idea to get drunk, smoke strong dope, and screw with a stranger.* Both sensibly fit last night's events, but really, he should have had both those ones down long ago. What other possibilities were there that weren't combinations of the above plus the age-old truism

story once in a while, usually while puzzling over what a strange man I turned into. Once I heard her tell a friend, "He always did things a little differently, as if he were seeing things other people didn't."

She's there in the world today, still my fond mother even though our relationship has altered in the natural course of events. What she doesn't suspect is that this incident created a perverse counter-reaction that reappeared in my late adolescence, and that it faithfully continued to reappear through the next thirty years. I had an irresistible impulse to run away, misbehave, and thus to challenge the beloved to carry out the threat to disappear. At a preconscious level, this was a three-year-old, alive and wilfully alert. He was sitting in that darkened shed, refusing to believe that the threat was not real, and challenging women who had no idea that the threat was ever made to prove that it wouldn't be carried out. Not surprisingly, in the real world, the women I ran away from, misbehaved toward, and then challenged to abandon me all did so. As they damned that males are stupid and gross *and* silly? He tried putting it—and himself—in a kindlier light. *Don't punch out noisy drunks* was lame and slightly inaccurate, because noisy drunks usually deserve what they get. So long as Ferris wasn't party to it, he was half hoping June went home and smacked Ethan silly. Leave him, even and … oh no. That was none of his business. That brought on another insight, this one slightly more obtuse: *Real sexual pride never involves cruelty to others. It will go to any length to avoid it.*

I have had some kind of pride, all right, Ferris thought to himself. There wasn't a whole lot of dignity in not wanting to puke on a stranger, and unpleasant as it was, cleaning puke out of a floor-mounted heat register so a casual lover doesn't find out you've lost your cookies in her bathroom doesn't exactly register high on the Richter scale of human pride events.

The only incontrovertible wisdom he could deduce from last night was that the world is full of jerks, and that he was indisputably one of them. He already knew that. No, that wasn't good enough. He'd spent most of his adult life comforting himself that he wasn't the *worst* jerk around. Now, suddenly, he wanted to ask himself just exactly how big a jerk he was, and whether it was necessary to remain one all his life.

He had plenty of practical motives for asking himself that. One-night stands weren't much fun any more. The adventure had dissipated along with the possibility of wisdom, and he'd lately become the victim of three- or four-day bouts

This isn't the universe according to the marriage counsellors and the relationship manuals with their ersatz give-and- of impotence whenever he encountered a new lover. It was embarrassing, but it was also a relief. He also was dimly aware, in his heterosexual moral fog, that unless he and his partners were prepared to

take, is it? Neither was the secondary adaptive mechanism I developed. If one's Beloved is going to disappear, then there had better be more than one Beloved.

Now, I'm aware that I've just recorded something of a Freudian cliché, but what interests me about it is not the occasion for psychomorphic dithering it presents,

but the testament it offers concerning the fragility of the human mind. As a rational adult I can see the point behind my mother's tactic. She was trying to solve a behaviour problem, and she believed, correctly, that she had the answer. She had no way of knowing that she was creating a piece of hard-wired emotional circuitry that would generate characteristic behaviors for the next forty years. Love and affection did not intervene with this piece of circuitry, nor did fear or self-preservation. Her simple, short-term stra-

use latex to seal all their orifices from intimate contact, one-nighters were getting hazardous. These once-simple honey-dips could be lethal. Oh well.

He finished the eggs and looked around. The woman was still standing in front of the kitchen shop window, her gaze fixed on the display. It occurred to him that she'd been holding the pose for almost fifteen minutes, and he wondered, idly, what *her* story was. A good thing to be wondering about, he decided. Better than sifting his own self-inflicted dilemma. But judging from the fixedness of her pose, maybe he should do more than merely wonder about her. Was something wrong? Maybe she was broke, maybe homeless, maybe her husband had beaten her, thrown her out of the house. Maybe a lot of things, none of them his business, all his human responsibility.

Well, better at close quarters, he decided, fishing some coins from his pocket and ambling down the street toward her. The starlings around her on the sidewalk, about twenty of them, lifted off in a curved sweep that took them across the street and above the buildings. He watched them, bemused by the joining of symmetry and scatter.

He'd planned to buy a newspaper from the box in front of the kitchenware store and make the decision about whether to speak to her at that range. He pushed three coins into the news-box coin-slot, pulled out a paper, and looked

tagem to keep a three-year-old from wandering away from the yard resulted in a closed neural loop that resisted experiential intervention and created more havoc with my personal life as an adult than anything else that happened to me during my unusually secure and uneventful childhood.

While this raises some scary possibilities—what would I be if I'd been kidnapped or otherwise abused—I'm not concerned at all with assigning guilt and culpability, and even less with idly obsessing about the cause/effect imbalance. I had to take this neurosis apart piece by piece over a period of years, and the experience was rather like disarming a bomb. Maybe because the trigger was so trivial and it took so long to understand, it has tipped me to a secret of sexual and erotic behaviour: the existence, in each of us, of a hard-wired emotional mother-board.

In a computer, the motherboard is the network of digital gates around the central processor that chops up the

sideways at her. She appeared to be in her late forties, stooped, thin, and nervous—nervous enough, actually, to sense that she was being observed. He was about to say hello to her when she looked into his eyes and recognized him—as a possible threat to her solitude.

Ferris recognized her, too—he had to repress a momentary shudder. Christ, he *knew* her. But who was she? Before he could decide what to do, she turned back to the window, shutting him out. Through the glass he could see a display of Henckels kitchen knives. It was the knives, not her, that touched off the necessary synapse: Her name was Eleanor Parker, yeah, that was it. He hadn't seen her for almost twenty years, and he hadn't thought about her for at least ten. She'd been beautiful then, dark-eyed, wild and, well…

He'd first met her on a street corner no more than two blocks from the kitchen shop where she was now standing. She'd been trying to fix a flat tire on an aging black Buick, and obviously didn't have a clue about how to go about it. Her car was stopped in traffic, and irritable drivers were honking their horns, pulling around her—the usual parade of impatient assholes, going nowhere, but in a hurry anyway.

Ferris pulled in behind her, turned on his four-way flashers, and got out. She was crouched beside the dead tire, fiddling hopelessly with the jack.

"Need some help?" he asked.

At first she ignored him. He squatted beside her, pointed to the rocker-panel hook the jack was supposed to fit into, and explained what had to be done. She

flow of granular electrical data into parcels of highly limited logical information. Human motherboards are conceptually similar to the ones found in computers, governing the unreflective general procedures by which we experience and express emotion and sexuality.

Human emotional and sexual impulses, however, are not like digital impulses, which operate at the speed of light but reduce everything to yes or no simplifications. Human impulses are obscure, obtuse, and by comparison, infinitely complex. Most of us know that already. What we seldom recognize is that they're often lodged in static infantile circuits that resemble digital circuitry, or that they engender extraordinarily practical behaviours once their closed logic begins its digital run. Mistaking nature for authenticity, most of us let those closed, infantile circuits determine our emotional and sexual identities.

In doing so, we ignore the most important difference between ourselves

fiddled some more, but then realized that he was there to help, and moved aside.

"It's my father's car," she said, as if that explained the flat.

"Open the trunk," Ferris said, trying to sound like he was all business. "There should be a spare tire."

"I don't think there is," she answered. "All I saw was the jack."

Ferris checked for himself. She was right. The trunk contained only an empty, rusted tire rim. He tossed the jack back inside, explained to her that they had to get the car off the main street, and got her to nurse the car around the corner into the alley. There, he jacked up the car, and removed the flat tire while she stood watching him, her pretty face a mask of wariness.

"This has to be fixed," he said, rolling the tire back and forth in front of her without meeting her eyes. "If you like, we can toss it into my back seat, and I'll drive you over to a tire shop."

"Who are you?" she asked. "Why should I go anywhere with you in a car? You could be anybody."

"I'm a guy who's trying to help you fix a flat," Ferris answered, irritably. Then he relented and told her his name. "Look, I'm just doing my good turn for the day."

She gazed at him intently for a moment, as if trying to decide if he could possibly be telling the truth.

"Okay," she said. "I guess I shouldn't be so suspicious."

"Oh, probably you should," he laughed as he tossed the dead tire into his back seat. "But you've got a flat to fix, and I seem to be involved. Hop in."

and computers and misuse the larger system of which our emotional and sexual motherboards are a part. That larger system—consciousness—is dynamic and educable. It can allow data to intrude, and it can learn from it—it is designed so that information effects change. Unfortunately most of us don't let this operation take place when we're trying to deal with the impulses that our mothers or fathers conferred on us before we were capable of enacting critical consciousness. Most of the time, we let the primitive, infantile subsystems govern the larger one.

What we do to protect ourselves and others from the effects of our preconscious motherboards is a test of our intelligence and humanity, and our efforts to break into and reshape their closed logic can be a life's work. Never mind the search for our lost general parents, or the often incompetent love we get from our parents; we need to find, understand, and rebuild our motherboards. Stated even more simply, we need to grow up.

Ferris quickly found a garage, and the two of them sat on the hood of his car and made idle chatter while they watched the repairman work on the tire. Her name was Eleanor Parker, she was a nurse, she worked in a psychiatric hospital.

"Day off?"

She seemed startled. "Oh. Yeah, sure. I'm working nights this week. What do you do?"

"Still at school, working on my Master's. Not very hard, I'm afraid."

She extended her hand. "Pleased to meet you. And thanks for the help. I don't know what I'd have done."

He looked at her hand and took it in his own. Like the rest of her, it was long, slender, and well-shaped. She was tall, very slim, and her hair was so jet-black he wondered if it were dyed. Yes, indeed, he *was* pleased to meet her.

One thing led to another. He drove her back to her car, put on the patched tire, they exchanged telephone numbers. Over the next few weeks, he saw a lot of her. She needed more help than most women did, and Ferris was a man who could do things. He helped her get a new spare wheel and tire for the Buick, he fixed her television aerial, got her recently installed phone to work properly.

Eleanor Parker was a strange woman, slightly aloof and thoroughly elusive about anything to do with her past. She lived in a dingy suburban basement suite sheltered by a canopy of evergreens. Her windows were always curtained, and no one seemed to be living in the remainder of the house, which was dark and curtained whenever he visited.

She was strangely secretive about her work. Never at home when he called her on the phone, she'd call him five minutes after he hung up and ask him over. She'd been "out" or "too busy to answer the phone." When he arrived, she opened her door as if he were a secret agent, saying things like, "Come in quickly, close the door, were you followed?"

They did nothing but talk. She did most of the talking, and it didn't always make sense. A story about a crazed patient in the psych ward would trail off in mid-narrative, or a theory about the sentience of evergreens would be interrupted by sounds outside the window. Ferris couldn't quite catch the spin of her mind, but it wasn't important to. He wasn't sure who or what she was, but the list of things she needed help with was a long one, and for the time being at least, that was sufficient.

She had a quirk that fascinated him. She did not like to be touched, unless she was in a public place. She seemed to feel free to touch him, but when she did it was only glancingly. When he left she would kiss him, caress his cheek tenderly, but if he reached for her she would recoil.

"Wait," she would say. "Wait until it's right."

December 11, 1969

COTONOU, DAHOMEY: Army Chief Lt. Col. Maurice Kouandete has overthrown the government of Dr. Emile Derlen Zinsou in a bloody coup d'état. It is the fifth coup in six years, and was precipitated in part by neighbouring Ghana's recent expulsion of foreign nationals.

SAIGON, SOUTH VIETNAM: Two U.S. Navy sailors were killed and two wounded when their river patrol boat was struck with rocket grenades and rifle fire sixty miles west of Saigon.

There were facts in her mind-spin, and he began to collect them. Almost all were disturbing. The Buick was her father's car, and her father was a police officer. Her mother? Long gone, not dead, but not to be spoken of. Her father was dead. Just six months dead and much mourned—as he had been much loved while alive. Ferris would have gladly let this recent tragedy explain her elusiveness. But she needed help with that, too.

"You remind me of my father sometimes," she said one evening as he was about to leave. "Don't go yet. I have something for you."

She disappeared into the bedroom—Ferris had not seen the inside of it— and returned with a sweater. It was hand-knit, mottled with blacks and green wool, almost iridescent, and very heavy. There was an odd excitement in her face as she draped it across his chest to see if it fit.

"It looks good on you," she said.

It was Ferris's turn to be wary. "What is it? Whose is it?"

"It was his," she said, simply. "His favourite."

"Your father's?"

"Yes. I think it'll fit you."

Ferris lifted the sweater above his head and pulled it over his shoulders. It was roomy, but the sleeves were the right length. It surprised him. From what she'd told him about her father, Ferris imagined that the man had been seven feet tall. Ferris moved his shoulders around inside the sweater, getting the feel of it. A small alarm went off in his brain, telling him that accepting the sweater wasn't wise. But what the hell, it was a beautiful thing, and he wanted it.

"I haven't told you how my father died," she said, as he moved to a mirror to admire the sweater.

"No," he agreed, "you haven't." She was standing behind him, looking at his reflection in the mirror.

She told him. Her father had blown out his brains with his police revolver. No warning, no note. She hesitated, as if there was more. No, it was nothing she could tell him, not yet. It was there to tell, but it was unspeakable.

The sweater began to itch, as if it were extending tendrils into the skin of his back and shoulders and chest. He wanted to remove it, to give it back, but he was caught, not just by the situation and his acquisitiveness, but by his own curiosity.

What was he supposed to do now? Should he ask her the questions, get her to reveal what else she was concealing? Or should he back away and run? He'd wanted this to be simple, to stay simple. At best it might become a brief love story. Eleanor was to play the woman, he would play the lover—sooner, he'd hoped, rather than later. It was the only story he knew—Boy meets Girl, Boy does amusing tricks for Girl, Girl loves Boy, Boy makes love with Girl, and then on to the Next Adventure.

But with the sweater, the plot shifted from Romance-in-the-Making to Theological Mystery, and a very peculiar one. Theology, even the conventional kind, wasn't among Ferris's interests. He believed that God was dead, that life cheerfully proceeded without divine help. But if someone believes in God, and God kills himself, as with Eleanor and her father, what then? Was Ferris supposed to renew this woman's faith in life by wearing God's mottled woollen husk? And what exactly was the connection between the death of God and her unwillingness to let him, a mere mortal man, touch her?

Concerns of the Moment

I n this depiction of middle-class brutalities, ineffectual human kindnesses, and singing avian plagues, I have not forgotten the militiaman sitting on the steps of a shelled building, sunlight gleaming from the brassy bandoleers draped across his shoulder, a cheap pair of aviator sunglasses perched across the bridge of his nose.

Late last night, twenty miles to the southwest in the village where he grew up, he and four companions surrounded the house of his former neighbours, called the adult males out and shot them. The men then entered the house, killed three small children cowering in a room off the kitchen, and took turns raping the children's mother. The last of them (not our man) raped her with a bayonet.

This morning, the same five had breakfast together. They drank watery ersatz coffee, munched on pieces of freshly baked bread, and

He sensed he would try to play whatever role the plot asked of him, but really, how could he succeed? He knew nothing of either faith or paternity except to believe that men are not gods, and that he, personally, was nobody's father.

"I've got to go," he said. "It's late." Fuck, he thought. Everything I say suddenly sounds symbolic. "Do you want me to leave the sweater here?"

"No, I want you to take it with you," she said, emphatically. "But you must take very good care of it."

He let her kiss his cheek, felt her lips linger there long enough to stir him, felt her knee move momentarily between his—and he backed discreetly out of the basement suite, closed the door behind him. As he drove home, waves of disquiet rolled over him. He'd accepted the sweater, and now he'd have to wear it.

———————————

What was strange got stranger, and stranger still. Each time he saw Eleanor he wore the sweater, and listened as different parts of her story tumbled from her. She'd had a lover. The lover had abused her, over and over again. Raped her. She spent three years in a mental institution trying to sort it out. And no, she wasn't a psychiatric nurse. She was a psychiatric day-patient, a patient on a

said nothing of the previous night's events. When their meal was interrupted by an artillery barrage from a rival militia unit occupying the hills to the northeast, all five scattered, cursing, to a nearby basement.

Two weeks from now, one of the five—not our man or the one who committed rape-by-bayonet—will be found lying face down in a ditch after a night of heavy drinking. When his companions find him and pull his corpse from the blood-fouled water, they will discover that he has been castrated, and that his bloated face is as pale and peaceful as the moon. Only his eyes, etched by algae and other organisms from the ditchwater, will reflect anything of the horror and death he has inflicted on others and had inflicted on him.

This is gruesome stuff, sure. And for sure, we all know what happens to warriors and hunters. Their fate has been the same since the Stone Age: myopia, indignity, and violence that breeds more myopia, indignity, and violence. What is worrisome is that their accessories have become progressively more lethal, efficient, and glittering. These days

deep, deep, manic ellipse. Keeping herself from suicide, she revealed, was a daily struggle. The ellipse had broken more than once, and now he was convinced that it was about to again, in spite of his help.

Ferris did what he could. He began by talking to a doctor at the psychiatric hospital to see what he could do to help.

The conversation wasn't very illuminating. "Make sure she takes her pills," the doctor advised. Then, as an afterthought, asked, "Who are you, anyway?"

"For the time being, I think I'm her father," Ferris answered, ruefully. "Surrogate one, anyway."

"You're in water that's deeper than you can probably imagine," the doctor said, frowning. "Just get her to take her pills."

Ferris nodded. He was pretty certain Eleanor wasn't taking any pills. Maybe that was part of the problem, but he wasn't about to suggest she start bombing herself. He'd accepted the sweater, but that didn't make him a cop like her father was. The last thing she needed was a policeman. In her life, they were everywhere.

Helplessly, Ferris stood by as her orbits deepened. He took to picking her up each night when her day-program ended—that seemed to be one thing he could do. He drove her back to the basement suite, fed her, and tried his best to calm her. Sometimes his presence seemed to please her, but mostly it didn't. The boundaries of her memory, her fantasies, and her nightmares were

there are so many accessories—and they have become so ubiquitous and indirect—that they have us all, literally, as hostages. They have also made the violence of life more impersonal, and thus harder to understand. A lever pressed inside a B-52 bomber at the airless verge of outer space releases a flood of explosives across a landscape of defenceless peasants, rice paddies, and grass huts; the executive click of a banking program impoverishes a Third World nation, triggering famine or the bloody overthrow of an elected government; a man in a ski mask steps out from between two buildings and attacks a woman he's never seen before. Finally, all are variants of the Stone Age warrior who sneaks up on another and crushes his skull with a rock or impales him with a pointed stick.

A militiaman sits on the steps of a shelled building, sunlight gleaming from the brassy bandoleers draped across his shoulder, a cheap pair of aviator sunglasses across the bridge of his nose.

blending into the details of the everyday world, and he had to piece together the final parts of her story from the few coherent fragments he managed to decipher from her manic gabble. It was like working on a jigsaw puzzle that had no boundaries. Each time he thought he was nearing an edge, the puzzle grew, becoming more bizarre and theological—and more erotic.

God was Eleanor's Father, that much Ferris knew. Then there was her Lover, who was also a Rapist. To this man Eleanor assigned no face, no identity. He was simply there, palpably, a third body in every possible pleasure she and Ferris approached, a body composed of ground glass. In the mottled black and green sweater, Ferris tried to be a lower-case father and tried not to be an upper-case God. Quietly, he longed to be her lover. It was a new, peculiar feeling, because he was not permitted to act, not even on his kindliest physical impulses. Like a heroine from a hundred-year-old novel, he had to wait, imprisoned by discretion, for the lover to imagine some small part of the world the way the heroine does.

Eleanor didn't make this any easier. Sometimes she teased him, fondled him the way a woman might a lover. But always she stopped short, grew frightened, manic, and became a child snuggling with her father.

Ferris wasn't with her when the last, least believable piece of her puzzle dropped into place. He was grocery shopping, pushing a cart down a super-market aisle when it hit him: It was her father—God—who raped her. It was

Because this militiaman is a European and therefore resembles us more closely than his counterparts in the Third World, he provides a transparent moment, the kind that permits us, temporarily, to see the most powerful of the accessories that terrorize us—women and children most of all, but men also. He is the perfect image of phalloc-racy, the shadowy set of conceptual instruments that are invisible most of the time, par-ticularly if we are male.

But here we can see it almost as clearly as we see this man's image. He and it are on the half-shell here, rawer than we're accustomed to, only partly concealed by what we know of his specific situation: a territory filled with xenophobic factions unleashed by the collapse of a communist regime that frustrated every instinct, tolerated unsuper-vised pleasure in no one, and suppressed every civility and community that did not orig-inate in its own cranky gearbox.

It's all too easy to simply declare this man insane, or buy into ideological explana-

the only possible answer, and it made the already tangled contrarium hopeless: Here was a woman who could accept no caresses that were not those of God. But because God was also a rapist, she could accept no caresses.

A few nights after the supermarket revelation, she called Ferris on the tele-phone, late.

"Please come over, Ferris. Now."

He begged off. "No, no, not now."

He was about to admit to her that it was too much, that he was too fright-ened to help her, too stupid. "No, no," she interrupted. "I'm frightened, it's so dark here.... Someone is outside.... Wear the sweater," she added.

She hung up before Ferris could answer.

He understood that there was really no one outside her apartment, but what difference did that make? For Eleanor, everyone was outside, everything was outside in the dark forest that surrounded her. Ferris couldn't participate in the surreality of her shattered sense of reality, with its fluid, wandering bound-aries between self, phantasm, and substance, but he'd become familiar enough with its logic to empathize. For her, the substantial world had been more brutal and surreal than anything she could dream up.

He put on the sweater and drove through the empty streets. When she opened the door, she was completely naked. She pulled him inside without a word.

tions that flatten him as utterly as communism once did, and as our own consumer nightmare flattens us. I'm not sure there is a significant *mystery* firing in the neurons of this man's brain. Something tells me to go beyond the usual summary convictions. Is his a hormone-fed mania, or does it run deeper, entwined in the latticing of our DNA, a primal and unavoidable biotrope? Or is it as shallow as ditchwater, the scum of repressed violence and unleashed opportunity, facilitated by military weapons developed in the collective insane asylum of *realpolitik*? Still, what aren't we seeing? What eludes us here?

And are we clear on the phallocratic mission? Let me remind you: All males are on a biogenetic mission to (a) drive other males away from the females and (b) control (and eventually impregnate) the females. Sure, it's the male prime directive and has been from the first stirrings of warm blood. Big deal. For the human species, it is now stupid, destructive, and biologically obsolete. And no one should be foolish enough

"I want you to look at me," she demanded, taking a stance with her legs slightly apart, her hands clenched at her side.

Ferris looked. Yes, she was as attractive as he'd imagined. Maybe more so. Her legs were as long, her waist as small. Her breasts were small and pointed, with dark, unusually large aureoles that distended with her erect nipples. Was that the flood of cold air as he entered the door, or was she aroused? And what had aroused her? Him? Or the sweater?

The reality of her carried other unexpected textures. Her pubic hair had been shaved. Was this the result of some medical regulation she'd been subjected to? Perhaps. But there was more. Across her lower stomach and thighs ran an irrational network of ridged scars, some whitened and smooth, others still angry and red. No medical procedure or regulation could have inflicted those.

"Don't touch me," she said.

She ordered him to remove the sweater. He did. She ordered him to sit on the couch, and he sat on the couch. She removed his shoes and socks, then, slowly, excruciatingly, his shirt, his pants, his undershorts. She swarmed over him, fingers brushing his shoulders, knees, ankles, her lips and tongue flicking over his neck and across his stomach, and lower, lower. She took his half-limp cock between her lips, and he felt her teeth, nipping the ridge, pressing down on the shaft as if experimenting to see how hard it was—or how easily severed.

to ignore its continued capacity for inducing violence.

Please don't mistake what I'm saying. The existence of this biogenetic mission does *not* excuse male excesses, asininities, or acts of violence. And if we are wise, we'll recognize that our militiaman (he could as easily be Cambodian, Azerbaijani, Guatemalan or, in a different world, a solid citizen from Oak Harbor, Michigan, or Prince George, B.C.) is the cipher to the proud factional tribalism that is now divorcing us, each and all, men and women, Croatian, Serb, and Muslim, white, black, and the endlessly multiplying gradations between, from the civility we will need to thrive on a crowded planet.

So let me tell you a different kind of story about him. A few years ago, he developed an attraction to tall buildings and to moonlight. It was an erotic thing, a weakness that made him liable to commit any romantic idiocy given the presence of those two ingredients. Maybe he lost touch with the earthly ground when he went beyond the third floor,

It wasn't hard because Ferris was terrified. On the arm of the couch, he could see a pair of scissors, and on the coffee table, a paring knife. Those were implicit threats. More real and immediate were her lips and teeth. Yet Ferris felt something in him give way, calming him. This was a truly mortal moment. She could, if she desired, bite down, and that would be it. Given the things that had been done to her, she ought to, almost. But as he acknowledged both his own vulnerability and her right to violence, he understood that nothing would happen. The revenge would have been symbolic, and Eleanor, for all her craziness, was not operating in a symbolic realm. Such things would elude her here as they had elsewhere.

So this was a human affair after all, where the totals were to be practical and physical. And inside her madness, Eleanor wasn't insane. She was, in a way that was unfathomable to both of them—and in the face of her swirling gods, devils and a thousand unnameable impossibilities—trying to make contact, to set things right.

Ferris reached out and put his hand on her shoulder, half out of desire and half to gain some sense of participation—to make it not only human but humane.

It was a mistake. The moment his hand touched her skin, she imploded, throwing herself backward across the coffee table. She scrambled toward a corner of the room, and she curled into a tight ball, her face hidden in her lap.

who can say? It was foolish and he knew it, but he was moved by it, anyway, moved beyond himself and the concerns of the moment.

On one chilly January night, when the moon was full well after midnight, he found himself in a darkened apartment on the top floor of an apartment tower with a dark-haired waitress he'd met some weeks before. He picked up the waitress at the club she worked in after it closed, and she led him to the high-rise tower so they could make love by candlelight.

At the apartment she opened a bottle of wine and lit dozens of cheap candles, and they removed each other's clothes, made love, and then talked for several hours. He began to see her as something more than a sweet-scented fellow creature he could fuck with. Her eyes, for instance, were almond-shaped and amber-coloured. And her nose was too big for her face, tilting slightly to one side. Her mouth was prettier when she smiled, even though one of her front teeth was slightly chipped. He also discovered that

"No," she moaned, "you can't touch me. You must never, *never*, touch me."

Ferris pulled his clothes on, sweater included, and tried to console her. It wasn't easy, because she didn't respond. So he talked. He told her he wasn't her father, assured her of that, and that he wouldn't, couldn't hurt her, he wouldn't touch her. But he could think of nothing by which to move her beyond her terror. What good to assure her that he was just a man, not a god or a rapist? Even to him it sounded hollow. How could she believe him after what her father had done?

A half-hour went by in this state of impasse, then an hour. Ferris began to relax. To amuse her he talked about himself, told her the story of his life in all its hapless banality and self-concern. It was a trivial story, but it was better than silence. She didn't say how it sounded to her, and he was pretty sure she wasn't capable of listening.

Somehow, he carried on a soliloquy that lasted several hours before his imagination and memory ran down. He lapsed into silence, dozing fitfully a foot away from her, close enough to touch, close enough to be touched. That was all he had to offer. Dawn began to break, and he heard birds twittering in the trees outside. Idly, he tried to identify them: chickadees, sparrows he knew, and one he didn't, a more cheerful, chaotic song.

"Do you know why birds sing?" he asked, not expecting an answer. He waited a moment, then answered his own question.

she wasn't quite a cocktail waitress. She was the granddaughter of an internationally famous classical scholar, had trained as a dancer, and had worked professionally until the car accident that broke her nose also damaged a knee beyond repair. He also learned that she was ambitious, intelligent, had a very slim, lithe body, and that she was determined to emigrate to America as soon as possible.

For reasons she didn't reveal, she wouldn't turn on the apartment lights and forbade him to. He suspected that the apartment belonged to a government official, a man of wealth and influence, possibly dangerous in the way such men are. But as the candles burned down, she lit others to forfend the darkness, and they talked more. He discovered that she was equally fond of classical myths and nightclubs, that she wanted to own a fast car and that she planned to live in bigger cities than he had ever seen. He began to wonder why she'd chosen him from the slick and money that passed her way. As far as he could see in the dim light of the candles—and of his life—there were no

"They don't have a reason. Scientists spent years trying to figure it out, assigning all kinds of goofy codes to the songs, trying to prove they had some practical purpose. In the end they gave up. The birds out there are singing because they like to sing—because it tells them they're alive."

She looked up at him, suddenly. Uncomprehendingly. "I don't want to go back to the hospital," she said. "If you leave me alone I'll get better."

Of all the thoughts that had passed through his mind in the last six or seven hours, neither dumping her into a hospital nor leaving her alone had been among them. Now, he understood that to her, they were the obvious ones, maybe the only ones. But were they sane ones? He didn't believe she'd get better if he left her alone. And he didn't believe the hospital would help her either. No, this was a woman who didn't have any options. Not sane ones.

"Isn't there *something* I can do?" he asked her. He waited for her to say something, but he didn't believe she would. Then he answered his own question. "There isn't, is there? No."

She had gone back into the crouch she'd been in for hours, like an injured bird with its head beneath its wing. He watched her for a few more minutes while the light outside brightened. "I've got to go," he said, at last. "I won't phone the hospital. I'll call you later this morning."

She made no answer to that.

He made the call around noon, but she didn't answer her phone. He

scars on either her mind or her body ugly enough to make her choice of him perverse.

So when the full moon drifted fully into view above the adjoining building, he made two contradictory and extra-rational determinations: one was to stay with this woman for as long as she would have him, and the second was to leave by the outside route as soon as she fell asleep, by leaping off the balcony.

He didn't awaken her to tell her what his alternatives seemed to be. How to explain so absolute a choice to a virtual stranger? But she must have seen something of the quandary in his eyes, because after they made love a second time she stayed awake and held him in her arms until he fell asleep. Perhaps, as the minutes ticked away, she watched the moon traverse the heavens, or saw Orion's bandoleer of stars drop beneath the horizon, recalling what she learned from her father of the tragic foolishness of warriors and hunters. Or perhaps it was more mundane, and she lay there thinking that she didn't want this man to kiss any pavement on her time and turf, the fool. And

wasn't surprised. He called her again and again the next day, and again and again on the day after that. No answer. On the third night, he drove to her apartment, wearing the sweater. The lights were on, but she didn't answer the door when he knocked. He drove around the neighbourhood for an hour, and when he came back, there was a note on the door. It read, simply, *"Go Away."*

He did, but he kept on wearing the sweater, and he kept up with the phone calls. But with each one now, the weight of the sweater grew. On the fifth morning, he realized that it had grown so heavy he could not quite lift his arms. He took it off, folded it neatly, and put it on the chair beside the telephone. He made one more call, and she didn't answer. A few days later he put the sweater in a plastic bag and left it on her doorstep.

Twenty years passed.

It came to him that after twenty years there was still nothing he could do to reach her, and so he walked back to his table to read the morning news. A starling landed on his table and began to peck at a slice of toast he'd left uneaten. He wondered if this aging wraith at the window, whose name was once Eleanor Parker, whose body had once been young and beautiful and scarred, still had her father's sweater, and how many others like him had worn it and, like him, taken flight.

As if in answer, she broke her pose to reach into the paper bag she carried.

maybe she merely experienced a moment of irrational, mammalian tenderness and gave in to it.

In the morning he awoke before she did. He sat up in bed, and for a few minutes watched her breathe. He then dressed and took the elevator to the world below, intact, and grateful. Before he left, he leaned over her and kissed the nape of her neck. She stirred, but didn't awaken.

He saw her several more times after that, but they stayed close to the ground and in well-lighted places. Then, one day, she was gone, moved to another city, another country, no goodbye, no parting message.

He stayed away from tall buildings after that, and as her presence in his life grew into a memory and eventually into a mystery, the moon seemed to lose its powers. And eventually there were artillery barrages to occupy him, brutal missions carried out in utter darkness, and other concerns of the moment.

It contained breadcrumbs, and as he watched, she scattered a handful on the sidewalk, smiling. One by one, the starlings returned, settling busily around her.

A Second Portrait of Fred Ferris,

This Time as a Sexual Being

*O*utside the window of the café, a flat-bed semi rumbles by, carrying three pallets, each shrouded under Desert Storm tarps. As it passes, out of scale with the streetscape, wind lifts the tarp from the rear pallet. Ferris sees that on it is a basketball backboard and hoop, the Plexiglas NBA type, and recalls that Magic Johnson retired a second time this morning, about equally the victim of his own promiscuity and his overpaid professional colleagues' fears of contracting AIDS within the paint.

Years ago, a supercilious professor told me I wouldn't understand modern life or literature until I'd read James Joyce's *A Portrait of the Artist as a Young Man*. I read the book and returned to the professor, suitably intimidated by Joyce's vast vocabulary but otherwise unenlightened, to ask for a clarification. With a slight sneer, and a mystifying "Aha!" he informed me that I'd also have to read *Ulysses* and *Finnegans Wake*.

I tried to read and understand those dilatory epics, but I failed both ways. They bewildered me only slightly more than they bored me. Still, I muddled on with life and with literature, eventually delving far and deep enough to decipher what the professor had been trying to say. Joyce's opus, properly considered, is a literary response to the scientific discovery of indeterminacy, which has put us all, whether we admit it or not, in a reality no objective instrumentation—be it God, ideology, or robotics—can guide us through. Joyce believed that we have been left alone to reinvent meaning with our imaginations and our language, and he set out to demonstrate how joyous and speedy this could be.

Now that I understand his mission, I applaud it, and him. Unless you count his personal life, which was marred by bad eyesight, a lust for strange and unhygienic erotic practices, some sadomasochism, and a willingness to get into IRA-type fights with his friends and loved one, he was a fine man. As a writer and innovator, he was still more admirable. He was also unique. He employed a working vocabulary of roughly eighty thousand words, and it is now apparent to any sane observer that he was an evolutionary dead end rather than a glimpse of humanity's cognitive future.

For sure, the writers who have emulated him have not met his challenge. Most of them, working with five thousand- to thirty thousand-word vocabularies, have dithered in the general area of their linguistic navels, trying to create the same sort of evocative music Joyce was able to produce, and forgetting completely that it is what gets written *about* that is important. The offspring of their literary labours have been as depressingly dull and stunted as these products produced by the army of academics attempting to manufacture a concordance to Joyce's last two indecipherable novels.

Their most noble ambition has been to reinvent the world, influencing and ordering our aimless walking up and down and back and forth by capturing people, processes, and objects in linguistic permutations as complicated and discriminative as reality actually is. Unfortunately, this noble ambition has tended to go awry—to socialist realism or to miniaturization.

My own grandiose ambitions—well, never mind what those are. Let me reveal just this one slightly silly one. It is this: Ever since I gave up trying to understand what Joyce was saying on a word-by-word basis, I've wanted to write a sentence, just once, that would bewilder the master as completely as he once did me. The paragraph at the top of this chapter contains two sentences that would mind-fuck Mr. Joyce admirably. As I was finishing the second I realized that eighty percent of today's common sentences would do the same.

I think the era of James Joyce is over. One reason is that the EuroAmerican artistic community has finally figured out what Joyce knew all along: that, for instance, "Victoria" Falls wasn't really "discovered" by a white man, and that naming it after England's crab-lice-tormented Queen did not alter the hue and volume of water rumbling over its impossibly aged rocky lip. This has rescued Joyce's imitators from their navels, only to send them squabbling over who has the right to use which voices and words, and in which tribalized context. (The rest of our civilization and its machinery, alas, seems undeterred in its quest to take us all, babbling and dithering, over the precipice.)

> **Queen Victoria:**
>
> The women who washed down the body of the deceased Queen Victoria are rumoured to have encountered a monumental infestation of crab-lice. Judging from the condition of the monarch's private parts, the infestation was of long duration — perhaps weeks or months, but perhaps years, even decades, given the technical difficulties and social proprieties of treating such a condition. Truthful or not, the story is a disturbing metaphor for the last years of the 19th century, and for the stultifying protocols of the British Empire at its apex.

The other reason for the end of the Joyce era is that the commoditization of things has utterly outstripped the inventions of language. We live in a world where a virtual myriad of manufactured things are neither named nor understood, where the effluents and poisons of their manufacture percolate silently toward the groundwater and slip unnoticed through our bodies and across the blood/brain barrier.

As an evolving species, human beings have barely responded to Joyce's challenge. By staying within assigned lifestyle enclaves and allowing themselves to be mesmerized by the relativist rhythms of the commodity shuffle, most citizens of our post-literate society can operate within a transient icon curriculum navigable by roughly four hundred words. Off in cyberspace are the corporations, piping in the mood Muzak and tuning the incitement-to-buy icons to ever more soothing and generic levels.

Instead of the collapse of authoritarian institutions before the dreamed-of onslaught of a Joycean run-on sentence structure that would connect every-thing and everyone and make reality open and unrestricted, most people have a cognitive range in which their individuality and creativity have become purely parenthetical, existing only between the dash-marks of the laconic corporate sentence in which money is the subject, spending it is the predicate, and share-holder profits are the object. *My girlfriend and I—even though we'd rather be screwing—want a BMW and jobs at the World Bank.*

Instead of the fully wired literacy imagined by Joyce and his disciple Mar-shall McLuhan, we're moving toward a closed global culture run by marketeers who live in—and operate by—the same logical manufacturing procedures as the technocrazies of the nuclear weapons industry. Articulation operates by enclosure, by imperializing technical sub-languages, cognition is ruled by semi-colons and a general denial of radiance. Know what I mean?

If you're still not convinced that we're in trouble, have another look at this sentence: *As he died, he [a Somalian refugee named Mohammed Osman] was not thinking about, say, the colour of Madonna's pubic hair curling out from the edges of her high-cut panties as she fondled the breasts of two skin-headed lesbians in front of a photographer there to take pictures for her new book on sex.*

As I said once before, I'm thinking about this—and probably not quite in the way I'm intended to. Madonna is synonymous with bankable commercial effrontery, the in-your-face about-face robotization of the amiable middle-class anarchism of the 1960s, the perfect moral liberty to make enough money to be able to mistreat, objectify, demean, or elevate whomever one chooses. I'm talk-ing about the rock singer again, the one who has become the symbol of post-Sexual Revolution sexuality, I'm trying to see what it is she is—to herself and to me and, maybe, to you. But the media incitements she employs so deftly cloud my perception, and it's impossible to get her right. And James Joyce doesn't help me at all.

Meanwhile, downstairs in the washroom, Ferris discovers that someone has left the following message:

IF you put an oilwell in Gino's head you would solve the energy crisis!

Nasty, nasty, Ferris thinks—and copies it down. The graffito is awkwardly placed, not above the urinal or on the toilet stall's wall, but scribbled on the inside of the washroom door at a contortionist's angle. It's so awkward he locks the washroom while he writes it down—no point risking the embarrassment of having to explain what he's doing if someone walks in.

Below the maxim is a long note, ostensibly addressed to Gino. It is small part philosophy, large part insult:

> Get a life, Gino. The age of John Revoltin and Saturday Night Fever is long, long over. Only a bisexual would find Madonna attractive. Ever see the biceps and thighs on that slut? She could put Schwarzenegger to shame. That slut is so worn out you could drive a Mack truck through her snatch and still have room to spare for a VW beetle and a Chevette.

Ferris sorts out the competing phobias at work in the message, settling a profile of the author. A "Gino," he deduces, is an Italian, and Gino is a specific person, probably an acquaintance, probably Italian. Our message-writer appears to have a cultural prejudice, but that ain't the half of it. The crack about bisexuals is homophobic, and the repetition of the word "slut," along with the remark about Madonna's vaginal elasticity indicates gynophobia. The passionate anti-Disco statement—and the implication that popular music is the unquestioned carrier of history—places the writer in his twenties, maybe younger: He's a teenage racist homophobic woman-hater. Hardly a unicorn in these depressing times.

Scribbled below this cosmography is a list of further criticisms aimed directly at Madonna under the subtitle "#1 Talentless Slut."

> Can't write or compose songs that do anything but torture the ears -- Disco sucks and keeps on sucking.
> Can't sing unless you call chirping like a chimpanzee on drugs singing !.!.!.
> Can't dance (unless you call spastic jumping dancing)
> Can butcher Stephen Sondheim songs
> Can fuck boyfriends pretend to be romantically involved

then dump them once their usefulness
is over
Can manipulate the market with slick
capitalist hucksterism and
"selling sizzle"
Can write pro-life (antichoice) and
pro-Roman Catholic pro-Vatican
propaganda.

Penned in alongside this Joyce-inscrutable list—perhaps to reinforce his will-to-criticism—is a reminder:

Gino assholes
like Madonna.

From this, Ferris deduces that the writer is an aspiring musical critic, a defender of Broadway musicals, possibly a crypto-Barry Manilow-worshipping sentimentalist and, for dead certain, a closet oral compulsive. He has anticlerical tendencies (Joyce would understand those) and probably had an Italian Catholic girlfriend who dumped him on his ear recently enough for it to still rankle. Did she dump him for someone named Gino? Ferris would bet money on it.

Another thought, equally idle, occurs to Ferris as he slips his notebook in his pocket and moves to the urinal to relieve himself. How upset would this guy be if Madonna was not of Italian descent, but a Presbyterian housewife from Illinois doing the same things?

On the wall above the urinal is another message. It has most of the same cognitive irregularities, this time from the opposite end of the spectrum. It's an advertisement:

Johnny S.
I like to suck white cunts!
$100/hr

Ferris finds several inaccuracies in this. First, if Johnny S. really likes what he says he does, why would he want to be paid for it? Second, Johnny S. seems to think that the proper technique is to suck women's private parts, a method that is arguably the least effective way to please a woman. Third, there appears to be some racially engendered confusion. Is Johnny S. a person of colour? If so, he has erroneous notions about the genitals of female Caucasians. Since these have as many colour variations as petunias or roses, one can assume that Johnny S. either hasn't seen many, or he hasn't paid very close attention to the ones he has seen. In Ferris's experience, the genitals of even the most fair-skinned women are not "white." They sometimes tend toward orange or dusky rose, and they are always significantly darker in hue than the surrounding tissue. Finally, why is Johnny S. declaring all this in the men's washroom, where no prospective customers are likely to see it?

Underneath the ad, Ferris prints the following message:

Don't hire incompetent workpersons.

Then he checks the toilet stall. It has some enthusiastic New Age advice:

RETAIN YOUR SPERM!!
FOR HEALTH AND LONGEVITY!!
No, REALLY, IT WORKS WONDERS
TO HOLD ONTO YOUR JAM
AND THE GIRLS LIKE IT TOO!

Almost as if the writer realized how silly his message sounds, beneath it he's scribbled a philosophical exhortation:

OPEN YOUR MICROCOSMIC ORBIT !!
ENLIGHTENMENT WILL ENSUE !!
IT'S TRUE !!

In tiny script, beneath it, Ferris pens this addendum:

How about we just stop pissing on the toilet seats.

Ah, everybody's a fucking expert these days. But can anyone say what sex is about? Does anyone know? Is it, to use computer metaphors, an optional piece of hardware that serves to provide pleasure and amusement while we engage in more serious behaviours, or is it the software by which we access everything in life that is essential? Or is it an impermeable black box that is in the process of triggering us, like the lemmings, over the cliffs into the wine-dark sea where, amidst the bleach bottles, gum wrappers, drug paraphernalia and manufacturing effluents, we will all perish?

Ferris and I have come to believe that all sexual wisdoms are situational. There are technical insights to be shared, and a few homilies that drag tracers of significance through the murk, but there are no large truths out there about sex that will relieve either the tedium or the terror of our condition.

Ferris has had it confirmed for him again and again that the sexual graffiti that get scribbled on the walls of washrooms and telephone booths are messages from our lowest common denominator. The messages are nearly never profound, and their single virtue is that they're specific. Most often they reflect current fashion—not the kind ad agencies track—and nearly always, they invoke the most ill-considered prejudices we harbour. Short-form newspapers, sort of, shouts of rage, squeals of frustration the papers always edit out. But put together, they're an eloquent testimony to our collective and private lack of understanding of what we're about, and what we should do with consciousness.

Like everything else about sex, sexual graffiti are best answered with a deliberate liberalism, not with a movement to stamp out asymmetrical ideas and behaviours. Therein lies Ferris's problem with it, and my problem with this book. How is it different than the sex manuals that insist that technique is everything? And how does it respond to the erotic anthologies and videos that liberate every impulse, but say nothing about sensory—and sensible—community? And what should I say to those zealots who would impose moral police states to regulate everything and everyone but their own erotic specialty?

I don't have those answers, and neither does Ferris. We are men who remember the marvels of sex, and we remember human kindness—and we do not inflate their importance or forget their healing powers. I move Ferris's hand to the wall. What he writes there, hesitantly, anyone can understand:

If you piss on your sexual partners,
it might make you feel
warm for a while, but it makes
the world cold.

Cure

Ferris can't quite decide why the first sight of the ferry dock makes him shiver. Is it fear or expectation, or is it simply the bracing spring air? With one hand, he grips the bouquet of yellow tulips he's carrying a little tighter, pulls his jacket closer to his neck with the other, and the shivers pass.

He doesn't expect the island to be the same after ten years. Islands change, people change, nothing remains the same. If it has taught him nothing else, travelling across four continents has driven home the ubiquitousness of change, although too often the specific message received is twisted between "Yankee Go Home" and "Everything changes—into a mall."

Yet from a distance, the island is at least similar, and it isn't until the ferry closes in on the dock that the changes become visible. Vince is waiting for him at the terminal, as expected. But he's standing beside a nearly new Volkswagen Jetta, not slouched down comfortably in the seat of a battered GMC panel. From this distance, Vince could be mistaken for an ordinary middle-aged man, his face obscured by a beard that is more grey than black. To Ferris, he's dead easy to recognize, and anything but ordinary. Vince is Ferris's secret life— together with Ava.

koo

Looking at him, Ferris shivers once again. That's the most familiar feeling of all, and it doesn't have anything to do with the weather conditions. Ferris has seen him waiting like this fifty, a hundred times, in every conceivable kind of weather, and the shiver has always been part of it. There is uneasiness and curiosity in it, and a tingling, *what now?* expectancy. But ten years have changed the shiver, too. The intensities have shifted. This morning, curiosity leads.

The ferry taps the dock, recoils a little, and the ramp mechanisms drop the heavy steel plates onto the decks. Ferris hangs back as the other passengers tramp across the plates and onto the wooden dock, an anonymous surge of eager human flesh that has debarked here the same way, in the same colourful chaos ten times a day since he was last here. How many crowds is that? Ferris tries to do the calculation in his head and settles at somewhere near forty thousand.

He leans against the ferry rail and makes an inventory. The mossy cedars and firs of the bay are more sparse than he remembers, and there are fewer of them. He glimpses several plush new buildings half-hidden among them, expensive homes defined by the unmistakable ostentation of wealthy people who want solitude, comfort, and convenience at the same time. The road leading down to the ferry slip looks more congested with cars and passengers than it used to be, but the sewery-salt odour of the marina is the same, and when he peers down through its murky iridescence, he can see neither improvement nor the bottom.

Ferris knows that the changes here, whatever they turn out to be, probably won't be for the better. Everything gets uglier and more vulgar. This island and its contents more than most places, probably. Less nature, more people, more toxins and shit. The crabs and shellfish all up the coast, he recalls, were declared unfit for eating several years ago, a combination of pulp mill dioxins and too much sewage washing through to the beaches from the new developments.

He steps onto the ramp, continuing his gloomy inventory. In the marina behind the ferry slip, the boats are bigger than they once were, more of them Fiberglas. And there are houseboats. He wonders how *that* happened. The islanders had once been willing to form their own navy to keep them out. Somebody has paid a lot of money for the privilege of having their living room roll around like a toy boat in a bathtub every ninety minutes when the ferries come in.

May 9, 1990

TALLINN, ESTONIA: Without formally declaring independence, the Estonian parliament reinstated key clauses from its 1938 constitution that declare it an independent republic.

TORONTO, CANADA: Twenty-eight-year-old Vietnamese Refugee, Ba Minh Hoang, who makes his living transporting other refugees across the Canada/U.S. border, was jailed for 21 months for criminal negligence causing death after abandoning Vasugee Krighan, 27, and Fong Yew Cheah, 38, in a small motorized liferaft on the Niagara River.

Vince catches sight of him as he reaches the end of the ramp and booms out a greeting. "Hey, hey! Cuckoo! Over here!"

Ferris almost flinches. He hasn't heard that nickname in a long time, not since the last time Vince used it. Trust him to bring it up before anything. He looks over and sees that Vince has a wide grin on his face—and that he's waiting for Ferris to come to him. Some things don't change.

They shake hands and then embrace, awkwardly. Vince glances at the tulips, but doesn't acknowledge them. "You don't change much," he says.

Ferris shrugs. "I've got a few creaks."

"No," Vince says, as if reading his thoughts. "You look young. Your face. And this," he pokes at Ferris's gut, "pretty good."

"Well, it isn't like I've had to work at it, " Ferris answers. "Good genetics, I guess."

Vince's face hardens momentarily. "Oh, yeah, sure. But you haven't led a hard life. All you do is travel to glamorous places and sit on your ass. Hop in." He gestures toward the passenger side of the Jetta.

Ferris leans through the open window and looks inside. The car is immaculate. "Nice car," he says. "What happened to your junk heap?"

At one time Vince had four mid-fifties GMC pickup trucks in his backyard to rob for parts to keep the panel he drove running. It wasn't that he liked working on cars, or that he was saving money. It was a gesture to his father, a master mechanic who could make or repair anything.

Vince doesn't answer for a moment, as if he can't quite remember. "Oh, shit," he says, finally, "that was a long time ago. Someone hauled them all to the dump when we sold the house."

Ferris opens the car door, tosses the bouquet into the back seat, and climbs in. When he closes the car door, it comes to with a satisfyingly soft thump. Vince clambers in, reads Ferris's mind once again.

"The old man's dead, you know."

Ferris doesn't know, but he isn't surprised. Vince's father had been in poor health for years, and he didn't much like doctors or hospitals.

Ferris had been fond of Vince's father and had got along better with him than Vince did. Ferris would have loved the old man, but that wasn't permitted. After Ferris's parents died, the old man had taken Ferris under his wing and offered him everything that familial love confers. He was about the only male role model Ferris ever accepted. He'd given Ferris his nickname—Cuckoo—joking that Ferris was trying to push Vince out of the nest.

"When'd he go?" Ferris asks, breaking his reverie. "How long?"

"A couple of years ago," Vince answers after a pause. "His heart blew up on him while he was pulling the transmission on a truck. Never knew what hit him."

"I liked your old man a lot," Ferris says, then revises. "I loved him. I'm sorry he's gone."

"Yeah, me too," Vince answers, as if it were the least important thing on his mind. "I miss him sometimes. And," he pauses again, "sometimes I don't. Sometimes I'm glad he's gone. He could be a miserable old bastard when he wanted to."

"We should have grown up to be men like him," Ferris says.

"We didn't." Vince stares through the windshield for a moment, as if considering what kind of men he and Ferris *had* become. "That's for sure."

He starts the car, and they drive off the ferry slip past the line of cars waiting to load.

"How's Ava doing?" Ferris asks.

"You know how it goes," Vince answers, noncommittally. "Up and down. You'll see."

Ferris wants to ask him if Ava is still beautiful, but it occurs to him that Vince might not understand what he's asking. There had always been a strange lack of interiority in the way Vince viewed Ava. He seemed to know that she was an attractive woman, and he admired her sexual athletics and her unpredictability—but Ferris didn't think he ever thought of her in terms of beauty. Not the way he did. And does.

They reach the turnoff that leads to the northerly part of the island. Vince yanks hard on the steering wheel—too hard—and the Jetta sloughs around the

168   I thought the *Kama Sutra* was silly while it was in vogue during the 1960s, and I still do. It—or rather, the set of attitudes that sparked the interest in it—didn't really increase sexual pleasure except among the already weirded out, and it was responsible for hundreds of thousands of stupid back injuries and a vast number of other twisted muscles, torn ligaments, and exotic infections. So what were those goofy attitudes? Let me list the main ones, from general to particular:

1. Sexual intercourse is the source of individual meaning, and anything (particularly when it also involves taking "organic" drugs) that prolongs or intensifies screwing is good.

2. The exotic is better than the familiar. (Much, much better…)

3. All erotic activities should lead to sexual intercourse and should (never mind what the *Kama Sutra* says about withholding) culminate in orgasm.

4. Placing yourself and/or your sexual partner into bizarre postures will enhance pleasure and will extend and enrich your sexual and domestic relationships. (It does, for better or worse, prolong sexual intercourse.)

5. Burning foul-smelling incense and slathering yourself and your sexual partner with slippery, patchouli-infused petroleum products will enhance sexual pleasure more frequently than it will cause low-grade (or acute) allergic reactions.

I could go on with this kind of dilation for an embarrassingly long time, but enough is enough. I don't agree with any of the above attitudes. The *Kama Sutra* enthusiasts, it seems to me, were correct about just two things. One of them—that

corner. Ferris can't think of anything to say, so he looks out the window. The island has, to use the misleading euphemism of real estate agents, developed. New homes sear the roadside, replacing the dense thickets of alder and fir that had been there since the glaciation.

The changes are so many that Ferris doesn't recognize Vince and Ava's old house when they pass it. Vince has to point it out. An addition has been built on, the yard backfilled, fresh paint. It looks like most of the other houses around it—an upmarket bungalow. When Vince and Ava lived there, it looked like what it was: a prefab starter home in a swampy yard filled with wrecked pickup trucks.

"When did you sell it?" Ferris asks.

"Four years ago, when Bobby moved out. I built the addition, and then we didn't need it…" Vince trails off into silence.

That sounds about right to Ferris. Vince was always good at starting projects, not so great at figuring out the correct scale, and lousy at finishing them.

Indian print bedspreads are less likely to show evidence of sexual activities than the purple satin brocade variety—isn't a very important insight. The other one *is* important: Sexual positions ought to be adopted in order to facilitate the maximum degree of satisfaction for everyone involved.

Whether or not we like to admit it, the issue of sexual positions has once again become important, but this time in a different way, and for different reasons. In recent years people have begun to search, quietly but with increasing urgency, for a politically acceptable sexual position. This position, to date, has only a theoretical existence.

What has touched off the search for this position is anything but theoretical, and it is *not* trivial. The underlying issue is that gender parity has become a democratic necessity—perhaps even a genetic one. Certainly it is an evolutionary imperative, without which our species is unlikely to progress much further. Women and men must have equal powers and pleasures both in and outside the sexual arena. I agree with this, and so do you, I hope.

Now come the difficulties: Leaving aside the wider context, how can the physical configurations of sexuality permit parity? How do men and women make love without one or the other taking a position of physical dominance? "Does someone have to be on top?" is not, repeat *not*, a rhetorical question. We can, physically, make love while lying on our sides. While this will satisfy our desires for equitable geometry, it unfortunately accords perhaps the fewest opportunities for stimulation

Twelve years ago, Ferris helped him put in a fancy new septic system, an experimental one that didn't work as advertised. Whenever it rained, the already swampy backyard turned into a private sewage lagoon, replete with floating turds and streamers of toilet paper. At least part of the cause was that Vince decided to route the eavestroughs into it, for reasons Vince couldn't quite explain and which Ferris never got his mind around.

They talk briefly about what they've been doing in the last few years—or rather, Ferris questions Vince about what he's been doing—teaching retarded teenagers—now challenged pre-adults—for some government program. Vince asks no questions and seems to have no curiosity about Ferris's doings. Several miles pass. The density of development drops off and the island begins again to resemble the island Ferris knew.

"What's the new place like?" he asks.

"Very different. You'll see in a minute. Here's the turnoff."

Vince makes a right turn off the main road and bumps down a steep gravel

and pleasure. And in the end, it has the same effect on domestic reality that the missionary position has had—after a while it becomes restrictive and boring, and if there are no alternatives, it will result in sleep, general indifference, and separate beds. From there it is only a matter of time until separate beds become separate bedrooms, residences, even separate cities.

The problem of physical configuration, with careful attention, some imagination, and good faith, can be got around. But there is a deeper problem, one that there is no getting around: *How can gender parity exist when sexual intercourse involves the violation of one gender's body integrity and not the other's?* The fact that a male is likely to inject a substance into a female that contains several million tiny half-baked but aggressive invaders, and that this substance is also a perfect medium for lethal viruses and a host of increasingly virulent bacteria is bad enough. How can men make love to women without violating them?

I know of very few intelligent persons—male or female—who are not troubled by this conundrum. I've encountered people from both genders who have, I suspect, chosen homosexuality because it offers sexual configurations in which positional reciprocality is equal—or where the violations of body integrity at least can be reciprocal. For the same reasons, still others are choosing celibacy. Heteros in settled relationships tend to deny that it is a problem—a little too vehemently—while those who are single tend to simply shake their heads about it. It is making nearly every hetero uneasy, and some, plumb crazy.

hill toward the water. They've moved closer to the ocean, at least, Ferris thinks. For a moment it looks as if they're right on the beach, but at the last minute Vince turns left into a deep draw sheltered by huge fir trees. It's like a park, protected from both the main road above and the ocean winds. Vince pulls into a tiny driveway that backs onto a shed-like structure, cuts the ignition.

"Here we are," he announces.

Ferris can't see any house, and Ava isn't to be seen either. Ferris retrieves the chrysanthemums from the rear seat and follows Vince along a treed path around the shed. Down a short but steep incline he can see a tiny cottage. It's covered in varnished shiplap, with deep eaves, and a roof of shingled cedar. Smoke drifts up from the chimneys at each end. Beyond it is another building, unfinished, but about the same size.

"This is a change," Ferris says, still wondering why Ava hasn't appeared. In the old days, she always came out to greet him, a habit he attributed to her Yugoslav ethnic background—it was not then necessary to know if that meant

I'm not sure there is a way out of it. There *are* crises that have no satisfactory resolution, and this may be one of them. Will we end up lying on our sides, performing acts of mutual or private masturbation in order to secure the configuration of gender equality? It's a possibility, and a perfectly serious one. So is the full latex solution, which solves the biofluid exchange deficit. There's a lot more of that sort of thing going on than there used to be, and I can't see anything wrong with it, aside from the fact that governments tend to like it, that it betrays most of the mammalian intentions of sexuality, which are designed to get us to care for one another and to have large amounts of the intimate contact that bonds us together. Despite the exhortations of the latex industry and every level of government that acknowledges that sex exists, we'd do well to remember that intimate—read "mucous membrane"—contact is *not* bad. That our children may never know how glorious it can be will be a terrible experiential and sensory deficit.

My best guess is that the answer does lie in that general direction, which is the opposite of where the *Kama Sutra* takes us. Certainly the politically acceptable position will remain theoretical until and unless we change the fundamental prejudice that all erotic behaviour is supposed to centre on and culminate in intercourse.

The acceptable position must begin with two human beings confronting one another, face to face, eye to eye. And that leaves us where we began: at the beginning *and at the end* of the political universe. Ready, set...

Serbian, Slovenian, Croatian, or Muslim. It was, as far as he could see, her only ethnic tic. Otherwise she was as disenculturated as any WASP.

Vince waves his arm forward in reply, and Ferris skids down the mossy slope after him, and in his wake, tramps his way to the cottagey wooden back door. There is a small bell over it, on a string, and Vince tugs the string before entering. Ferris isn't sure whether to expect Ava, or Goldilocks and the Three Bears. Vince pushes the door open.

Over his shoulder Ferris can see a sign that says "NO SHOES." Vince bends over to remove his, and there is Ava. Her dark hair is peppered with grey, but God, she's still beautiful. Ferris drinks her in, transfixed by a sense of relief. Without being conscious of it, he's been imagining all kinds of horrible transformations—weight gain, accident scars, the coarsening of the features that women sometimes get under extended stress. For ten years he's seen and heard nothing of or from her except a single telephone call he made five years ago. It wasn't a long call. Ava cut him off in the middle of the opening pleasantries, saying that she and Vince were having problems; no, there was nothing Ferris could do, please stay clear.

"Ferris," she says. "You're here. It's been a long time."

Before Ferris can hand her the bouquet, Vince straightens up, completely blocking his view with his bulk. "Take off your shoes, Cuckoo," he orders, curtly. "Things have changed."

The last time Ferris saw Ava, he had anal intercourse with her while Vince had vaginal intercourse with her. As Ferris waits for Vince to move out of the doorway so he can remove his shoes and continue the conversation with Ava, he recognizes that something about that night was disturbing enough that he's completely blocked it out. He can't, for instance, remember the physical configuration of it. And that in itself is strange. In the past few days, a thousand other details of those years have flooded his memory, but not that one. It has vanished, including any memory of pleasure.

When he first met Ava, more than twenty-some years ago, he thought she was the prettiest—no, the most beautiful—woman he'd ever seen. And moviestar beautiful rather than model-beautiful. She was tall, dark-haired, and darker eyed, with full breasts and hips, statuesque. Her breasts were too large for modelling, and she carried and cared for herself indifferently—without any sense of glamour. She rarely wore make-up and Ferris couldn't recall seeing her in high heels. Here, he can't even remember seeing her dressed up, except the day she and Vince got married. That was the day Ferris met her.

It took a while, but when he got to know Ava, he liked her. She seemed bright enough even though she didn't talk much. Ferris put that down to the fact that no one talked much around Vince. He dominated most conversations, and when he talked, you listened.

The pleasure that anal intercourse offers to homosexual men ought to be no mystery. Even if it is currently out of fashion, body-to-body copulation is one of our primal instincts and the anus is the only available orifice to male homos. That heterosexuals sometimes practise it should be no great mystery either, although the motives are slightly more complex—and at times, extremely unpleasant.

First of all, anal intercourse offers a different set of erotic sensations: For the perpetrator, it is more indeterminate at the head of the penis because there is no cervix to bump against, and smoother and more constricting along the sides. For the woman (or male homosexual recipient), the sensations it produces are likewise indirect. The physical pleasure women experience seems—as with conventional intercourse—to depend on the degree of labial engorgement prior to entry, and on simultaneous clitoral stimulation. Male receptors derive some pleasure from the mas-

He never asked them when they got into group screwing, which of them initiated it, or exactly why they were doing it, but it had started before he entered their orbit. A few years after they got married, Vince began to talk about it—proudly, as if it were a badge of their openness and modernity. At first Ferris thought he was bullshitting. Talk is cheap, and Vince was a talker. And even if he was telling the truth, well, so what? It was the aftermath of the 1960s, when everybody thought they had the duty—and maybe even a basic right—to grope anyone they found attractive in whatever configuration appealed to them at the moment. The more bizarre the better.

Oh, Ferris had his fantasies about such things, but in strictly democratic terms, as a foursome, in which he and whatever partner he was with would sleep with others. Like most men (and maybe women) in those days, he was as interested as the next person in sleeping with new partners, but giving up bodily possession of his own in the deal was just too threatening. He'd occasionally entertained fantasies of a threesome involving two women, but not with much enthusiasm. He assumed that such a configuration would be centred on the male, and he had enough doubts about his stamina and gifts as a lover that he didn't indulge the fantasies very far. Two men and a woman hadn't occurred to him.

The first time Vince asked Ferris to join them, he said no. Thankfully, Vince didn't persist beyond calling him a reactionary. Ferris didn't say so, but he was quite willing to be reactionary. It was easier just to screw around, thanks. He preferred to have his adventures one-on-one, where the social politics were a little easier to sort out.

———————————

Ferris dutifully removes his shoes and tries to evaluate what he's seen so far—Vince's relative silence on the drive over, the look on Ava's face as she greeted him. He's asked for the visit, so he can't fault them if they don't want to be hospitable. It occurs to him that he'd asked Vince, and that Vince has never denied him anything. Judging from Ava, she has misgivings about him being there.

Well, what should I expect, Ferris muses as he parks his shoes beside Vince's larger ones and picks up the bouquet. He's already frustrated by the palpable barrier between them, but he doesn't know what to do about it. Lord only knows why it's really there—it's been ten years, they've had a rough time domestically, and he still knows nothing definite about why.

sage of the prostate gland—an acquired taste, as anyone who has ever had a prostate infection will attest to—and I'm told that receptors rarely achieve orgasm without alternative stimulation.

But let's not kid ourselves. Few heterosexuals—male or female—would engage in it simply for the sake of variety. It is attractive because it is intercourse without a goal other than pleasure—i.e., there is no possibility of depositing sperm at the entrance to the uterus (it was a surprisingly common form of birth control until fairly recently) and it is hence a respite from biology as well as an affront to it. In fact, to engage in anal intercourse is to mess around with nature, and the sensations it offers—pleasurable or not—will always reflect that. Where it is pleasurable to both partners, the pleasure resides in the extreme intimacy of it, and to a lesser extent, in the biological affront it constitutes. In other words, it's mostly in the head.

Heterosexual anal intercourse can be explained by two separate socio-erotic impulses. Among mem-

He has a theory, if you can call it that, based on what Vince told him on the phone. Eight years ago they adopted a foster child about a year younger than Bobby, an eleven-year-old girl with learning disabilities. It was Vince's way of bringing his work home, and Ferris's guess is that it went badly. How or why, he doesn't have a clue. It occurs to him now that the one time he talked to Ava, also on the phone, they were probably in the midst of that mess.

There is another possibility, a simpler one. Maybe they're just wary of him, and of what he might want. That makes a certain sense, except that wariness isn't something he's seen in either of them before. When you've been in every nook and cranny of another person's body, and that person has shown no hint of reluctance or displeasure, you don't expect them to respond to you with suspicion, not even after ten years. Or at least Ferris doesn't.

He's a bit simple-minded about certain things, our Ferris. He thinks, for instance, that intimacies are permanent even though he will tell you that nothing lasts forever. Some tangled circuit in his brain insists, against logic and common sense, that anyone who has cared for him once always will. He understands that the world and human beings aren't perfect, but he retains a perfect ego anyway. Is this familiar to anyone out there? Is there another name for this? Stupidity?

———————

bers of cultures and subcultures where organized religion is a primary rationale for degrading the status and societal prestige of women (and therefore fearing for their "secret" powers), and where there are powerful prohibitions against "spilling seed," anal intercourse is a "favoured" form of sexual violence. In Latin America, for instance, where the borders of criminal sexual violence, sexuality, and political violence are foggier than here, performing anal intercourse is a badge of macho honour. I understand that this is also the case in most war zones, even among cultures normally too prudish to admit that women have anuses. Whenever it occurs under these circumstances, it is obviously an act of violence designed to humiliate the victim, and (usually but not always) her kin. It also serves to dehumanize the perpetrators, making them more pliable for subsequent acts of atrocious behaviour.

There's an unintentionally revealing story Norman Mailer wrote in the late 1950s if you want an unfiltered look at how hetero males

Ferris follows Vince into the tiny kitchen. Vince, Ferris notes, brushes past Ava without touching her. Ferris stops in front of her and presents her with the bouquet. He most definitely does want to touch her, to look at her, to see for himself. For a moment he just looks at her, and she stares back without taking the flowers out of his hand, a slight smile on her lips that doesn't touch her eyes. He brushes back a stray lock of her hair and leans in to kiss her cheek.

"Well," she says, taking a step backward but not quite flinching, "do come in and sit down. Would you like some tea or coffee?"

The three of them negotiate a pot of herbal tea, and while Ava finds a vase for the bouquet, Ferris looks around. Despite the hominess of the cottage, it is Spartan. There are no paintings or prints on the walls, and no personal mementos to be seen. Vince and Ava, Bobby, the foster daughter, and everyone else—parents and friends alike—have been disappeared.

Ferris ambles over to the couch, sits down, and surveys the cottage. The orderliness of it is startling. The Vince he knows isn't like this, not in any way. He's always been a bouncer—a project here, an idea there—the projects never quite complete, the ideas never entirely coherent. Ava lived amidst his chaos without any evident discomfort, or, now that he considers it, deep interest. She wasn't a compulsive housekeeper or much of a cook. She seemed to be in her own private universe, even as a parent—not that he saw much parenting or much of Bobby—the boy was always visiting "elsewhere" when Ferris visited. Ferris suspected that Ava was competent but slightly indifferent as mothers go. But if she didn't exert much control in the household,

thought about the practice a generation ago. The story is titled "The Time of Her Time," and in it, the macho protagonist performs the then-exotic (now stupid) feat of simultaneous anal and vaginal intercourse with a bitchy young Jewish woman he wants to somehow "defeat." He does this, improbably bringing her to orgasm by penetrating each of her orifices on alternate thrusts.

Curiously, neither the plot nor the erotic activities in the story are as revealing as some of the subsidiary details. Absurdly, the story's male protagonist lived in New York City where he ran a bull-fighting school out of a rented loft. He referred to his penis as "The Avenger" and seemed strangely concerned at winning the paternal approval of Ernest Hemingway. I was a young man when I first read the story, and in my naïvete I missed the implications of a man naming what should be an instrument of pleasure as an instrument of violence, and I wasn't then aware of Hemingway's repressed cross-sexual longings. I'd read *Death in the Afternoon* not long

in the bedroom she was definitely in charge—and the bedroom had very elastic proportions.

There was the time she greeted him on arrival with a blowjob: no formalities permitted, not a word of explanation. Ferris stood in the doorway with his back to the road, his arms braced against the doorjambs and watched her slip his cock in and out of her throat with an exquisitely firm touch, grasping and sucking on the in-stroke, and vibrating her tongue across his glans on the out.

Anyone driving by would have recognized exactly what she was up to, but it didn't take very long, and the road remained empty. When she was finished, she stood up, kissed him, and slipped his own come into his mouth. Then, grinning, she told him it was an experiment—she wanted to see how fast she could make him come.

before, and while I sensed that there was something fishy about Hemingway's evident lust for the practice of violently impaling bulls with pointed objects and shouting loud *Olé's*, I didn't quite recognize what was, as it were, at stake. Similarly the hostility toward women in Mailer's protagonist was hard to distinguish from the casual contempt for women that was common then, in both literature and life.

Today, most heteros who admit to having engaged in anal intercourse (very few) will claim a different understanding of it. They attest that it invariably occurs during periods of profound and increasing intimacy, and regard it as an attempt to establish a still-greater degree of intimacy. If performed with caution and restraint, they continue, the shared carefulness and the proximity it has to violence can be the source of extremely intense pleasure. I agree.

There's almost certainly less of it going on today than a few years ago, and for at least two reasons. One is that the colon is the human body's

Watching Vince and Ava dither in the kitchen, Ferris has another a moment of doubt. Why *did* he come here? With some fatuous hope that nothing changes? Aside from a salting of grey hair, Ava seems to be the same woman—physically. But she is wary, chastened, closed, and now it comes to him, unerotic. Why?

Ferris is suddenly assailed by a flood of erotic memories. The way it started, for instance: Vince invites him for dinner. Ferris is between relationships, so he comes alone, dressed in bluejeans and shirt and tie, bringing a bottle of wine and flowers—they were chrysanthemums, so it would have been autumn. Ferris always keeps his seasons straight that way.

He's expecting a family dinner, to yap with the kid, and leave early. When he arrives there are only the two of them. Bobby is staying with an aunt.

At the dinner table the conversation rolls around to sex. Vince is doing the talking, Ferris isn't saying much, and Ava is impersonating the Mona Lisa, watching them both with an amused expression on her beautiful face. The flashpoint is sexual jealousy, which Ferris uncomfortably admits to feeling. Who doesn't?

"I don't," Vince claims. "I've never felt a twinge of it."

"I don't believe you," Ferris says.

Vince grins. "That's just your threatened sexuality talking," he answers. "Ava can fuck with whoever she wants. So long as she experiences pleasure, I do too."

"I suppose you sit on your hands and watch."

"Sometimes," Vince answers as if it were a completely mundane matter of fact. "But usually not for long."

Ferris eyes Ava, imagining her moaning and bucking in a stranger's embrace while Vince calmly watches. It's an arousing image, but one that makes his spine contract. It's Ferris's ex-girlfriend making it with her new man, and Ferris is being forced to watch—or is it Vince watching him and his ex?

Across the table, Ava unbuttons her blouse. She's not wearing a brassiere. She begins to fondle her nipples. They're inverted, and as Ferris stares, they grow erect beneath her fingers. Vince is watching her too, saying something Ferris doesn't follow. He sounds like a television game show host. With an effort, Ferris focuses on what he's saying.

most fragile and permeable membrane. Transmission of the AIDS virus, if it is present in deposited semen, is highly probable, and I'm told by my homosexual friends that even with protected sex, ejaculation now mostly takes place outside the body—just to be on the safest side of "safe" sex. Interestingly, one informant noted that this has resulted in an aesthetic improvement, because the presence of semen in the colon often caused unpleasant chemical reactions.

The second reason that anal intercourse is growing rare is more obtuse and political. All sexual intercourse involves violation of body integrity. In heterosexual relations, the male must penetrate the female. And this, given the social and interpersonal tensions of this era, has grown especially problematical. There is now, in a sense, no culturally acceptable way of having any kind of penetrative intercourse. The initial permission required for intercourse is among those, like the conferring of permanence, that this society no longer has the moral authority to grant,

"Well," Ferris hears Vince saying, "why don't you show Ferris what I'm talking about?"

Ava murmurs an "Uh*hum*" that is neither concurrence nor question, and stands up, sloughing off her blouse as she does so. She walks around the table, slips to her knees in front of Ferris, and begins to unzip his fly, nuzzling his crotch as she does it. Woodenly, Ferris helps her, undoing his belt and freeing his erect penis from his jeans. She inhales it expertly. Within seconds he's on the verge of coming, and she senses it. She pulls back, holding the head between two fingers, and looks up at him.

"Oh, no you don't," she says.

She leads him to the couch, where she slips off her skirt and sinks back against the material. She's not wearing panties. Ferris crouches between her thighs and lifts her legs over his shoulders. He tries to give her head, but she isn't very interested. She grabs his hair and looks into his eyes, the same amused look on her face.

"I want you inside me," she says. It's an order.

It's like a pornographic movie to Ferris, and he has to remind himself that this is really happening. He looks over at Vince, who is still sitting at the dinner table with an I-told-you-so smirk on his face. Ferris tries to slow down, to think of other things as he strips off his clothes, but it's impossible. His sense of irony has deserted him, and for the first time he can remember, there is no part of him standing aside, watching and analyzing. Vince is the watcher, here.

For a while, anyway. Ferris glimpses Vince removing his clothes, and as he kneels in front of Ava again, Vince moves past him to sit on the arm of the couch, his erection bobbing against her face. She slurps it hungrily as Ferris penetrates her.

Ferris comes in a few strokes, and in a state that is about equal parts tumescence and culture shock he watches his first live blowjob. At a distance of less than two feet, it goes on too long and it looks awkward. Eventually Vince pulls away, and as if Ferris isn't there, he pulls Ava off the couch onto the rug and mounts her.

---

and won't be able to until the disequities between men and women have been thoroughly corrected.

The pleasure of anal intercourse, finally, lies with the same permission that is at the core of all sexual intimacy. It may, in fact, contain the essential secret (and conundrum) of sexuality. All mutually erotic congress is an act of trust, and anal intercourse requires an extreme degree of trust. This notion has been emphatically confirmed for me by several homosexual friends. The necessary degree of trust now rarely exists between heterosexuals.

That people create intimacies and grant permissions to one another anyway, in defiance of the cultural tensions (and occasionally, common-sense parameters) that prohibit it, may explain the attraction of anal intercourse and other, more directly and/or symbolically violent acts. The border between social pathology and permissive ecstasy is more blurred right now than at any time in human history. It is a dangerous one to inhabit, and it will become more so in the next few decades.

Ferris doesn't quite know what to do, so he covers his confusion with a feigned empiricism. He lies on the rug beside them, watching Ava's face as they fuck. It's easier to watch her than him, somehow, or *it*. She remains composed and conscious, taking his hand and pulling it in to fondle her nipples as Vince pumps away, lost in his own groaning, grunting ecstasy. He takes what seems like forever to have an orgasm, and through most of it Ava's eyes are locked on Ferris, beads of sweat rolling off her forehead and neck, her hand rhythmically gripping his wrist as Vince's thrusts pound into her. When Vince finally does come it sounds and looks like he's dying. Ferris is half convinced that he and Vince are from a different species. But he doesn't get to think that one through. Ava reaches over, grabs his hair and pulls him to her. He kisses her lips, licks the sweat from her face. Behind him he feels Vince running his tongue along his spine. He closes his eyes.

Ava comes out of the kitchen with a teapot and three mugs on a tray. Vince follows with small cream and sugar jugs in matching ceramics, and some spoons. She slides the tray onto the coffee table, and Ferris realizes that she's left the vase back in the kitchen.

"That's milk there," she says, motioning at the cream jug. "I trust that will be fine."

The way she says it lets Ferris know she's not interested in the answer.

"Milk's fine," he says.

Vince eases his big body into the chair across from the couch, and Ava pulls one of the wooden chairs from the table and sits down opposite him, beside Vince.

"What do you think?" Vince asks, leaning over to pour the tea.

Ferris isn't sure what he's referring to, then realizes that he's being asked his opinion about the cottage.

"It looks pretty good," he say. "But very different, no? The old place was…"

"Bigger," Ava intervenes. "There's just the two of us, you know. And we live very quietly."

"I'll show you the workshop later," Vince adds. "You'll like it."

"You did all this yourself?"

"We did it," Ava says, emphasizing the "*we*."

Ferris can't quite stifle a smile. The Vince he knew would have cut off both thumbs before a quarter of this got completed. "You mean, *you* did it."

"I took a carpentry course, actually," Ava answers, a dry smile crossing her face momentarily.

Vince hands Ferris a mug of tea, with milk and sugar already in it. Not the kind of detail he'd have expected Vince to remember, but he does. And Ferris doesn't point it out. Instead, he recognizes that this is the most formal the three of them have ever been with one another, and the tension is exquisite. On the tail of that thought rides another: We want this to be over, all three of us. In our different ways.

Ferris doesn't know where to begin. Nothing new in that, Ferris muses. Well, there were always interminable awkwardnesses to this. How can you have casual conversation with a married couple immediately after you've had sex with them? You can't talk about the weather, because there isn't any. The world disappears, replaced by one's own overdrawn senses. You place your fingers in front of your nostrils and there is her scent, yours, and a third. There is a drop of come on your leg. Whose is it?

Then there were the other, trickier questions that Ferris couldn't quite ask: What is this for? Why Ferris and not someone else? Where is this supposed to lead?

If Vince had answers to those questions, he didn't offer them. He travelled in Ava's erotic wake, revelling in the foam of her mysterious agenda like a dolphin in the backwash of a ship. For Ava, there didn't seem to be any questions. She was inside, and of, the events, and one event simply led to the next.

This book concerns itself almost entirely with heterosexuality. For that, an explanation rather than an apology: As a perspicacious gay friend told me recently, the only sexual mysteries left are the heterosexual ones. He admitted to being completely befuddled by what heterosexuals think about sexuality, and about just exactly what they do in bed—aside from, he jokingly added, being depressed about it afterward. He was exaggerating, but only a little. Heterosexuality in the 1990s *is* confusing, and heterosexuals are more confused than my gay friend.

It hasn't always been this way. As recently as twenty or thirty years ago, there was a settledness about heterosexuality that had been, for centuries, unperturbed, unquestioned, and unquestionable—relatively speaking. Heterosexuality had a mainstream, a tiny avant garde that studiously flaunted normality, and a vast oppressed backwater that included nearly all women. Heterosexuality's

Not Ferris. The minute the event was done, he wanted to know where, and why, and what. And the only answers he got were what came next.

There were *explanations* to be had, of course. The first was predictable, and it brooked no further inquiry: *Why not?* That was the battle cry of their generation, but in this case Ferris couldn't quite separate the question and its answer from *Why me and not others?*

That got explained indirectly. There *were* others. A woman, whose name he was given along with explicit descriptions of what had gone on. She was Ava's choice, Ferris gathered, although no one said so. Ferris wanted to know whose choice he'd been, but he didn't ask.

The other explanations made his head spin. They'd wanted him for years. They loved him, in fact. Both of them, yes. Love, and friendship. Why not?

This revelation muddied things further. In theory he too loved his friends, Vince included. Maybe particularly. But neither love nor friendship would have occasioned him to invite Vince to sleep with his women, alone or with Ferris watching or participating. What did Vince get out of this? Was it just for the erotic kick he got?

"All those things are part of sex, Cuckoo," Vince explained one night when Ferris pushed the subject. "Ava wanted you. I did too."

"We didn't pick you out of a police line-up," Ava added. "Don't make this too complicated or it'll screw you up."

"It is complicated," Ferris said.

exclusive and absolute hold on normality was backed by church, state, and perhaps even by a situational common sense.

In the last five hundred years or so, the expansion of the species across the planet's uninhabited territories made most offspring wanted—if not adequately cared for by their parents or by society—and the need for economic and cultural mobility had, in the past century, made the nuclear family (the most efficient vehicle for successful breeding and mobility) a practical necessity—if not an enriching experience.

Very abruptly, times have changed. We're elbow to elbow and up to our necks in production debris, unemployed workers, and children without any future. Heterosexuals are no longer confident of their biological purpose, and the fabric of both the extended and nuclear families is in shreds. The result is a confusion about heterosexual practice, even a sense of futility and nihilism. The visibility and élan of sexual minorities, meanwhile, is open and on the upswing. Being hetero just ain't what it once was, and every hetero knows it.

"Well," Ava said, "you know what they say."

"What do they say?"

"They say that when a married woman wants to sleep with another man it means there's something wrong with her marriage."

"What do they say about men doing the same thing?"

She laughed. "They say it just means he has testicles."

"Yeah, well, who the hell are *they*, anyway?" Ferris said, getting irritable.

"They're the part of you that wants to believe what they're saying."

That didn't quite answer the question Ferris couldn't bring himself to ask either of them: Why does Ava *love* me?

The question, after ten years, is still there. In fact, it has grown. Now he wants to know *how* Ava loved him, not just why. And his perfect ego, stupid as always, wants to know if she still does.

———————————

Both Ava and Vince are gazing at him impatiently.

"Well," Ferris says, pausing to sip the tea. "I guess we should get on with it."

"I'm not sure what we're supposed to get on with," Ava answers, irony distributed about equally through the sentence. It coats each word with ice.

"I guess," Ferris says, hesitantly, "I want to know what's become of you. And I still don't quite understand *us*."

Question the validity of that description if you want, but one thing isn't questionable: Today it is far easier to find out what gays are and do than to figure out what it is to be comfortably and pridefully heterosexual. Several decades of non- and sometimes anti-hetero activism has produced a graphic and thorough body of open information about homosexual erotic and social habits, values, and practices, one that is now breaking down into extraordinarily detailed specialization of erotic and socio-political interest. No comparable database about heterosexuality exists. Several anecdotal "tee-hee" surveys exist, along with several more that are riddled with pedagogic and ideological nonsense. "Serious" literature is still stuck in the conventions of the nineteenth-century English novel, primarily offering descriptions of how much fun Planet of the Guys used to be for the guys—or how distasteful for women. With rare exceptions, heterosexual erotic literature is sexist, and the films are aesthetically awful and educationally useless, depicting women as brainless, cooing hose-monsters and men as walking hoser-poseurs. Our most

Another hesitation. Ava arches her eyebrows, Vince looks out the window. Ferris knows he sounds like a fifteen-year-old explaining why he's come home late with the family car.

"What happened, like."

Ava rolls her tongue around across her top lip. Ferris recognizes the gesture, but here it means something quite new.

"*You* disappeared," she says. "That's what happened. Not a word, no good-bye, no nothing. Why do you want to know what happened? You were there. And then you weren't. Were we supposed to come looking for you?"

Ferris shivers again, involuntarily. Was it really that open? A free choice, openly offered despite the nature of their arrangement and its strange discretions? Maybe.

He senses that it was, and then again it wasn't. It explains how easily he walked away from it, and it explains why they didn't come looking for him. But it doesn't explain either what they did together. And it leaves out the intervening years, and it says nothing about the obvious truth that a ménage-à-trois isn't exactly a configuration built for stability, emotional or any other kind. It was asymmetrical, unbalanced. With them—or maybe it was only with Ferris—the imbalances shifted constantly, creating new ground that was always somehow weirder. He'd get his head around one part of it, and the norm would move beyond, out there.

Vince doesn't say anything. He looks over at Ava and smiles, wearily. She

widespread and influential medium, television, has almost nothing at all to offer on the subject.

Any attempts being made to secure reliable empirical data about heterosexuality face a basic difficulty. Embattled groups that have power—real or imaginary—are notoriously *not* forthcoming about what really goes on among them, and the information they do divulge is usually loaded with mystifications, exaggerations, and other projections. The most interesting current hetero information is partisan and politicized, largely written by erotically dissident women in an attempt to get men to recognize their historical and present insensitivity, or to organize alternative structures.

Meanwhile, whatever homosexuality—male androsexuality or lesbianism—really is (and no one agrees on what it is) and whatever its possible genetic sources and animal-behaviour precedents and parallels, it is probably most usefully approached not as an aberration from normality but as one of humanity's more

smiles back, wryly, as if she's explaining something obvious to an obtuse child. "Maybe it's time you told us what was happening, Ferris."

Ferris puzzles over the solidarity he senses between Vince and Ava. It doesn't have anything to do with sex. Its basis is an almost monastic separateness, a formality that precludes sexuality rather than preludes it.

If he's reading it right, it's a dramatic change for Ava. The one certainty about her was her readiness for sex, anytime, any place, the weirder the better. She simply liked to have cocks around her or inside her, preferably more than one. Well, "simply" isn't the right word. She seemed to take her greatest pleasures from controlling him and Vince—from making them lose control, to be exact, and in being able to dictate where, when, and how they got off. She liked to see them come—liked to see the imminent orgasms, the helpless heedlessness of them, in their eyes. Sometimes Ferris thought he detected a kind of contempt for their immense, brainless neediness.

He's pretty sure she didn't have orgasms herself. And God knows he tried to make her have them. For nearly a year he became obsessed by it, going down on her literally for hours, licking and stroking every fold of flesh he could get his tongue on, keeping himself glued to her clitoris while Vince fucked her, whatever he could think of to get her over.

It never quite happened. She'd reach a plateau of pleasure, cruise it for a brief time, and then subside back to her zone of control. Vince seemed oblivious to all this, and Ferris didn't ever ask either of them about it. It

wonderful adaptive inventions. It meets a startling number of the criteria I've posited in this book for a more livable world and for the continued survival of the species: It is relatively non-violent, doesn't contribute to overpopulation, seems less addicted to—and less impressed by—testosterone. In general, it seems to me rather admirable.

If that's how I see it, I can hear a few of you asking, why don't I just go off and engage in homosexuality instead of pestering the hetero hordes about their lousy behaviour. The answer is simple. *I don't feel like it.* I mean that literally rather than colloquially—I *can't* feel like it. Given my hard-wiring, the choice is not any more open to me than it is to homosexuals. And as a poet I know once said, you can't be arbitrarily arbitrary. Besides, it is possible, and I'm seriously—not blithely—recommending this, to admire something you aren't or can't do when you're convinced that it is admirable. In fact, I'll go a step further. Maybe we ought to do what we can—with things like school sex-ed, liberal legislation, etc.—not just to make

was, after all, her show, and if not, then their show.

After an arduous session one night, Vince went off for a shower, leaving him to cuddle Ava. She suddenly sat up on the bed with her back to him.

"I'm in love with you, Ferris," she said, very slowly and carefully, as if she were pronouncing some sort of curse. He felt his heart constrict. Vince had already established that she loved him, but this was different. The situation was already crazy, and this zoomed it a lot crazier. Here was a woman, someone else's wife, a woman he'd been intimate with in almost every way except the conventional ones, and now she seemed to be saying she wanted to have an affair with him, and maybe a lot more than that.

"You know how I feel about you," Ferris answered after a tense silence. It was a careful answer, as careful as he could make it. Ferris wasn't sure what he felt for her, and he didn't want to use the word "love." Love is something people settle into, a comfortable, conventional intimacy. This wasn't comfortable, and it sure as hell wasn't conventional. He'd tried to convince himself that it was just sex, something they did without needing to talk about it. He knew that this wasn't quite accurate, but it made it easier to cope with.

"I don't know," she said, still not looking at him. "I don't know what you feel at all, Ferris, and I don't know what you think. You come here and we do all this, we make love, we fuck, but what does it count for?"

"A lot."

That was true. It did count for a lot, but what "a lot" meant, he couldn't have said. And here was a problem. It was great sex, great. No other word sufficed.

things safe for people who are trying to normalize their homosexuality but also to enable those who are somewhat interested or curious—bi's and semi-bi's—to get some experience with it in a context from which the hysteria and misinformation have been removed. At very least, homosexuality ought be accorded generous respect as a human practice on the basis of its record.

I've said almost nothing in this book, by the way, about lesbians, but I do note that a significant—and growing—number of women, have espoused—as it were—lesbianism with apparent success, happiness, and without measurably adding to the human atrocity/misery toll. For any heterosexual male to presume to speak about lesbians and their erotic and ethical stances is tantamount to walking on quicksand, and if I get through another three sentences on the subject without spewing sand I'll be lucky. Since lesbians are currently the most politicized sexual minority, discretion commands me to be brief and to the point.

And it satisfied his hunger for transgression, his need to affront convention. But how important was that out in the world? Not very, if he could walk away from it for weeks and months at a stretch. And what did it say about how he felt toward either of them? Not much.

"A lot?" she repeated. "You leave here in the morning like you're escaping. Where do you go? I don't know anything about your life. Do you ever think about me—about us—when you don't have your face buried between my legs?"

It was a deadly question—and he didn't have to answer it. Vince came out of the bathroom, still wet from the shower, with a towel around his head and shoulders. "So," he asked, "what are you two talking about?"

Before Ferris could dodge, Vince told him what he thought the conversation was about. "Ava wants to have a child with you. I think it's a good idea."

This wasn't what he and Ava were talking about, was it? He glanced at Ava and could read nothing, either way, from her expression. Maybe this is how she explained it to Vince, or maybe it was how Vince explained it to himself, made it into a practical reality. Vince's version was the more frightening, but either way, it scared the shit out of Ferris.

"You already have a child," Ferris said, tentatively. "If you want another, why don't you just go ahead and have one?"

"We didn't think about it until a little while ago," Vince said. "I had a vasectomy last year. Didn't think we'd want more kids. But Ava really loves you, Ferris. So do I. And why not?"

First, I will be very surprised if, in a generation, there are not more lesbians than male androsexuals. In part, this reflects the growing social autonomy of women in general, in part the diminished necessity of reproduction and their growing freedom from social institutions geared to keeping them barefoot and pregnant, and in part, the lousy treatment women have received from generation after generation of male lovers. I've always found it difficult to blame even the most separationist of lesbians for their choice. I might make the same one myself if I were a woman, and I could make it solely on the way most men continue to treat women in bed.

Still, if anyone thinks I'm saying this simply to play humble before an aggressive minority, they'd do well to read this book more carefully. The erotic practices I've recommended in this book—directly and tacitly—are much closer to the erotic behaviours of lesbians than they are to the heterosexual practices of the recent past—or to current or past practices popular among homosexual males.

Ferris's head was spinning. On this one, he could think of several dozen reasons why not, the best of them practical. Whose child would it be? Who would raise it? He was number three in this relationship in every way, and so far that had been fine. But what would happen if they were to throw a child out into the mix? Would the child have two fathers?

Oh, no, Ferris could see that this was altogether too crazy.

"This is a pretty amazing proposition," he said, trying to compose himself. "I need some time to think about it."

"Oh, sure," Vince said, very serious now. "Think about it."

Ferris takes a sip of tea. "I'm thinking about that time you asked me if I wanted to father a child with you," he says. "I never understood that."

Vince shrugs. "What's to understand? At the time, it was a serious offer. But you would have had to make a commitment, and you didn't. So it passed. That's when I began to realize just how screwed up you were, actually."

Ferris looks to Ava for confirmation. She looks out the window, and then back at him. "It was a bad idea," she says, slowly. "We had a lot of those, if you recall."

Oh yes, indeed. The worst one was Ferris's, kicked off from that incident. He decided that he wanted Ava for himself. Or at least, he wanted to see what it would be like between just the two of them. An affair, or whatever it might be

Notwithstanding the above, it seems to me that most of the public issues that now divide heterosexuals and homosexuals are either unimportant, or they're stupidly and excessively sectarian. Heterosexuals, admittedly, are all the things homosexuals accuse them of being. We're breeders, we're arrogant, we're often unadventurous and technically incompetent with our sexuality, and we tend to get depressed after sex instead of experiencing the exhilaration claimed by homosexuals. Hetero males are particularly easy targets for ridicule. We wear unfashionable clothing, don't speak foreign languages when ordering in fancy restaurants, don't work out enough, think only team sports matter, and then treat sports primarily as occasions for drinking beer, talking dirty, and swearing at our spouses. Indeed, hetero males are almost as bad as heterosexual women say they are. I'm sure you get the point without my having to run through the even sillier list of heterosexual complaints about homosexuals.

called in the circumstances. The nomenclature would need to be peculiar, but then his feelings for her were peculiar. Until that moment putting a name to them hadn't seemed relevant, or rather, it hadn't seemed possible.

Ava went along with it, for as far as it went. They met several times in anonymous hotels. Ferris was all over her, and she was either bored or diffident—Ferris couldn't decide which it was. He did everything he could to make her lose control of her reserve, to orgasm, but even though he licked and sucked and fucked her until she was raw he couldn't get her half as close as Vince and he did together. She let him do whatever he wanted, affectionate and slightly impatient at the same time, as if she were humouring a child. Whatever he thought he was doing, it was wide of the mark, and Ava gave him no hint of any alternative. Maybe she felt guilty because Vince wasn't there. After a while, Ferris did.

Alone, he and Ava discovered they had little to talk about. By unspoken agreement, they didn't talk about Vince or about the ménage-à-trois. They didn't talk about being in love, or about having a child, although Ferris imagined that he might be getting her pregnant. They didn't discuss how either of them got to the hotel, or how she would get back to the island afterward, they didn't discuss work or children, and they barely talked about the weather. They were left with a present that had to subsist within the walls of the hotel room, and a future that they might be risking by being there.

They met in the hotel lobby, rushed to the room, made love, and lay in the darkness without speaking. If this was the real thing, it wasn't nearly as exciting

Homosexuals, meanwhile, do have some excesses to answer for. In politics, excessive behaviour is occasionally necessary to alert the repressed and the apathetic, or to liberate the oppressed. More often than not, the excesses get out of hand. Some of the radical sexual practices gays have adopted have had unforeseen side effects, and, sorry, nobody is being *entirely* candid about their consequences. Homosexuals who've admitted to having had between five hundred and two thousand sexual partners during the 1970s and 1980s were common—and vocal. AIDS has now silenced most of them.

I suspect that any competent immunologist could have told us that no species is capable of surviving that degree of intimate individual contact without radically increasing the incidence and variety of infectious diseases. They would have pointed out that it was a form of incest—immune system incest, which is the kind that really counts. No one asked the questions. We're now learning the hard way:

as the unrealities they were cheating on. Ava didn't get pregnant, and they stopped meeting without having to admit they were going to. Ferris was disappointed and relieved at the same time.

Now, here, he has a sudden instinct that Vince had known about it all along, and that if not, he certainly knew now. "I had some dumb ideas in those days," Ferris says, looking at Vince and feeling guilty.

"You mean like trying to take Ava away from me?" he says. "Yeah, I knew you were trying. I wasn't worried. I thought you'd figure it out for yourself soon enough."

"How did you find out?"

"Ava told me she was seeing you. I told you we trusted each other completely. You didn't believe it like you didn't believe a lot of the rest of what I said. More tea?"

Ferris decided to leave "the rest of it" alone. "Another cup is fine. Why didn't you stop it?"

"Why would I? Ava was crazy about you ... and I thought you might see what we were offering you."

Ava fills Ferris's cup, tops up her own and Vince's, and goes off to the kitchen to make more. Watching her do this simple thing, Ferris tries to fathom how she sorted out complexities like the ones he'd created for her. Did she sort them out at all? He could hardly fault her if she didn't. He hadn't, not really.

From the beginning of it, Ferris had difficulty living with the idea that he

Given the fragile biological construction of human beings, cultural and sexual exogamy might be quite a bit more than a lifestyle option. Practised judiciously, it is the backbone of a healthy culture and a healthy psyche. Practised en masse and without protection, it is lethal. The homo vanguard went too far, and that is a tragedy from which we all must share the catharsis.

Having mucous membrane contact with everyone in one's peer group was, I'm told, a liberating experience and quite probably an excellent organizational procedure. It was an amazing thing to have done—courageous, thrilling, and foolhardy at the same time. Heteros don't like to admit this, but many of us were secretly envious while the Bacchanalia was in full swing. And let's be clear about this. If heteros hadn't been so obsessed with holding the family, the military, and the banking system together, we'd have been doing it too.

Let's be clear about a couple of other things, while we're here. Homosexuals

was sexually involved with a married couple. How many times had he sat on the ferry on the trip back and told himself it was too weird, that he couldn't handle it any longer?

Yes, but it was also the ferry rides, together with the isolation of the island, that protected it, and him. No one knew he had this other life. To his friends, Ferris was someone who sometimes disappeared for a few days, that's all. Not generally available on weekends. If a friend asked where he was, he mentioned business. If business associates asked, he used his friends as an excuse.

After the "affair" ended, it got harder, and he didn't return to the island at one point for almost eight months. He found several new lovers, tried hard to stay interested in them, but couldn't. When he starting coming back to the island regularly, there were no recriminations, no oblique punishments, no reluctances. But there was a subtle erotic escalation, so subtle that he didn't notice it at first.

Ferris was conducting his own subtle escalation. He was competing with Vince, holding off his orgasms until after Vince had his, or breaking off to watch them fuck, nestling close to Ava, cuddling her, kissing her breasts or face or neck, holding her eyes with his while Vince came. Then he'd have her to himself, and he put on performances that were as much for Vince as for Ava.

They weren't always comfortable performances, because Vince had some unsubtle ways of watching. He'd lie with his face next to Ava's vagina, slipping Ferris's cock out of her and into his mouth for a few strokes. Or while Ferris was fucking with Ava, Vince would play with his balls, or lick his asshole. Several

didn't invent AIDS. Recent discoveries tell us that the virus has been with us for at least two centuries. It has been unleashed by our globalization of economic, social, and biophysical systems, all of which carry exogamy to extremes without examining the long-term consequences. I'm not being flippant about this—after two hundred thousand deaths, there's neither cause nor occasion for that. The situation in Central Africa, where more women than men are dying, indicates that AIDS in the West is only temporarily a homosexual phenomenon. If globalization is not to become our doomsday machine, we are all going to have to alter a lot of our behaviours, sexual and otherwise. And we'll have to do it without becoming xenophobic or likewise morally insane. The response of North America's homosexual community to AIDS can serve as a model for sensible and humane adaptation.

The only other question I want to raise about homosexuality has to do with lifestyles. Is sexual orientation enough to hang a personal or community identity

times Vince insisted on joining in on fellatio—at least once, due to last-second manoeuvres, Ferris came in Vince's mouth. Vince seemed to enjoy all of this, and Ferris, well, didn't.

Meanwhile, the configurations and combinations were escalating, getting wilder and weirder. Each round of love-making seemed to require a new configuration. Some of them were simply contortions—easy enough to adapt to. Then came vibrators and dildos, an uncomplicated fourth partner. There was a decipherable symmetry to the escalations. Each time, Ferris was offered the more extreme posture. At the next session, Vince began there. Oils appeared, anal intercourse was introduced. At that, Ferris at first balked.

"Don't be a prude," Vince said. "It isn't painful if it's done right. You lubricate properly, and come into her from the front, just like conventional fucking. You'll like it. She does."

Ava, lying between them on the bed, arched her back and licked her lips.

Then Ava wanted them both in her vagina at the same time. It was a difficult, contorted manoeuvre, and Ferris was convinced that it was painful for her. A few days afterward, he phoned and asked her point-blank.

"It was pleasant," she said, her voice cool. "Should we be talking about this on the phone?"

"It didn't look like it was pleasant," he said. "It looked painful. And it felt painful."

"It hurt you?" she answered, her tone still cool.

"No, damn it. It hurt you. I hurt you."

on, as nearly every element of the gay community has? Homosexuality has become the gender equivalent of ethnicity, in which individuals define their political and cultural identities by a single—and political—point of reference. I'm aware that doing this has helped to raise the pall of political oppression, but it has also created a commercialized sub-community, and a new generation of gays who are about as radical as Rotarians.

As someone who received the best parts of my academic and artistic education from homosexuals, I may suffer from too-high expectations. I may also be doing, in a slicked-up way, what liberals have always done to partially liberated minorities: demanding exemplary behaviour across the board, asking that they retain the degree of social and political alertness they had while they were more marginalized and threatened. Maybe I should recognize that in a civilization (or is this now just an economy?) that is trying to make citizenship and mediocrity mean the same

"Ferris, sweetie," she said as if instructing a child. "Sometimes it's hard to tell the difference between pleasure and pain. In any case, if I'd wanted you to stop, I would have said so."

"You would have."

"Yes. Don't you understand that?"

He told her he did.

Ferris realizes that he's staring at Ava, remembering being in those strange and stranger embraces with her, helplessly recalling her scent and taste and the myriad erotic postures in which he's seen her exquisite body. He knows more about her, been more intimate with her than any woman he's been with. At the same time, he knows almost nothing about her, nothing comfortably human. Doesn't intimacy leave indelible traces? Where are they, here?

"Don't, Ferris," Ava says. "I don't want to be looked at like that. Not by you, or Vince, or anyone else."

"I'm sorry," he says. He *is* sorry. "That certainly isn't why I'm here."

"So why are you here, exactly?"

Tough question. Mentally he goes over the list: curiosity about the events of the last ten years, an old friend's and lover's distant concern, some personal curiosity about how a beautiful woman has aged. All acceptable motives. But there's a surprise item on the list, and it isn't acceptable: Ferris isn't sure he

thing, homosexuals are doing better than the rest of us. There's no reason why homos can't be as mediocre and boring as heteros, but still…

I guess what worries me is this: To willingly enter a sequestered zone where only one's peer group rules matter carries a set of dangers we seem to be forgetting only fifty years after we had a world war to free ourselves from them. History demonstrates how quickly a tribal domain or lifestyle enclave becomes a ghetto, a concentration camp—or, on the aggressive side of the scale, a *fascista*. In its extreme forms, tribalization reduces everything to scale, power, and prestige, making it easier to exterminate rivals and strangers—and be exterminated by them. It is the opposite of democracy, which seeks to create and celebrate distinction and difference. A few decades ago we were headed toward a democratized community of the whole, a megacommunity of copper-coloured polysexuals with a range of preferences wider and more colourful than the rainbow. Where did we lose that?

An Authorial Crisis

Here, as elsewhere in this book, I'll go the direct route: A private crisis occurred during the writing of this chapter, episode, story. The crisis was unexpected, precipitated by Ferris's confrontation of the erotic emblem of simultaneous anal and vaginal intercourse. The practice he was referring to is a troubling one—morally, politically, and now, perhaps, medically. Current gender relations make it more troubling again.

You don't have to accept the story's implication that Ava instigated it. This is, after all, being written by a male, and everyone knows how good they've been at blaming their victims. Even accepting that Ava was the instigator, it's reasonable to speculate that the roots of her erotic predilec-

wouldn't tumble into the sack with them right now if they proposed it.

He frowns, tries to rid himself of the thought. "Tell me what happened with the child you adopted."

Ava looks at the floor, and Vince sinks back in his chair with a sigh.

"There's not much to tell," he says. "She had learning disabilities, you knew that. She didn't improve, and by the time she was fifteen, we had a major behaviour problem on our hands. All sorts of incidents, one thing after another. Eventually she was caught breaking into the house of one of our neighbours, and she got sent to a juvenile home. We sprung her, but after that, it was worse. She'd be here for a few days, and then she'd disappear for weeks on end. Then she stopped coming. We don't even know where she is, now. In jail, I think."

"I'm sorry," Ferris says. "What about Bobby?"

"What about him?" Vince replies. "He's around. He has his own place in town, works, goes to school part-time. He just outgrew the island, that's all. This isn't much of a place for young people."

"Are you two happy?"

Ava answers. "Sometimes. Yes." There's a long hesitation. "We've been in therapy for three years. That's helped a lot."

"What for?" Ferris asks, without thinking.

"It got out of hand," Vince answers for her. "There was nothing in our lives but sex. It was an addiction."

Their distance makes it feel more like there's a continent between them and him rather than a few feet. The distance was there when he arrived, but now it is tangible. And it is growing, solidifying.

tions lie in an abusive pre-history that she—and the story—doesn't elucidate. Why else would a woman gather all her pleasures from control rather than orgasm?

You could also impose ideology over situation and opine that the whole thing is a cover-up for the fact that all-men-are-exploitive-crapheads-so-let's-beat-the-shit-out-of-them, including this author. To substantiate that, you could point out that the sexual practice depicted is a frequent plot denouement (I'm carefully avoiding the word "climax") to a high percentage of blue movies.

Any and all such responses will find considerable support in different quarters. My comment, here as elsewhere, is that ideological posturing rarely results in the demilitarization of a war zone.

"We didn't understand that, not really. Nobody does, anymore. We thought the pleasure we wanted, or whatever it is life is about, was somewhere else, something else, some*one* else. That's what you were all about, what that whole thing was about. It felt like a big mountain we were climbing, but we were only climbing out of ourselves. We discovered that what matters is the village at the base of the mountain. Now we get up in the morning and work on things. One day at a time."

Ferris can feel disappointment straining against his discretion. Vince has just given him a cliché-ridden Alcoholics Anonymous speech. It's evidently a sincere one, and the small smile on Ava's face as he speaks confirms her agreement.

"But you know, Ferris," Vince says after an awkward silence Ferris doesn't break, "we're okay, now. It started to come around when we realized that life isn't supposed to be easy. None of what we did was a total waste of time. We had to go through it and come out on the other side. I think that's what you're doing, too, in your own way. It's too bad you have to do it alone."

Ferris shrugs. Maybe, just maybe, it is that simple. The way they lived, the dangers must have kept growing, while the payoffs got smaller, or at least harder to find. Eventually, the accumulated discretions and indiscretions must have toppled over on them in some terrible way. Maybe in the real world, maybe just in their minds. But maybe they just got tired of the complications, and stopped. So maybe the unfinished business he came here to settle isn't unfinished, and there are no revelations forthcoming.

Well, not quite. Ever since he got on the ferry this morning, he's been wrestling, somewhere in his subconscious, with the puzzle of how Vince and he

Meanwhile, let me clarify the fiction/reality interface. Whether the incident under scrutiny is drawn from my experience or is an invention doesn't matter. It should suffice if I admit what everyone who writes or reads fictions knows, or ought to: that creativity does not occur in a vacuum, and that characters in a novel are neither inventions nor replicas of living persons. I'll go an aggressive step past that and admit that the inclusion of this incident is deliberate, and that its inclusion is something to which I've given extremely careful thought: i.e., these things happen out there, and they can't be dismissed by political side-taking or censorship.

To me, what matters more than the incident's origin and pedigree is that it is the instrument by which Ferris discovers and tries to confront his private sexual frontier. For

performed simultaneous anal and vaginal intercourse with Ava. He's certain it took place, because he can distinctly remember the sensation of his and Vince's penises touching through the thin membrane between them. What's bothering him—what's been bothering him for a long time—is the configuration.

It was part of an obscure fidelity Ferris kept, and he'd been subtle enough with it that he was certain that neither Vince nor Ava were aware of it. But throughout everything they did, Ferris had not once entered Ava unless they were face to face. Now, suddenly, he realizes the configuration he wants isn't physically possible. He's been deluding himself. Vince had been on his back, she kneeling forward on his chest, and Ferris was squatting behind her. In the crudest possible sense, Ferris had fucked her up the ass, impersonally, like a dog would. And for ten years, he'd been blocking the memory of it.

"What's wrong, Ferris?" he hears Ava asking. His consternation must have shown in his face. "Were you expecting more?"

Ferris looks at the ceiling. "No," he says. "I just thought of something. It's obscure stuff. Nothing to do with you."

He wants to tell Ava he's sorry, but what he's sorry about is so oblique there's no way he can make her understand—even if she wanted to. It's the truth, but sex delivers an almost infinite number of truths, all equal. It's also true that he didn't return after that because he was frightened to. Beyond unrestricted pleasure he'd glimpsed its opposites: violence and pain. And in Ferris's mind, they had crossed the boundary.

Or maybe that's what *I'm* seeing and saying, and Ferris is nothing but a sexual cuckoo that vacated the nest when it got too hot inside. I'd like Ferris to see

him it is the frontier in just about every sense he can name—erotically, politically, morally. It happens that it is—big surprise—mine as well. It is as far as I can take you, and as far as I will go.

Yet it is our private *frontier*, and not a wall. Beyond it is a zone of sexual practices we can't distinguish from violence. We don't understand them, and we can't operate within them. The eros is incomprehensible, the social and emotional triggers and routes alien, the ultimate moral and political dimensions frankly insane. But because we—Ferris and I—are on a frontier, there are no border guards or customs officials to tell us when we are on one side or the other, and that makes the experience an extremely contemporary one, one that might challenge others to find theirs. As a result, my story deliberately has

it, but what's the point of inflicting my erotic insights on him—or on Vince and Ava? I could do all sorts of comforting things here. I could make Ferris grovel for forgiveness, join their chapter of Sexaholics Anonymous—or form his own. I could force him to admit that he'd started a primary relationship soon after he left, and when that failed, another, ad nauseam. Or less comforting, I could make him confess a secret he's kept even from himself: that sex was never so good as it was with them, not before, not after.

But there's nothing discreet for him to say, nothing more he needs to know or say about this. By a different route, he's come to the same conclusions they have. It's time to go.

"I should catch the next ferry back," Ferris says. "But you're right. Life isn't supposed to be easy. I just wish I'd known that twenty years ago."

Ava smiles. It's a real one this time, and as Ferris gets up to leave, she reaches over and grasps his hand. "So do we," she says. "But we didn't."

It's too early to leave for the ferry, so Ferris and Vince wander out to the workshop, where Vince shows him an array of power tools and a birdhouse he's planning to elevate next to the living-room window. It's a mess, big enough to house a raven, but Ferris doesn't say so.

On the ferry back from the island, Ferris writes this in his notebook:

What if our erotic lives are not written on water, but are a kind of graffiti scribbled on the planetary and cosmic slate, an inscription of meaningless insights and temporary states of emotions and prejudice by which we are nonetheless going to be mercilessly judged, not by a divine being but by the volume of darkness and misery we generate with them.

no dramatic resolution, and the characters, Ferris, Ava, and Vince, have to do what we all have to do in circumstances that don't add up: go on living.

Each day, unless we are simple-minded, lucky, or extraordinarily privileged, we live amidst similarly unresolved contradictions. We make situational decisions that turn out to have absolute resonance, or we make what we think are absolute decisions that are rendered irrelevant the next day by events we didn't predict. That's how life works, and I don't think art should pretend it is any other way.

As I write this, for instance, the Bosnian Serb militia are shelling a Muslim-held village somewhere in the hills of Eastern Bosnia—or is it Western Serbia. Innocent people are being killed or injured, their property is being destroyed, their ability to make a livelihood

"Well then," he says aloud, "I will generate no more darkness."

The man sitting next to him looks up from the book he's been dozing over. "What did you say? Were you talking to me?"

Ferris laughs. "No," he says. "Not directly. Thinking out loud, I guess."

He pulls his bag onto his shoulder. The ferry is nearing the mainland terminal, but he's got time for a pee before it docks. After that, he has distant places to go, faraway people to meet and write lies about.

Over the urinal is scribbled the following barely literate message:

I just had fuck a chery Nazi asshole.

I guess the confusion is universal, Ferris thinks to himself as he tries to come up with an answer to the graffito. Trouble is, it exists in specific conditions. Some of them lead easily to violence, others get resolved by small bursts of insight, and some simply remain unanswered and unrelieved.

He feels the gentle bump of the ferry meeting the slip, hears the rumble of the motors as they reverse. He leaves the graffito unanswered, and seconds later he's back in the crowd of travellers hurrying to the next destination.

is being impaired, as is their psychological ability to live normal lives. For those who survive this event—a group that, in this media-enriched global community, ought to include you and me—months, years, perhaps even decades may have to pass before we can forget and be healed.

Or minutes. Seconds after seeing the bodies of the latest shelling victims lying in their own blood in some shattered street, some of us may click off the television news, roll over in the bed, and become aroused at the sight of a lock of our sleeping mate's hair.

What I'm trying to say here is this: Sex has its limits. While it does a better job than anything else I can name of satisfying our longings for being, it provides nothing for our longings for meaning. Most of us recognize that it is the great *I Am*. When it is good, it can be the great *We Are* and occasionally, the great *This Is*. These latter two are there to protect us from the backswing, on which always rides the *Great Nothing*, but only by allowing us to see it as the great *Sweet Fuck All*.

Sex is not a social or interpersonal beast of burden. It is just sex. No more and no less. It doesn't get the laundry done, doesn't get food on the table at dinnertime. It can't substitute for common interest, mutuality of taste and values, and it doesn't replace good faith, discretion, and kindness, as anyone who has slept with a rotten person and enjoyed it knows. Not for long, anyway.

I could put all these insights into Ferris's head and have him leg them out. That would have presented me with two technical alternatives. In one, he would have jerked back and forth like a puppet, carrying out my concocted, wilful mission. In the other, two thousand pages from here, he would still be chasing after the meaning of his sexuality, women's sexuality, and the perfect conduit between them. By the time he finally finds the perfect woman, he won't be able to make any more than casual contact with her because there will be almost nothing permissible left that can establish an intimacy. (Eventually, on his way to pick up his OAP cheque, he will be run over and killed on a street corner by a woman in a dilapidated Toyota. It will be neither personal nor symbolic, and the ending will have been constructed after my death by a friend eager to settle my estate.)

Those literary alternatives are too logical, and too far removed from the dynamics of our condition. And anyway, both this novel and the conversation that accompanies it are an attempt to depict the state of sexual and gender chaos we endure and will continue to endure for the foreseeable future. Let me strain the limits of artifice in less conventional ways, flinch, and get on with it.

Animal

magine the poet William Blake at the beginning of the nineteenth century, sitting in the scruffy Lambeth garden he believed was inhabited by angels and demons, writing his famous metaphor about how the Tygers of Wrath are wiser than the Horses of Instruction. You don't have to agree or disagree with him. Instead, try to imagine what that kind of blue-eyed optimism about human life might feel like.

Ferris and I live in a world without angels or demons. What interests us instead are the activities of animals and human beings. We agree on the analysis—and update—of Blake's metaphor: The demonic Tygers he saw all around him are long extinct, and we're left with a few common tigers, mostly in zoos. These days, only pigs and sheep are angry, and horses no longer give lessons. (Hard to, when they're being pumped full of steroids to make them run faster.)

Stories

We're also interested in the distinctions that can be made between human beings and animals. As this story breaks into our conversation, Ferris is saying that he can't see any distinctions. I'm more generally more optimistic about this, as you probably recognize. I'm trying to get him to come to terms with what happened between him and Annie.

All Ferris will say about that extended episode in (or as he sees it, "out of") his life is a single sentence: *I married Annie but it didn't last.*

That's more neutral than what he'd say if I pumped a few drinks into him. He'll elaborate then, but only slightly: I *married Annie,* he'll say, *but she was a nightmare.* Another couple of drinks and he'll go slightly further: *I knew marrying Annie was stupid but I couldn't figure out any other way to make her happy.*

All three of these statements are partially true. To Ferris, the first one has the virtue of, well, greater discretion. My objection to each of them is that they aren't enough for even a small, piercing tale, which is what this needs to be.

Need? Yes. I still think there's a need to resolve the Mexican Stand-off this novel began with and to uncover what, if anything, Ferris learned from it. I would prefer a large canvas to draw it on, one with self-sacrifices, reconciliations, epic emotions, and some glamorous, galvanizing insights. At very least I'd like some civilized, generous behaviour. But Ferris refuses to co-operate. On this subject, all he has is silence, one or two tactical wisdoms, an unresolved miniature Cold War and a portrait of small animals acting small and becoming smaller as the surrounding wilderness looms heavier and darker around them.

I've caught him just after his return from a trip to the Far East, where he went to research an article on the wonders of Laotian cuisine. He didn't find any, wrote the article anyway, and then skipped off on a side trip to Vietnam, following a French film crew through the Mekong Delta and then on to Ho Chi Minh City. He was trying to get a leg up on a guidebook for this soon-to-be-rehabilitated tourism opportunity. Once there, he was equally startled by the country's beauty and by its abject poverty. Out of respect, he left his notebook in the hotel and flew back to North America.

Ferris says this about Annie, when I prod him: "If she'd been an animal, she'd have been a small chestnut mare of uncertain breed and breeding running heedlessly through a dark forest. For two years I ran with her. Somehow, I survived. End of story."

Unsatisfied, I keep on prodding. "Nightmare or not, didn't you love her?"

His face tightens. "Yeah. Sure. But it was a private existential project, and I don't want to discuss it."

"If she was what you're suggesting," I answer, "then what were you?"

He grins, lamely, not enjoying himself. "How about a half-blind dray horse drunk on hormones and confused by the musky perfumes of the forest?"

"That isn't a nightmare. That's comedy."

"It was a nightmare because I was trying to run in her wake," he says, letting himself become a little bit amused by his metaphor. "Okay. I suppose maybe there was a comic side to it. Being part of her life was sort of like living in a television commercial—the kind where a horse slo-mo's across an idealized landscape—a beach or a hillside—so you'll think that smoking a certain brand of menthol cigarettes is going to make your life feel like you're on the horse… Except that this wasn't a television commercial, and I wasn't riding on the horse. I was the sweating glue-factory candidate who kept on crashing into the tail end of the slo-mo sprints and collapsing the sets. There's an element of slapstick there, but slapstick is only fun from a distance. When you're on the business end of the stunts, it's no fun at all."

I take up his third opening statement.

"Sure," he admits. "I knew marrying Annie was stupid and mutually dooming. Does that make me the villain? What was I going to do? She wanted to get married. I was nuts about her, and I did what she wanted."

"Too easy," I say.

Ferris raises one of his eyebrows. "No," he says. "Not easy at all. Horses, even when they're existentially motivated, are dumb, but they're not perverse. They can be ridden into brick walls or over cliffs. Sometimes they'll toss their rider when they recognize what it is they're facing, but mostly they don't. I didn't."

"If a horse jumps off a cliff," I ask him, "does anyone hear it whinny as it plunges to the rocky canyon floor?"

"Not in my case," Ferris answers, pretending to look pathetic.

We're getting close to silliness here, or worse, "guy talk," and I say so. "Sheep," I add, "have as much insight into their personal behaviours as you and Annie displayed."

Ferris shrugs that one off. "Lust turns people into animals. Love doesn't always, but it can."

Human beings aren't *dumb* animals, and in the human universe, no behaviour is so simple that it can be excused with single words: love, lust, stupidity, perversity. I tell Ferris I can't let him off that easily. "What was your subconscious agenda? What was Annie's, come to think of it? What kinds of human beings were you and why so stupid and wrong-headed?"

"That's too many questions at once," he says. "But you're right. Annie wasn't a simple person. On her good days, she was an obtuse one, hard to please, and she didn't have very many good days. It wasn't until it was too late that I figured out that what pleased her changed every second or third day."

"So what were the human qualities that turned her into a nightmare?"

I keep running into people—solemn, deadly serious people—who suggest that we live under a patriarchy that is male, evil, and destructive. If the species is to progress or simply survive, they say, the Patriarchy must be eradicated. Usually they call for a return to some adaptation of the matriarchies that appear to have governed kinship groups prior to the first Aryan tribal migrations into the Mediterranean and Western Europe about five thousand years ago. If these serious people are ecology-minded they will call for something they call an omniarchy: rule by—depending on the hagiography they use—archetypes, ecofeminists, vegetarians, or virtuous folks who wear Birkenstock

"Well, that one. And maybe the fact that when I first met her, she was a dream."

He stops, allows the dream to haunt him. It's an admirable thing to do, and I like him for it.

"It's hard to describe what it was like—this woman comes out of nowhere, and her life fits mine like a glove. Maybe that's where I was at fault. I accepted it, and I accepted her—and it forced her to try to make the dream real."

"You mean that she became a nightmare trying to sustain the phony dream?"

"Something like that. And really, there *were* some good times. I just don't remember them. She was only a nightmare toward the end, and then what spilled me on my ass were her quick shifts back and forth from loony-tunes to rational behaviour. Except when she was freaking out, she was ultra-rational. Maybe I was the crazy one."

"Yeah," I reply, "but you understand rationalism, don't you? It generates meaning on the basis of what the operator assumes—before the facts or the situation—to be true."

Ferris looks at me with glazed eyes. "Maybe," he said, "it happened because relationships are all nightmares these days. Maybe we should just fuck occasionally, and go free."

"All relationships? That's a little too easy," I tell him. And between you and me, even if it does contain a grain of truth, this is about Ferris and Annie, an animal story, not the prelude to a string of sociological generalities that'll just make us all feel helpless. To get you to understand Ferris's *personal* nightmare, I have to induce you see the specific logic of it: the animal moves Annie had, and the animal Ferris became in response.

Try this. When they split up the marriage, there is a nasty, expensive court battle over the distribution of their communal assets. Ferris wants

sandals. Ultimately, they're talking about government by well-educated middle-class professionals of one sort or another, generally ones who resemble themselves.

Not to ridicule these well-intentioned, serious folks, but it is very hard to eradicate things you can't locate except by way of your own ambitions and prejudices or cultural/personal wounds. The Patriarchy they so despise exists, and any sensible person knows it does. Unfortunately it rarely shows up in an eradicable form long enough for anybody to get at it. It doesn't have offices, troops under direct command, or identifiable leaders and figureheads. It doesn't have firm values or an ideology, and its intoxicant-of-choice, testosterone,

his half, Annie wants everything, and lawyers are soon slithering around them like bullsnakes in a peat bog. This part of his nightmare goes on for months, petition and counter-petition, screaming, all-hours jackdaw phone calls and public scenes between.

On the day of the final hearing, Ferris finds himself sitting, exhausted, broke, and feeling extremely vulnerable, in a courtroom. He is there to listen to his lawyer's summary arguments to the presiding judge, and to witness the judge as he decides if Annie is going to get to screw him financially, and if so, how completely she'll get to do it.

Except that Ferris isn't really listening or witnessing. He's gazing at Annie, actually, thinking how attractive she is. Luckily for him, the judge calls their fight a draw. Ferris doesn't hear a word of the judgement. He's admiring the rich red of Annie's hair and recalling how her eyes look in the dark, and to hell with the fact that she's given him considerable justification to despise her. But he isn't feeling any such emotion—and he isn't hearing a word of the court's judgement—until his lawyer elbows him.

"Hey, Ferris," the lawyer says, "wake up. It went our way. You're supposed to be jumping up and down with joy."

"Oh," Ferris answers, distractedly. "I guess. Great. That's great. You did great work."

He is having mixed emotions, second thoughts, a crisis of conviction. He's won the court battle, but it doesn't feel like he's won anything at all. A painful episode in his life has just been declared legally finito, over and done with, and he's missing all the hoopla.

No, that isn't what he's missing. He's missing Annie. She'll be so pissed off at losing the court decision that she'll never speak to him again.

He watches her stand up and stretch her arms in the air, languid, oddly indifferent to the proceedings.

isn't even a controlled substance.

In short, patriarchy is easy to hate, easier still to sneer at. But when you try to spear it with a stick and hold it up for all to see, it slithers away.

In a recent (1988) essay written in a typical delirium of moral comfort, eco-theologian Thomas Berry has called the current version of the Patriarchy—and I'm paraphrasing only slightly—rule by wealthy white guys. It's a tempting definition, because it implies that if we can just smear some squash pie and brown rice on their business suits, they'll have a change of heart and give up their business suits and the nasty behaviours that seem to go with wearing them.

She even, remarkably, smiles at her lawyer. She'd been fucking him all through the trial, Ferris thinks to himself. Oh well. None of his business now.

But as the entourage of lawyers, clerks and clients files out of the room, Annie doesn't seem interested in fucking her lawyer. She lags behind, catches Ferris's eye, shrugs as if it all means nothing, and smiles. As they reach the door, she "accidentally" stops in front of him so that he bumps into her from behind.

"I'm sorry," he apologizes, warily, half expecting her to pull out a knife and stab him in the throat—or at least to bite his head off like she's been doing while their divorce was before the court. He's also attempting to mind-control the erection that is beginning to distort the front of his trousers.

"Don't worry about it," she says. "I'm fine. Everything is fine. You want to have lunch?" She turning her body sideways so that, in passing, her hand momentarily grazes his bulging fly.

He loses. "Sure."

Two hours later they are in bed, fucking, as they used to say in Ferris's home town, like mink.

Now, let's be clear that this isn't a semi-romantic anecdote about two people trying to rekindle a marriage. It's about an expensive piece of ass, a declaration of Ferris and Annie's joint membership in the Bimbo Brigade (a gender-indiscriminate organization exclusively reserved for the human species). In their defence, I can only suggest that in joining the BB, they are part of western civilization's fastest-growing enclave, and they are exercising the privileges of membership. In other words, they are in character, behaving like stupid animals.

Let me counter his definition with a more serious one: *Patriarchy was, is, and will remain the organization of human relations by violence.* It probably arose during the late Neolithic period not because a bunch of white guys decided they wanted to someday own BMWs, carry cellular phones, and possess other emblems of advanced capitalist evolution, but because human populations had begun to crowd against one another and life, as a result, was getting nasty. The crowding engendered an unremitting phenomenon every political system since has been a reaction to: territorial tribalism, of which violence is the primary and ultimate instrument. Tribalism hasn't ever been pretty,

There is a slightly kinder explanation. However stunted and perverse Ferris and Annie's moral values and interpersonal solidarity, they are also the victims of a social fact that seems to be eluding everyone these days. Without specific reasons for solidarity, they did what most people do when their relationship begins to display its structural weaknesses. They formalized it by getting married.

Quite frankly, I don't know why people get married and expect the institution to protect them from their unexamined appetites and attitudes. Marriage just isn't the necessary adjunct to domestic happiness and order it once was. Most of the time, it isn't even helpful. These days, there are far more and better incentives for people to act like myopic hedonists than to opt for the domestic solidarity, endurance, or other kindly uses of the brain a good marriage demands. There are just too many consumer distractions, too many incitements to singularity, too many entertainment-lined alternatives. That's why, as with Ferris and Annie, a trip to the altar more often turns into a trip to the zoo.

Hardly anyone cares if couples stay together except their parents, a few right-of-centre religious leaders, and an unemployed former U.S. vice-president who isn't exactly known for the depth of his analyses. And marriage failure may scar our real estate portfolios and make us bitterly unhappy, but it still isn't quite like getting hit in the face with a rifle butt. I may harp on that point, but it's valid. And divorce is little more than a make-work activity for an over-sized legal community. Neither marriage nor divorce has any serious moral implications.

Let me go all the way. In the latter part of the twentieth century, most marriages are short, banal experiences or long, obscure co-dependencies. The institution is fouled by obsolete romantic expectations that are generally exhausted before the marriage vows are mumbled, and the rituals have been supplanted by legal statutes but for a couple of thousand years it kept marauders out of the compound while the deep thinkers dreamed up other ways to do things.

Now, matriarchies, which are excellent at organizing family-sized units and better still at successfully fostering large, healthy families, were ill-equipped to acquire and defend the territory that an increased and colliding population demands. Quite simply, those skilled at violence took over, and here we are today with Serbians trying to eradicate their tribal enemies (and vice versa), Lithuanians and Estonians trying to kick out Russians from their newly liberated tribal zones, blacks and whites trying to wipe out each

that sanctify little more than the accumulation and disposal of property, tax avoidance schemes, and wildly insensitive procedures for protecting children when the marriage blows apart. Few couples seem concerned about anything other than who owns the property and children once the domestic worm takes hold.

But another kind of story sometimes begins when a marriage is over. These are nearly always animal stories in which domestic animals pretend that they're graceful and wounded and wild, and act pretty much like vermin.

Which brings us back to Ferris. He really doesn't have a story to tell about *being* married, animal or otherwise. He can't quite remember what went on, actually, aside from the crazy incidents. What he remembers about those is primarily his own terror. To him it was pitch black, and he can't quite recall what the comforts were.

"I tried to make it work," he says, "I tried to get it. But there wasn't anything to get—tree trunks, momentarily visible, not there when I tried to grasp hold. Shadowy inhabitants, species unknown. Pathways and trails that led a short distance into the dark and petered out, usually in quagmires of one sort or another. It was my time to be banally, wordlessly human, and I did it as best I could."

Once more I prod, this time suggesting that his metaphors are too complicated.

He decides to play the buffoon. "Well, I don't know much," he says, "but I know a guy who got married four times. One afternoon, over coffee, I asked the guy why so many times. He laughed at me, maybe a little longer and harder than the question warranted.

other in South Africa, managers raiding the assets of shareholders, bankers trying to impoverish everyone, etc. The list is agonizingly long, and if I go on we'll end up in a fist fight when I impugn your tribal affiliations. Can you hear the artillery battalions marshalling in the background?

"'Well, you know how it goes. It seemed like the thing to do at the time.'

"My expression must have convinced him that I truly was curious

What I'm saying here is that I can't lay hands on *the Patriarchy*, and neither can you. I can't even get my head around it without imposing some sort of factional ideology. Much more easily and usefully, I can conceptualize hordes of extremely energetic tribal airheads waving their sticks at one another. And on a daily basis, I

about it, because he went on to answer my question seriously.

"'About fifteen years ago,' he said, 'I began to notice that there were fights I wasn't winning with my women anymore. Or maybe I realized I didn't want to win or lose the fights I was getting into. To win I'd have to be the sort of asshole women complain about all the time. But if I lost, I'd be under the same sort of house arrest women used to have to put up with.'

"'And still do,' I added. 'Are you talking about domestic violence here, or what?'

"'Oh, Christ, no,' he said. 'I mean the kind of fights that involve principles—the fair fights—for attention, or control over the space and time people have in common. The things we think our lives are all about.'

"'For instance?'

"'Okay,' he said. 'A simple one. It's Sunday morning. I want to play baseball, and she wants us to ride bikes around the park. So there's a problem. I can do fine without her help or company, but she can't be and do herself without my company. I don't really give a damn about the ballgame, but I insist that I am, well, me. So I end up doing nothing. I won't go to the ballgame, but I'll be fucked if I'll ride around the park either.'

"'Why act like a jerk?' I asked. 'Why not work it out?'

"'I know I sound like a jerk,' he said. 'But this kind of conflict isn't as simple as it looks. She can't go alone because there are perverts in the parks, she can't hook the bike rack onto her car, or hook the bike safely to the rack. You know the routine?'

"I did recognize it. Annie'd irritated me with it any number of times.

"'There's a whole generation of women out there,' he continued, 'who've deliberately tossed out the domestic skills their mothers traded with their fathers to keep households working—cooking, sewing, things like that. Part of it was shitwork, see acts of violence becoming more and more acceptable as political acts. It scares the hell out of me because nearly everyone seems to be ignoring this, particularly the neotribalists who want to eradicate the Patriarchy. The Patriarchy is the result of a global deficit in deep thinking about alternatives to violence. And so are these new-fangled tribalists.

Behind tribalism, I can see something else that may precede matriarchy and patriarchy alike. It is something we now ignore studiously, and, I think, unwisely. Much as we would prefer to think otherwise, a large part of human behaviour is an instinctual response to what animal scientists like to call our "genetic mission." In

maybe most of it things like keeping things in order. I dunno. Maybe most of it was. But part of it was nurturing. The problem we got now is that the generation of women around now don't do any of those things. Some of them refuse to do any of it on principle, others don't know how. They never learned those things because they were out getting professional degrees or whatever.'

"'You have a problem with that?' I asked.

"'Nope,' he answered. 'What I've got a fairly major problem with is that these same women expect men to continue doing the things men have traditionally done, like lifting boxes, using tools, and manipulating sophisticated technologies—keeping cars and appliances working, and so forth. Those skills are as foreign to women today as they were to women a couple of generations ago. Meanwhile, most men—well, some anyway—have learned traditional "female" domestic skills. Most of us have learned to cook and clean, and some of us can even sew. I can, for instance. Men have also learned to nurture.'

"'We're better for having learned those things.'

"'Sure we are,' he said. 'Hey, I *like* hanging around the house. I was a better cook than any of my exes.'

"'Better at cleaning the house, too? Gimme a break.'

"'I did my share,' he said, then emended. 'Most of the time. And anyway, that's not the point. I did all the other stuff, the renovations, the gardening, the police-work. And when I tried to count that into the total load, I got nothing but grief.'

"'Well,' I said, 'that all sounds fine as theory. But I think you'd have trouble getting many women to accept that the division of household labour was equitable—then or now.'

"'I wouldn't try,' he said. 'I'm not sure myself that it ever was, and with women working and having careers it sure as hell isn't now. Everybody knows that. But what no

fact, ours is depressingly similar to those of other mammals, where males are missioned to drive out or kill competing males, and to breed with as many females as possible. Female mammals are genetically programmed to protect their offspring against predators and secondarily against other genetic lines and marauding males. In most mammals, derived behaviours are important survival mechanisms, and a key element in natural selection. Among human beings, most of these instinctive impulses are now superfluous and counter-productive, particularly the male ones.

The genetic programs that affect and effect our behaviour are lodged fairly

one wants to see is that when a relationship between a man and a woman gets intimate and domestic, a reversion to the old domestic arrangements often occurs, or at least to an approximation of them. And if the couples are really sharing the domestic work, the picture starts to get out of focus. Men start finding that they're doing their half of what women once did, and all the things men used to do, except for providing all the money. So the wrangling starts. The men start cutting back on the domestic stuff, the women get pissed, or the men don't cut back, and *they* get pissed. Wars break out, small, nasty wars. They're totally fucking nasty wars because after centuries of losing domestic battles, women nowadays will fight to the death rather than lose them. It isn't necessarily you they're trying to defeat, it's their gender's history. Hard to blame them, but where the hell does that leave men who've gone beyond playing Dagwood Bumstead?

"'I got to the point where I couldn't let a woman win a domestic battle just because she was female. I didn't like the idea of it, and I learned that whenever I let them win, I'd get accused of being patronizing. I was fucked either way. So when I saw those kinds of squalid conflicts becoming general, I walked out. Made myself do it.'

"'And then?'

"'That *really* pissed them off, of course. But fuck it. I couldn't see any alternative. Sure, my own gender has been tyrannical for centuries, but if I stop and look at it, and if I admit that it's wrong and put a stop to behaving that way myself, I'm sure as hell not going to let things get turned around so that the old victims get to be the new tyrants. I don't know about you,' he said, too quickly for me to interrupt, 'but I'm running into a lot of women who are wondering where the men have gone. What they don't see is that they often don't have much to offer the men they want beyond sex—which they believe, correctly, isn't a favour that deeply in our subconscious and preconscious circuitry and, in most of us, sublimated by learned behaviours. But no one should be arrogant and foolish enough to think that they do not influence our social and sexual behaviours, particularly among heterosexuals.

Not to get mystical about genetic missions, of course. Like tribalisms, they're utterly superfluous to a civilized society, and they deserve to be ridiculed whenever derived behaviour can be identified. But they're at the root of a lot of things we don't like to think about: why men are violent toward one another and to women, why men screw around when there's no visible reason for it, and why mothers are

ought to be traded in a domestic relationship. The kind of men they want—and who would want them—sure as hell don't think sex is a commodity women should trade on. Only the worst kinds of jerks will accept sex that way in a relationship.'"

"That's a nice story," I say to Ferris. "But you didn't follow that man's advice. You hung around, you fought those sorts of battles with Annie over time and territory and, maybe, you accepted the sexual favours."

"Sure," he admitted. "You've heard all this before. I lost most of the battles, lost my dignity. Fuck, maybe I lost my mind. For sure, I gave in to her sense of reality even when I was pretty certain she didn't have one. If that's a crime, then I'm guilty. I let her control our common space because I was never very clear about what it was, and God knows there were a hundred times when I accepted her logic even though I thought it was crazy. I told myself that she was a woman, that she had her reasons, and if I loved her I ought to hang in and put up with her demons, go through her hell with her. I told myself that peace and sanity were just around the corner even though after a while I didn't really believe it.

"My kindly cowardice just made her crazier. She accused me of being a patronizing passive-aggressive bastard, and she was right, I suppose. But what was I supposed to do? It never quite occurred to me that I was up against anything more than this very singular woman who was looking to brawl, by her rules and on her agenda.

"I knew there was no way I could do it forever. It was leading straight into hell for both of us, to crawl-on-the-floor-drool-and-puke humiliations. When I figured *that* out, I turned around and marched back the other way, abandoned her to her demons. Doing that ended the marriage. It just took a while for it to end."

Notice how abstract this all is? Ferris had neither anger nor understanding, and he's trying to make it look like he had both. What he isn't

prone to be idiotically overprotective of their kids. Somewhat further afield, they've hung Abraham Lincoln on the clothesline for more than a century, and they helped the Nazis, fifty years ago, to manipulate an entire nation into trying to exterminate everyone who didn't have blond hair and blue eyes. More recently, they have been a large part of the reason the former Soviet Union and the United States ended up with forty thousand megalethal penis substitutes pointed at one another, and they explain why the collapse of the Soviet Empire has resulted in practically everything but a flowering

saying, and won't, is that it is after they divorce that the true animal stories commence.

Here's how it went. For reasons of her own, Annie kept coming after Ferris through the one sure route she had: wiggle her ass and *cherchez le beast*. Ferris never let her down. He didn't think it was because he was such a great fuck. He'd become too wary of her to let that part of his ego dangle free. He didn't quite believe she was trying to rekindle the marriage, either, even though she talked about it a lot. To him her talk about getting back together was detumescence gibberish. He had a suspicion that sex was the one thing about him she hadn't grown to loathe.

For Ferris, any flimsy pretext would do—for a few days or weeks. He told himself that he liked sleeping with Annie, that he was addicted to her saliva, her bodily fluids, her pheromones. He told himself that she was his cross to bear—and then laughed because he wasn't remotely Christian. He even convinced himself, each time he dived in her aromas, that this time, maybe, they'd get it right. So he was an animal. These are animal stories, remember?

Alas. Each episode was shorter than the last, and nastier when it blew up. Each time Ferris would bail out more quickly. By the third or fourth of these episodes, he began to understand the dynamic, and he didn't even stay for the full blowout. But however depressed he got, he left with the taste of her on his tongue, and to him it was the taste of honey. He was like a bear with a beehive. He kept sticking his face into it, and he'd hang in until the stings grew too painful to stand. Animal metaphor. Sorry.

Eventually, he lost his appetite for the honey. Or rather, he killed it. Now here's an animal story. The version he told people at the time—the official story—is that Annie bet a mutual friend that she could get him back, and the

mutual friend ratted on her. Ferris couldn't quite explain why the friend told him, and few asked. When they did, he said it was, maybe, that she felt more sympathy of peace and democracy. Similar instances abound throughout history— and more locally on our television sets and in our late-night bars and workplaces.

The presence of these vestigial genetic missions doesn't excuse lunatic behaviour, and they certainly don't exonerate sexual violence. But they are part of the explanation, part of our make-up, and part of the reason we still find it easier to point weapons and accusing fingers at one another instead of developing a mutuality that can put an end to such stupid tyrannies.

for him than loyalty for Annie—or maybe she just wanted to win a bet. Ferris claims that when he heard this, he decided he wouldn't go near Annie again, and he stuck to it. That's a story he even tells himself sometimes. But he knows it isn't the real story. That one is quite a lot less glamorous.

It begins ordinarily enough. She coaxes him back into bed with her. Nothing novel in that. He can't quite see why, and he's nervous about it. Just days before, she phoned him for no reason, screamed obscenities at him, and refused to forward mail. He's given up trying to explain her behaviour. Nearly anything can set her off—jealousy toward a new girlfriend of his, a relationship with a new man that she'd managed to screw up. Maybe she needs some pictures hung or an appliance repaired, who can tell? None of that matters anyway, not to him or to this story.

What matters is this: They are making love, and he is giving her head. One of the things he likes about her is that her cunt is unusually appealing to him, sweet-scented, with thick labia that blossom at the slightest touch. As he is about to widen the zone he glances at what he is into, and into which he is about to dive deeper. Next to her sphincter is a quarter-inch ball of shit, stuck to a hair.

Ferris isn't Jonathan Swift, so this doesn't mortally offend him. It doesn't deter him at all, actually, except that he temporarily narrows the zone a little. He and Annie fuck their brains out all night, and they keep it up for several days—as is the now-established custom. They even make the usual stupid plans to live together again.

But then some chance remark or neural flip turns Annie into a Tasmanian Devil—or threatens to—and Ferris is out of there. Except for this small erotic glitch, this tiny ball of shit, this unexceptional breach of hygiene that he knows happens a million times each day across the planet, there is nothing to distinguish this episode from the ones before it.

Then a second event takes place, this one inside Ferris's mind. As he leaves, escaping once again, he recalls the shitball. He picks it from her buttocks, and he plants it on the end of Amor's nose, then smears his finger on along the point of the God's arrow. It takes a split second. Annie knows nothing about it, and Ferris himself barely records its occurrence. But the next time Annie tries to get him into bed, he forces himself to think about that quarter-inch ball of shit. He imagines that it is up there once more, stuck to a hair right next to her behind, and that it will always be there. He tells himself that it is her soul, his erotic soul, whatever.

"No," he tells her. "Not this time."

He doesn't say "not ever again," because he isn't sure it will work more than once. But the next time it does work.

And somewhere, deep in the forest, an animal that is not a horse and not a tyger lies down quietly on a bed of moss and begins a sleep that will last forever.

This time, Ferris is waiting for a train. It's delayed, and he has several hours to kill. The station is old and elegant and relatively empty, so this isn't quite the disaster being stuck in an airport would be. He could park himself in the deserted rotunda and do some serious people-watching. If that fails, he'll find a café somewhere nearby, and it won't be filled with the frantic assholes he'd encounter in an airport.

His travels have made him most comfortable in uncrowded stations and deserted markets, more comfortable still in cafés, restaurants, and cafeterias— the kinds that don't lay tablecloths. For a time he came to believe that a travel writer's job was to tell the truth about places and people, and he wrote about them in public places as a matter of principle. He did some of his best writing there, with the people he was writing about milling obliviously around him.

Their presence reminded him that writing is a public activity, and that a writer's best intentions are to liberate his or her readers from lies. Eventually the market divested him of that illusion, but the café habit remained. Now he edits in public, or plans how to deliver his next parcel of half-truths.

Serious people-watching requires attention to detail, and he quickly discovers that the people passing through this particular station aren't heavy on detail. He wanders off in search of a storage locker for his bags and a café where he can collect his thoughts, work over his notes for the article he's writing about the four-hundred-year-old Kashan Gardens of Iran. He's finished the first part of it and already has it teeming with the sorts of icons travel agents thrive on: quince and walnut trees, melodiously trickling streams running across turquoise tiles, couples strolling beneath the cypresses. Nary a mention of Koran-waving loonies, tanks or screaming mullahs, or the bizarre melange of Muslim fundamentalism and Disney cartoons that makes up the country's popular culture.

He finds a locker, stows his suitcase in it, and, shouldering his book bag, wanders through the labyrinthine corridors of the station. Before long, in an alcove (or is it a time warp?) he uncovers a spacious cafeteria. With its vaulted ceilings and darkened wood tables, chairs and panelled booths, the place seems to have been preserved from the 1940s. If the tables had been crowded with soldiers triumphantly returning home after defeating Nazi Germany, he wouldn't have flinched.

For sure, it's a welcome respite from the too-bright decor virus of the fast-foods era, but at closer examination it isn't quite a time warp. There is an electronic cash register, some glass food cases, and the uniformed employees wear plasticized ID tags that carry a corporate logo and a first name: Tracy, Waldo, Bruce. Worse, the food being offered is the same food he's seen in cafeterias across the continent, sealed in preformed plastic wrappers, prepared in the same anonymous factory somewhere in the American midwest and air-freighted in daily by astral projection and fax machine.

There aren't any returning soldiers, only scatter of depressed-looking people, a few grim-faced railway employees killing time as they shadow jobs they expect to disappear any moment, and one or two too-aggressive Global Village Visigoths who act slightly guilty, as if they're buying transport for the victims of their latest business deal. It's vaguely depressing, and Ferris knows why. Despite their often grand architecture, railway station cafeterias have become the nearly exclusive precinct of the derelict and the transport-poor—those who can or need to travel, but can't afford to go very far or at real speed. People here do their travelling dressed in polyester, the combat fatigues of the marginalized and the alienated, the dress uniform of consumerism's endless, comatose infantry divisions.

Masturbation, Pornography, and So On

Things have loosened up since the 1950s, when masturbation was regarded, almost universally, as self-abuse, and in some circles as a quasi-criminal activity. Back then, it was widely believed that for men, masturbation led to physical weakness, mental illness, hair growth on the palms of the hands, eye glasses, and increased susceptibility to the Communist Menace. It was also believed that women didn't masturbate at all unless they were, well, nymphomaniacs. If there'd been any reality to these notions, civilization as we know it should have been overthrown by hordes of weak-eyed hairy-palmed ninety-seven-pound Communist lunatics pursuing and being pursued by

There's only one person in the cafeteria who interests Ferris. At a table next to one of the tall windows sits an attractive woman. She is tall, slim, with tangled dark hair cascading across her shoulders. She appears to be in her thirties, and she's pretty in a Karen Black sort of way—square jaw, deep-set eyes.

He forgets about the Kashan Gardens and sits down a few tables away, ostensibly to fiddle with his notebook but really to watch her, close enough for accurate observation but still distant enough that she won't think he's hitting on her: writer's distance.

She's wearing a white cotton blouse and loose turquoise pants. On her feet are red spike heels that make her appear taller than she is—even while she's sitting down. They also make her feet seem larger than they really are.

Ferris has a mild fetish about women's shoes and feet. Like all fetishes, this one operates outside the boundaries of strict rational choice and, occasionally, of good and conventional taste. He's traced it to his mother, and it appears to be a component of the peculiar Oedipal warp he has to work with. When he was growing up, his mother was a blonde-haired mesomorph with large fleshy hands and feet, and a generous bosom. As an adult he has a singular erotic aversion to women who resemble her in any way—his way, perhaps, of not attempting to replace the original target of his Oedipal impulses. Whatever the cause, he's drawn instead to slim, dark women with small, slender hands and feet, and long fingers and toes.

When he was a young man, these preferences often—and sometimes hilariously—alienated him from "normal" male sexual camaraderie and banter. While his friends slavered over breast sizes and the other voluptuary fetishes of *Playboy* magazine, Ferris quietly and unashamedly examined the hands and feet of the women around him. I say "quietly" because commenting on, say, the A-width shoe size or the length

nymphomaniacs.

It does explain the 1960s, sort of, but the truth is that human beings have always amused themselves by fiddling with their private parts, and without any adverse physical effects. Today, only those who want to keep women barefoot and pregnant object to women masturbating, and only a few others who would dearly love to fill the world with paranoid anal-retentives like themselves find "spilling seed" objectionable. More sensible folks recognize that even though masturbation can be messy (physically for men, emotionally for both sexes) and despite the fact that there's something fundamentally silly about it, it is a good way for males to unload excess

or shape of a woman's digits wasn't something he could share with anyone.

Men do not, as women seem able to, search for the whole person of the other, at least not erotically. The male erotic universe most resembles an automotive parts department, with idealized goddesses as the service managers and Playboy bunnies in the showroom reminding the customers that the women they know aren't quite the stuff of their—or is it Hugh Hefner's?—dreams. Not to make a sympathy case to excuse Ferris's particular and peculiar fetishization of female body parts. It's probably no more savoury than the common tits-and-ass criteria males generally use to characterize women. But he keeps his tastes to himself, and more than once they've given women who'd long since consigned themselves to the Plain-Jane department a renewed (if slightly puzzled) sense of their beauty.

There will be howls of derision and denial from several quarters—those remaining male fools who still want to blather on about archetypal blonde goddesses, and another kind of fool who believes that men ought to be able to recognize the beauty of an Inner Person through the seductions and clamour of the marketplace. But this is how male sexuality and intelligence really work, and probably always have: A man sitting in the cafeteria of a railway station in a strange city wonders about the condition and shape of a strange woman's toes, comparing her to an obscure movie star, and feeling vaguely guilty that neither of them resembles his mother in any way.

Ferris looks up, distracted at the intellectual wrangle I've written him into, discovers that the woman he's been thinking about is staring at him. She's caught him red-handed, but at what he's not sure. He looks back at his note pad and rereads what he's written: There is a description of the room, of her, and the confessions of cultural guilt and of Oedipal dysfunction I've just inflicted on you. In the

testosterone, and for hetero women a safe alternative to being dependent on husbands and boyfriends for stress reduction, physical release, fun. It's a small advance in our general level of civility that we're no longer obliged to feel guilty about it.

Properly regarded, masturbation is the answer to the old Zen problem: *What is the sound of one hand clapping?* It makes sense to me that way—in moderation, and provided that it stops short of onanism, isolation from others, or evangelical fervours. I've always suspected that those guys—male or female—who insist, loudly, that they never masturbate are probably doing it more frequently than anyone,

real world, a sequence of behaviours like this one would be impossible to explain to a stranger, let alone those one is intimate with, and he wonders what to do here. Should he go over and introduce himself? Continue his confessional vein and explain his interest in her shoes—perhaps ask to see her feet?

Of course not. She'll think he's a lunatic, and if not that, then a pervert, perhaps a potential rapist, the kind that lurks in railway stations preying on women who have nowhere to go or are simply passing through strange cities without much money, obviously, or they'd have a car or be travelling by air. Ferris knows that women who wait in railway stations are likely to be poor, alone, and thus vulnerable, and so is this Karen Black lookalike. Any way he comes at it, they're all like her, only not so attractive. And despite his attraction, hers is a story Ferris can never know, because he's barred from legitimate, dignified contact from her.

At the height of this ridiculous crisis a strange transformation occurs inside him: The serious writer unexpectedly emerges from his travels. It occurs to him that this ought to be about her, not him. Whatever he's become in the twisted curriculum of this dying but still-thrashing patriarchy, he has a deeper duty to enact—that of understanding those things in the world that are not created and governed by his ego. Ferris *is* a writer, *not* a rapist. And he has the rap sheet to prove it, even if most of the items on his rap sheet are half-truths about remote locations accessible only to those who possess a Gold Visa card. This woman is *other* than him, and therefore the focus of his creative imagination, not a potential real-world victim of his inherent male exploitativeness and violence. He glances in her direction again, quickly, but, he hopes, not quite furtively.

Damn. She's watching him openly now, a slight smile on her face, as if she's aware of everything he's been thinking.

Her steady regard and enjoying it least.

This isn't to say that all is well. "Normal" as it may be, masturbation is also a symptom of the immense loneliness of human life. And yes, I know those political arguments that say masturbation is cheaper, simpler, the entanglements are easier to escape from—and now that the Communist Menace is gone, why not? All those things being true, it is only a small abstraction to suggest that masturbation is a signal of our failure to achieve even an approximation of social justice, and that in some best of all possible worlds, involuntary loneliness would not exist. I'd prefer to live in a world where no one masturbated out of loneliness. Wouldn't you?

Pornography is different, for several reasons. It was once a protest against sexual repression, and it usually appeared as highly stylized visual or written materials—art, in other words. Modern plunges him into near panic. His instinctive response is to disappear. Since that isn't possible, he pretends that she doesn't exist. Then he remembers his imaginative duty. He's required to respond more reasonably, to ask—if not her then at least himself—the right questions. Why, for instance, is she here? What is she thinking about right now? Why is she watching him? What kind of moment is this in her life? What does she think and dream about in her best moments?

pornography isn't art, it isn't a coherent protest against anything, and it is so commercially ubiquitous that, for instance, among the heaviest consumers of porno films are adolescent children, who rent their porn videos from the corner store. Contemporary pornography is perhaps the purest illustration of just how far the commoditization of life has reached, and a depressing part of the apparatus that has overpowered our traditional education system with specious consumer rights and inducements to entertainment. Pornography atomizes everyone involved—producers and consumers alike—to an insidious array of body parts and their friction-coefficients.

The industry, like most others, is interested only in keeping a tested, banal product flowing off the assembly line, and not interested at all in artistic merit, social development, or improving our minds or our erotic

Practical reality saves him—someone else's economic reality, actually. He can't sit at this table scribbling in his notebook indefinitely because the owners will be forced to intercede—economic ruin will befall them if everyone did what he's doing. Ferris is obliged to buy something and consume it. Coffee, he decides, maybe a piece of pie. That'll keep capitalism's floor-space econometrics off his case for an hour or so.

But in order to do that, given the layout of the cafeteria, he'll have to walk right by the woman. Either that, or make the obviously hostile (because she's still watching him) gesture of walking halfway around the room to avoid going past her table.

He gets up from the table, still not sure which route he'll choose, and the shift in perspective concedes two new details. The first is that the tabletop in front of her is clear except for a paperback novel spread open, cover up. The second detail is a bulky navy blue overnight bag on the chair next to her.

Okay, so if I were going to try to pick her up, Ferris quickly calculates, I'd

abilities. The only variety it offers is the binary choice of whether to consume or not to consume it. Still, since we aren't about to ban other similar industries (the fast-foods industry comes to mind) banning pornography is unlikely and illogical.

On the other hand, arguing that its presence in the community has a positive side is difficult. It's pretty clear we'd be better off without it. In its current form, it reflects both an inequitable (and inaccurate) distribution of erotic power and an unhealthy societal obsession with maintaining that disequity. Its production and consumption have, not surprisingly, become a major industry, one that is probably controlled by organized crime. Unintentionally, nearly all pornography winds up showing us how psychotic the status quo has grown, and this—and not the erotic depiction of human beings—is the main reason that authoritarians from both ends of the political spectrum are trying to suppress it.

Those aren't the only things wrong with pornography. From an aesthetic and political perspective, the folks down in production, and some sashay over and ask if she'd like some coffee. That would be easy, because she's looking right at him as he approaches the junction where he'll have to choose between walking by her or going the long way. Then again, not so easy. "Pickup artist" isn't among the several identities Ferris lives with.

At the crucial moment, he manages to go both ways at once—he smiles at her, a shy grin and a shrug of helplessness at the same time—and he takes the long route. Maybe she'll think he's going to the washroom. Maybe he will go to the washroom. Maybe she'll steal his book bag while he's in there and be gone forever when he returns, in possession of several weeks of impossible-to-decipher private ideas, details, observations, along with the sole copy of part one of the Kashan article.

No, he decides, the washroom is too risky, and he strides straight to the cafeteria line-up via the long route, feeling foolish at his choice, and now, paranoid about leaving his book bag unguarded. As he reaches down to pick up a tray, he sees a pair of red spike heels with a woman's (possibly extremely attractive) feet in them moving in behind him. It's her. More wary than he is of theft, she has her overnight bag with her.

So now what? Ferris thinks. Does he make some inane remark about the plastic sandwiches in the display case in front of them, does he commiserate about the weather or about having to wait for trains, or does he just keep his mouth shut? Maybe she's the sort of person who adores cafeteria sandwiches and

of the clientele (Jimmy Swaggart, for instance) are leaving rather a lot to be, er, desired, particularly if you happen to be female. Additionally, the technical information it provides is often erotically very misleading to

and for both sexes. Partly that means that anyone who learns to screw by watching pornographic movies is going to have a physically awkward and unrewarding sex life. Human sexual anatomy is not designed to accommodate camera angles, and the neural circuitry that experiences desire does not have a built-in soundtrack with disco

music and loud moans of "Yes!" or "Fuck me harder!" on it.

But pornography does more than merely mislead and disinform us about sex. It feeds the darkest side of the extraordinarily glamorous and unattainable erotic images that have become a ubiquitous presence in our lives. Who among us hasn't had fantasies about a supermodel or a movie star? Pornography pushes that relatively innocuous commoditization a step further, into a destructive strain of erotic voyeurism: *There is always some-*

gloomy weather and waiting for trains. Who is he to presume they're in agreement about anything? This woman, remember, is a perfect stranger, and these are the 1990s, when nearly every presumption about women is either an insult or a harassment.

"Hi," she says, smiling. Nice smile.

"Hi," he answers back.

"Do you think these sandwiches are plastic right through?" she asks, deadpan.

"Not quite," he answers, picking up the cue. "There was some organic material in there when they were packed in Ohio. But that was several weeks ago."

The woman laughs, not deeply, and they move slowly along the line, both of them poking casually through the display case.

"I hate waiting for trains," she says. ""Particularly when the weather's like this."

"I can think of better places to be."

He's lying, because suddenly he can't think of a better place to be. He fills a mug with coffee and chooses a piece of blueberry pie.

"This'll be safe," he says to the woman, feeling increasingly chatty. "It won't have anything *but* chemicals in it."

The woman doesn't quite get the joke, and he mumbles something about the pie being at least two months old. "Anything organic would be mouldy by now," he adds.

She doesn't respond. When he looks back, she's fallen behind him in the

one else we'd like to fuck with. It is distinct from erotica in that it posits a normative sexual universe that borders both on onanism and violent exploitation without ever hinting that the sexuality is a primary instrument in the search for the other.

I don't see any way that one can be turned so it comes shiny side up. Pornography degrades our everyday erotic lives, and it distracts us from those we live and love with. Period. For women, it may have an additional effect, encour-aging screwed-up fantasies of fuck/subjugating other women. As with Frantz Fanon's idea of colonialized people taking on the behaviour of the oppressor, if you can't beat them…

Having said this, I would never propose that we ban any of this stuff, and I won't support any form of sexual censorship. A world that active-ly suppressed masturbation or pornography would be much worse than one in which it is tolerated. And yet I'd prefer to live in a world where there was no need for either. So call me a utopian.

line-up, fiddling with the zipper of her overnight bag.

"Pardon me?" she asks when she sees he's looking at her, jerking the zipper closed. She has an oddly distracted expression, as if he's spoken to her in a foreign language.

Ferris is distracted, too. Close up, her hands are larger than he expected, almost bony, and the skin is rough and red. Enlarged veins are puffed across the knuckles, the joints slightly arthritic. They will, he calculates, probably puff further and twist as she gets older.

A swift run of images crosses his mind in no particular order: his mother washing dishes, applying Jergen's lotion, hands at an elevated scale as he runs his much-smaller fingers tenderly across her arthritic knuckles, the bottles of vitamin A—or is it Vitamin D—she used as a remedy. When he comes back to the world, the strange woman whose hands touched this off is waiting for an answer.

"Oh, it was nothing," he says, gesturing at the cup of coffee and piece of apple pie on her tray. "Can I buy you that coffee?"

She seems startled. "Oh, sure. Whatever."

He's in trouble again. Does he buy her piece of pie for her as well? He isn't sure. Is it a presumption if he does, or an insult if he doesn't? When he reaches the cashier, though, she's pulled in close behind him, and he grins at the cashier, hands over a ten-dollar bill and indicates that he's paying for both trays.

The cashier, a big blonde woman who looks like she lifts weights, glares at him, and then, for some reason, rolls her eyes. Just for a second he has a premonition that she's going to judo-chop him in the throat, but the woman merely makes the correct change and hands it to him, all without saying a word. Very strange.

He lets the woman with the red spike heels and puffy knuckles step ahead of him with her tray, and he follows her, this time via the short route, to her table. From the back, the red spike heels look even bigger, but somehow, they're also becoming more attractive. She plunks her tray down on the table and places the overnight bag carefully on the seat beside her as he passes, heading back to his own table.

"Hey," she says. "Why don't you join me? Leave the tray here and bring your bag over so no one steals it."

It's a tricky moment. Ferris doesn't want to join her. Other men may meet attractive women in railway station cafeterias, but not him. Not only does he not know what the right thing to do is,

Which leads me to the "and so on's." Given the way my life has gone so far, I have more opinions about these than experience, so what I have to say about them may need to be taken with a grain of salt. The first one is the erotica/porn controversy, which I think works pretty much as Germaine Greer's cynical insight has it: *What gets me off is erotica, what gets you off is porn.* Ultimately, erotica is a quasi-legal distinction invented during the last century to help pry open the guarded portals of expression.

an instinct tells him that there is no right thing to do. Going back to his table alone and writing about her now would be prurient and voyeuristic. Making a break for it would be cowardly. What's he going to do? He still has two hours to kill.

Damn, he thinks, slips his tray onto the table across from hers, and goes to get his book bag.

"I'm Sylvia," she says when he returns. "Sylvia Eighty. Have a seat."

He tells her his name and sits down. The paperback she's reading is a Danielle Steel novel.

"Are those novels any good?" he asks, gesturing at the paperback as he sits down. "I've only seen her stuff on television."

It's the last thing he wants to know, but they talk about the novel anyway. She tells him she likes Danielle Steel because the books are romantic: the heroines get men, money, and love all at once, and somehow manage to stay vulnerable and feminine and sweet while they're getting their heart's desires. Ferris can think of a few logical flaws in the formula, but he doesn't tell Sylvia what he thinks they are.

They make other small talk. He soon discerns that for all her friendliness, Sylvia Eighty isn't very forthcoming about anything important or interesting and has nothing at all to say about herself. The small talk gets smaller and smaller. He doesn't reveal much either, just where he's going, and what he thinks about some predictable items—the weather, waiting for trains, etc. As a matter of policy he rarely admits to strangers that he's a writer, and he doesn't here. Whenever he does, it guarantees a string of impossibly difficult questions: What kind of writer are you? What kind of books do you write? It also guarantees that anything they tell him from that point will be either a glamorized lie or an inflated opinion. Conversations turn into interviews, and private secrets blossom like algae on a pond. A decent life will descend into maudlin melodrama in front of a writer faster than in front of a South American prison torturer.

> Now that those portals are off their hinges and everything is rushing through, maybe we ought to drop erotica and move on in our intellectual evolution: No idea and no person or persons should have public powers of censorship. We should be adult enough to take on the individual right (and the duty) to judge any representation of reality on the basis of its internal merits—including any and all representations of sexual reality. Rights ought to be backed by an education system, not censors, morality squads, or customs officials.

But there is one small blessing here. Maybe because Ferris is talking to her, or because her feet are under the table where he can't see them, his foot fetish quickly fades into the background jumble. He'd like to ask her about her name—Sylvia Eighty—which sounds like a military code for a bomber squadron, and he'd like to know who she is, where she's from, and where she's going. But something about her tells him not to ask, and she doesn't seem at all curious about him. She just wants company for a few minutes, even if it's alien company.

At this distance she's still pretty, but her features have a certain coarseness, the kind people get from watching too much television and going to too many shopping malls. There's a heavy silver ring with an obliquely shaped turquoise on her left ring finger. It isn't a wedding ring, but at least it isn't a skull and crossbones. And her eyes wander a lot, scanning the tiny universe they're in for presences that are invisible to Ferris. Oddly, one of the presences seems to be in the general vicinity of the cash register. Sylvia's eyes keep darting back to the

S adomasochism? I wish it didn't exist, and I account the current (and curiously commercialized) outbreak of it as a side effect of neoconservative politics and economics. In a culture of entrepreneurs that valorizes cruelty and aggression in the marketplace, the representation of the accruing social damage is certain to be played out at the boundary where sexuality meets art. We should treat S&M, along with the spectrum of erotic fetishizations, as a mirror to our political and economic relationships, be tolerant of its effects in ourselves and others—and slightly embarrassed by it.

cashier, and when Ferris looks, damned if the blonde woman isn't participating. And she's glancing over at them too often for it to be idle curiosity.

The conversation is stuttering badly when, mercifully, Sylvia Eighty glances at her watch and announces that she has a train to catch. To where, he still doesn't know.

From a core of sentimentality Ferris thought he'd expunged long ago comes the image of ships passing in the night. He giggles helplessly to himself, thinking it should at least involve trains and stations. And tunnels, maybe.

Well, they're passing at some distance, because Sylvia Eighty isn't even curious enough to ask why he's giggling. This isn't a significant moment in either of their lives, Ferris decides. He'd have been better off alone with his imagination, concocting any story about her he cares to—or laundering Iran for the travel industry.

"Well, nice knowing you," she says as she shoulders her overnight bag.

"Have a nice trip," he answers. It's been that kind of conversation, and he's glad it's over. Maybe he ought to read a Danielle Steel novel to see how chance encounters are done in that world. Maybe he's been missing all the cues. As she turns and walks to the cafeteria exit, his eyes dip down to the red spike high heels. They're looking pretty terrific.

The cashier intercepts Sylvia Eighty before she gets to the exit. Sylvia struggles, but the cashier grasps her forearms and won't let go. Ferris can see Sylvia wince, but she doesn't really try to elude the cashier's grip. A few seconds go by this way, with the two women standing by the doorway, almost as if they're comforting one another.

A male security guard arrives, a beefy guy, standard issue right down to the crew cut, and he and the cashier open Sylvia's bag, poke around inside it. The guard lifts a plastic-covered sandwich from it between two fingers, then thinks better of it, and drops it back inside.

Christ Almighty, Ferris thinks, almost aloud. She's stolen a sandwich. She's probably destitute, too broke to buy anything. That's why she followed me up to the cash register and hit on me. Now, at least, the encounter makes sense, even why she dropped behind me while we were in the cafeteria line. She was using me as her blind while she put the sandwich in her bag.

He'll have to intercede. Maybe he can buy her way out of this, claim that he thought he'd paid for the concealed sandwich and merely hadn't bothered to check his change. My mistake, so sorry, let her go. Then he'll find out what the real story is. He storms toward the cash register, a man with a mission.

"You stay the fuck out of this," the cashier warns him. The security guard concurs, and so, with a shrug, does Sylvia.

Something about her concurrence and her posture makes Ferris hesitate. She leans against the security guard, shudders, a weak smile playing across her features. She has an unmistakable trace of erotic gaiety about her, as if being held in restraint by the two uniformed employees is profoundly, sickeningly, pleasurable.

A police officer appears just as Ferris resolves to interfere anyway. Once again Ferris stops. Sylvia and the police officer seem to know one another. She smiles at the officer, and he grins back.

"Jesus H. Christ, Sylvia," he says. "When are you going to stop doing this?"

It isn't quite a question. It's more like the kind of admonition one would direct at a misbehaving child. As a reply, Sylvia shakes loose from her captors and offers her hands to the police officer, wrists together, for handcuffing. The officer locks a set of silvery handcuffs around her wrists as if he were placing jewellery on them.

Ferris has had it. He approaches the police officer, his shoulders squared for a confrontation. At very least, he wants an explanation. "I'm sorry to bother you," he says to the officer, "but can someone explain what's going on here?"

Phone sex is a temporary industry that is being fed by the hysteria about AIDS and enabled by recent advances in telephone switching technologies. It is acoustic pornography and it is probably less harmful—individually and sociopolitically—than its visual equivalent. It will almost certainly disappear with the advent of true videotelephones. Along with pornography and sex ads, it is a symptom of the loneliness that results from commoditizing human needs in a market economy, and another signal that the general search for collective social justice has been interrupted.

"Who're you?" the officer demands to know.

Before Ferris can respond, the cashier answers for him. Good thing, too. At this moment, he's a little confused on that point.

"She used him for her blind," she explains, more to Ferris than to the police officer. "He didn't have a fucking clue."

"Yeah, I guess that's true," Ferris admits to the officer.

"Still doesn't," the cashier adds.

"Well," the officer says, looking Ferris over, "I'd hate to think anyone would be knowingly stupid enough to get involved in one of Sylvia's pranks."

Ferris is getting annoyed. "Hey! *Hey!*" he says.

"Hey, hey, yourself," the cashier mimics, punching a muscled finger against his chest. "You were warned to stay out of it. Your pal here is a kleptomaniac."

"A *wealthy* kleptomaniac," the police officer echoes, laying a lot of emphasis on "wealthy." "There's no need for you to get involved. She *likes* to steal, and she likes it better when she gets caught."

Ferris looks at Sylvia, hard. "Why use me?" he demands. "Why get me involved this way?"

She has an extraordinarily dumb smile on her face. Then she tosses her head and looks away. No answer.

"She needed a witness," the cashier answers for her. "And don't go getting Freudian on us here. Just back off and leave it be."

Just for a second, Ferris considers announcing that he's a writer, and that their goofy show doesn't add up. He doesn't do it because he doesn't want to face the inevitable questions—or possible arrest as Sylvia's script assistant. There's a script to this somewhere, but it's anyone's creation but his, and no one has left it lying around for him to look at. He's trying to break into a closed system here, and what he thinks of as his investigative rights and duties don't count for much.

"Poets and thieves," he mutters to himself as he gives up and walks back to his table. By the time he gets there and looks back, the police officer and the security man are herding Sylvia gently out a back entrance.

Ferris spends the next hour at his table, drinking coffee (which the cashier brings and doesn't seem interested in charging him for), trying to sort out the loose ends. There are plenty: who Sylvia Eighty is, what he just witnessed—or was part of, why, from beginning to end, he was behind the eight ball.

Almost everything is a loose end, actually. The biggest one, he eventually recognizes, is in his head, and he has a small suspicion that maybe it *is* his head.

While he's become knowledgeable and adult about the specificity with which men desire women, he's grown confused about the ways in which men are now *permitted* to desire women. There's the strident "special interests" factions that call for community but won't discuss the rules of community, the economic system that seems to agree that anything short of armed looting is valorous entrepreneurialism. And women themselves, who want to be loved and admired for their beauty but are blocking every possible path to it short of a three-page blank application form. And then there's Sylvia Eighty. What impulses drove her to her erotically charged kleptomania?

Ferris's impulses are, by comparison, fairly simple. He wants to slay dragons, rescue fair damsels, ride by the lake in his best shiny armour beneath the friendly sun, etc. But here, and lately in general, he's found himself surrounded by dense brush where he can feel the breath of dragons around him but can't quite admit to himself what they are even when they've blacked his armour. Is this woman, Sylvia, a dragon? Is he? Where is the lake and the sunshine?

He's not even sure if legitimate paths of desire exist at all. The old paths nature dictates—most of them variations on "grab the babe, throw her on the ground, grunt"—remain intact, but they're under censure—and with justification. What's the current saying? *WASP hetero males have had their two thousand years in the sun.* At least at the radical edges of this culture, it's become more or less impossible to put the words "male," "intelligent," and "desire" into proximity with one another. And Ferris wants to operate at the radicals because they're the only level at which this culture is anything more than half-considered sentimentalities and consumer manipulations—and the dictates of different people's private, obscure fears about touching and being touched by others.

He knows that the turning of consciousness among those at the radicals of a culture precedes the turn of the larger wheels. He accepts that the wheel is slowly turning, and that it has already put a few progressive hetero males on the muddy side of the turning. This is hardly a profound insight. Most men sense the wheel turning, whether they admit it or not. So far, most are simply frightened about it. To Ferris, that's a frightening thought in itself. A threatened male of any species all too easily turns into a violent one.

Ferris may be discovering what women have known for centuries—that it is deadly difficult to be spontaneous or generous or articulate with your spine pinned between a wheel and the mud. It is difficult to be anything except passive, confused, and angry. Yet even from that uncomfortable position, Ferris is generally curious about women, and situationally curious about Sylvia Eighty. What *is* her story?

Why does she hang out in railway stations wearing red spike heels and stealing barely edible sandwiches she doesn't need? Was the whole thing staged? Seems like it. The police officer arrived too quickly and knew too much, and the cashier and security guard appeared to know what was going to happen before it took place. Perhaps they were merely actors, employees hired by Sylvia so she can safely play out her fantasy. Or was Sylvia too an actor, hired by someone else, someone operating on yet another thoroughly mysterious agenda?

And what role did he play—or fail to? Was he supposed to have been more aggressive, a frothing Knight Errant out of his own fantasies, or more appropriate to the sets, an asshole biker with a baseball fan hat done up to the tightest notch. And was he supposed to have proffered the elixir (sex? love? money? simple curiosity?) that would have prevented the sequence of crime and arrest? Other daffy scenarios flood in, the last of which gets him giggling once more. Was he party to some clandestine research test for the next Danielle Steel novel?

We know that Ferris is easily amused, and talented at amusing himself. But here he isn't quite amused. He's confused and his laughter isn't genuine. It is one thing to have his identity as an adult male placed in doubt. That happens almost daily, and he generally accepts the justice of it. What a male is *is* in doubt, and there's controversy over whether such a thing as an adult male even exists. The planet certainly isn't in need of more hyper-erect dicks, pointed sticks, or automatic rifles with the safeties off or disabled running around looking for trouble. But if the new operators are the career- and cause-focused Stalinoids currently pushing the wheel to turn, the improvements will be minimal.

Ferris can draw only one secure insight from all this. The conditions that kept him from meaningful participation in Sylvia Eighty's drama are part and parcel of the strangest civil war that human society has ever fought.

We would do well to note that civil wars are the most violent of warfares human beings engage in, and the most difficult to stop once the lines are drawn and the values, goals, and stakes officially articulated, the artillery units dug in and the supply lines secured. The stakes in this civil war are very high indeed, and they are very complicated. Scenes like this one will have to be played out millions of times before the strife can end and men can cease to be caught red-handed by everyone and everything they desire, natural or unnatural. Ferris has no idea where or what he and other men will be at the end of it, or what or where—or who—Sylvia Eighty will be.

And let's drop the pose of omniscience once and for all: neither do I. He's lost, and there are no roads left that go home, except through what he left home for.

The Widow's Café

TW

**F**ar up above the clouds, I can hear Ferris talking to himself.

Here's how it goes:

"As far as I can see, the lost do *not* get found. On that count at least, the Christian moral system has lost track of its mission. The lost aren't cherished, beloved, and they aren't offered anywhere near enough affection or esteem. They're a non-tribe among neo-tribes, a vast demographic growth sector hiding within the market matrices, and they'll eventually overrun whoever still has illusions about where they are.

"Oh, sure, the lost were welcomed to the hearth in the uncrowded days of the past when strangers were rare and unthreatening. But where the hell are the hearths these days? We've replaced them with homeless people and tourists' facilities. Most of the people and places that welcome me also want to eat me, or the welcome is corporate or tourist-bureau, the product of entrepreneurs or bureaucrats, and who wants that phony embrace? Who wants to be a purchase opportunity, a walking wallet? We've become a vast tribe of wanderers, embracing every strangeness just long enough to fleece it. But we don't make homes and hearths, and we have an aversion to our fellow-strangers."

Between you and me, I think he's being a little disingenuous about this. He's just come from a week in the western Arctic, sent there by the airline he's flying on to write a piece about the purity and glory of the tundra in summer: wild-flower cliché heaped upon evanescence-of-summer cliché, written without seeing much of what he was writing about. He began the week by spending most of his time hermetically sealed inside a double-sided tent, reading Elmore Leonard novels and sleeping. On the third day, a romance fiction editor showed up, supposedly scouting locations for a new series of ethnically complex romances.

I won't subject you to the mutual seduction routine or the snappy dialogue, except to say that the editor carried equal quantities of cosmetics, hydroponic marijuana, and anthrotexts on Inuit custom written by white men at the turn of the last century, that she was allergic to blackfly bites, and that she was used to men who wore more expensive colognes than the local Inuit did. She assuaged her need for authenticity by pretending that Ferris was Inuit—"A spiritual eskimo," as she put it.

Aw sure, Ferris liked fucking with her. Her idiosyncrasies interested him, at least while he was inside her tent. What did she have going? Well, she insisted on smoking a joint before sex, she *commanded* him to tug on her labia, to stretch them out while they were having sex, and that the labia were unusually elastic. To him, she was graffiti, marginalia. To her, he was a research adjunct, a dope side effect. They were both glad when his week was up, ready to move on to the next novelties, right, left, march.

Still, this is the right place to entertain such thoughts as he has, on a transcontinental flight thirty-nine thousand feet above the planet's polluted upper atmosphere. Hard to be more lost than this, suffering from oxygen deprivation, breathing the collective airborne viruses and bacteria of two hundred other strangers, distractedly taking in a Sean Young flick, a mediocre potboiler selected by the airline's programmers for its non-discriminatory violence, a titillation no one on the flight will recall beyond the terminal.

Permissions

As we head toward a millennium that we may not, as a species, survive for very many years, the nature of human sexuality shows signs of making a fundamental shift that might be cause for cautious optimism.

The last thousand years could be described— by an optimist—as the Millennium of Liberation. Our species spent its most creative energies in the pursuit of freedom—freedom from subsistence, from political and religious oppression, freedom to speak our minds and to express ourselves sexually and biologically. A lot of crazed optimists are currently positing the idea that capitalism is the engine of this pursuit, arguing that it defeated the Evil Empire of the Commies because it was better tuned to our liberationist instinct. As a long-time lower-case commie who has spent years observing, at close quarters, how capitalism exploits us and turns us into assholes, my opti-

His connector flight from Edmonton departed at noon, and when he checked in, he broke a long-standing habit by choosing a window seat. The Weather Net at the hotel said the prairie skies wouldn't be cloudy all day, and he wanted to see if the deer and the antelope still played. Beyond that, he was curious to know if he could recognize the Great Lakes. It was a bad choice. Two thin bands of cloud imprisoned the aircraft, volcanic dust from Mount Pinatubo in the upper atmosphere, and a gauzy haze at thirty thousand feet that obscured the landscape below. Worse, it trapped him next to a businessman who spent the flight alternately poring through technical reports and skimming an obviously new hardbound tome on how to mind-fuck his customers and competitors. For the first hour of the flight, Ferris surreptitiously fought the businessman for possession of the elbow rest. Stupid game, and eventually he lost.

Beneath, on the moonscape of midcontinent, he glimpses a network of tiny settlements, farms, villages, and towns connected by ruler-straight roads. Is that what they are? Today he has his doubts. Maybe they're part of a totalized human eroto-net, small eructions of consciousness abstracted by the nothingness of overflight. Down there might be a woman in her thirties, overweight and unkempt, lighting a cigarette and settling in for the afternoon soaps, her husband just pulling onto the highway in a green GMC pickup truck fifty miles away after a nooner with the county supervisor's wife. Ferris considers this fantasy, asks himself what he would do in any of the identities he'd idled into existence. If he let them breed, they would quickly build to a hundred, a thousand, eventually to every human being on the planet, the eroto-net. He lets the wife and husband fade for a more interesting thought, loses that, and finds his mind turning to Sylvia Eighty.

He might not recognize her now. Months have passed, almost a year since she used him to screen her theft—or whatever it was she actually did do in that cafeteria. He tries to picture her, and keeps getting Karen Black as she was fifteen years ago. No, Sylvia is slimmer, her face thinner, her eyes less deep-set. (Or is this, he asks himself, getting mixed up with Sean Young from the in-flight movie?)

Ferris crunches the reverie. Helplessly, he's been stripping Sylvia Eighty of all the things he doesn't or can't know about her, and she is drifting steadily toward a B-movie identity. That means she is about to become a pair of red high heels and some veins on the backs of her hands. He begins over, this time constructing her more deliberately, then stops again because the construction materials belong to other women, ones he's been intimate with—and (admit

---

mism is more limited. I'd go so far as to say that yes, we now *know how* to free ourselves from subsistence and political oppression, but that we haven't because capitalism inherently requires losers/victims for its winners to paw and crow over, and it likes them on the streets as an example to the rest of us. I also think we've placed sharp limits on the various kinds of freedom of expression because we're afraid of their extremes. Occasionally, as with sexual and biological expression, there are reasons to be afraid.

I've talked, directly and indirectly, about the pitfalls of absolute sexual freedom throughout this book, hinting that freedom of biological expression is a mixed blessing. So let me state it plainly: I think that the headlong pursuit of free expression is obsolete. With six billion human beings crowding the planet (about 5.8 billion more than the biosphere can handle), we are soon

it!) Sean Young from the plane's movie screen. He lets both women go, half-uncreated, and sleep takes him. It isn't until she touches his arm—no, it is the flight attendant with Sylvia's hand, the familiar mood ring, the manicured red nails, the same distended veins and slight arthritic puffiness across the knuckles—that he reawakens.

"Excuse me, sir," the flight attendant says. "We'll be landing in a few moments."

going to have to make changes in our personal and public values and behaviours that are currently unthinkable. The sexuality of the twenty-first century isn't going to be a vanguard-directed revolution but evolution driven by the hellhounds of dire necessity. If we expect to survive as a species, we'll have to liberate ourselves from precisely the kinds of sexual and social behaviours we've just liberated ourselves to pursue: the unleashing of gender and bio missions, and the kinds of inarticulate desires that are locked away from situational reality by expressive and infantile phobias and fetishes.

The Sexual Revolution of the 1960s and the subsequent rebirth of radical feminism may be offering us glimpses of what the future may ask of us. Both have inherently demanded a shift from the myopic, passion-driven sexual forms of the past to a egalitarian sexuality grounded on mutual

238

Ferris looks up into the face of a middle-aged blonde-haired woman with pale blue eyes and a too-thin nose. Midcontinent is gone, and the sky is dark save for a faint gleam in the west.

———————

Ferris dislikes airports, and he doesn't hang around for the ambience after his bags come off the plane and onto the baggage claim conveyer belt. He catches a limousine to his hotel, etc.—uninteresting details and generic behaviours I won't describe.

Don't be irritated. These things shouldn't comfort us as much as they do. They're what we're forced to wade through to get to the few specific moments that seem to be our own, the ones in which we're not merely lost or riding someone else's media-born notion of what life is supposed to resemble. In this case, for instance, the specifically large ears of the limousine driver, soft-lobed and red, as if the man has been hearing things that embarrass him. Or the no-smoking stickers plastered on every visible surface of the limousine that end any possible conversation Ferris might instigate. Do the stickers on the window beside him render the passing industrial landscape a non-smoking zone? Does he want the driver to beat up on him for being a smart alec?

Ferris slept through the airline's in-flight dinner, and now he's hungry. There is a restaurant in his hotel, but it's a chain, the menu is unappetizing, and he has a long-standing principle about not patronizing restaurant chains. He likes to be where he is, whatever it is, not in some corporation's food chain. After checking in, he sends his bags up to his room and walks out to the street. He hails a cab without any clear idea where he's headed.

"Just go," he tells the driver, settling into the back seat. "I'll tell you when I want out."

Ferris sees the cabby stare at him momentarily in the rear-view mirror. No doubt the cabby is wondering if the strange order he's been given holds any danger.

"It's your buck," the cabby shrugs, evidently deciding Ferris isn't a threat. "Try to give me a little warning before you want to stop. Brakes cost money."

Ferris doesn't answer. He rides for a mile or two, and then, when the cab stops at a light on a street corner, a projecting neon sign halfway down the block catches his eye. It's small, oval-shaped, and its blinking message is very simple and symbolic: Open. He asks to be let out, slips a sawbuck over top of the seat and gets out.

permission and conscious consensus. What neither of those "movements" recognizes, unfortunately, is how oblique the trail from current sexual practices to mutual permission and consensus is.

As in every other age, there are those who are attempting to invade this obliqueness by ideological fiat or by creating an interpersonal police state. That we continue to burden sexual values with their social and political counterparts is more than unwise. Given what we now know about the delicacy of the human mechanism, it amounts to a perverse disregard for the difficult and potentially tragic bind we're in. The asymmetrical erotic behaviours we play out as individuals are the products of individual trauma and external political and social pathologies, sure, but they can't be redeemed or resolved in a legislature or a police station. In most cases they can't be altered at all. It's tempting just to fiddle with

He stopped because the street ahead isn't generic—it isn't rough or seedy, and it isn't genteel. It is what it is: local, and rare for that reason. The franchises haven't invaded it. There's nothing special about this street, but Ferris has unusual criteria: He's never seen one like it. Most of the storefronts have been settled for a long time. A drugstore on one corner sides on a beauty salon and a hardware store. Across the street is a credit union, and next to that, a bookstore with a discreetly hand-lettered sign in its window advertising old, new, and antiquarian books. Next door is a 1950s-style pink neon sign announcing The

Widow's Café. Beneath it, directly above the entrance, is the sign that originally attracted his attention.

Ferris peeks through the window before entering and sees the expected restaurant layout and decor, a long Arborite counter stretching along one wall to the kitchen, with booths along the other. He counts three customers at the counter, another seven or eight grouped in three of the booths. Three women stand side by side behind the counter, chatting animatedly. It looks okay. He pushes open the door and enters.

"Seat yourself," a voice calls out. The speaker is halfway down the counter, the largest of the three women behind the counter. He assumes that they're all waitresses. They're uniformed, but each in a different kind and colour. The speaker is in pale yellow, standard waitress issue with dark brown lapels, the second in bright red, a pantsuit. Both are middle-aged. The third waitress is younger, and her costume is white on black. She looks like a French maid. Odd.

them, to go on indulging the preconscious and the infantile in a sophisticated parody of what human beings have been doing to one another since the dawn of time. This is not *mutual permissiveness. It is virtually its opposite: the SOS we've had for far too long.*

Private sexuality operates in a different environment than the overcrowded, decaying political ones we see around us in everyday life, and we ought to give ourselves a break about this. Until social and political justice can be achieved—and gender equality along with it—we should acknowledge that even while our gender and social politics inevitably influence our sexual politics, they don't and can't dictate the contents of our private erotic paradises.

So what is mutually permissive sexuality? Well, let's get the vulgar stuff out of the way. It isn't what happens when someone permits anoth-

Ferris chooses the second booth in from the door, checks to see that there isn't a no-smoking sign. There isn't, so he sits down, back to the window. As he removes his coat, the waitress in yellow approaches him and slides a plasticized menu in front of him.

"What's good?" he asks, looking up at her. She's in her late fifties, with dark eyes and strong features. Eastern European, he decides—probably Hungarian, judging from the olive skin and the heaviness beneath her eyes. A beauty once, now handsome in the way large women sometime become. And oddly self-assured in the way she holds his gaze.

"Everything is good," she booms back, as if to make sure everyone in the restaurant knows it. It's a judgement on life, not merely a culinary recommendation. Ferris peruses the menu while she stands over him, waiting.

"Well, I can't decide," he says without looking up. "Can I have a cup of coffee while I think about it?"

"Take your time, take as much time as you like," she says, but makes no move to leave. Ferris glances up. She is gazing at him. Not quite staring, but, well, *looking him over*. He meets her eyes for a moment.

"I'll get your coffee," she announces, and strides away imperiously. He watches her go, interested, and sees her say something to the other two women standing at the counter as she fills a cup with coffee and slips a saucer beneath it. Whatever she says amuses the others, because all three laugh uproariously for several seconds.

"Cream?" she calls out in her booming voice.

Ferris nods, not wanting to try his own voice. This seems to amuse the waitresses, and laughter breaks out again. Something slightly mysterious going on here, he thinks to himself. But what?

er person to do something to or with them that is beyond the limit of emotionally or bio-safe behaviour. At best that is thumbing one's nose at convention, satisfying one person's desire to sacrifice their identity or body to another's apparent need: the SOS, slicked up.

Mutually permissive sexuality is much better than that. It is that elusive sexual experience that occurs during those moments when our clawing, egregious needs subside and we experience the enriching *other* at level ground and at depth, without fear or ambition. I don't know about you, but when that happens I get a glimpse of paradise, even though I insist that no such thing is attainable.

Still, we're not confronting paradise here. We're up against the twenty-first century, where things are going to be so crowded that securing permissions will be the key to every access. And the key is right in front of us.

Three waitresses having a good time is odd, but hardly mysterious. Or maybe it is. As Ferris watches, the door opens and a young man enters—tentatively, the same way Ferris did. The Hungarian woman gives the newcomer the same loud directions she gave Ferris, then changes her mind and directs him to a booth close to the back. He's young, blond, and good looking, and the three women watch him intently as he passes. The young waitress elbows the grand Hungarian and laughs out loud. The Hungarian nods assent to some inaudible remark, but makes no move. This one belongs to the elbower, and before the new man settles, she's on him, pushing a menu in front of him while she scrutinizes him at close range.

Ferris glances at the waitresses still at the counter. They're in conference. The waitress in the red pantsuit points at the new man, flips an elbow in Ferris's direction without looking at him, and shrugs.

"They think you're attractive," a voice says from behind him.

"Who does?" Ferris replies without thinking.

He looks up, and Sylvia Eighty is slipping into the seat across from him. She's carrying the same black overnight bag she had the day he first encountered her, which she shoves into the corner of the booth beside her. She's smiling, as if being here is a natural event. As if she and Ferris were old friends.

"It's nice to see you again," she says. Her voice seems deeper than he remembered.

"It is," he answers. "I mean, it's nice to see you, also. I didn't expect…"

She cuts him off. "Don't ask," she says.

Ferris doesn't. "I had a feeling I'd run into you again," he says, making conversation. He's partly telling the truth. He hoped he would, somewhere, but he didn't think it would happen.

"Yeah, sure you did." Her tone is ironic. "You've done nothing but think about me since, I suppose."

"No. But I have thought about you some. Tell me about those women."

She unzips the bag, pulls out a small compact, and renews her lipstick in front of him. "They're widows," she says, then amends case. "*We're* widows. Like the sign outside says. Also shareholders. The one in yellow bought the place ten years ago when her husband died."

"Why a restaurant?"

Sylvia grins at him, licks her lips, looks suddenly vague the way she did the first time he met her.

"It's hard to explain…" she says.

"Try. I really am curious."

"Well, she liked men—likes them, around her. You know. But she didn't want to live with another one."

"Too much hassle?"

"Yeah, sort of. But she set it up as a company, and instead of hiring employees, she sells shares. The other women there are shareholders…"

"You said 'we'," Ferris interjects.

"I'm one of them, yes."

"You're a widow?"

"Yes." The irony returns to her voice as suddenly as it left. "And no. We, uh, redefined what a widow is. My husband didn't die. He was an asshole."

Ferris says nothing, so she continues.

"He was threatened. I'm sure you know the routine. Thought he owned me. Took me years to cure him of that, and when I did, he decided he owned my orgasms. Had to steal those back."

Ferris shrugs. At least one mystery is becoming slightly clearer. "So you work here too?"

"Sometimes," she says. "I'm not as far out of the circuit as they are. They're strictly looking *at*. Part of me is still looking *for*. But not very hard."

Ferris can't resist. "Looking for what?"

She tosses it back. "Well, what are *you* looking for?"

Long pause as they both search for the answer. "I don't know anymore," Ferris admits. "Women. The right woman, I guess."

"You and several billion other goofballs," she answers. "Tell me something that isn't a cliché."

"Okay." Second long pause. "I'd, um, like to have a few orgasms I can live with."

Sylvia Eighty's eyes narrow. "What do you mean by that? You don't live with orgasms. You consume them. Like a sandwich, only better."

"I used to think that. But it's more complicated. I want orgasms I don't feel guilty about, ones that don't make women flinch, wondering what's next. And I'm tired of being drugged by my sexual needs. I still like the drugs, but I'm tired of the addiction. I wouldn't mind an orgasm that didn't feel like a fix once in a while."

"You sound more than tired. A little angry, I think."

"Aren't we all?"

"Not around here. Do those women look tired and angry to you?" She gestures at the three women standing behind the counter. They're talking animatedly, obviously having a good time. Ascendantly so. Gay.

Ferris experiences a twinge of resentment. "Okay," he says. "I'll bite. Why are they so happy?"

"Because they're free."

"Free to what?"

"To do whatever they want. They're free from biology, for one. From goofball men, for another. Free to educate themselves on their own terms. To educate their senses, amuse their bodies, whatever."

An old brainteaser from Ferris's youth comes back, and he toys with it for a split second: *Everybody feels gay except Gay/ And Gay feels nothing at all.* Not anymore, not here. *Nobody feels Gay except the Gay, and she feels fine.*

Ferris frowns. "What are we talking about here? Are those women lesbian?"

Sylvia rolls her eyes. "And what if they are? What if," she enunciates her words carefully here, "they're simply gay women?"

"They can be whatever they want to be," Ferris replies, also carefully. "Of course."

Sylvia snorts. "No. It isn't for you to confer that freedom anymore. Or me. They're gay because they're free, not the other way around. Because their pleasures are their own, and no one and nothing can control them."

"Within the limits of sanity. And public order."

The Punch Line

Over breakfast recently, a cherished friend and fellow-writer told me how, years ago, she accidentally entered a room where I was sleeping. She hadn't expected to find me there—it was midmorning, and she thought I'd be long gone, out in the world, walking up and down and back and forth, about my business. When she found me still awash in my dreams, her first impulse, she said, had been to leave. But another impulse overtook her, and she plunked herself down on a chair beside my bed and for several minutes sat and watched me sleep.

I sipped my coffee and waited for the punch line, which I assumed would have something to do with me snoring, or about how she'd been tempted to stick kitchen utensils or a lit cigar into my open mouth. Perhaps because we've never been tempted to become lovers, we've enjoyed this sort of playful, chiding intimacy. But this time, instead of joking around, she simply remarked that she'd found me very beautiful on that morning.

Men don't like to admit to it, but we have that same wish to have our beauty discovered that until very recently seems to have governed much of women's spare time. And I'm talking about upper-case Beauty, the kind that graceful animals like leopards, horses, and antelope have, not GQ/Vogue magazine-style good looks. I was, therefore, about equally pleased that my comrade had discovered my beauty and embarrassed by her evident sincerity. To that point in the conversation, we'd been talking about her recent break-up with the man she'd lived with for a decade, and about my break-up—not quite so recent—of another long-standing relationship. We'd been talking in generalities—and in circles—about why our relationships didn't seem to last, and we were getting theoretical about how many of our generation seemed oblivious to how quickly they used up the non-renewable fund

"Ah, and who decides what's sane and what isn't? And in the name of whose version of public order?"

Ferris laughs despite himself, remembering the episode in the railway station cafeteria. "I don't know," he answers. "It sort of depends on what you think life is meant to achieve. I always *thought* it was aimed at order, overcoming chaos. But I see progressively less evidence to back it up. Not here, not anywhere."

"You have a police department mentality," Sylvia sneers. "The purpose of life is to achieve orgasm."

Ferris thinks about that. Hard, fearful thoughts. Right. This is what every man fears—or is supposed to. Women who are multiorgasmic, women who think of nothing else, just as men have thought of nothing else for centuries. But she's talking about something else: omniorgasmic women, a new species

of good faith and good will that is any relationship's greatest initial asset.

I'd been saying how intermittently and badly we put to use what little we do discover about one another. This, I opined, was because most men don't understand, trust, or like women very much these days.

"And vice versa," she'd said.

We agreed that it was hard to trust the opposite sex, and that this had something to do with the fact that successful relationships—while they last—are now based not in the social or economic necessities of the past, but in intellectual and erotic permission. On the heels of that agreement, for reasons I didn't understand, she was complimenting me on my beauty.

Wondering what was going on in her mind, I turned her strange anecdote back on her with the playfulness with which we were so comfortable. "That was a long time ago," I said, mocking up some world-weariness. "Being beautiful only counts if it's now. Anyway, I'm a sensible egomaniac, happy to be merely silver-haired and wise."

"No, you're not," she answered, snapping back to the ironic tones of our friendship. "You're a male jerk fishing for compliments."

Pleased at putting me in my place, she returned without a hitch to what we'd been talking about a moment before, commenting that men and women now seem to find it easier to interpret the opposite sex through ideology than to find sensible ways to get along.

"Well," I said, "now that it's been proved that ideology doesn't make successful politics, I guess people are applying it to gender and sex."

"That won't work any better," she sighed. "Ideology only makes sense when

that is capable of innumerable orgasmic events, some as physical couplings, or self-induced, even continuous orgasms.

"You seem to have a certain weakness for the police department yourself," he says, unable to stop himself.

"Well, why not?" she answers. "What's wrong with a little perverse sublimation? One way or another, men think of nothing else. I mean, no offence intended, but either men are thinking about getting off, or they're womanizing, or else they're sublimating it, turning it into dynamos or missiles, or whatever. But now, you see, women are going to outdo you. We'll outfuck you, we'll outsublimate you, and while we're doing it, we'll have thirty more orgasms a day."

Ferris experiences a moment of clarity. "Sure," he says, "and you'll end up as

you apply it to people you don't know and want to keep away from you. That way you don't have to see the suffering you're inflicting. It works best of all in a war zone."

"But a war is going on," I said.

I could see she didn't like the direction the conversation was going any better than I did, but we were both powerless to halt it. There was uncomfortable silence, and then she plunged into the deep water.

"Sex with men just isn't working for me," she admitted, "and I don't know how to get around it. I don't like it much, or them, once they get close."

I asked her what she meant by "close." Body parts? Genitals? Or was she talking about the intimacy that seemed to be eluding everyone—the kind that comes from mixing familiarity with trust?

She wasn't sure.

Which specific elements of male behaviour and sexuality was she troubled by?

Again, she wasn't sure.

I was getting nowhere with this line of questioning until, on impulse, I asked her how she felt about about oral sex. She grimaced.

"What," she said, "would possibly possess me to put a man's penis in my mouth?"

The look on her face told me she was as surprised by what she'd confessed as I was. Still, it was a question, and not a rhetorical one, and I scrambled to come up with a straight answer. There wasn't one, so I pushed it back to her. I asked her to clarify. Was she talking about what had happened with her old lover, or did her distaste run deeper than that? Then, before she could answer, I realized that it was

pleasureless as we are, as brainless and fucked up. And that'll be the end of us, with gender-Armageddon. There'll be no community, no congress. Just new kinds of pleasure-enclaves and their enterprise zones—or killing fields, like in what used to be Yugoslavia."

"What's wrong with women playing the same games men have played?"

"Men have been indulging themselves at the expense of whoever happens to be in their path. It's a lousy, destructive game."

Sylvia stops him dead. "Is that what you see here?"

"No," he admits. "Anything but."

"Well, then, maybe this is the way the future will be. With all different kinds of women. Some will hate men, sure. And maybe you're right about them, they'll turn into monsters. Others will simply turn away, and live among

neither. It was neither a question nor a statement of erotic preference. It was an ideological statement.

It didn't occur to me that she was being ironic, making fun of me. If that's how it was meant, it had trapped us both—i.e., it was a real problem, beyond our liberality and our private erotic preferences. I was caught by it because I share her dislike of male sexuality. For me this isn't much of a problem, since most of the time I think and act, sexually at least, out of empathy for, and interest in, women. Additionally, the distaste I have for my own gender is an innate heterosexual sensory prejudice— it's easy for me to admit that males are jerks, and that our obsession with our own fragile equipment is pretty silly.

For her, though, this distaste, even though it is an ideological one, is a very serious problem, because she happens to be as heterosexual as I am. She desires what she finds distasteful. It doesn't help her that, along with a generation of other women, she is now able to legitimize her distaste. As an individual, she still has to find love and be loved, and given her sexual orientation, she's unlikely to be comfortable accepting it from women.

So what were we chasing here, beyond a conversation about sex that went a little deeper than usual? What did we uncover?

Both she and I have been through the sexual revolution. We—the two of us and the rest of our generation—failed to liberate ourselves enough to change the way human beings relate to one another and to sexual desire. Maybe we did everything wrong, or maybe we just didn't have enough time to get it done. It doesn't matter much now. The hidden rules of sexual antiquity—the ones that pertained until the invention of penicillin—have supervened in unexpected ways. It isn't God or the

themselves. But there'll be women who choose men. Choose them and need them to be around. Most of the time, anyway. And then there will be women like these widows, women who like men but don't need them."

"Then there's you," Ferris says. "Where are you in this?"

Sylvia Eighty laughs. "I'm just a girl who reads Danielle Steel novels in train stations to ward off nosy guys."

Ferris feels his face reddening.

"I'm a woman who's here with you," she says, after taking a moment to enjoy his embarrassment. "And I'm wondering the same things about you. Where did you think I was?"

"Now what?" he says.

"Well," she answers, "let's find out. We can start by getting out of here."

Church or the government that has ruled against unlimited sexual openness, much as they'd like to. It is our own bodies, and the limits of our immune systems.

Circumspection is one thing, fear and loathing are another. Even though it's evident that what we were doing in the 1960s and 1970s didn't work and wasn't biologically wise, the thought of a return to the sexual repression of the past or even a step sideways into an erotic era governed by bizarre sublimations fills me with dread. Why? Because sublimation and repression never breed anything good or creative when they are exercised by fearful people. And if we're to avoid an all-out gender war and an erotic Armageddon, we're going to need a new kind of non-partisan openness and creativity. That's going to be hard, because the era of erotic empiricism is over.

Despite its inability to come up with a new rule book or even a body of workable data, I'm regretful that the empirical era is over, and that all we're likely to be able to do with the data we did amass is to enlarge the scope of onanist behaviours. I remember a very sensible friend saying twenty years ago that the only immoral sexual acts were those that were impossible to perform. Can you imagine anyone saying that now?

Yet for all my pessimism and dislike of our collective erotic past, what may save us is yet another of those hidden rules of antiquity. The neo-reptiles among us aren't going to like it, but a very old principle is going to come into play, this time from an opposite and unexpected end of the conflict. It's the one that says that sexual desire can't and won't disappear, however much we come to fear it. What that means is that however dangerous sex becomes, and however much women and men dislike each other, some substantial percentage of men are going to go on desiring intimate companionship—male or female, and some women will go on desiring pretty much the same. This is because we are physical beings, creatures of the body for whom sexual desire can disappear only at the moment of death.

I remember an incident that took place years ago while a film maker of my acquaintance was dying of leukemia. I overheard several of his women confidants, including his lover, discussing how to best assure him of sexual pleasure and solace in his last days. He was in an oxygen tent at the time, his body failing, his lungs starving for air. For some time, his lover had been habitually and openly giving him her breast to fondle, but here the women were arguing over masturbation techniques, insisting that he should be having orgasms right up to, and into, his last hours of life. At the time I thought that their concerns were inappropriate, a little gross, and maybe even silly.

Now I understand that they were right, as far as they took it. Add a thousand more levels of complexity, a hundred thousand instrumentations as seemingly bizarre, and you'll have a sense of how alive we are, and how we are alive.

All Those Things

That

He slips his left arm from under her torso and pulls the bed sheets down with his right, tosses them beyond her ankles. His lips begin above her right breast and move downward, caressing her nipple, grazing her rib cage, the soft spread of her belly, then up across the ridge of her hip. He runs his tongue along her flank and lifts her right leg over his shoulder, kneeling between her legs, which open without reluctance.

There is redolence here, hers mostly, but more complicated than a single scent. It is familiar and strange, this redolence, the scent of the present tense escaping a hundred entwined pasts, of the adored but also other, not him—and not all the others. He takes it in, breathes deep, and getting her, he arrives. He slips an arm under each of her buttocks and shifts the angle of her body, pulling her into him as he drops his mouth to feed.

He doesn't hurry. There is nowhere else to be but now. Beyond is darkness, uncertainty. Better here. Nor does she urge him. Now and again she lifts her head to watch, or entwines her fingers in his hair, or tests his shoulder for the unique bones and muscles there as he grazes her, slowly tasting each scented nest and fold before settling in, and down. It is a slow thing, this, meant to last forever, to postpone everything, to render lovers crystalline and organic in the same suspended instant.

Can I distract you one last time? I want to point out, again, but in a slightly different sense, that Ferris and Sylvia don't exist except in these pages. It isn't just that their moment is mine, their experience and knowledge mine. It's that even though I created him to answer the questions about sex and gender that puzzle me, and to act out these puzzles in ways I'd prefer not to have hanging over my public identity, he's no longer strictly my alter ego.

Sylvia is freer still. She isn't a composite, and quite deliberately, she isn't my anima. That person is in the real world. As I write, actually, she's one floor above me, playing a computer game called Jezzball, scoring nearly double the scores I'm capable of—and preparing to tease me about it.

This isn't the customary bull about how Ferris and Sylvia have taken on a life of their own, that I'm not in control, and isn't imagination remarkable, etc. Imagination *is* remarkable, but I'll spare you the insult to your intelligence of suggesting that I'm not responsible for these two, and for what they do. I'm completely responsible, and I'm in control enough that you can rest assured that in the next pages they aren't going to rob a bank or hide in a doorway and mug an innocent passer-by. Yet I'm not in control in several ways I expected to be.

No, I'm not contradicting myself. I'd love to be negotiating a universe based on facts, or at least operating in a field where I can see the parameters, understand the laws and valences, decipher the rules. From where I am, none of those comforts are available.

Ferris, you see, may have started off as a projection of my personality and experience, but along the line his track and mine began to diverge, altered (fiction writers would say predictably) by the particularities and events I conferred on him. The gap was widened much more by some radical changes in my private life and outlook, ones that divested me of a future I'd come to think of as fated. What I'm saying is that it was *my* life and expectations that went for a loop. I suppose I could still rein Ferris in, bring him in line with what I've learned, candy-ass the poor bozo in mid-flight, make him me. That would now be inaccurate, because he isn't me. More complicated than that, the "I" subtext you've been listening to along with the third-person narrative of this book isn't quite me either.

That's right. The voice you're hearing right now, the analytical "I" that may seem to be the person named on the jacket cover and title page as the author, isn't. That "I" is every bit as much a literary creation as Ferris and Sylvia are. I'm not saying this to be a slinky postmodernist relativist. I'll still take full responsibility for every word of this book. But at the same time, I have to admit that I discovered, along the way, three unexpected but fundamental truths about erotic life. Each one has influenced the compositional dynamics of this book. The first is this: *Our lives, sexual or otherwise, are not fated.* Human beings are at perfect liberty to change themselves. Freer than birds, more transformative than the caterpillars that turn into butterflies. Most of what we regard in ourselves as fated is the product of our habits (good or bad), our cowardice or misguided use of will.

That's the easy one. The second isn't so easy: *Sexual discretion is an endless, automatic, and incalculable process*—that is, a full or true sexual confession is an oxymoron. Can't be done. Whatever confessions I set out to make, abject or proud, aren't.

Third, and still more complicated to explain: *The human body doesn't have a memory.* On the surface, this might not seem like much of a revelation—

memory is a neural function, stored (for limited recall) across the blood/brain barrier. What I'm suggesting is that the body prevents recall of physical sensation, unless (as in the case of torture) the neural/physical trauma is so great that the integrated personality is incapacitated.

Ergo, the sexual memories in which people in our culture invest such importance are illusions, reflections off a slippery surface on which our momentary insights, satisfactions, and dysfunctions alight for an illuminated—or traumatic—moment. But always, they are atomized by the impact of the next similar bodily experience that crosses into our neural nets. The brain may pick up fragments to adorn our ongoing self-portraits, but the exact details—*always*—are gone. Hence, I discovered, it simply isn't possible to recall erotic experience with any degree of faithfulness. When I tried to recreate my own, my body simply refused to co-operate, claiming that it is capable only of experiencing its present capacities and limitations, and sorry bub, *it* doesn't remember a thing. Write your book without my help.

> **Two Incitements:**
>
> "The most dangerous people are those who know each other."
> – Walter De Keseredy, Guelph University sociologist, Feb. 8, 1993
>
> "Chastity is the only safe and virtuous way to put an end to the tragic plague of AIDS."
> – Pope John Paul II, 1993

The implications of this reach well beyond the covers of this book and my frankly unimportant problems with character, event, and composition. One thing it implies is that the current round of well-intentioned docu-confessions in which writers (most of them male) undertake to record their sexual disasters and conquests are without verity—an epistemological fraud (Frank Harris did this sixty years ago, but the current generation seems to think that its good intentions will spare it the same silliness).

It also means that those of us who've spent our adult lives swimming in the privileged mainstream of twentieth-century consciousness are guilty of trying to make sex something it can't be. It is not the hoped-for undistorted window through which we can distinguish the meaningful sense of communion and community the century has denied us. Nor can sex be an integral—and integrating—cipher to daily life. At its best, sex has translucence—it feels as if it spreads its light and dark through everything, but it just isn't the window onto reality some of us would like it to be. It's like a window on a fast-moving train, and unless you're one of those rare human locomotives whose behaviours are indistinguishable from their ambitions, it isn't possible to see what's coming at

you from it. If you do, you'll be so alone there won't be much erotic experience, at least not the communal kind.

What I'm saying is that we simply do not recall physical sensations accurately. We make up our understanding of them conceptually—or if we're easily frightened—by slathering them with sentimentality or bashing them into shape by ideological fiat. But we do it without exact recall of the sensations experience confers. In some ways, this is a good thing. It is why we're not permanently terrified by accidents, medical operations, or the casual violence of nature. Thorough recall of sensation would put us cowering *under* the beds, not luxuriating in them. The human body experiences physical sensation through the autonomic nervous system, which sends filtered and unreliable information to the brain through pathways that are routinized and closed to recall at the same time. After that, dopamines and other, more obscure hormones anneal and counter-load the pathways. There's a rather dark corollary to this: The more hypersensitive one's receptors, the more accurate one's recall, the more likely one is to be neurotic, phobic, or crazy.

Of course, we're able to remember that we have experienced private pleasures and wounds, moments of ecstasy, declarations of love and affection. We can identify the people and things that were the targets, proprietors, or perpetrators. But when and while we do this, the body is silent and unhelpful, stupidly awaiting the next travellers to send off into our unmapped and barely understood synaptic nets.

It is the translucence of erotic experience that makes us lose perspective, our sense of its limits and possibilities. Again, this is partly efficient design. Common sense tells us that if we had profound memory recall of orgasm we'd be permanently distracted by it, unable to function or to think about much else. And it is precisely here that our peculiar enculturation has created a major difficulty.

Technically speaking, an orgasm is a neurophysical tremor caused by overstimulating selected nerve endings. Biogenetically, it is ultimately the product of a sub-program originally designed to get our ancestors' minds off the search for food and onto reproducing themselves. For us, orgasms have become a cultural commodity, the fulcrum of personal identity and meaning: a great, fabulous outburst of the elusive present tense. Orgasms have become the answer to the humiliations of bodily life, the carrot we hang just beyond the pebbles or boulders we push uphill, the antidote to our black depressions—the thing that gets us off, the pinnacle of and respite from, everything: the only pure product the present gives up to us.

Herein lies the difficulty. Human beings are creatures of consciousness, to which the present is only a moving point of reference in a matrix of experiential accumulations and intellectual projections. Consciousness is a responsibility that orgasm seems to deny because, for a brief interval, orgasms make us forget everything.

As a civilization, we've reacted badly to this. When we're not concocting elaborate valentines to sentimentalize our orgasms, we're buying into an elaborate commercial apparatus that translates life into a series of org-ops and their purchasable accessory products. Even when we're not having enough orgasms, we erect magnificent gargoyles that we alternately excoriate and glamorize. It's a waste of time, because we're sentimentalizing half-memory, glamorizing our own lack of perspective. If you're not sure what I'm talking about, try to remember exactly what an orgasm feels like. You'll find your body squirming to produce one—and your mind blank expectancies. You have to repeat the physical experience to reclaim it with the mind. And the moment you do, you're back where you started.

That the body lives only in the present while the mind lives mostly in the past and the future is a fact of life. Call this a disability if you want, whine about the need to heal the mind/body split. You'll be wasting your energy. Calling it a disability is almost as silly as choosing the reality of one over the other. Orgasms would be more rewarding if we recognized that they are neither fraud nor possession, and that their evanescence—together with the body's refusal to record them—is what makes sexuality a survivable exploration. Better yet, we could recognize that orgasm is just one of number of the building blocks of human sexuality. The other important ones are mammalian intimacy—a need that is lodged as deeply in our animal inheritance as our orgasmic drive—and a third: the need for wisdom.

Precisely because it is grounded neither in accurate memory nor sharable facts, sexuality is the arena of a doomed but compulsory search for wisdom. That most of us hunt for sexual wisdom in the realm of the absolute present isn't quite the absurdity it is at first glance. By itself, the present isn't enough. One hundred billion orgasms from here, human beings will still be trying to discover the wisdom of them. It's the human contrarium—why we're such interesting animals—and consciousness will ensure that the search will go on as surely as the body will forget every spasm that passes through it the instant it subsides.

It is also why the question that was originally mine but is now equally the question Ferris and Sylvia ask keeps turning up like a bad penny: Even if sexual wisdom is an epistemological absurdity, what *is* its essential nature? There's a miracle at work, too. Some of us learn wisdoms willy-nilly and they don't appear to be the product of decay or exhaustion. Instead, they generate new questions: How does sexual wisdom exist in relation to all the other things we are and do and know? How do we make it stand against the brutish animal imperatives we begin with and fall back to when culture fails?

And then there is this additional question that I've added to the stew: How do we enact a non-coercive, generous sexuality in the midst of a gender war?

And so it goes, on and on, until human consciousness reaches and understands infinity—or blinks out. What creature could ask for more than this?

———

This is Sylvia Eighty and Ferris we're observing. For as long as this moment (day, week, year) lasts, she is his lover, and he is hers. Don't ask why. Call it my author's gift, or my indulgence, or my heavy hand. And don't ask when it began, or how they got from the Widow's Café to here. This could be weeks, months after we last saw them, or as easily, forty-five minutes later. Here as elsewhere, I'm not very interested in seduction. I'm interested in consummation and what it consumes, and in what distracts us from the obvious, the banal, the Mall. I'm interested in the illuminated promontories where the chiaroscuro of gender politics meets the soft creamy light where we are animals seeking the comfort no body can possibly deliver and, miraculously, delivers anyway, the electric eye-to-eye that temporarily denies meaning to everything else but the moment we are wrapped inside.

To Ferris, everything that has happened in his entire life seems to have led him here. He is like you and me that way, and there is nothing mystical about it. He is trying to live competently in the present, and that is the hardest of human tasks. Never mind solar winds, cosmic drift, or the myopic geoeconomics of the G-7. He brings the accumulation of his experience and knowledge to this moment, each one of his successes and failures. Despite the absolute insecurity of the data, the endless, arguing interferences, the distracting shadows of sensation, and the guilt-darkened colossus of his past mistakes, he's trying to do the right thing—while gratifying his senses. As we all are, right?

Harder to say with certainty what Sylvia Eighty is doing here. She is part madness, part incisive sanity: It's hard not to recall her as a wealthy, cracked woman stealing sandwiches in a railway station cafeteria. Harder still to forget the orgasm she stole as her two lovers held her in their grasp in the cafeteria doorway, as if all there was to erotic life is theft and capture, a life of clichés, brutalities, and banalities sweetened only by stolen moments. I know this much: just being here is an act of courage. Behind her lies god knows what traumas, an abusive ex-husband, but she has put them and him behind her. She knows nearly nothing about Ferris and has only his half-hearted attempt to rescue her in the railway station cafeteria a year ago and the quick judgement of her three colleagues at the Widow's Café to recommend him. Would you go with this man?

No matter, the past. They are eye-to-eye and I am imagining that eye-to-eye. This is sexual consciousness on the half-shell, extensible and evanescent, the dissolution of ratio and control. Ferris can sense the perfume she has dabbed on her throat, he notes the patina of tiny moles from her neck up behind her right ear, the slight weakening of the muscles above her breasts, the unexpected broadness of her belly and hips. A faint line of coarse hair runs from her navel to the swelling of her Mount of Venus, the pubic hair jet-black and unexpectedly sparse and straight. She has sculpted it to expose the labia and clitoris, which protrudes a little, hot pink and glistening, from its darker surroundings.

This is her, Ferris insists, her, the woman Sylvia. She is not Everywoman, not the answer to his prayers—he has none—certainly not an airbrushed *Playboy* fantasy. She is not a passing fancy either, their desire for one another is not the accumulation of their taste and needs that enabled it. Not now. This is particularity, voltage, and focus, what the meat market wants to steal from us, this is the wildness of consciousness in the wilderness of the body, the reason human beings turn and return to sex, and dream of its turns and return. Around them, anima and animus drift by oblivious, fatuous milkcows and slaughterhouse cattle of commoditized individuality, the doppelgängers that supposedly tie us to the collective, to the irremediable perverse polygamy that haunts everyone. But not here. Not now. Particularity. Voltage and focus.

Good luck. What he wants comes and goes, ululates as ghosts are said to. At this moment, Ferris is trying to give up some of his ghosts, but a ghost, once freed, is a free spirit. He'd like to give up the smoke-and-mirrors part of himself that is never quite up to the rigours of being, always clutching ancestors, mother, departed lovers, the technical devices we all use to avoid the nakedness of the particular. This time, a miracle, he is only up to this one woman, the sum total of what he has seen and that which is her and of which he knows little beyond what he can imagine, her red fingernails, the slight puffiness of her knuckles, her ankles that have turned out to be slighter than he remembers, her feet narrow and highly arched, her toes long and graceful, distractingly, thankfully so. Of course, of course…

This is a lie. There *are* infinitesimal points of distraction. Others appear in the bed with them, unbidden. Some are his, some hers, the cheated and the lied-to, the half-loved or incompetently loved or the not-loved-at-all, the passing fancies and selfish choices, the phantoms daemonic and benign, the poor benighted remnants and closed summaries of slippery things and impulses, the traceries of people travelling through their own inscrutable wilderness or Club Med. What matters about these distractions is not their presence but the *degree* of distraction and abstraction they create, the ossified postures and poses by which he and she have ordered and disarmed them, by which the ghosts have been reduced to coherence, and the degree to which they skew focus, how loud their whispers are and accusations, threats, blessings they whisper. All of us are subject to these same sensory delinquencies. They are conferred automatically, part of the gift and curse that human beings must simultaneously uphold and transcend—or return to the trees that will be logged off when we arrive.

Try to ignore them, that is all we can do, I whisper. Sylvia glances down at him, querulously, and laughs. She thinks he said it, and her laughter is accurate. Better than him, she knows that any command for silence, however earned, will be met by their howls of derision: "You want us to *what?*"

Call this her wisdom, this much *her* senses have earned. She embraces her ghosts, they are part of her erotic architecture. But she says nothing of them to Ferris. She merely lets her head fall back on the pillow, and arches her back. Move me.

Ferris lifts his head from between her legs, marvelling at the zone of darker skin, the tracer mark our dumb simian ancestors must have needed, not discoloured but rooted beyond the course of ordinary things, here the colour of earth he remembers from a childhood neighbour's garden, but opening to pink, to a light that he tastes and smells rather than sees and comprehends, the ciprine that is unlike any other substance under heaven, oh, here I go mystifying, and that is distraction, too.

———————————

He stops, lifts his mouth from Sylvia's swelling clitoris to caress the stretch marks along her inner thighs, the olive pigment of her skin there broken up by lighter striations almost to her knees, did she lose weight too quickly at some point or is this years of habitual exercise, tennis anyone?

Well, she hasn't played much tennis lately, judging from the subtle cavities along each of her tendons, or, let's see here, yes, the pouchiness along the backs of her legs. But then, no tennis tonight, either. And who cares? Each slight infirmity and flaw is a tendril of desire her body invades his with, and he runs his lips across them, then turns her on her stomach, finds everything he can, a varicose vein behind her knee, a blemish on her left buttock, and, jackpot, a nest of stretch marks across the saddle of her hips. With each one acknowledged, a new intimacy is created, a sense of safety, a step beyond graffiti. These are not surfaces a single night can mark, a stupid indifference won't scar them, or a single night of pleasure, whatever its depth, will addict.

Ferris stops cold. What has he been thinking?

Other thoughts rush in. What if he were another man, would it be the same? Will her back arch the same way, will the depth of her orgasm be as great? And what real improvement am I to the technical devices available? Does he merely resonate at a frequency she finds pleasant, and is there a difference between resonance and vibration?

He stills his terror. He knows, after all, what everyone in this civilization eventually learns, no matter what their gender or occupation: Any lover can be replaced. There is always something or someone more attractive, a woman with a prettier body, a man who is bigger and harder, with more endurance and skill and imagination. That, and not the creation of wealth, is the ultimate triumph of the marketplace. It is a triumph over local responsibility, and the things of the human spirit—loyalty, kindness, intimacy...

"Hey," she's saying. "Hey."

And what's going on in her mind? Is she auditioning him for a lifetime or for another episode in the nightmare in which she's forever drifting through a mall on private solar winds, a snowflake caught up in the storm of confetti at the marriage of heaven and hell? So, okay. Aren't we all snowflakes? Or are we confetti?

He buries his face in the pit of her stomach, catches a hair between his teeth and resists the impulse to sever it. She fluffs his hair, then places her hands on his shoulders, not impatiently, but to say, quietly, get on with it, I am eager for this, I want more, and more, and more.

When he's in position once more she presses the inside of her knees against his skull and he moves in, her fingers pressure the back of his head and he pushes his tongue into her vagina, pulls up slightly into the folds of her labia, gently tugging the vaginal roof. He feels her labia engorging, filling with blood, and he plays on those, first on one side and then the other, they're the instrument now, cello to the clitoral violin that enriches the harmonies so that her orgasm arrives more as a symphony than a scream of the pierced that shuts out communion, he has brought her imperfect body to it by accepting its wholeness, he has not merely moved her to sensation,

And she wants to stay on the plateau and go higher, her clitoris is blooming, she's impatient, holding him into her. He plays this, pulling back a little, teasing her, moving lower to stroke the lower edge of the opening, darting his tongue inside her, poking his nose against her straining blossom, showing her he's in no hurry, making no pretence that he's in control, merely playing her until she gives the signal by pulling him roughly back, and he settles in over her clitoris, a mouthful of it as if it's her nipple and he's milking it, except now it's she who's pulling away, it's too intense, and he pursues it, pursues it, won't let go … and at the last moment, a split second before her spasm, which seems to her to be starting at the base of her spine and radiating outward like a rolling earthquake tremor, he pulls sharply away and holds her on its trembling edge, flicking his tongue across her clitoris until orgasm erupts into her and through her at the same time, the trembling wave that has been rolling forward and up for thirty seconds, or is it thirty minutes, and now breaks over her in a sharp infusion of violet pleasure so intense she wants to split open and draw him into her, hold him there, forever, forever. But alas, the sensation reaches its crescendo and ceases, and she floats down to him on the aftershocks of the first.

They could go on with this for hours, you know. Days, weeks, months. Ferris is learning her, and learning has a curve. Suddenly, he sees its end, a delicate strand of boredom that right now is barely detectable, one among many that will eventually thicken and grow. It will resemble a serpent for a while, its sinuations mobile and compelling. But finally it will more resemble a service pipe, heavy and impermeable. Damn.

Did you see it? I didn't, not at first. I had hopes for this, for her, for them both, and maybe I didn't want to see it. I wanted it to be a miracle as specific as my beloved's grin when she loses at cards, or leans across the bed to retrieve the newspaper on Sunday morning, the thousand and one discoveries that tell me that the learning curve is renewable and infinite. But of course, that's private, and like I said, none of anyone else's business.

Ferris and Sylvia won't stop here. Later on in the event I'm describing, they'll probably make love by the methods the church and state prescribe. They won't feel like missionaries, but they won't feel like it's the triumph of one gender over another, either. They'll feel deeply, deliciously mammalian, gratefully human.

They'll have a few months, maybe more. Then one morning he'll find himself feeling anxious, and he'll make a bitchy remark about the Danielle Steel novel she's reading—a reading habit he's been thoroughly unsuccessful in trying to cure her of. Or she'll make some remark about his lack of ambition, or his slovenly habits, or the fact that he was out far too late the evening before.

And that's all there is for them, except for the anarchy of redolences, that for them, grow more complex and alluring, a bridge to the next redolence.

Meanwhile, water flows beneath the bridge, bubbling with chemical wastes and human sewage. And traffic flows across the bridge, incessant, purposeful, the succession of journeys we make that are also aimless because we are of the devil's party, we walk up and down and back and forth, and up and down, and back and forth. And I hope that the artillery barrage in the distance will come no closer because that would be too, too easy.

Ge

nd

This book is set in Garamond

and News Gothic

We

The text stock is 55lb White Hibulk

ra

rs